ALSO FROM JOE BOOKS

Disney Frozen Cinestory Comic
Disney Cinderella Cinestory Comic
Disney 101 Dalmatians Cinestory Comic
Disney Princess Comics Treasury
Disney • Pixar Comics Treasury
Disney Big Hero 6 Cinestory Comic
Disney • Pixar Inside Out Cinestory Comic
Disney Gravity Falls Cinestory Comic Volume One
Disney Gravity Falls Cinestory Comic Volume Two
Disney Gravity Falls Cinestory Comic Volume Three
Disney Zootopia Cinestory Comic
Disney Descendants Wicked World Cinestory Comic Volume One
Disney Descendants Wicked World Cinestory Comic Volume Two
Disney Alice in Wonderland Cinestory Comic
Disney Star vs the Forces of Evil Cinestory Comic
Disney Princess Comic Strips Collection Volume One
Disney Darkwing Duck Comics Collection: Orange is the New Purple
Disney Star Darlings Cinestory Comic: Becoming Star Darlings
Disney Elena of Avalor Cinestory Comic: Ready to Rule

Don't miss our monthly comics…

Disney Frozen
Disney Darkwing Duck
Disney Pirates of the Caribbean
Disney Princess
Disney Star vs the Forces of Evil

Disney
DESCENDANTS
Wicked World
Cinestory Comic
Volume 3

JOE BOOKS LTD

Published simultaneously in the United States and Canada by
Joe Books Ltd, 489 College Street, Toronto, ON M6G 1A5

www.joebooks.com

First Joe Books Edition: January 2017

ISBN 978-1-77275-460-5 (paperback edition)
ISBN 978-1-77275-502-2 (ebook edition)

"Rather Be With You"
Written by Jeannie Lurie, Aris Archontis, Chen Neeman
© 2016 Walt Disney Music Company (ASCAP)/
Wonderland Music Company, Inc. (BMI)
All Rights Reserved. Used with Permission.

"Evil"
Written by Dan Book, Shelly Peiken
© 2016 Wonderland Music Company, Inc. (BMI)
All Rights Reserved. Used with Permission.

Joe Books™ is a trademark of Joe Books Ltd.
Joe Books® and the Joe Books Logo are trademarks of
Joe Books Ltd, registered in various categories and countries.
All rights reserved.

Adaptation, design, lettering, layout, and editing by First Image.

Library and Archives Canada Cataloguing in Publication
information is available upon request

Printed and bound in Canada
1 3 5 7 9 10 8 6 4 2

Disney

DESCENDANTS

Wicked World

Cinestory Comic
Volume 3

CHAPTER 19: SLUMBER PARTY

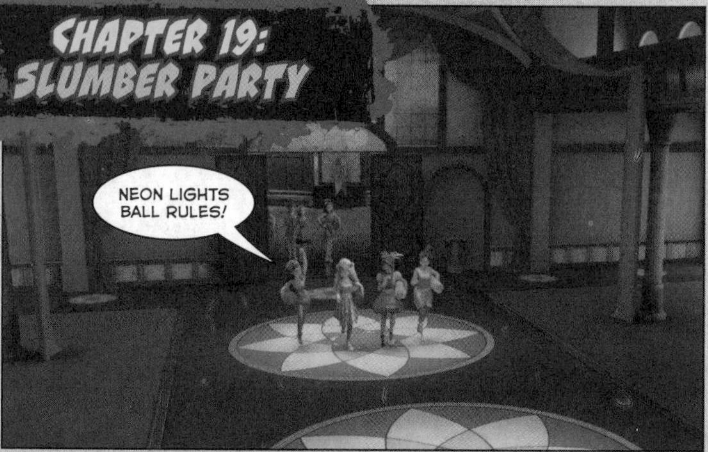
NEON LIGHTS BALL RULES!

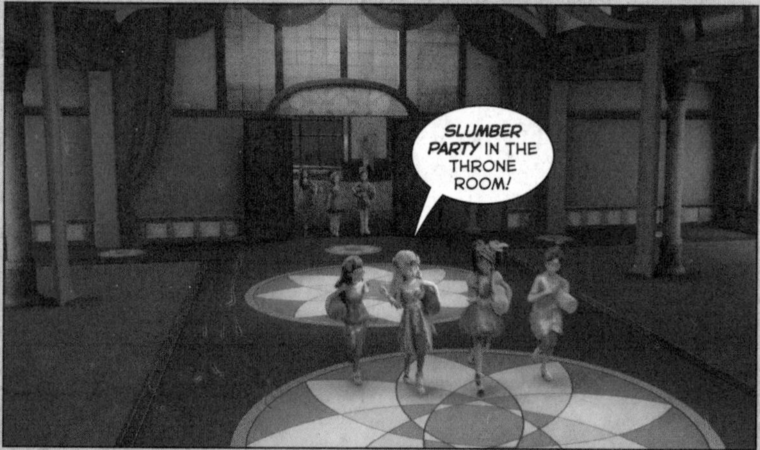
SLUMBER PARTY IN THE THRONE ROOM!

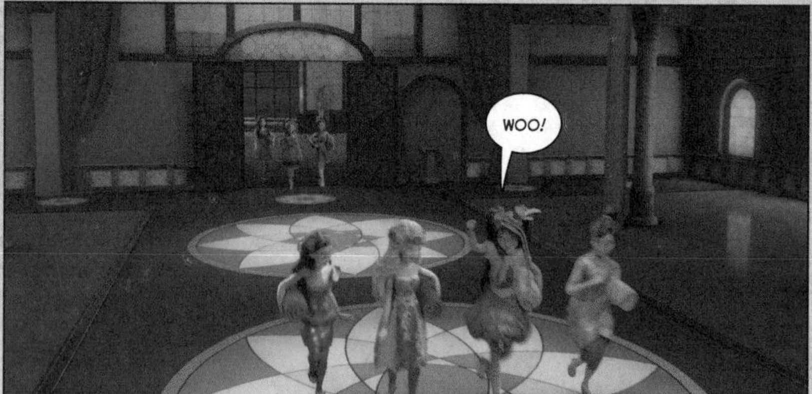
WOO!

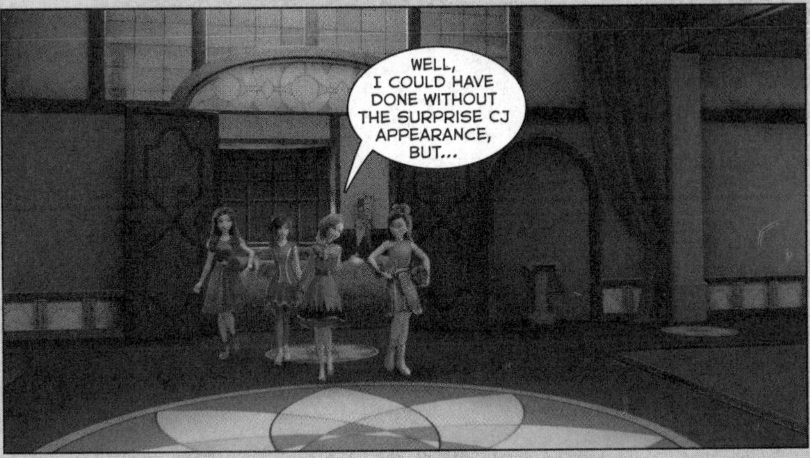
WELL, I COULD HAVE DONE WITHOUT THE SURPRISE CJ APPEARANCE, BUT...

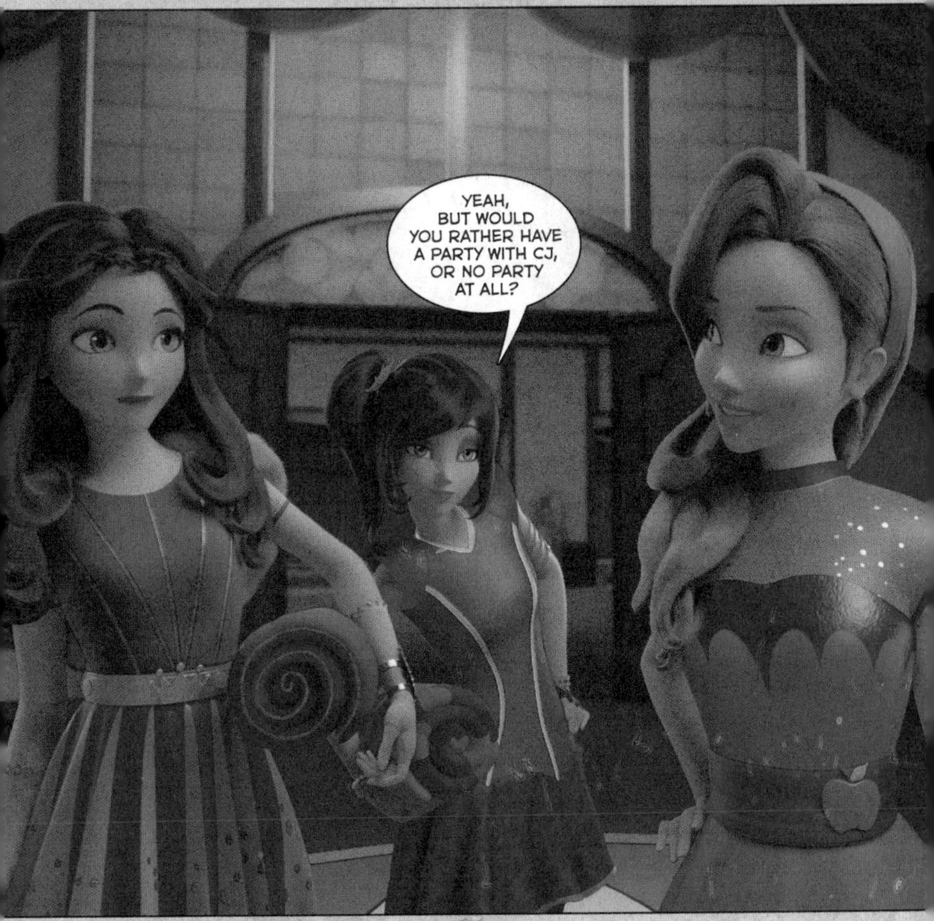
YEAH, BUT WOULD YOU RATHER HAVE A PARTY WITH CJ, OR NO PARTY AT ALL?

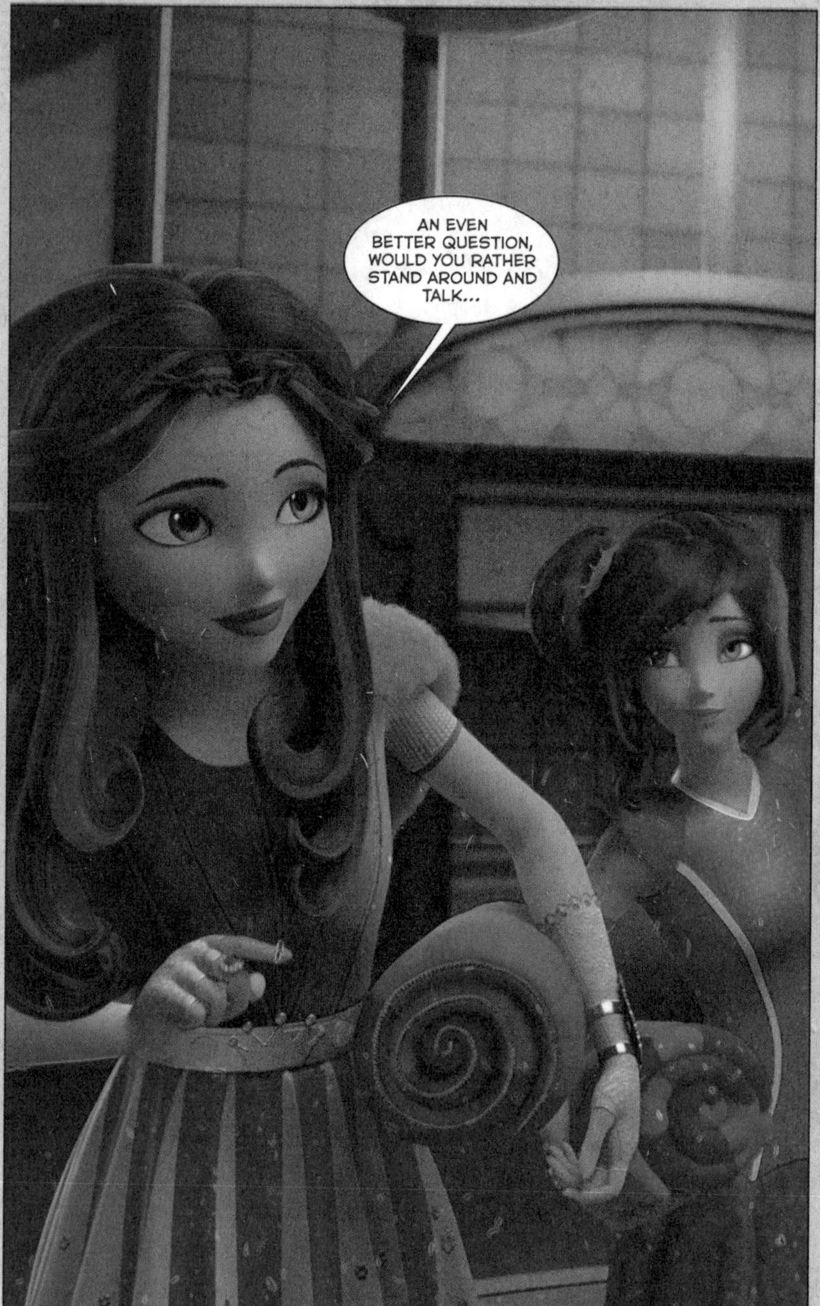
AN EVEN BETTER QUESTION, WOULD YOU RATHER STAND AROUND AND TALK...

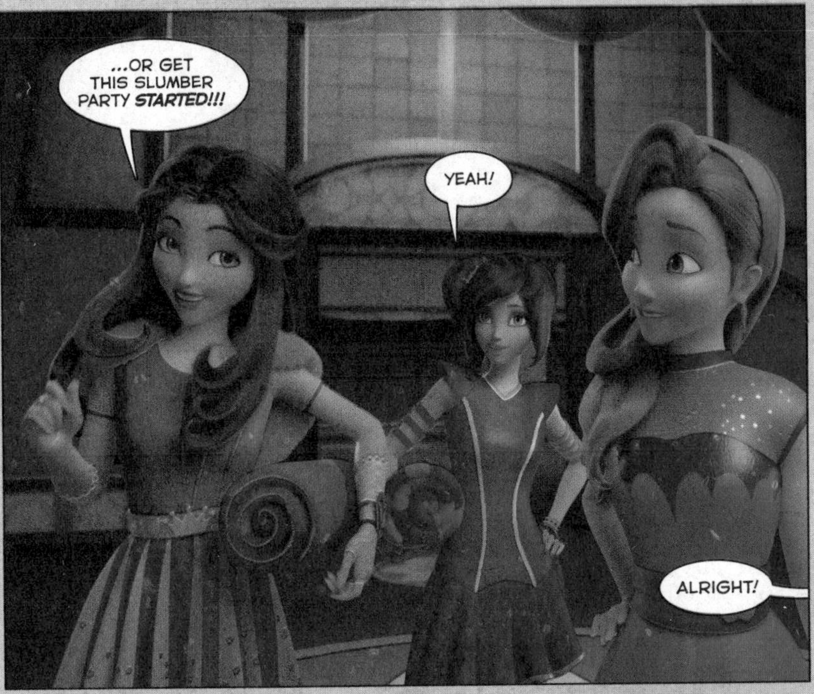
...OR GET THIS SLUMBER PARTY STARTED!!!
YEAH!
ALRIGHT!

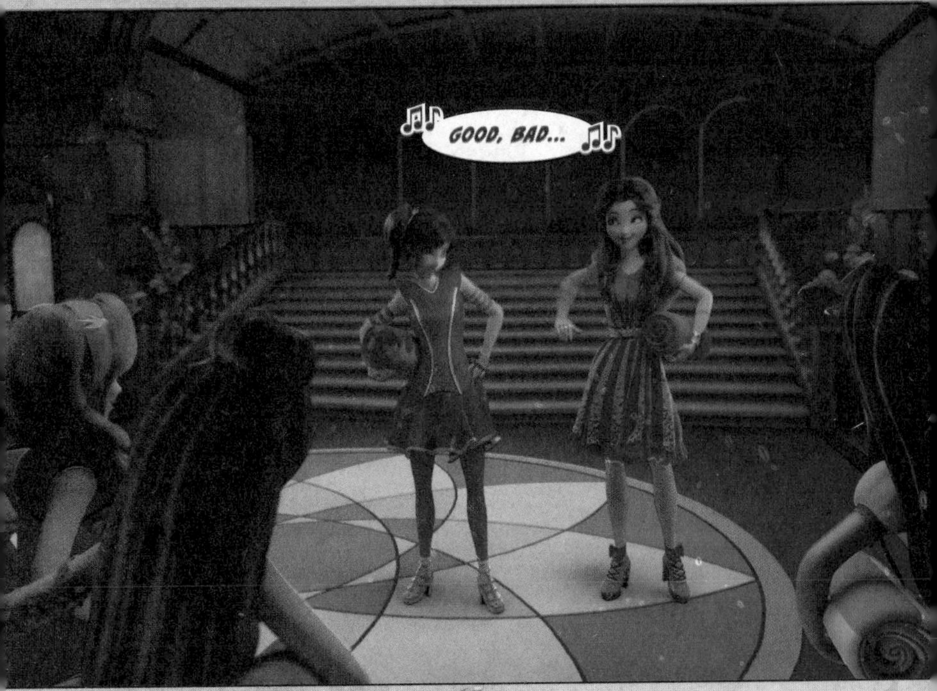
GOOD, BAD...

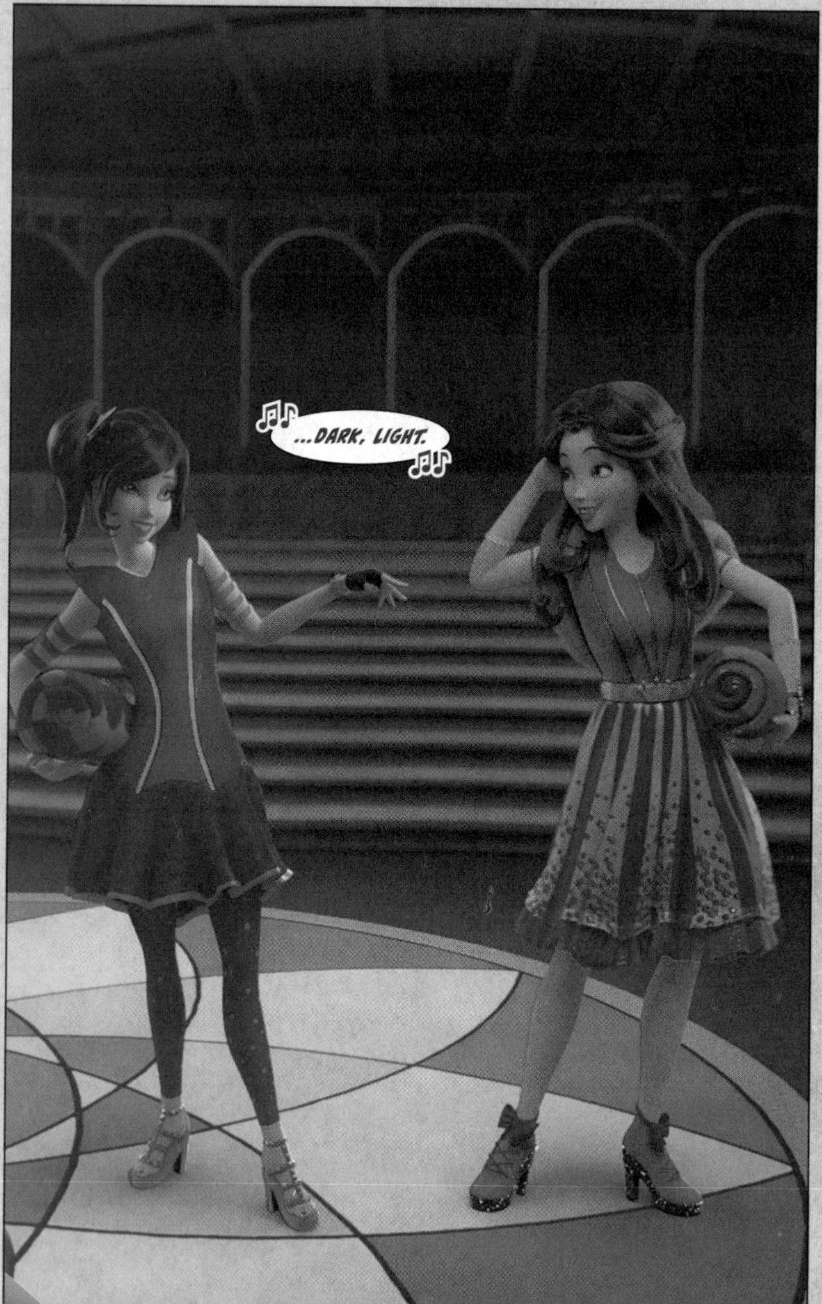
...DARK, LIGHT.

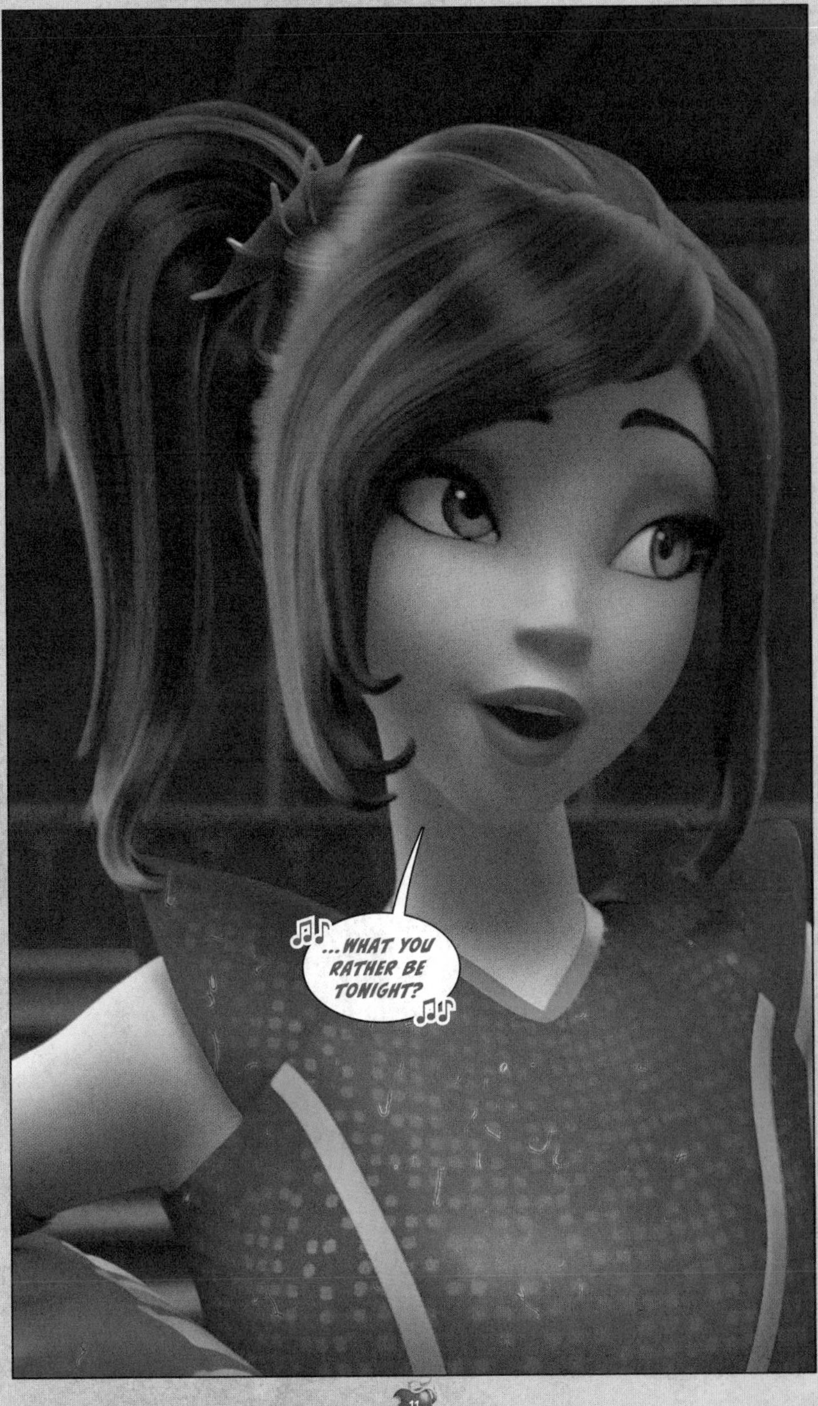
...WHAT YOU RATHER BE TONIGHT?

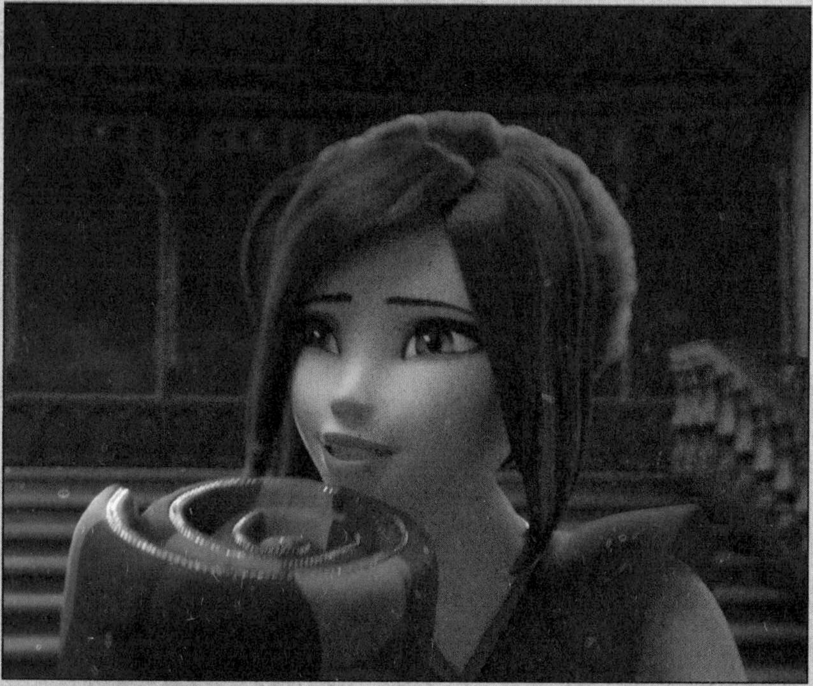

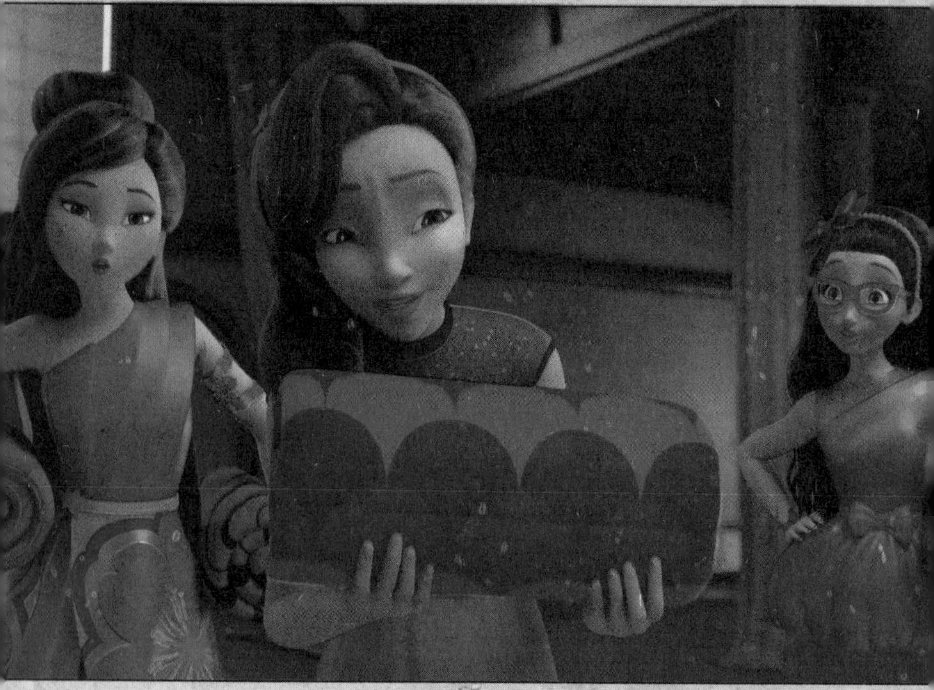

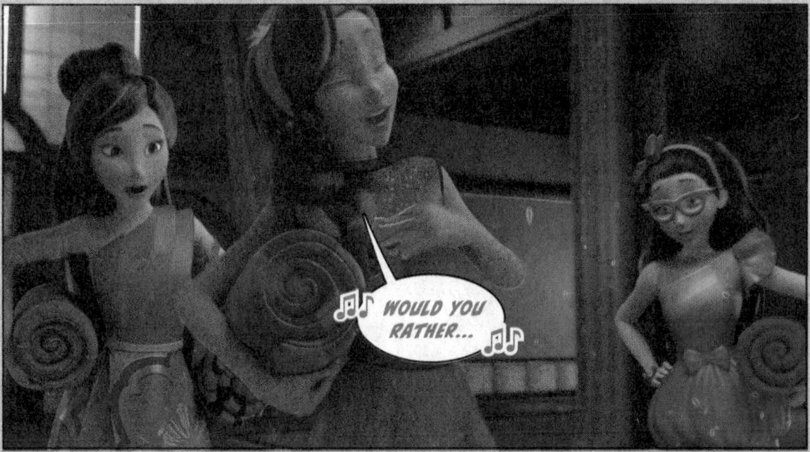
WOULD YOU RATHER...

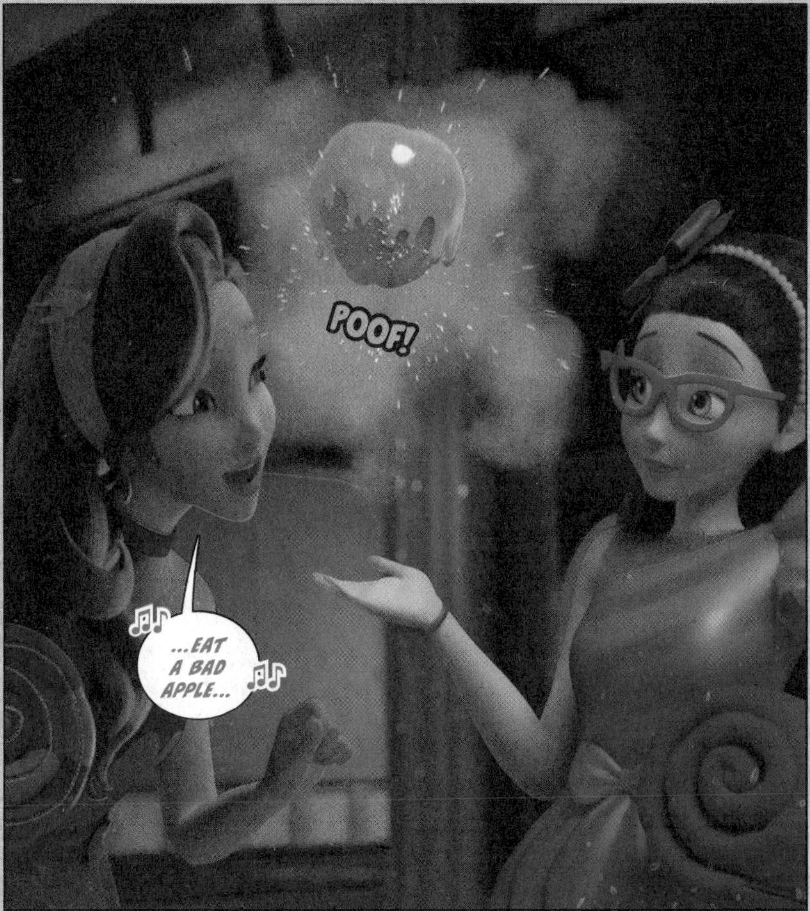
POOF!
...EAT A BAD APPLE...

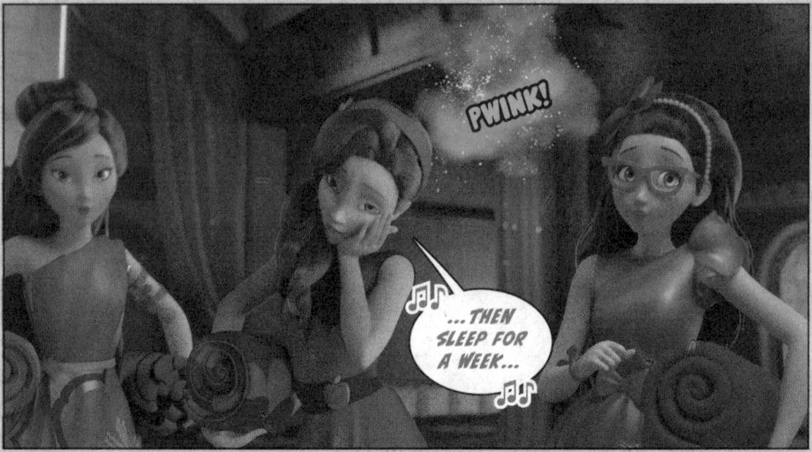
PWINK!
...THEN SLEEP FOR A WEEK...

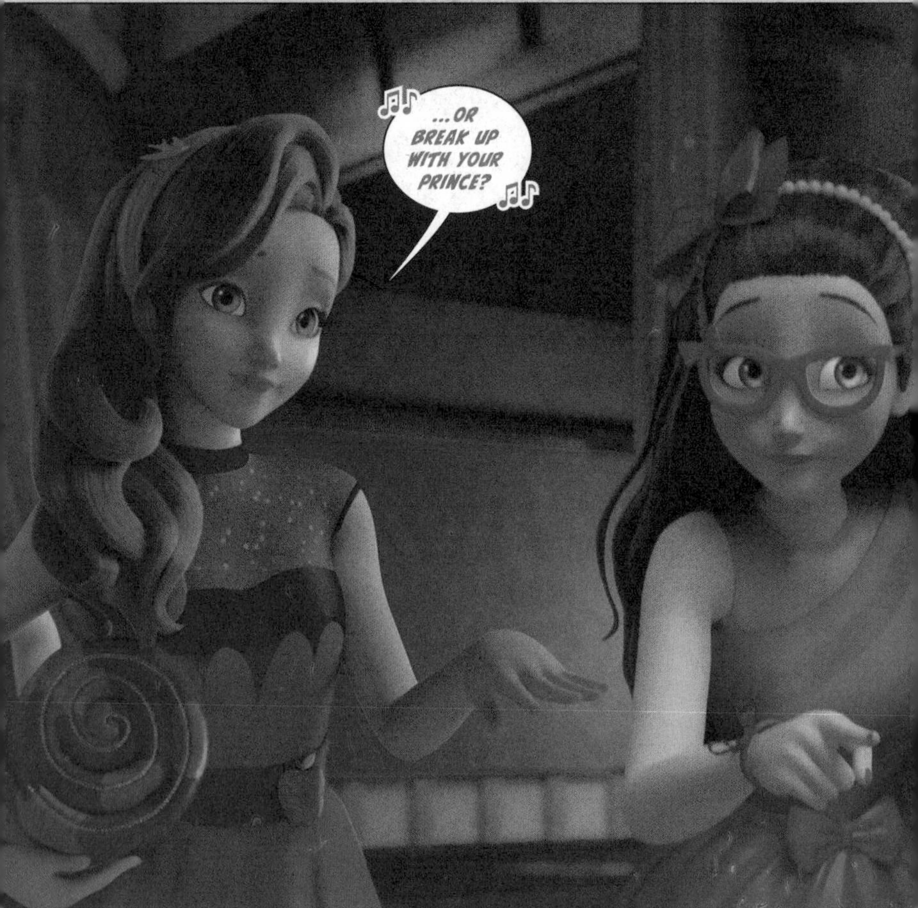
...OR BREAK UP WITH YOUR PRINCE?

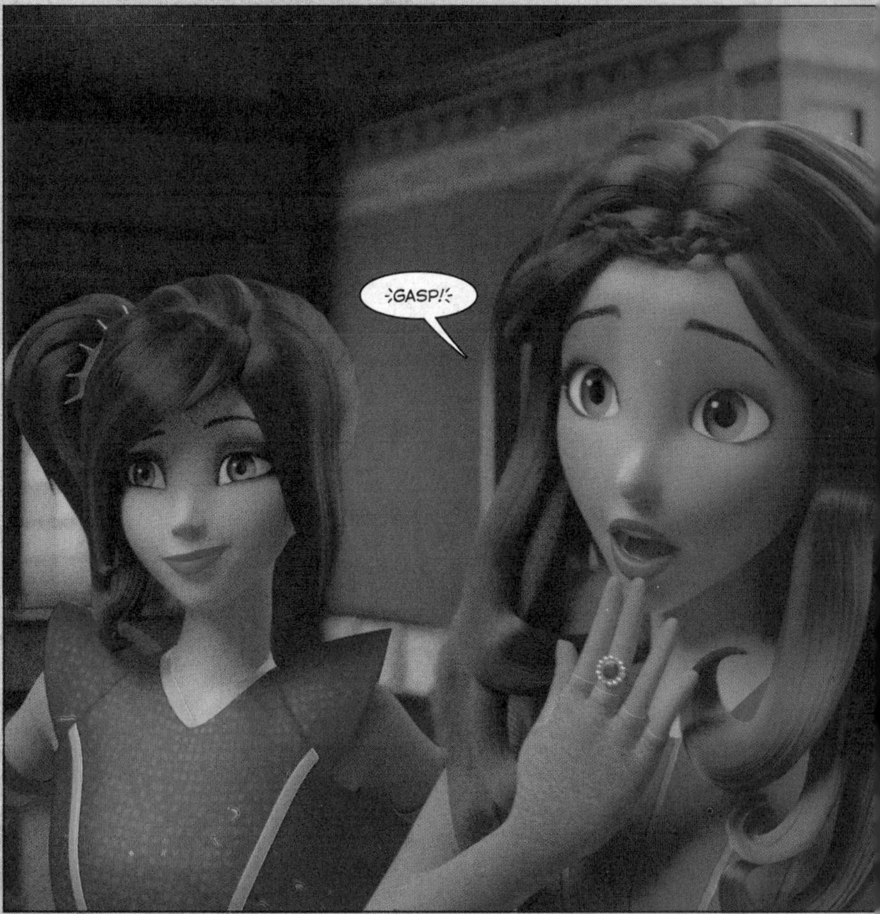
GASP!

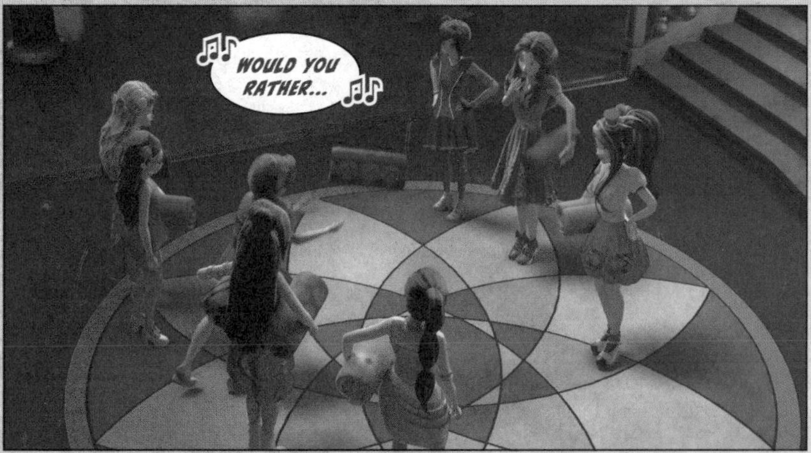
WOULD YOU RATHER...

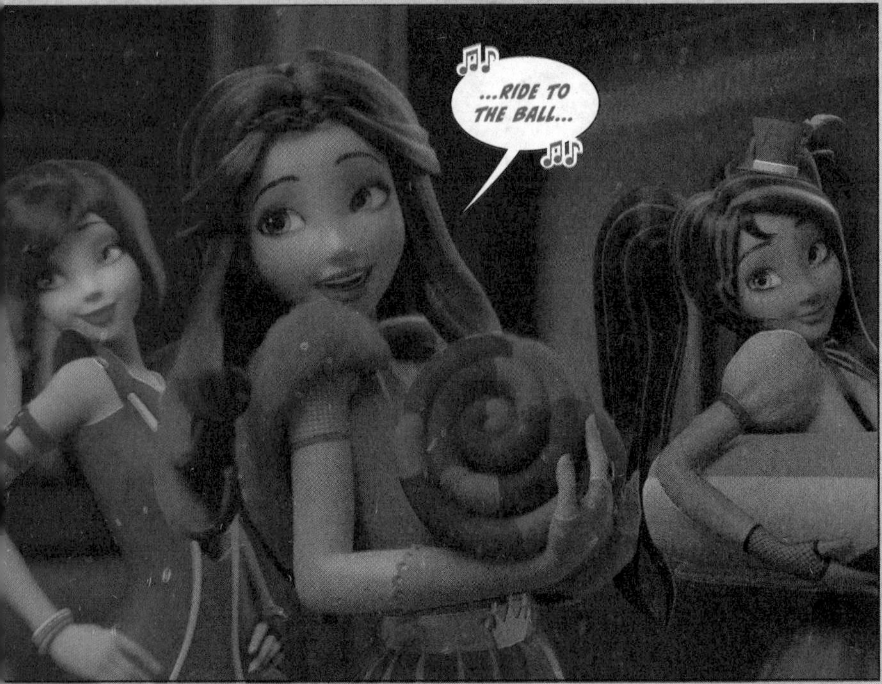
...RIDE TO THE BALL...

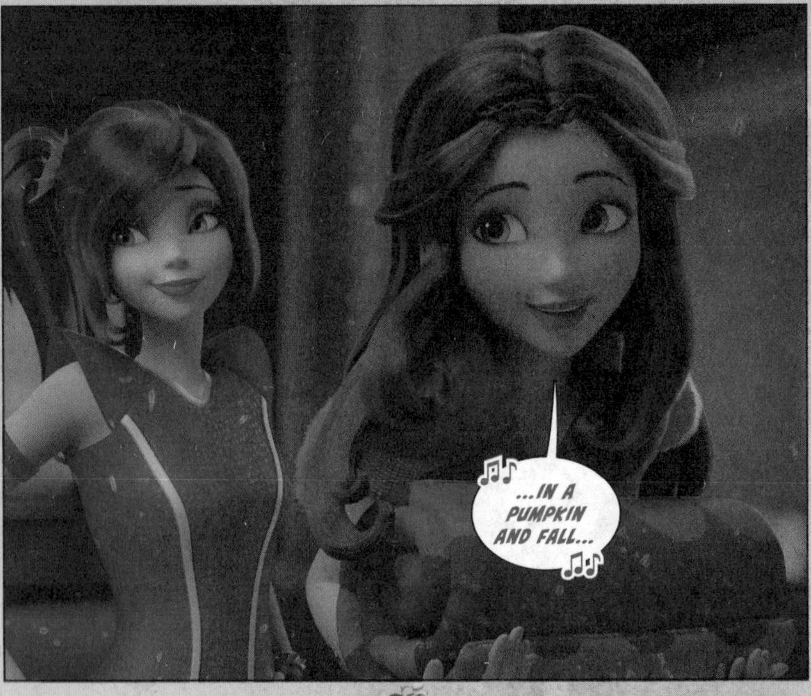
...IN A PUMPKIN AND FALL...

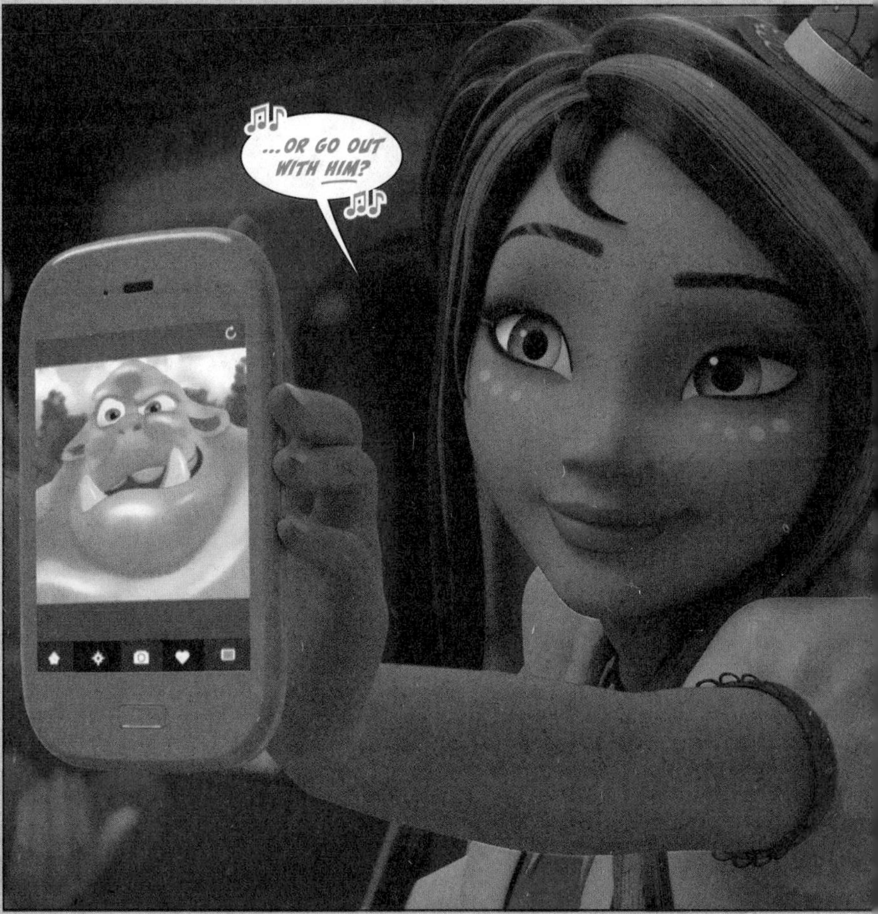
...OR GO OUT WITH HIM?
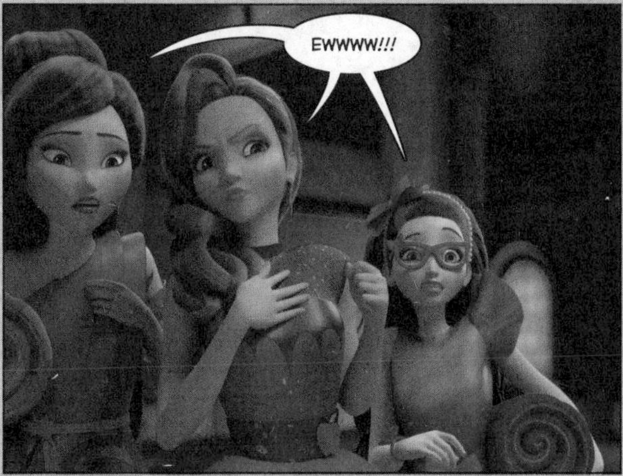
EWWWW!!!

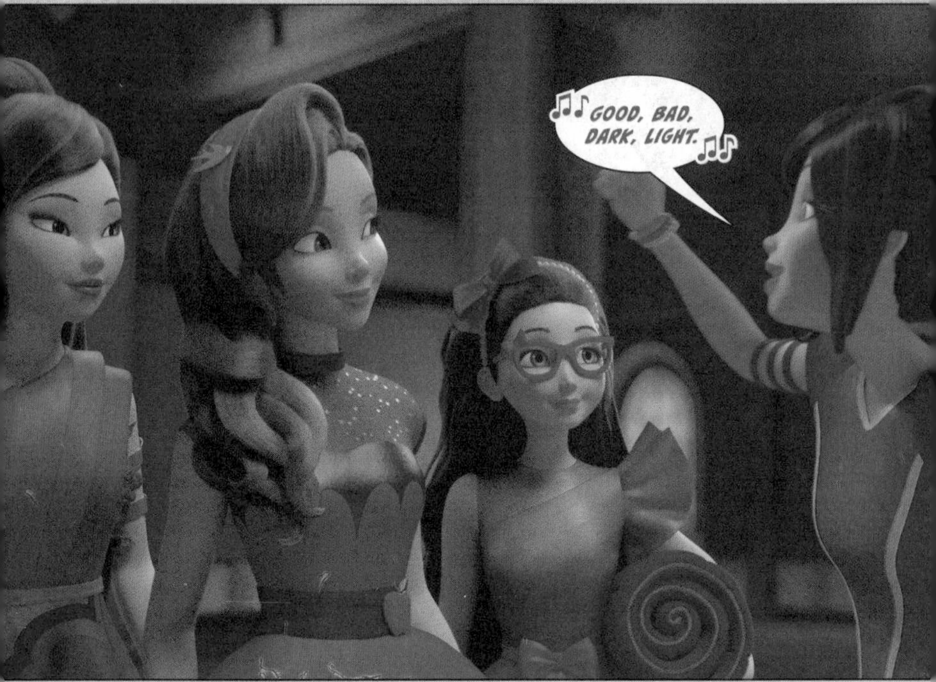
GOOD, BAD, DARK, LIGHT.

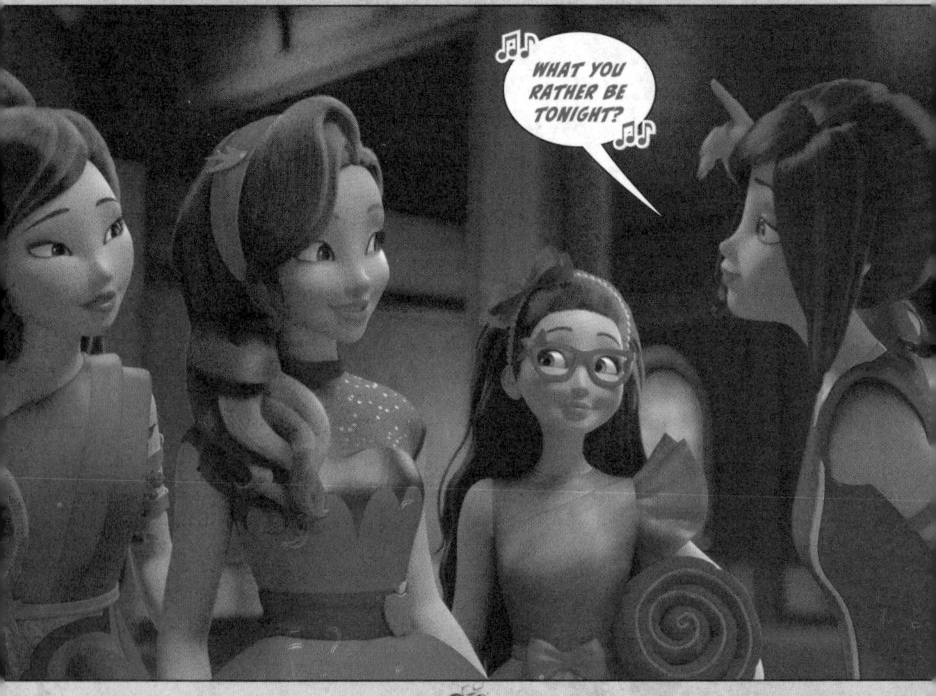
WHAT YOU RATHER BE TONIGHT?

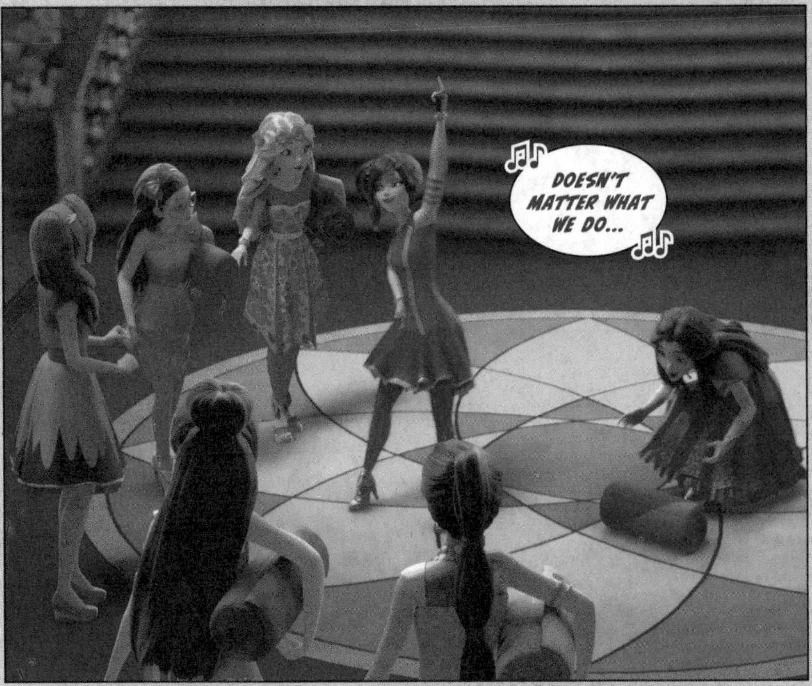
DOESN'T MATTER WHAT WE DO...

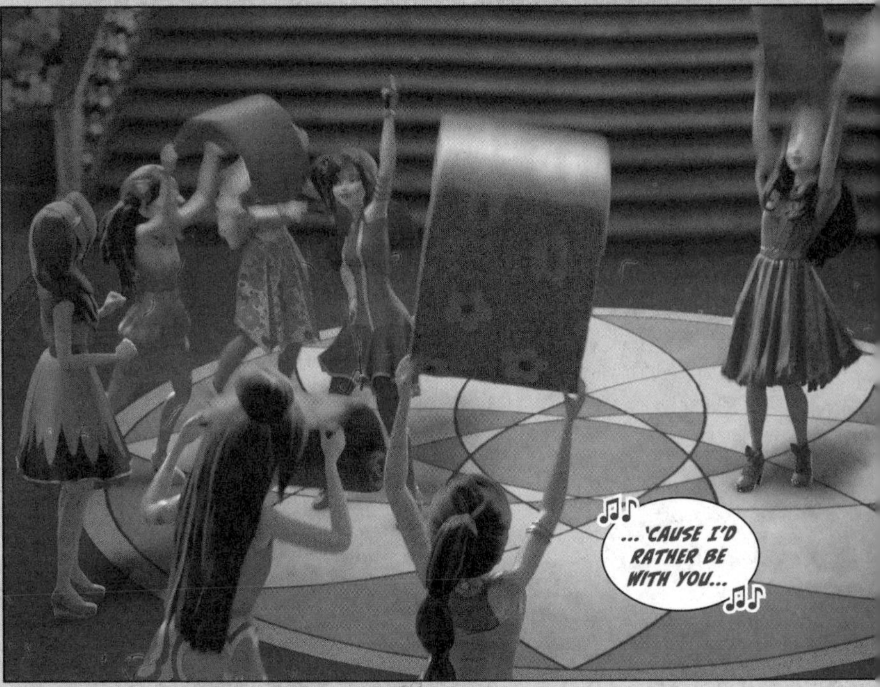
...'CAUSE I'D RATHER BE WITH YOU...

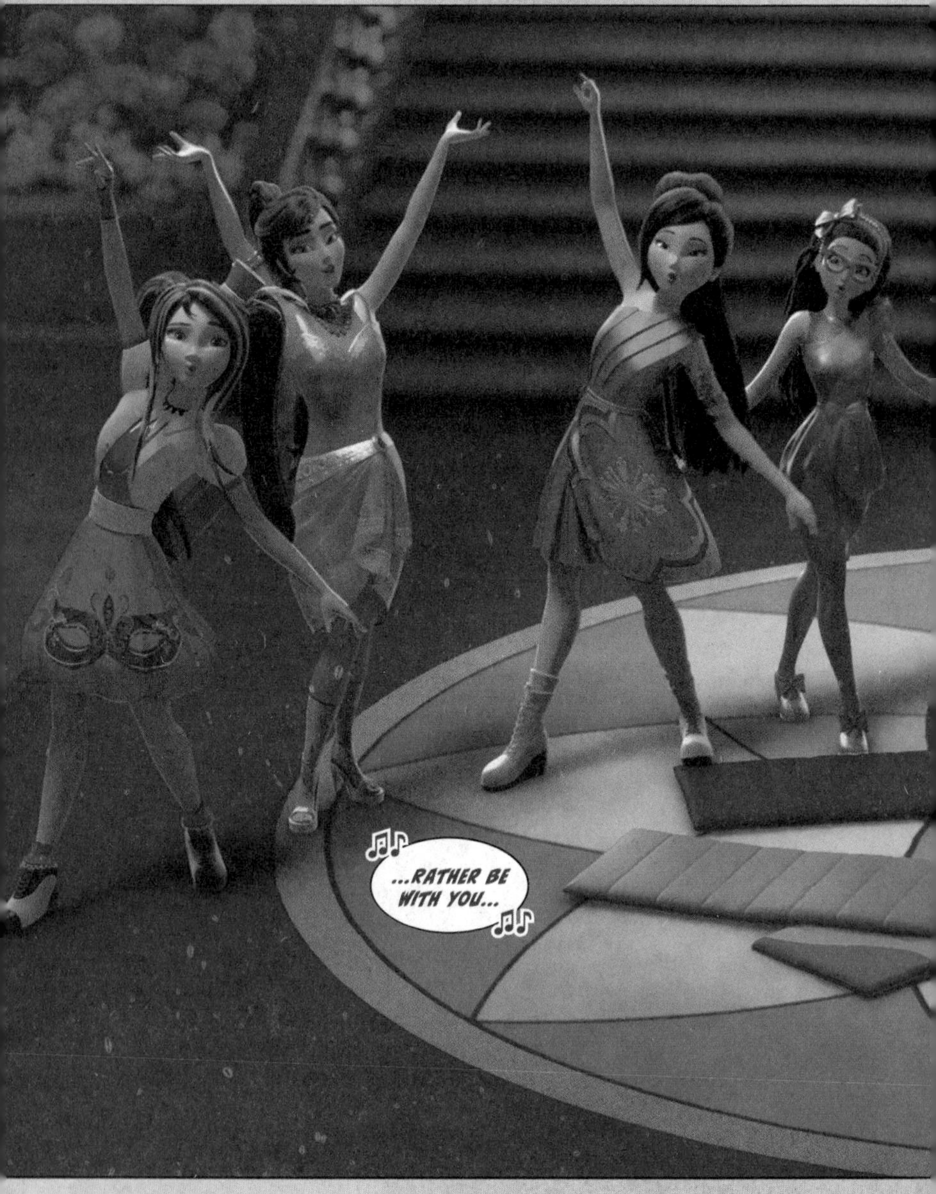
...RATHER BE WITH YOU...

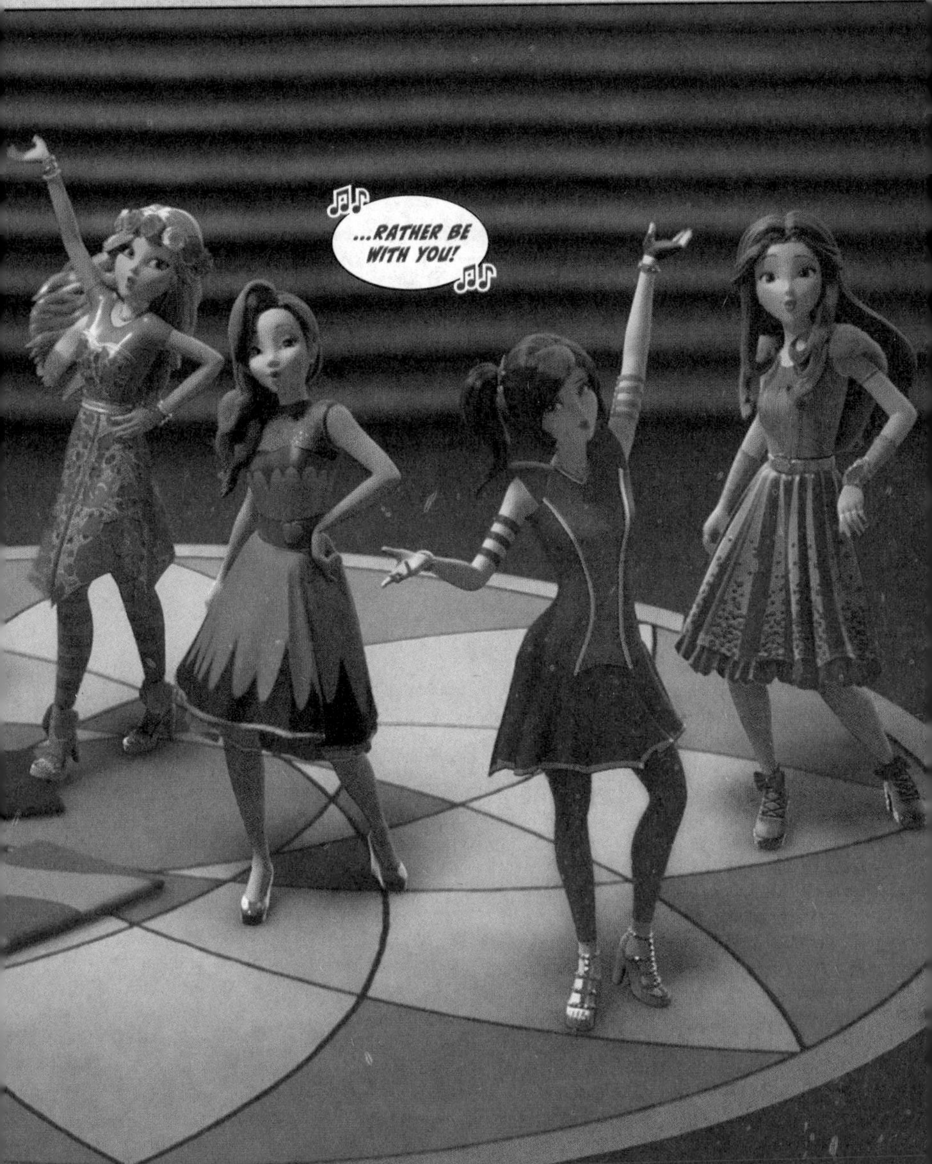
...RATHER BE WITH YOU!

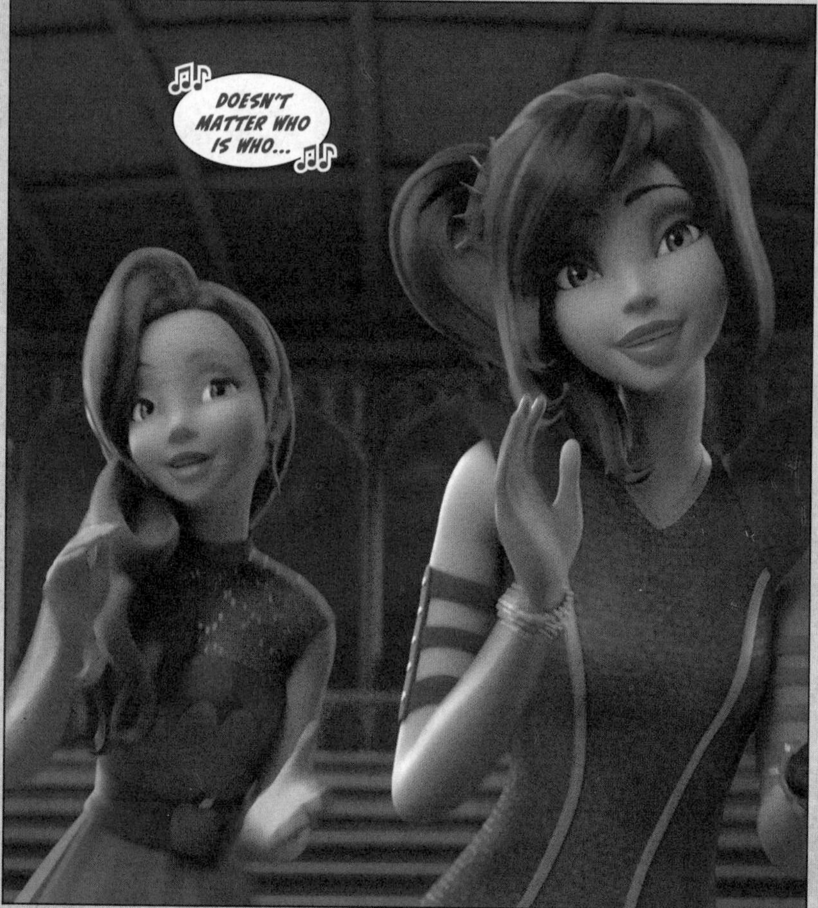
DOESN'T MATTER WHO IS WHO...

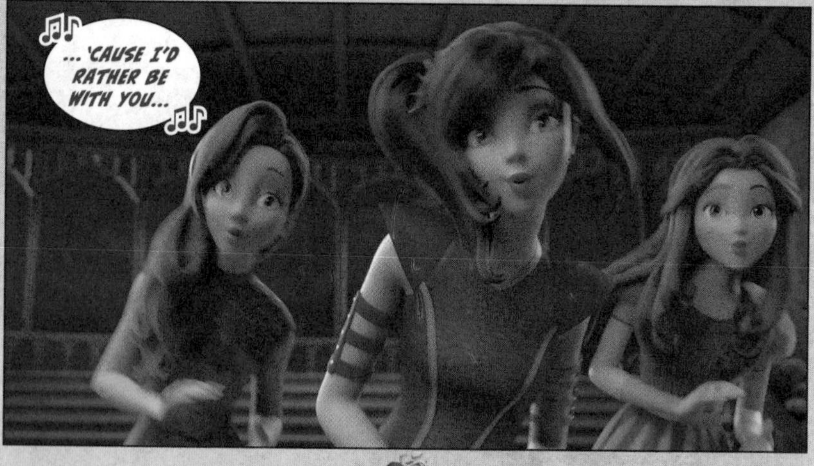
...'CAUSE I'D RATHER BE WITH YOU...

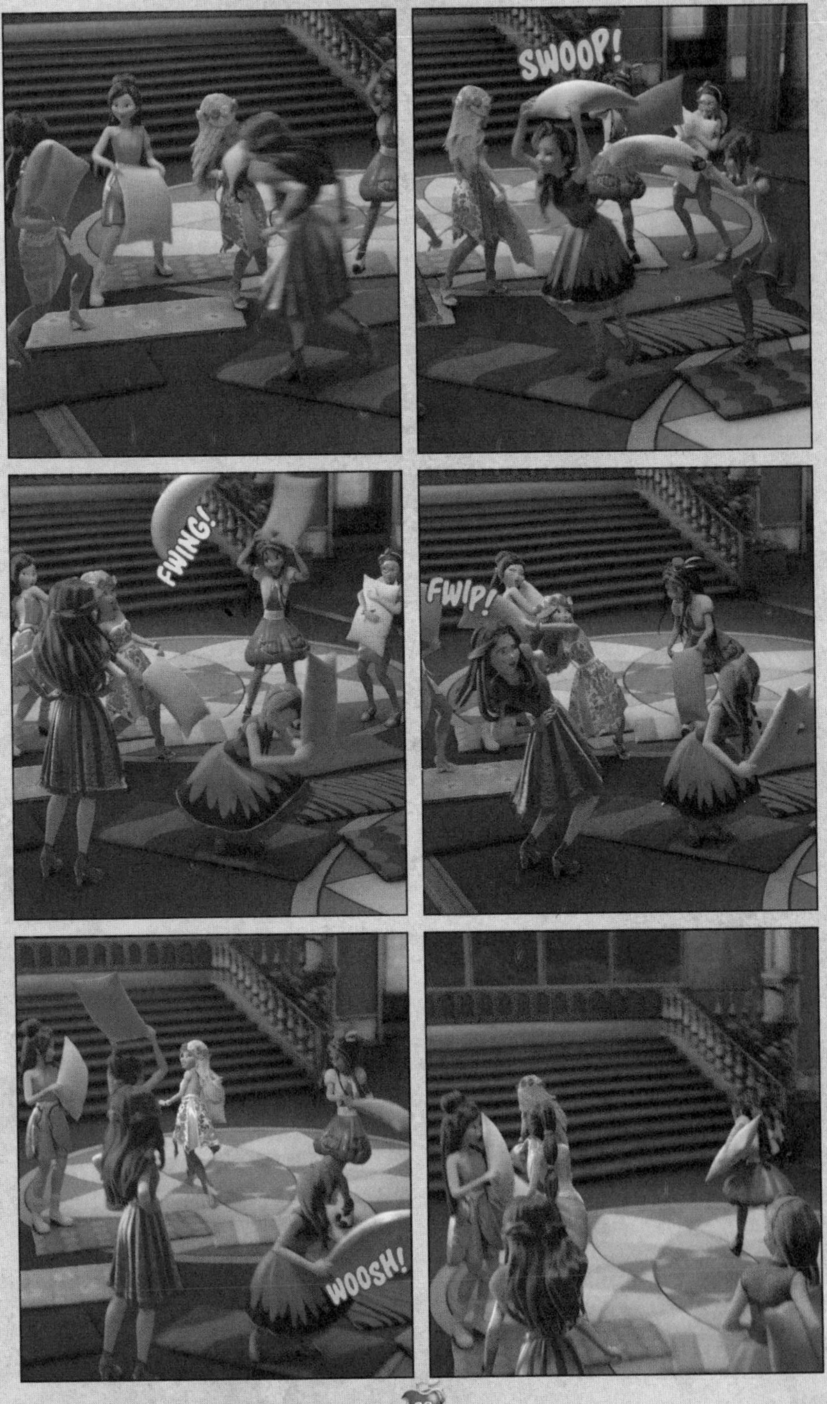
SWOOP!
FWING!
FWIP!
WOOSH!

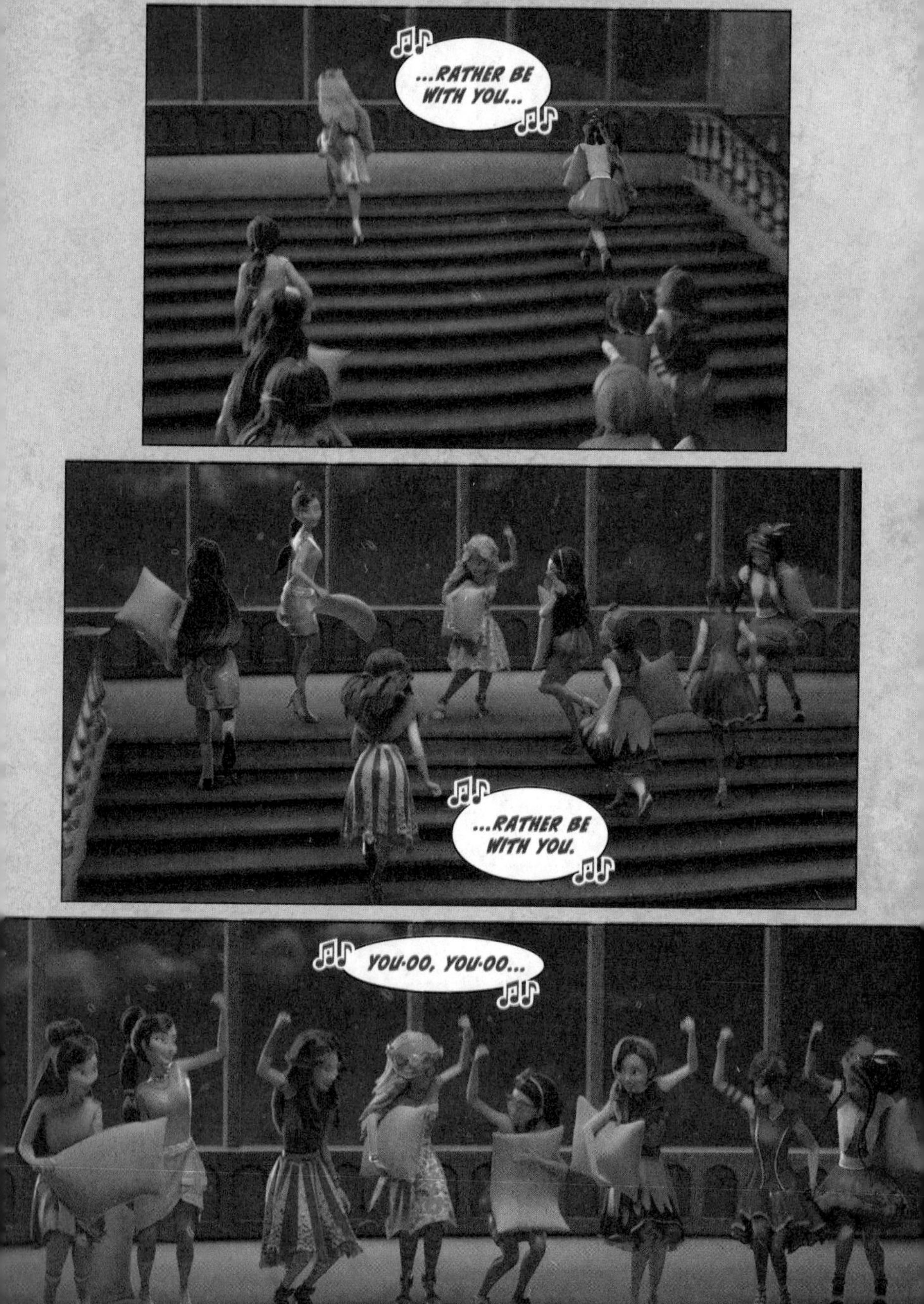
...RATHER BE WITH YOU...
...RATHER BE WITH YOU.
YOU-OO, YOU-OO...

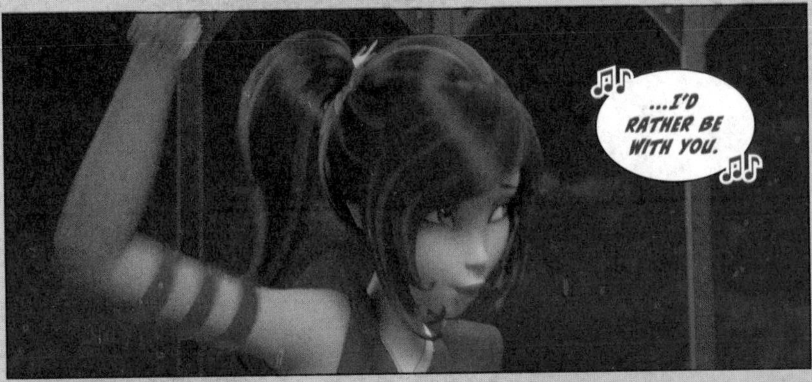
...I'D RATHER BE WITH YOU.

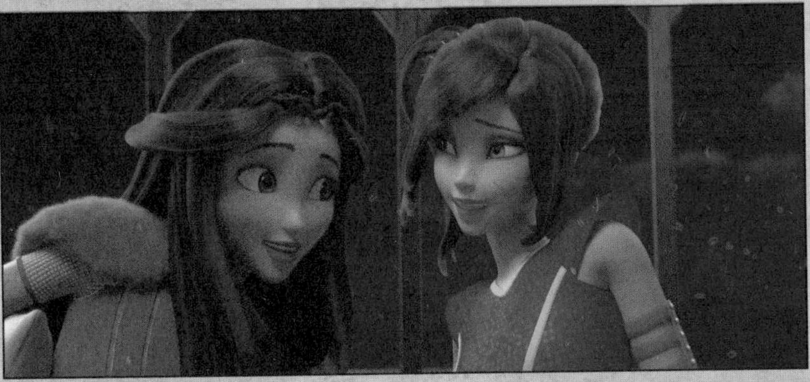

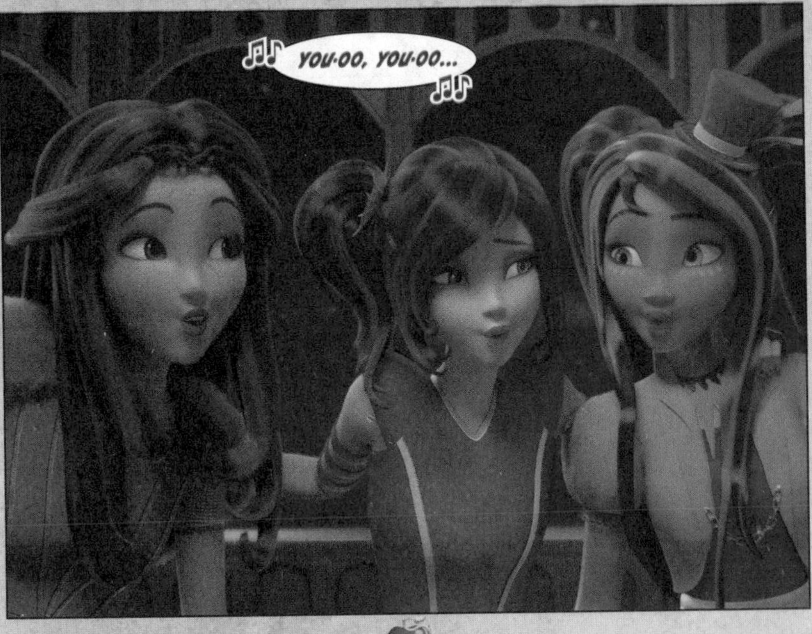
YOU-OO, YOU-OO...

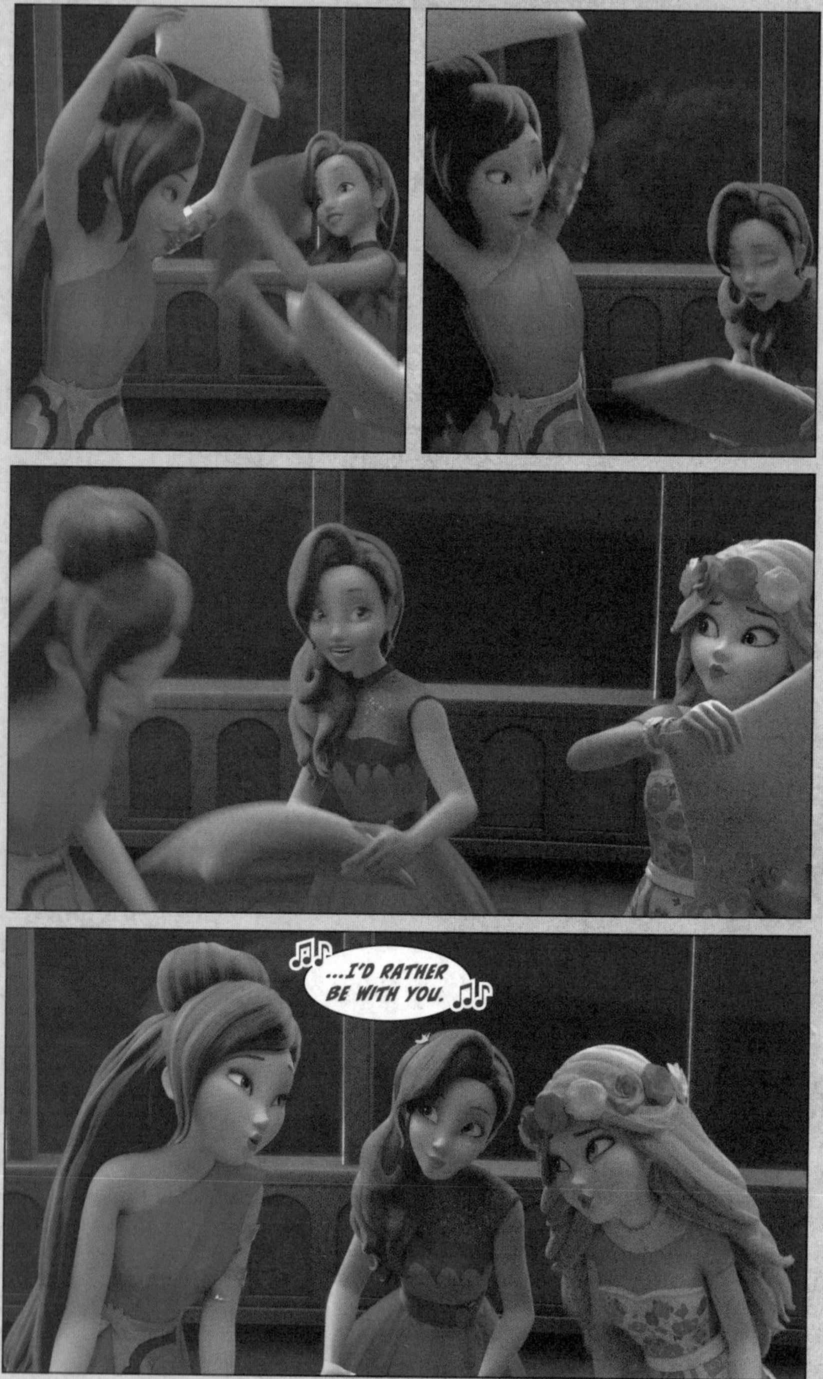
...I'D RATHER BE WITH YOU.

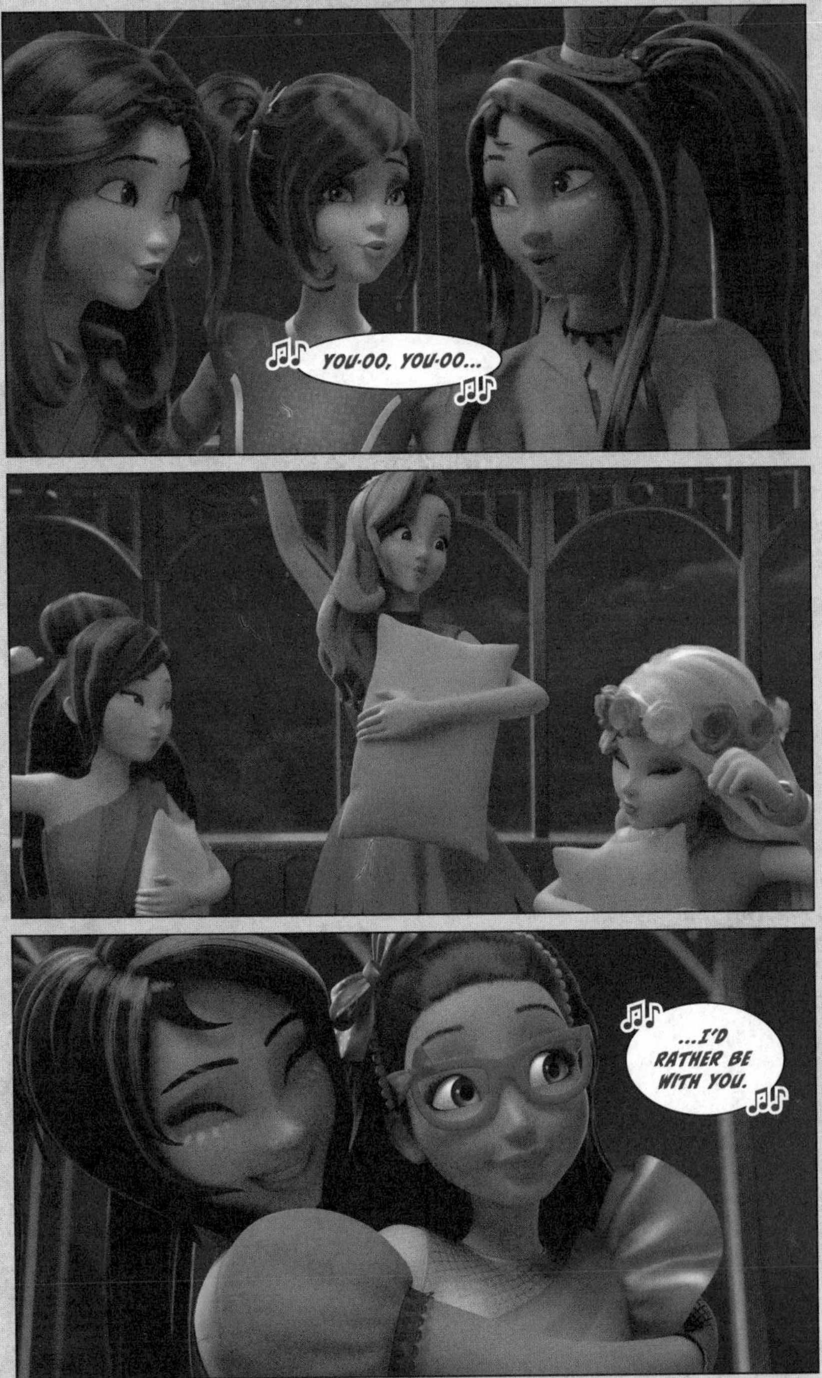
YOU-OO, YOU-OO...
...I'D RATHER BE WITH YOU.

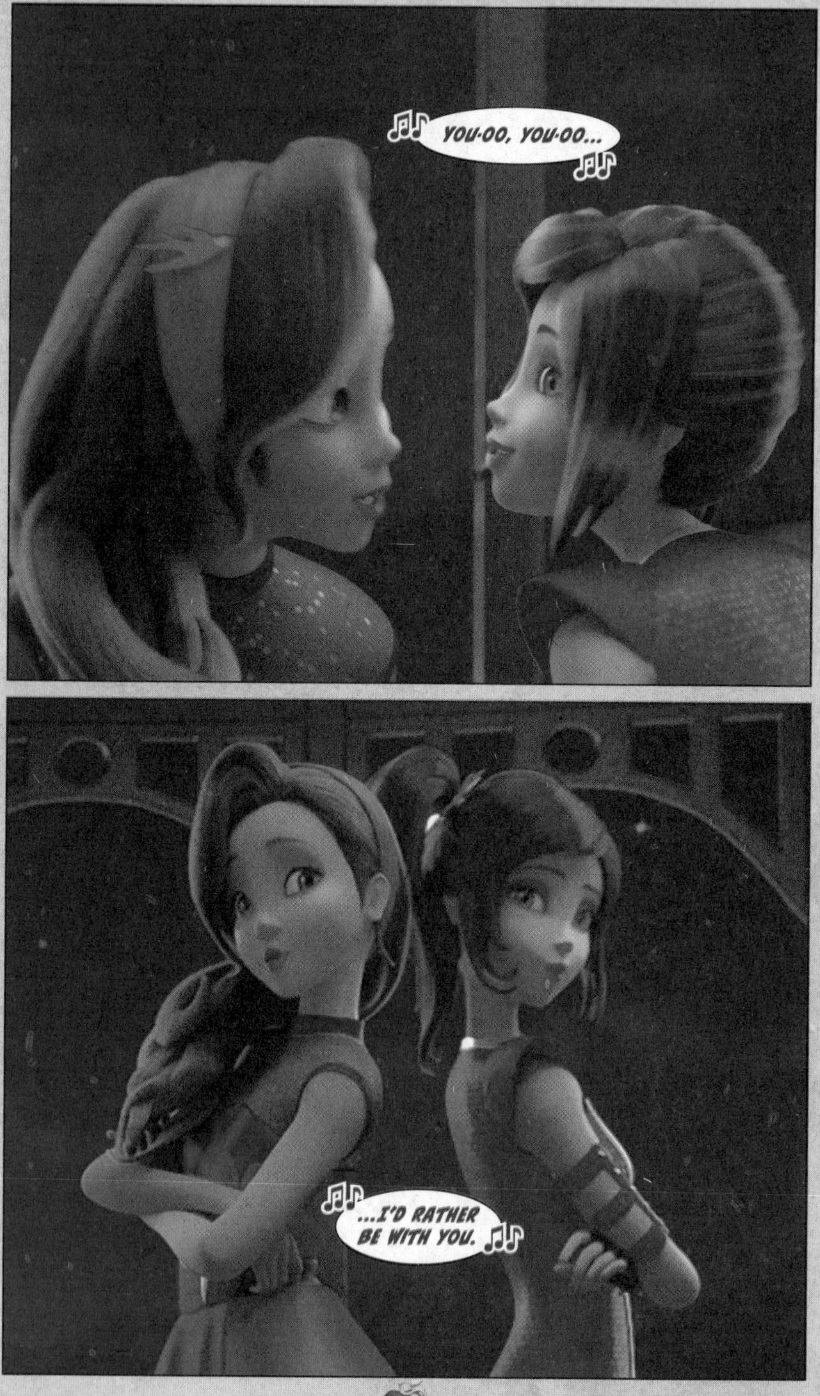
YOU-OO, YOU-OO...
...I'D RATHER BE WITH YOU.

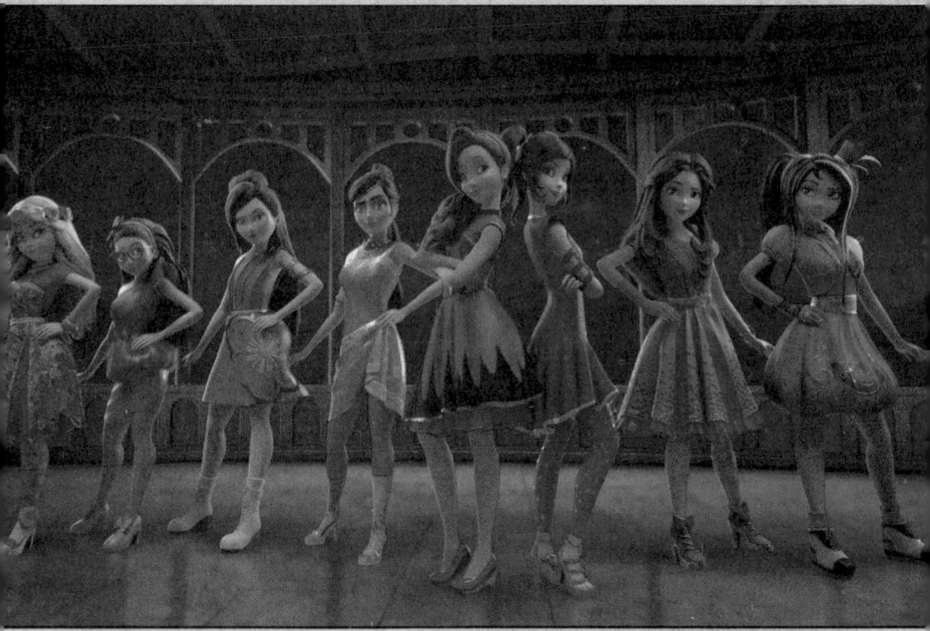

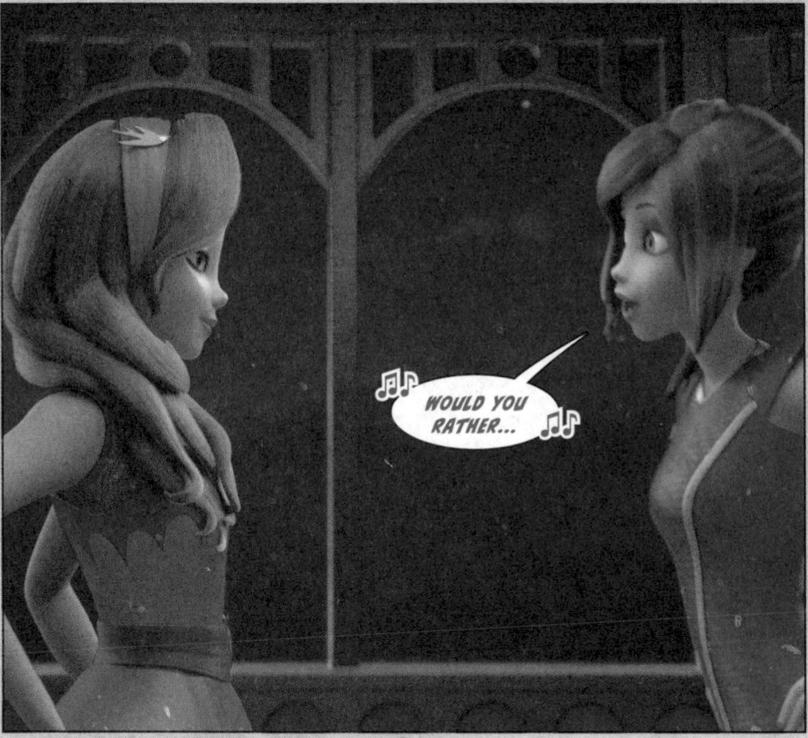
WOULD YOU RATHER...

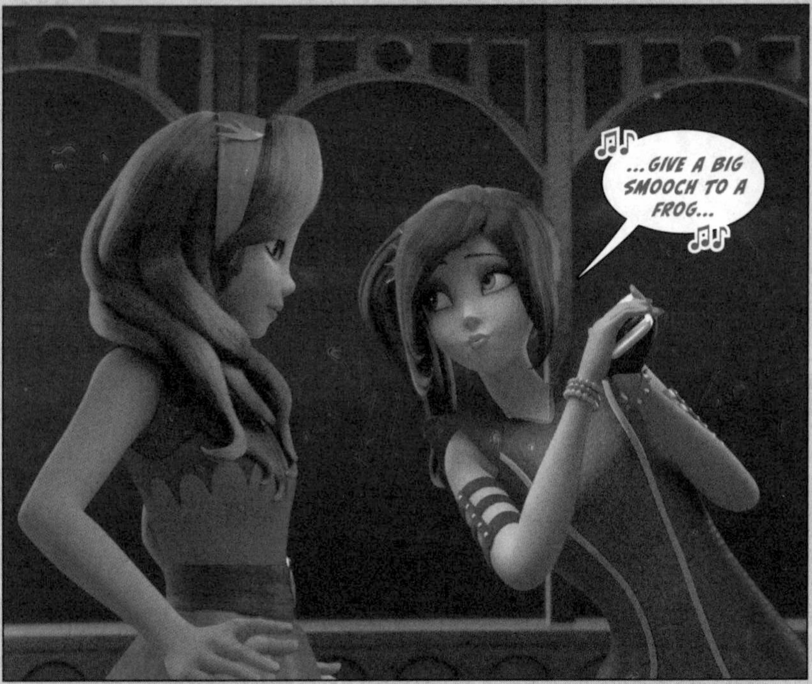
...GIVE A BIG SMOOCH TO A FROG...

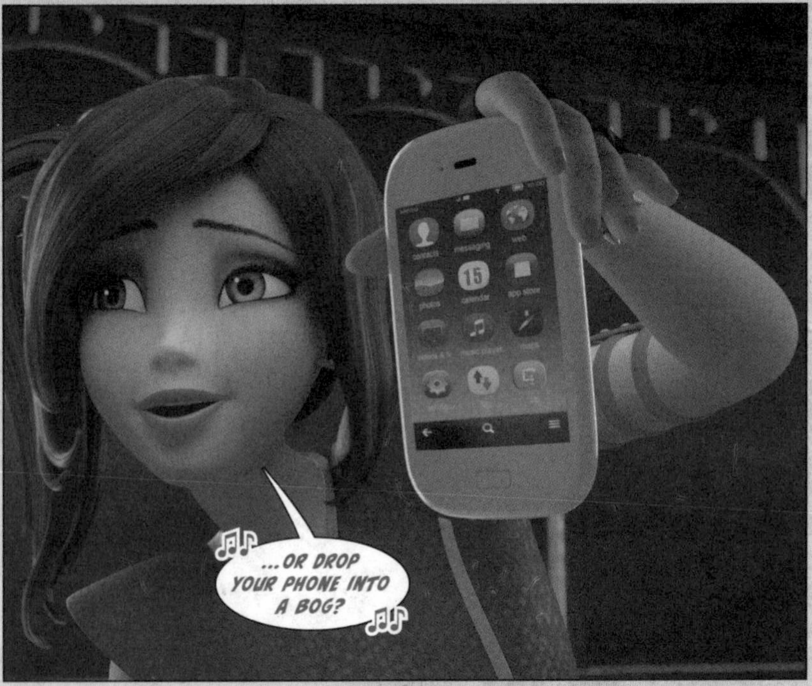
...OR DROP YOUR PHONE INTO A BOG?

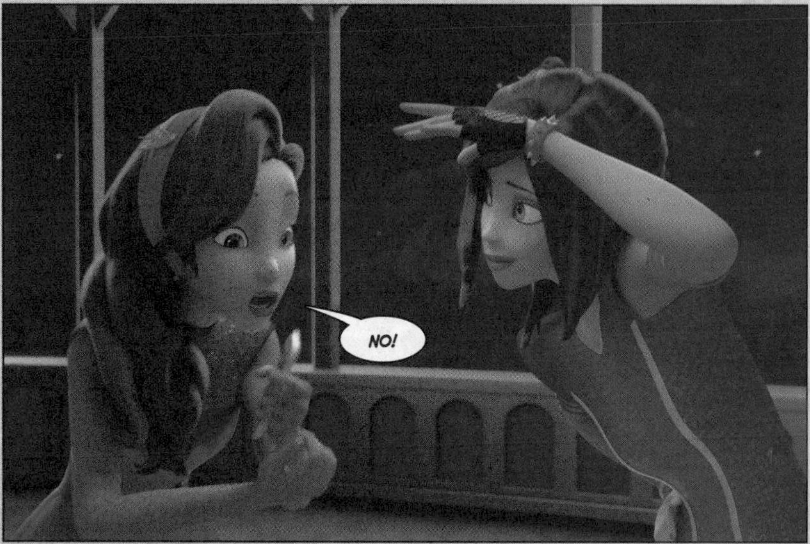
NO!

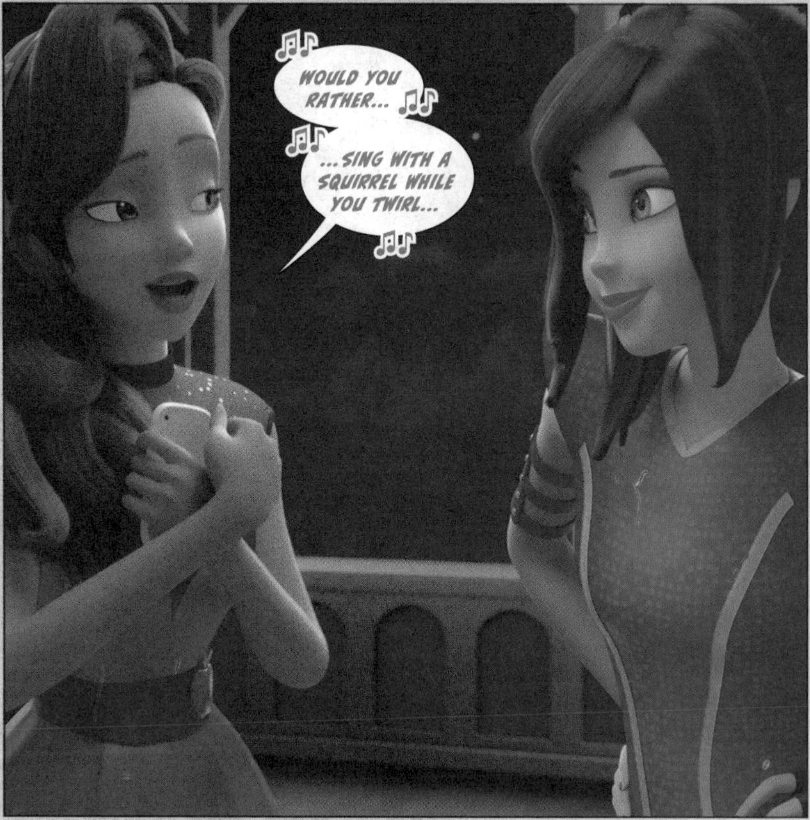
WOULD YOU RATHER...
...SING WITH A SQUIRREL WHILE YOU TWIRL...

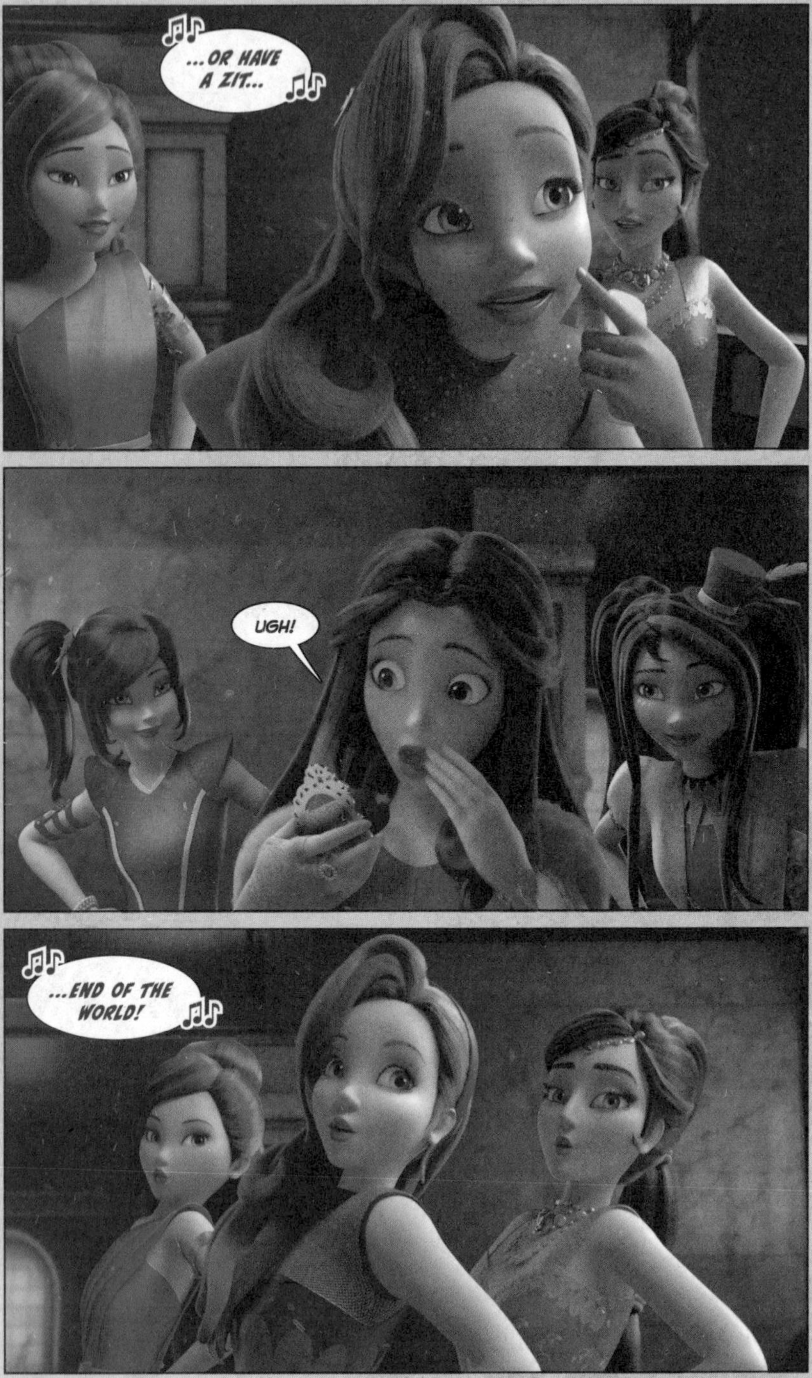
...OR HAVE A ZIT...
UGH!
...END OF THE WORLD!

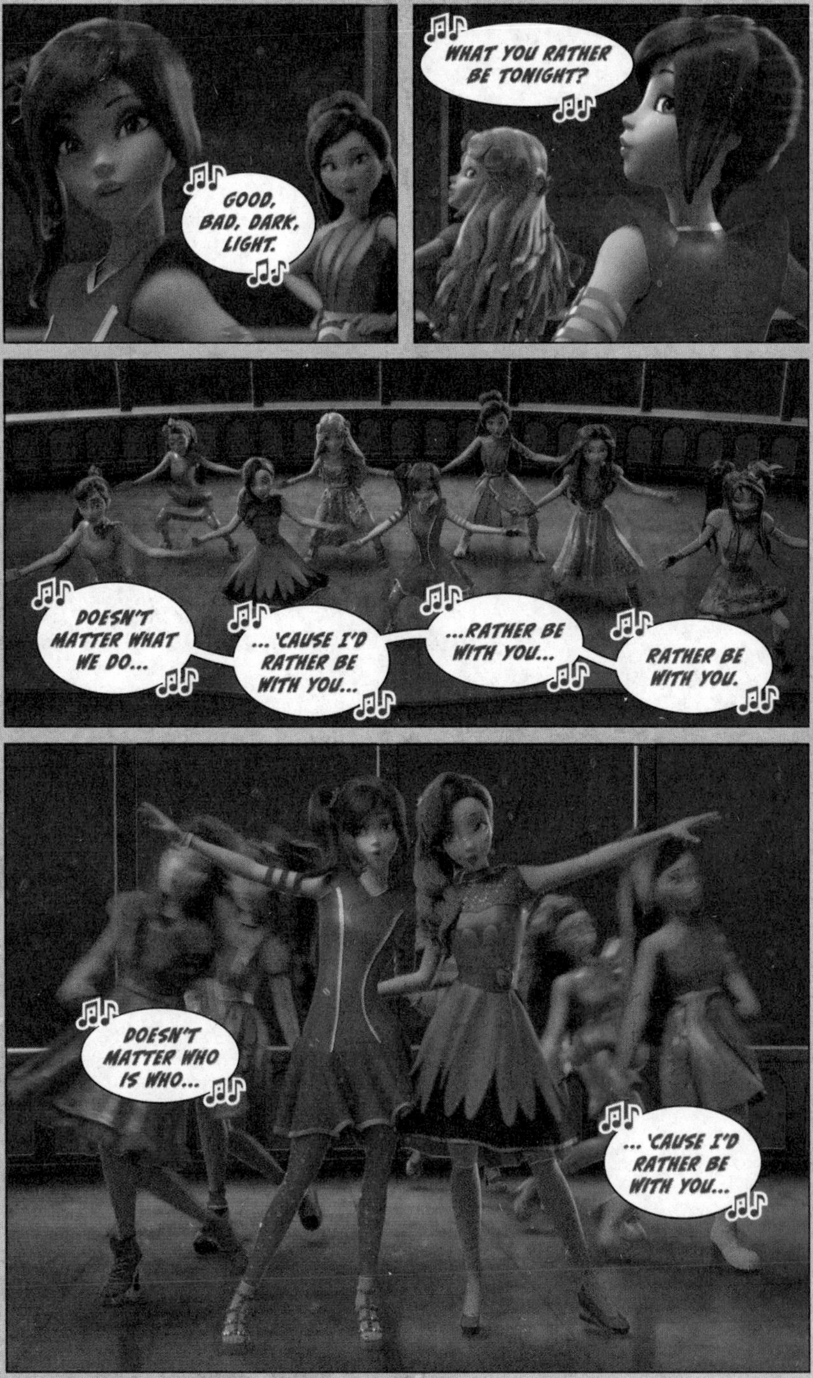
GOOD, BAD, DARK, LIGHT.
WHAT YOU RATHER BE TONIGHT?
DOESN'T MATTER WHAT WE DO...
... 'CAUSE I'D RATHER BE WITH YOU...
...RATHER BE WITH YOU...
RATHER BE WITH YOU.
DOESN'T MATTER WHO IS WHO...
... 'CAUSE I'D RATHER BE WITH YOU...

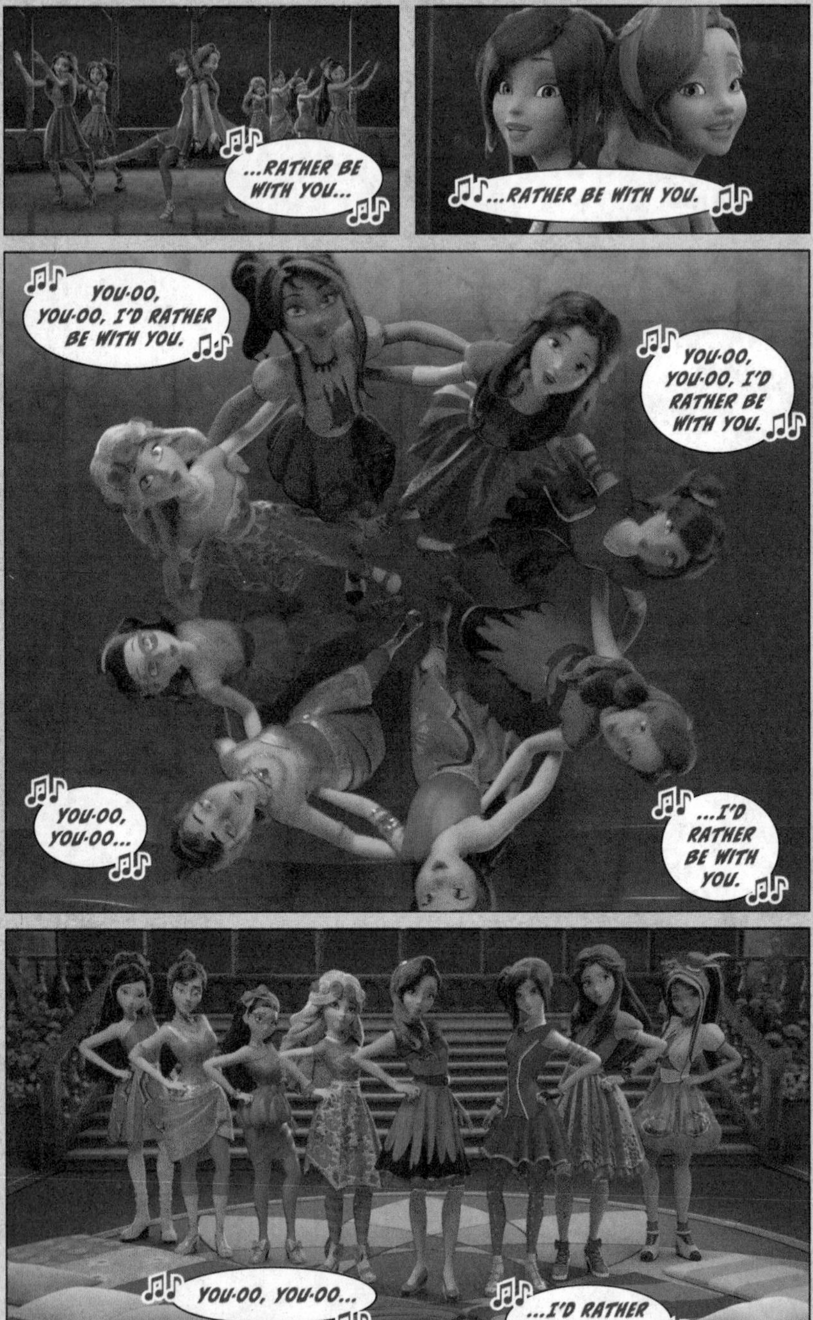
...RATHER BE WITH YOU...
...RATHER BE WITH YOU.
YOU-OO, YOU-OO, I'D RATHER BE WITH YOU.
YOU-OO, YOU-OO, I'D RATHER BE WITH YOU.
YOU-OO, YOU-OO...
...I'D RATHER BE WITH YOU.
YOU-OO, YOU-OO...
...I'D RATHER BE WITH YOU!

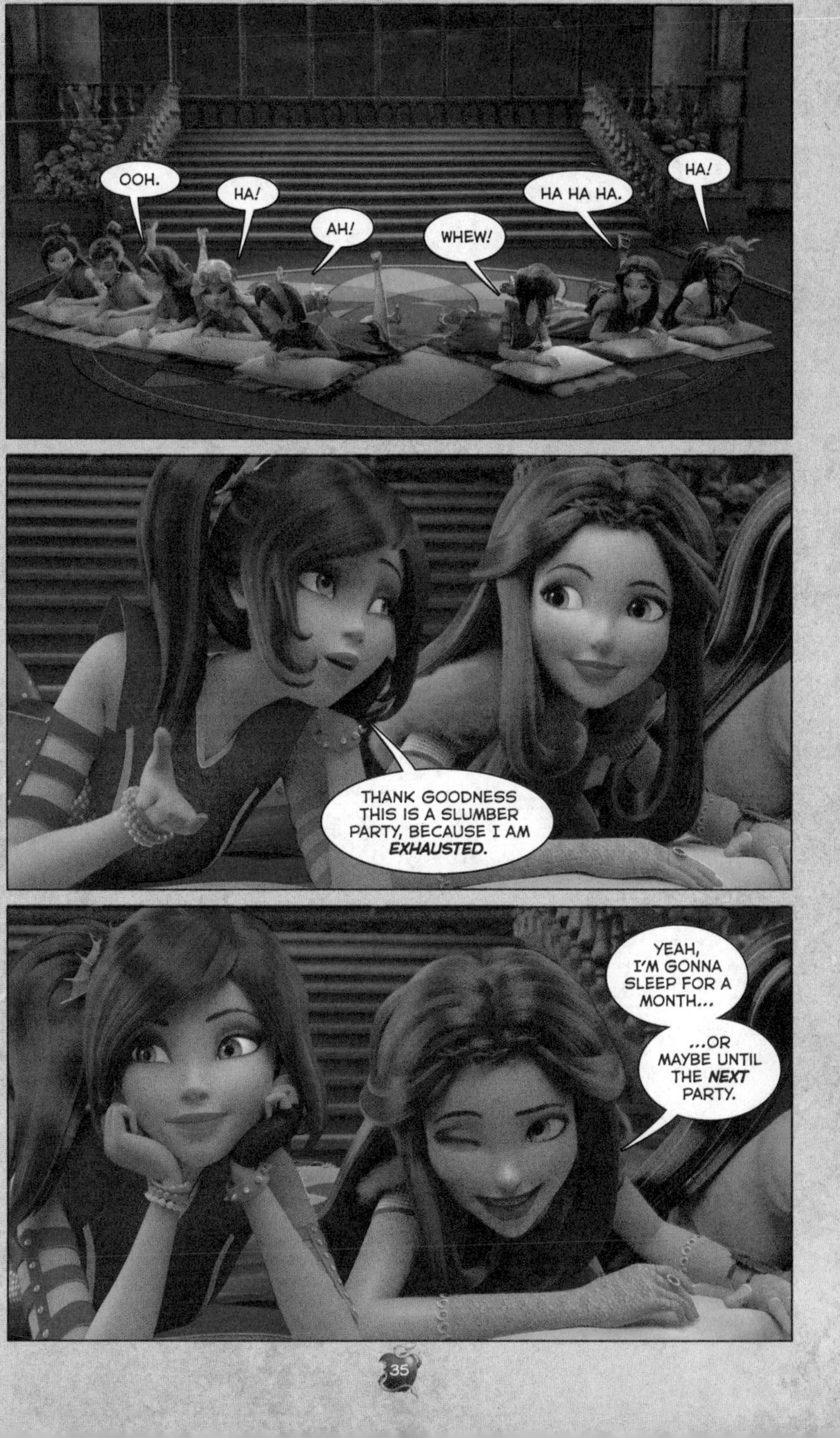
OOH.
HA!
AH!
WHEW!
HA HA HA.
HA!
THANK GOODNESS THIS IS A SLUMBER PARTY, BECAUSE I AM ***EXHAUSTED.***
YEAH, I'M GONNA SLEEP FOR A MONTH...
...OR MAYBE UNTIL THE ***NEXT*** PARTY.

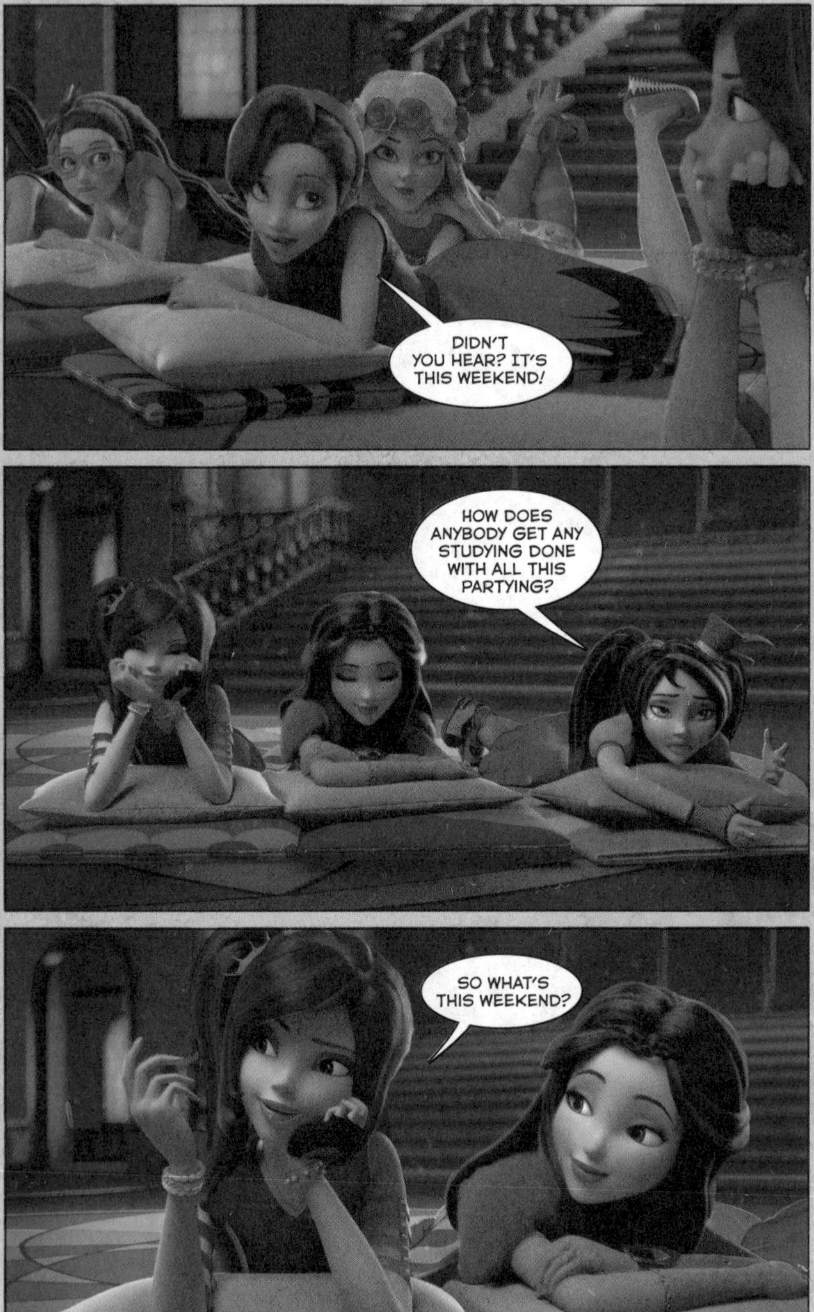
DIDN'T YOU HEAR? IT'S THIS WEEKEND!
HOW DOES ANYBODY GET ANY STUDYING DONE WITH ALL THIS PARTYING?
SO WHAT'S THIS WEEKEND?

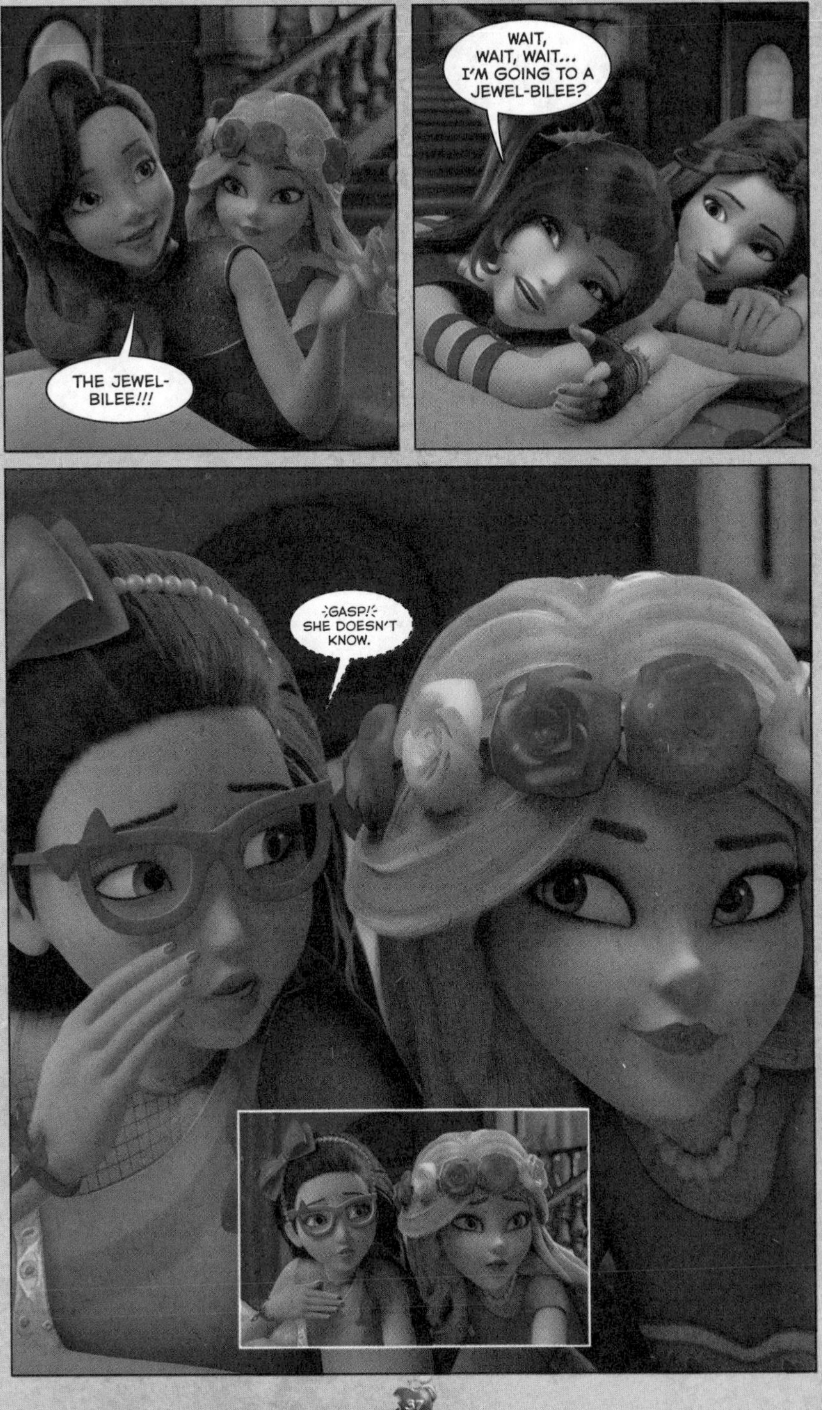
THE JEWEL-BILEE!!!
WAIT, WAIT, WAIT... I'M GOING TO A JEWEL-BILEE?
GASP! SHE DOESN'T KNOW.

CHAPTER 20: ODD MAL OUT

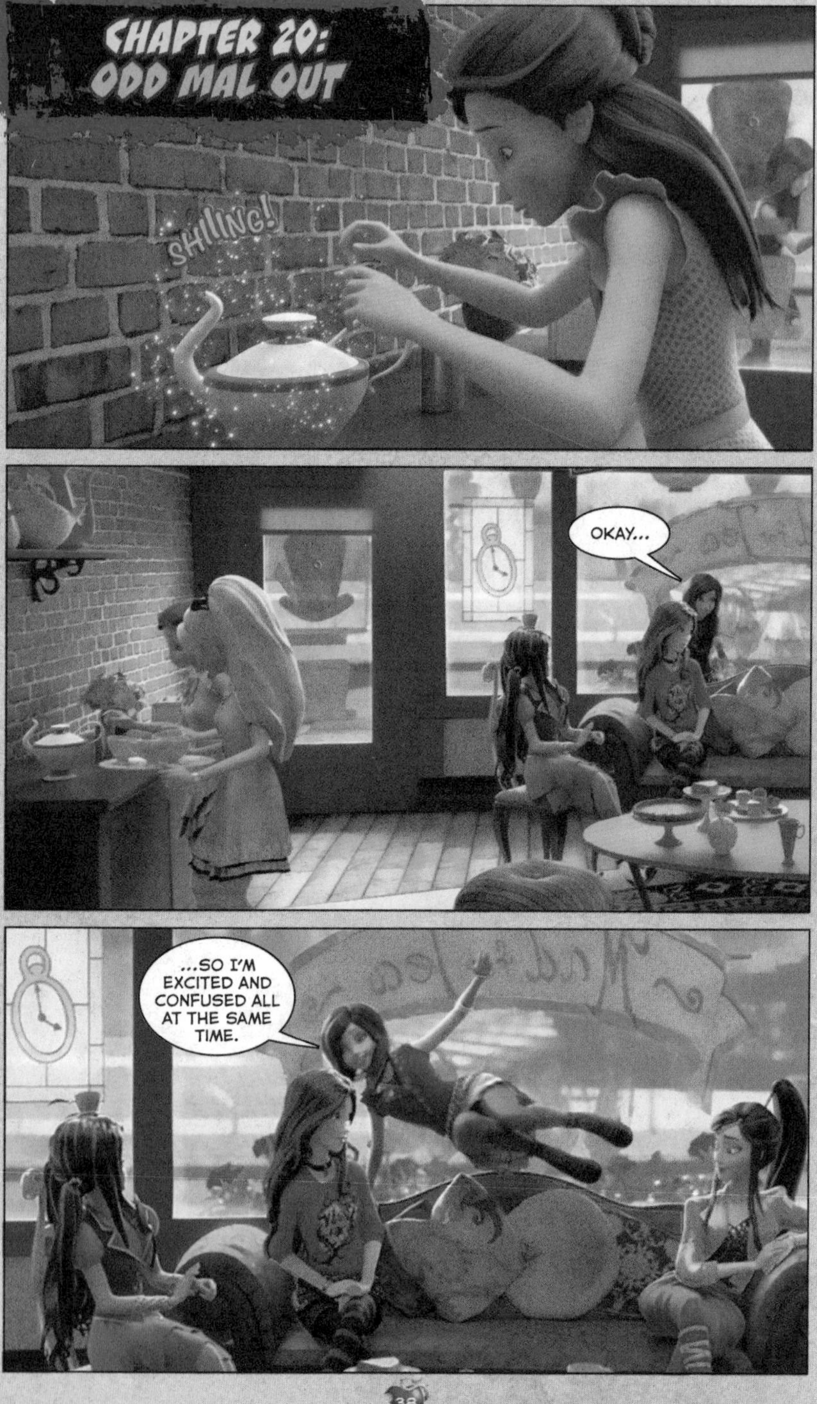

SHIIING!
OKAY...
...SO I'M EXCITED AND CONFUSED ALL AT THE SAME TIME.

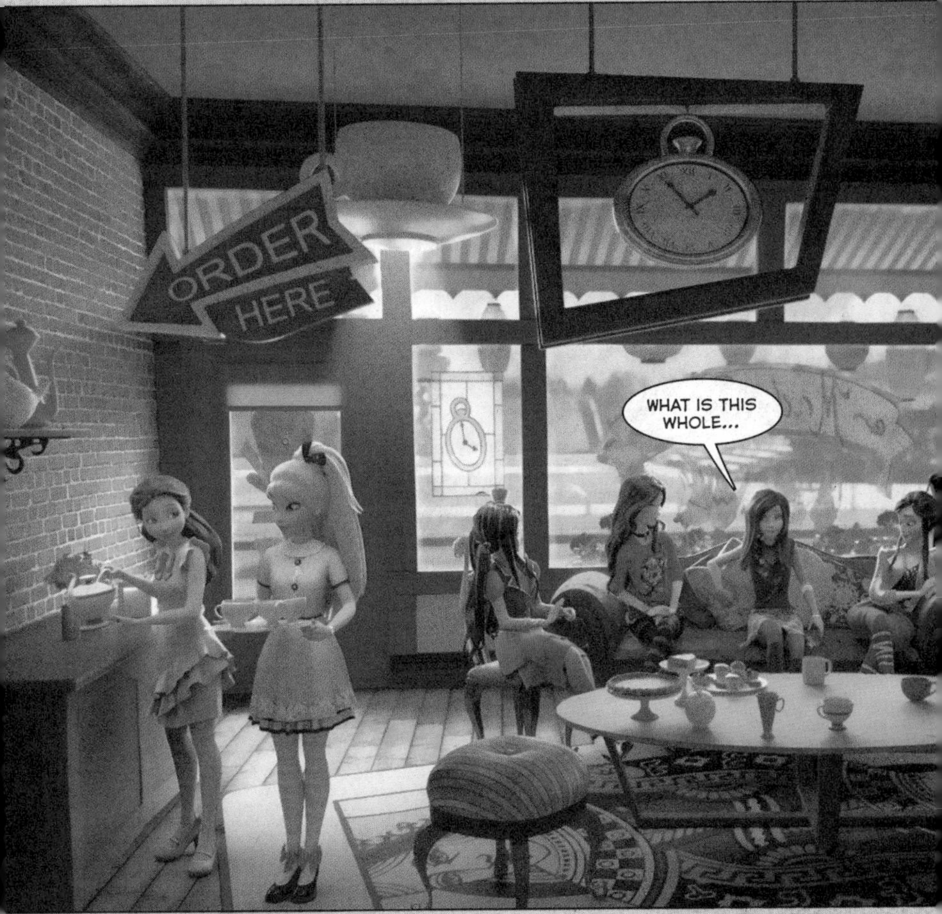
ORDER HERE
WHAT IS THIS WHOLE...

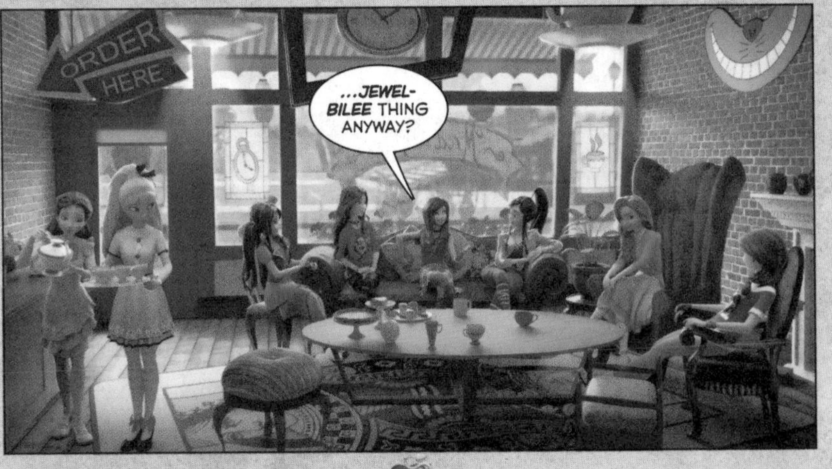
ORDER HERE
...JEWEL-BILEE THING ANYWAY?

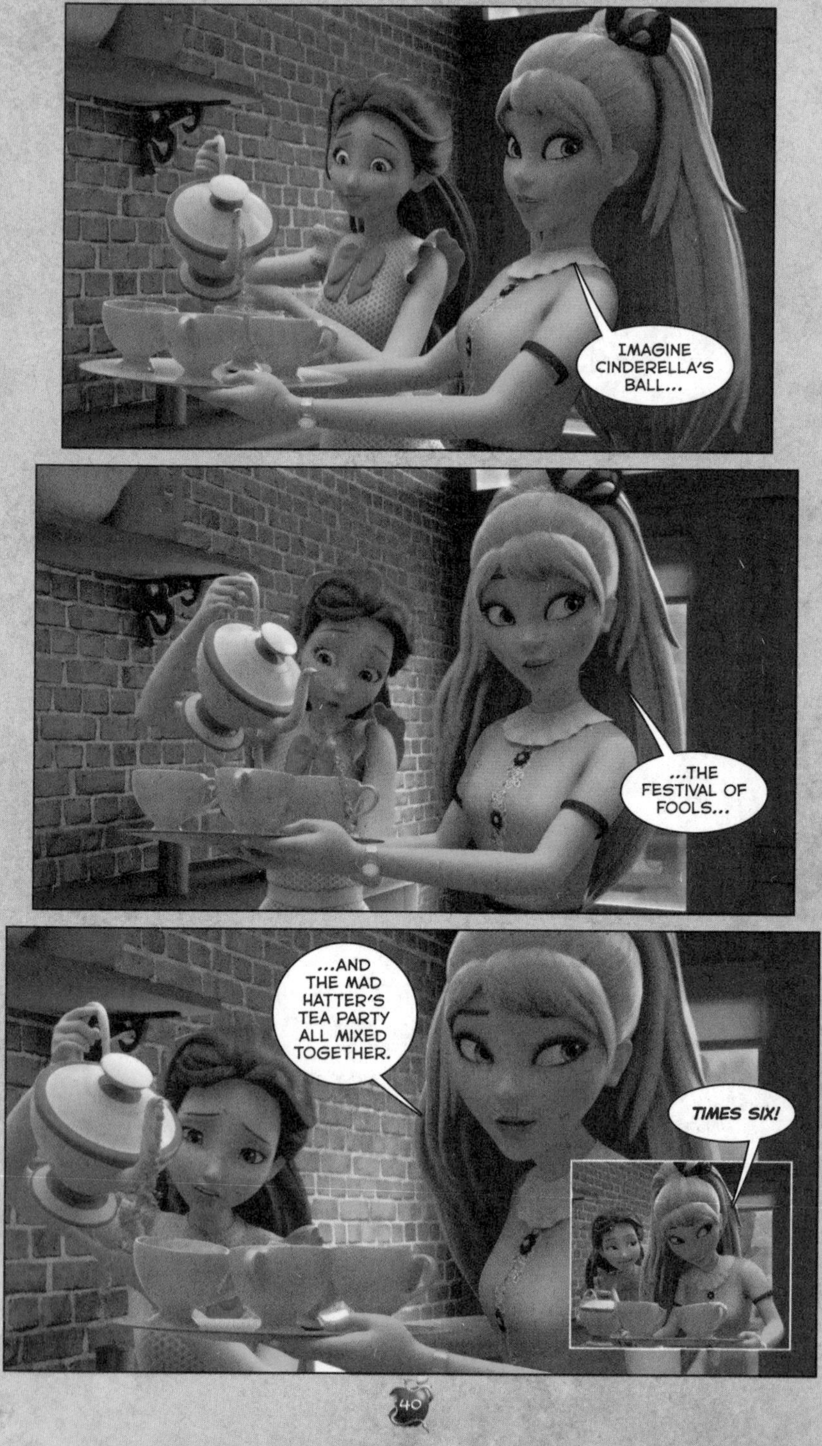
IMAGINE CINDERELLA'S BALL...
...THE FESTIVAL OF FOOLS...
...AND THE MAD HATTER'S TEA PARTY ALL MIXED TOGETHER.
TIMES SIX!

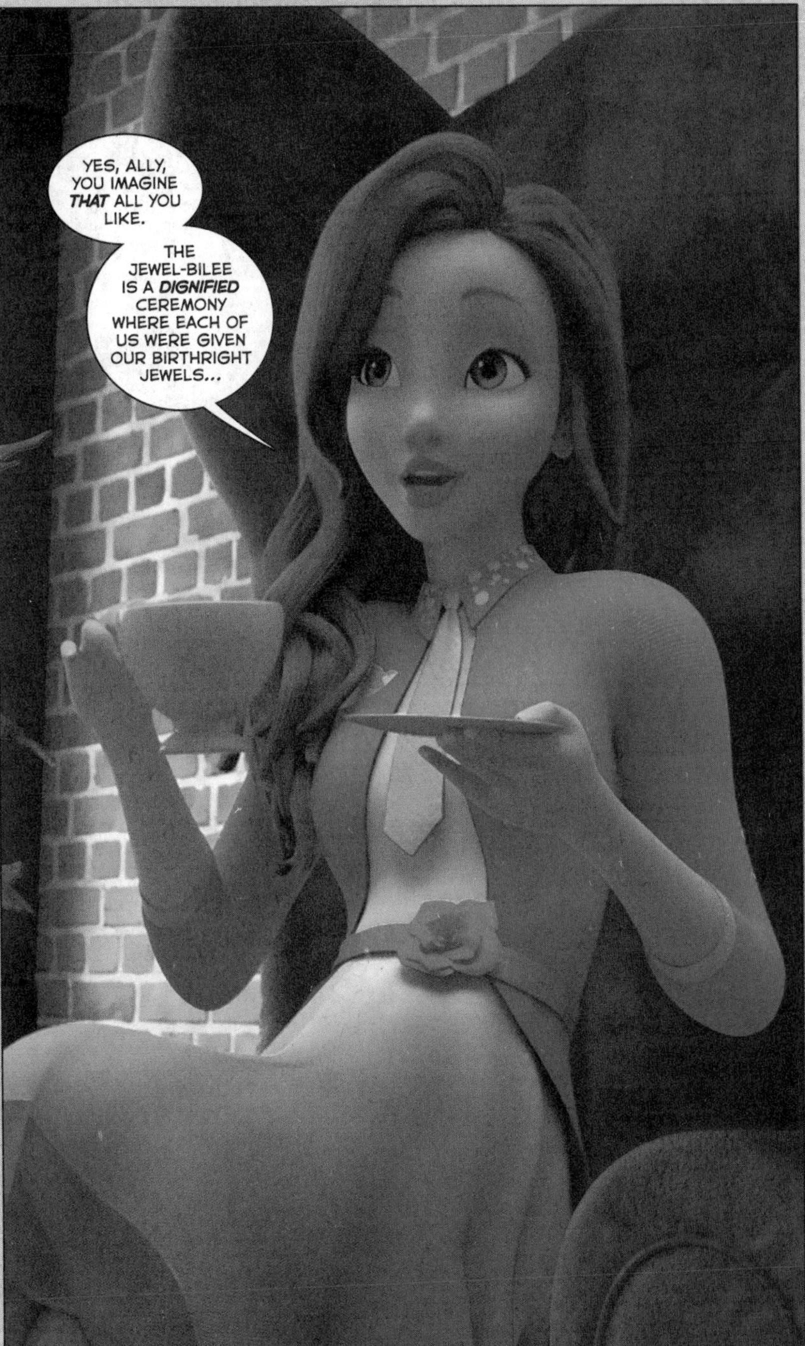
YES, ALLY, YOU IMAGINE *THAT* ALL YOU LIKE.
THE JEWEL-BILEE IS A *DIGNIFIED* CEREMONY WHERE EACH OF US WERE GIVEN OUR BIRTHRIGHT JEWELS...

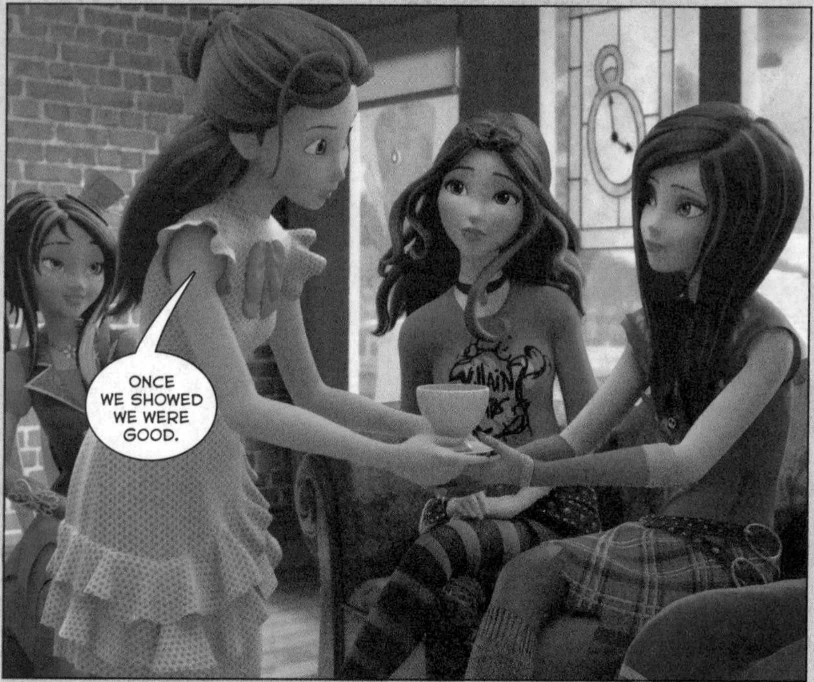
ONCE WE SHOWED WE WERE GOOD.

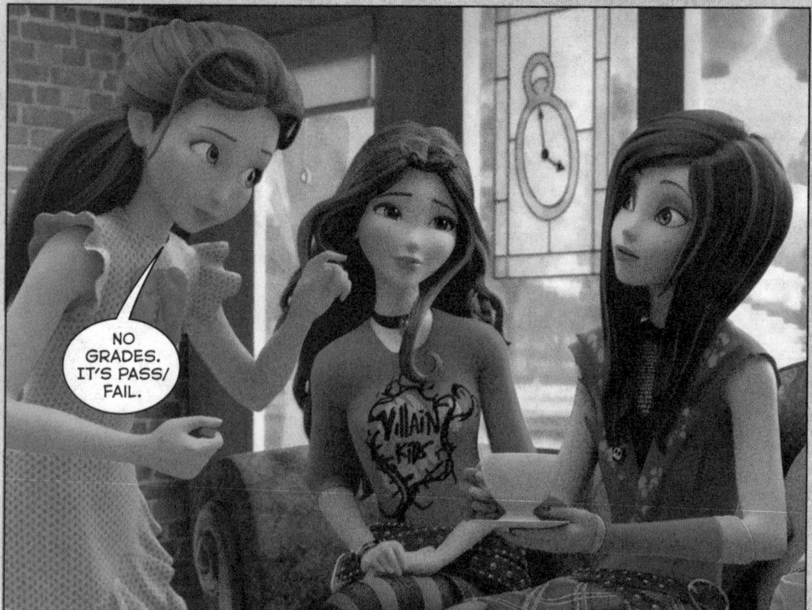
NO GRADES. IT'S PASS/ FAIL.

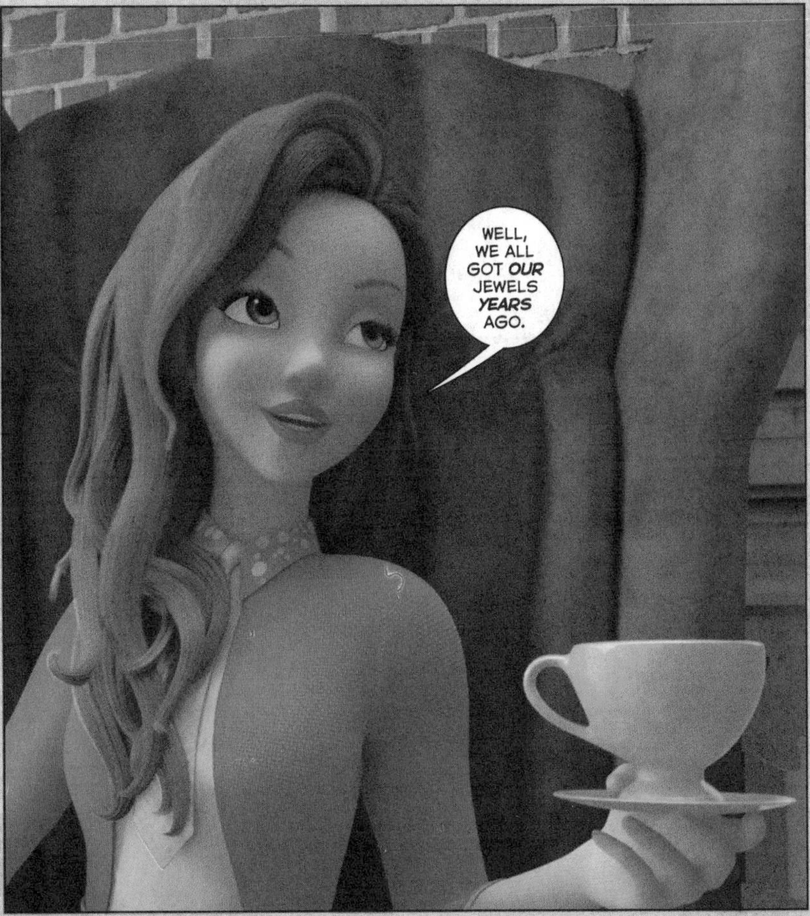
WELL, WE ALL GOT **OUR** JEWELS ***YEARS*** AGO.

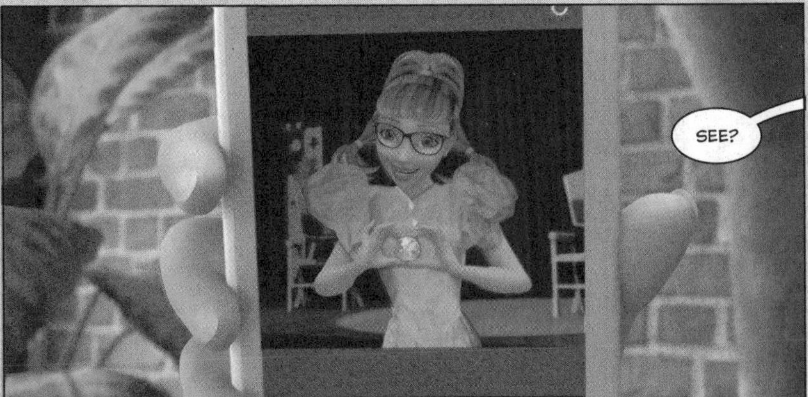
SEE?

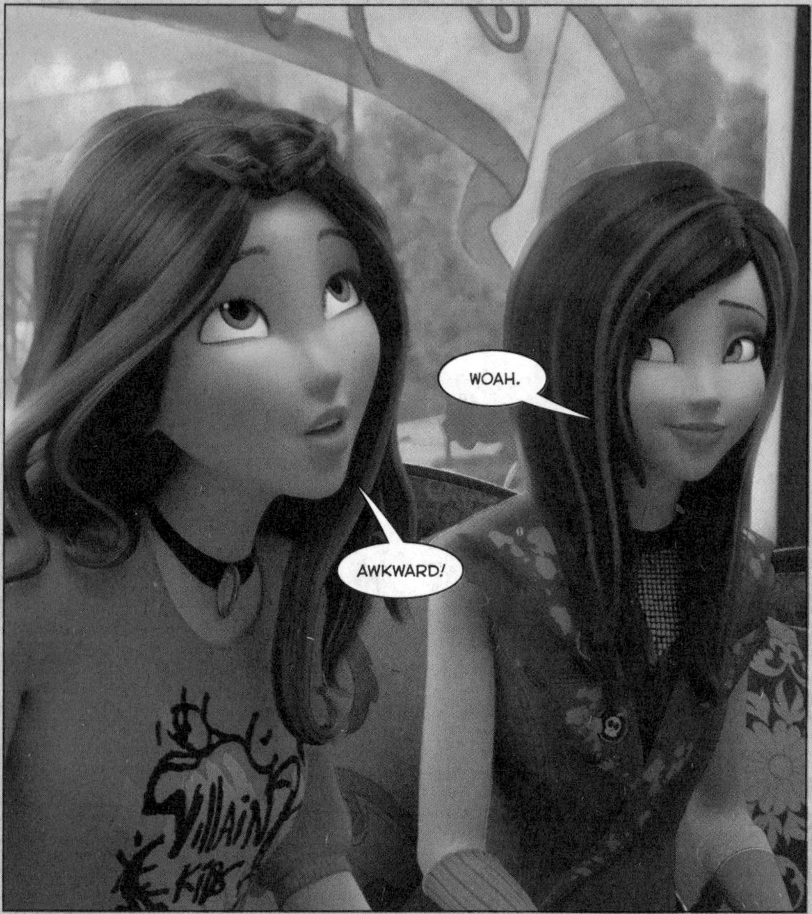
WOAH.
AWKWARD!

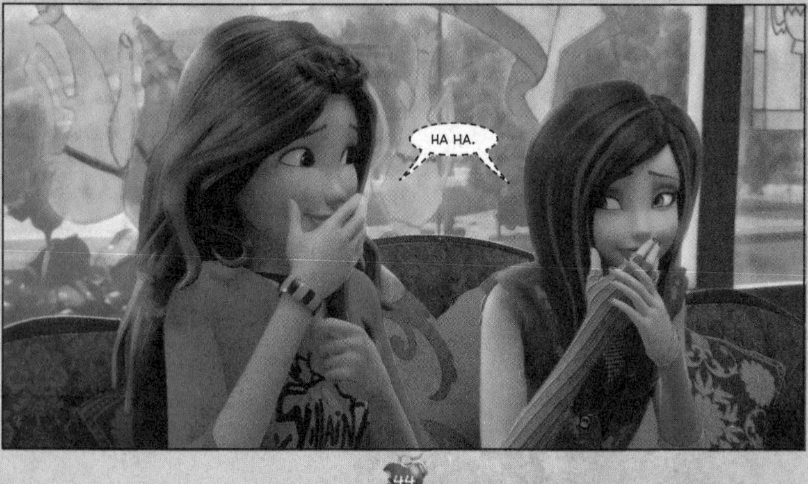
HA HA.

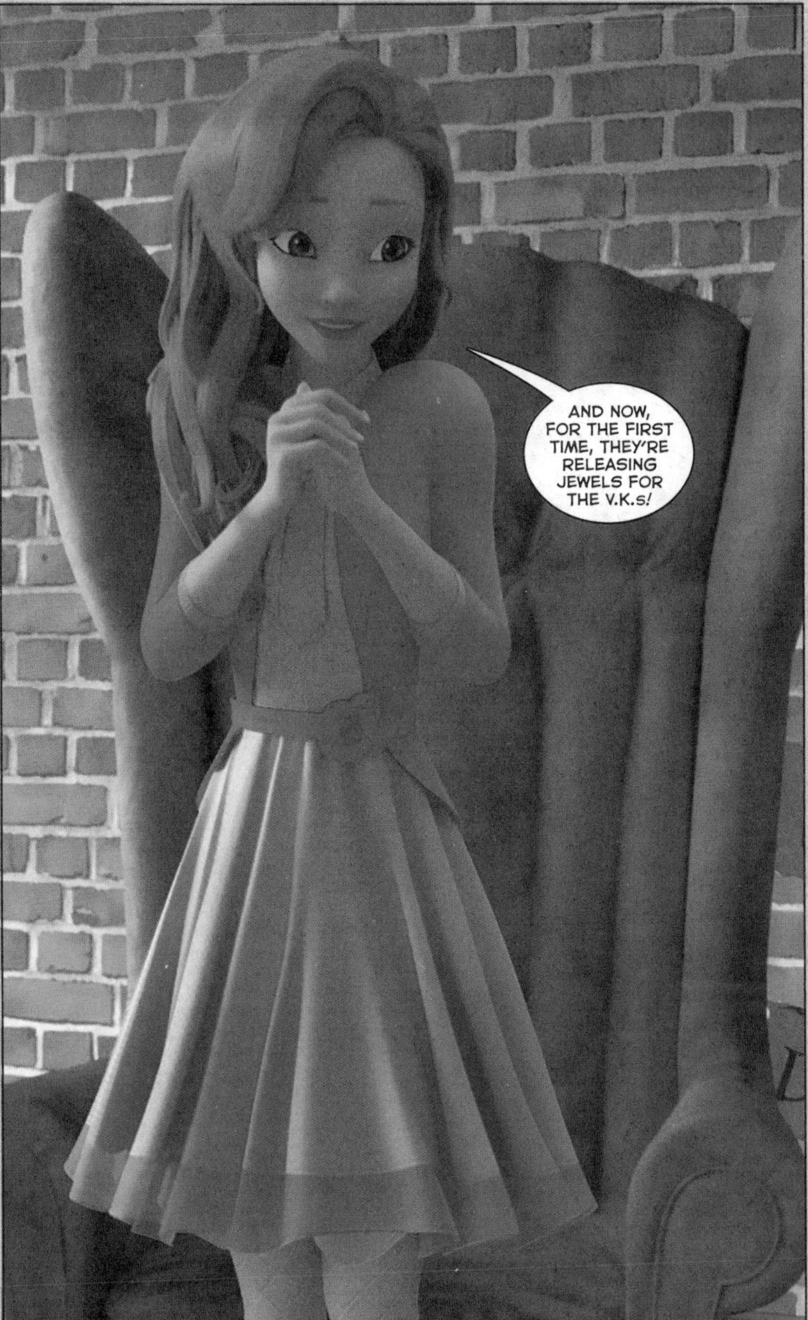
AND NOW, FOR THE FIRST TIME, THEY'RE RELEASING JEWELS FOR THE V.K.s!

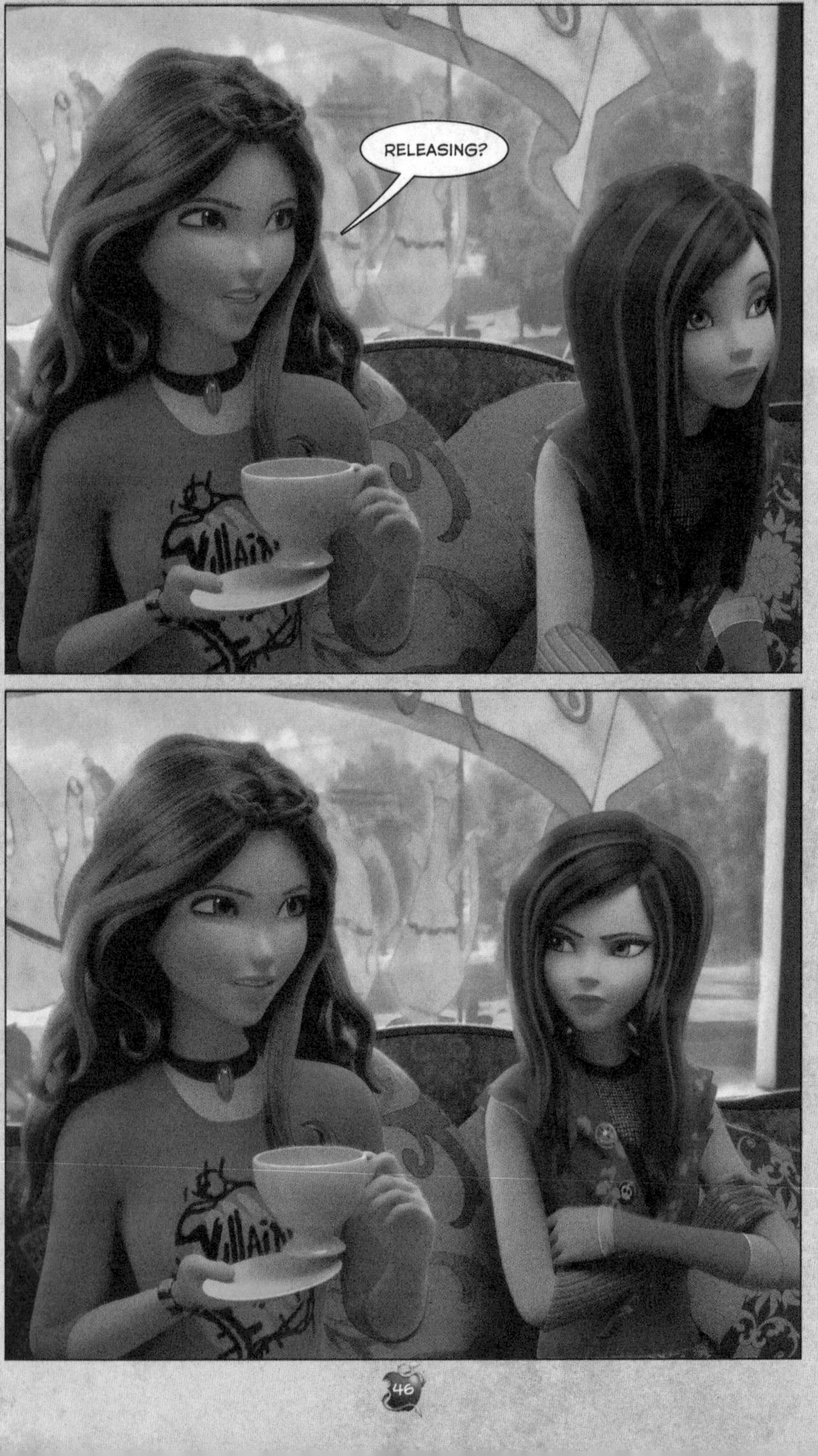
RELEASING?

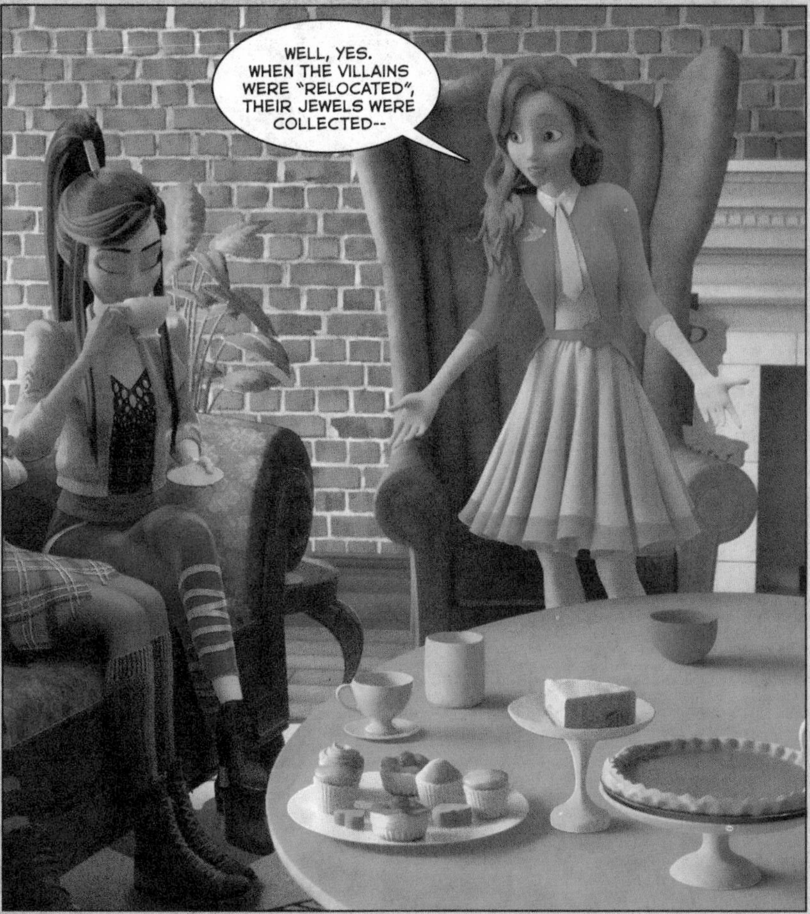
WELL, YES. WHEN THE VILLAINS WERE "RELOCATED", THEIR JEWELS WERE COLLECTED--

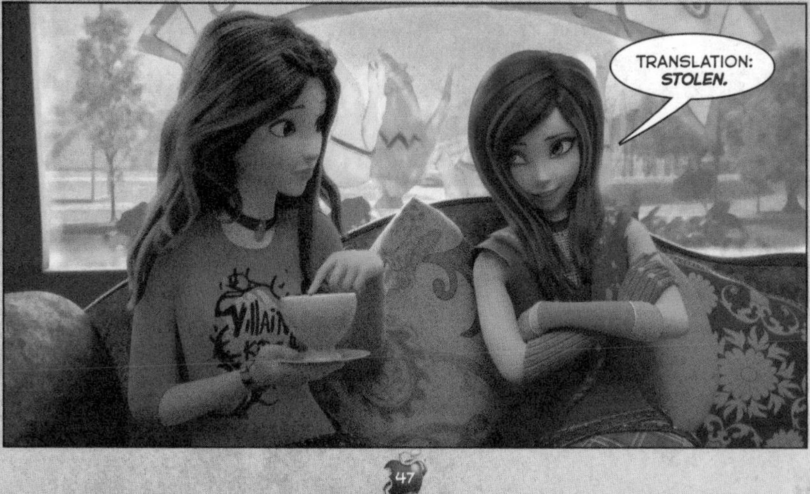
TRANSLATION: *STOLEN.*

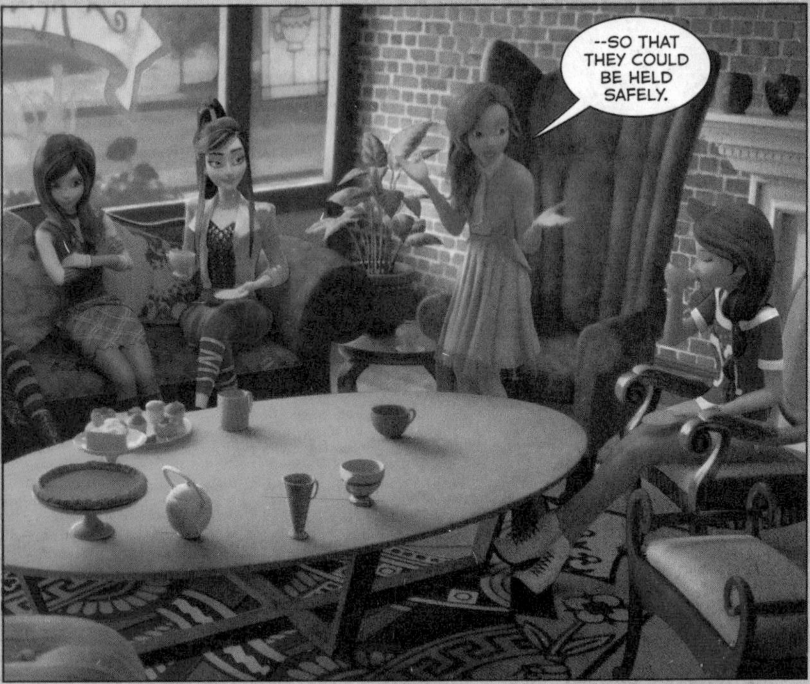
--SO THAT THEY COULD BE HELD SAFELY.

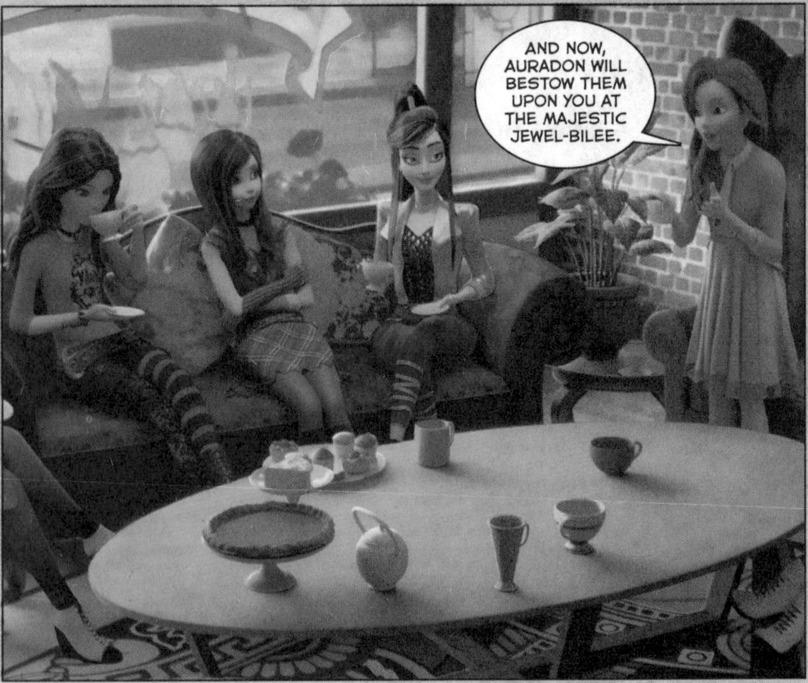
AND NOW, AURADON WILL BESTOW THEM UPON YOU AT THE MAJESTIC JEWEL-BILEE.

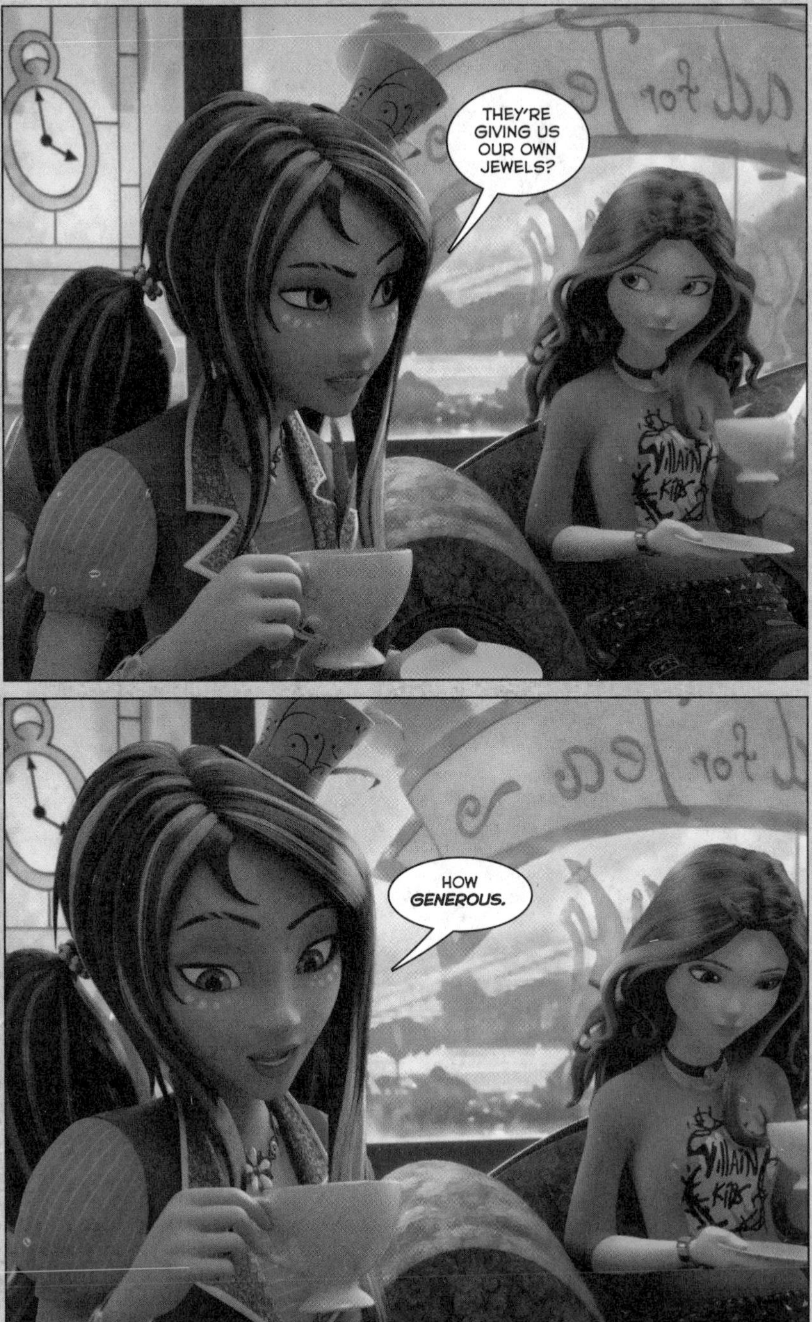
THEY'RE GIVING US OUR OWN JEWELS?
HOW **GENEROUS.**

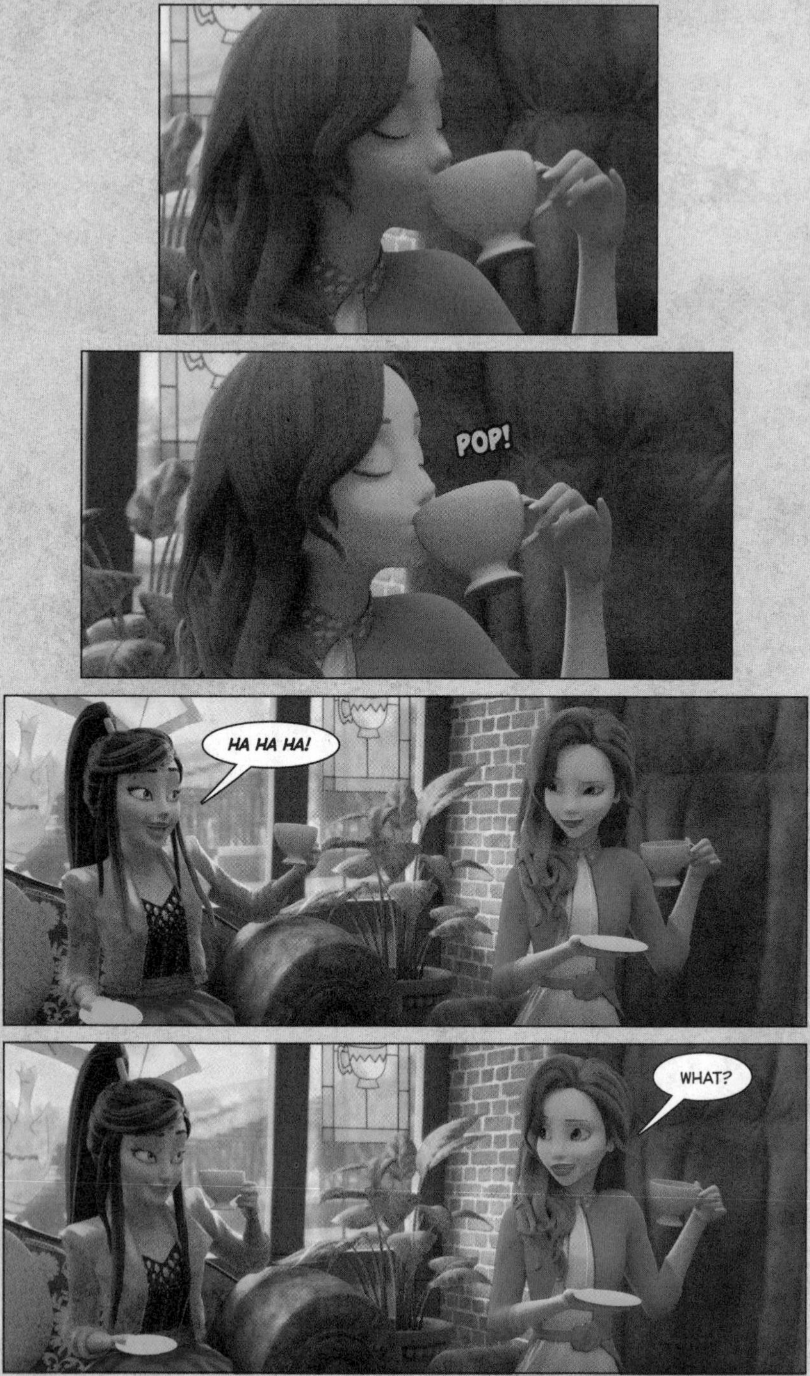
POP!
HA HA HA!
WHAT?

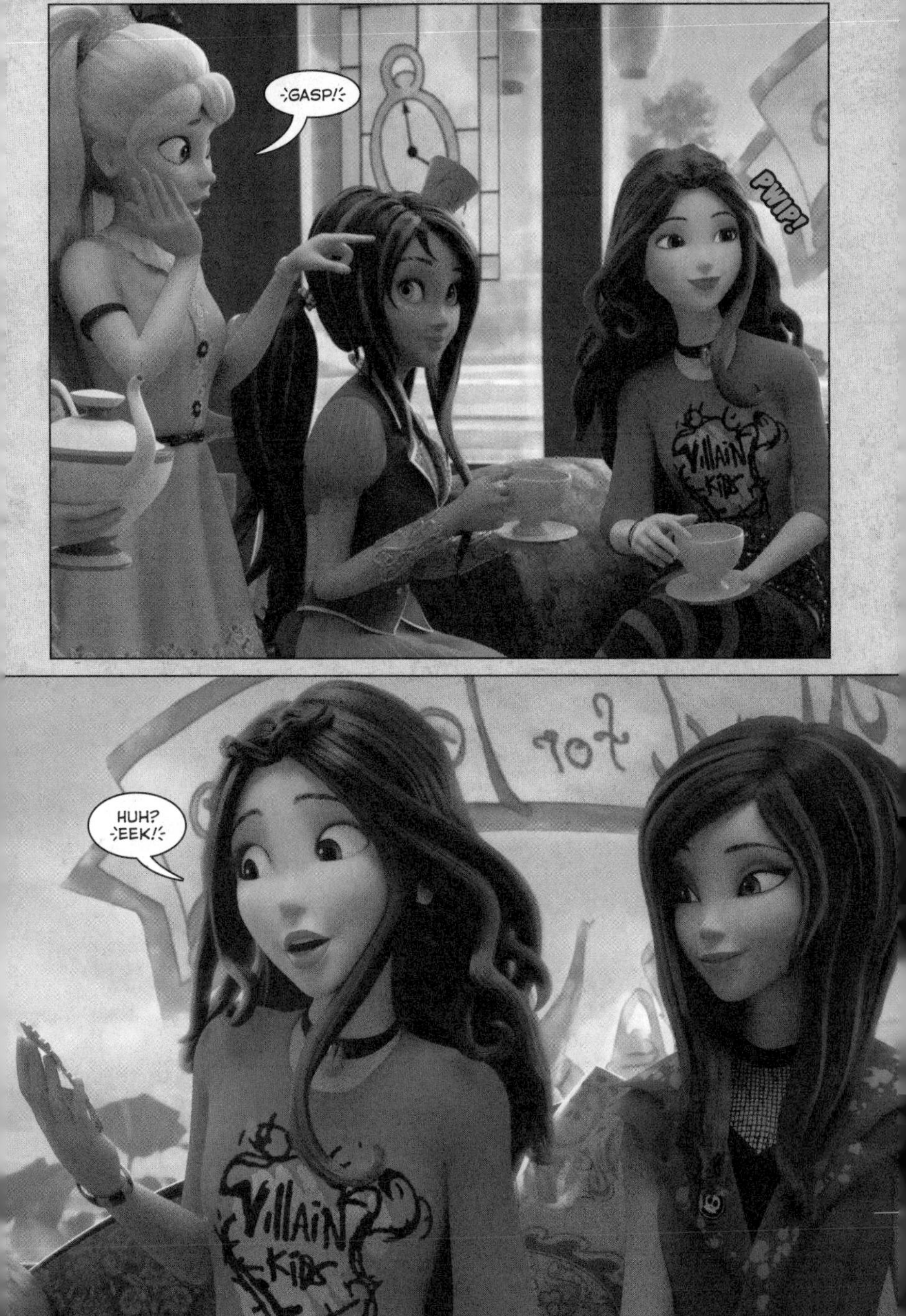
GASP!
PWIP!
VILLAIN KIDS
HUH?
EEK!
VILLAIN KIDS

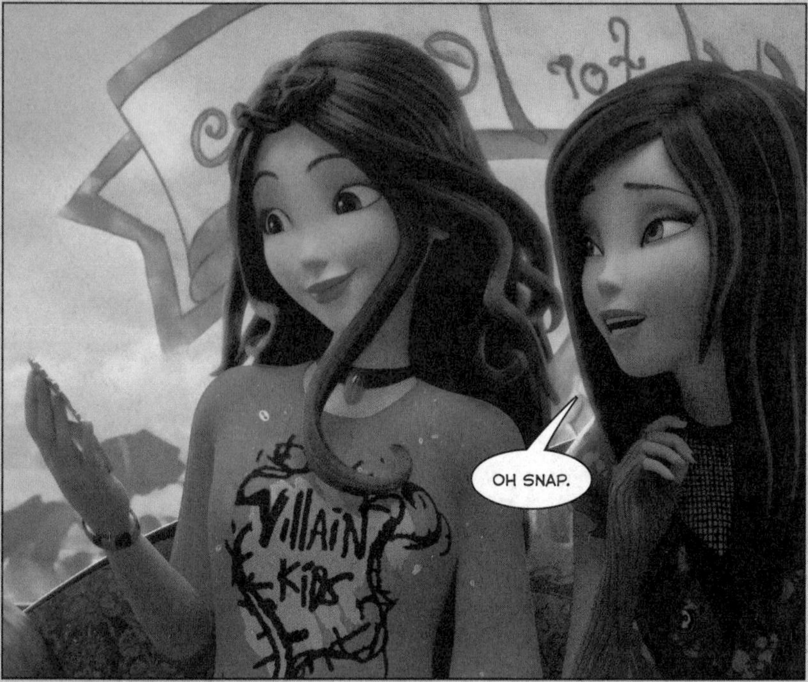
VILLAIN KIDS
OH SNAP.

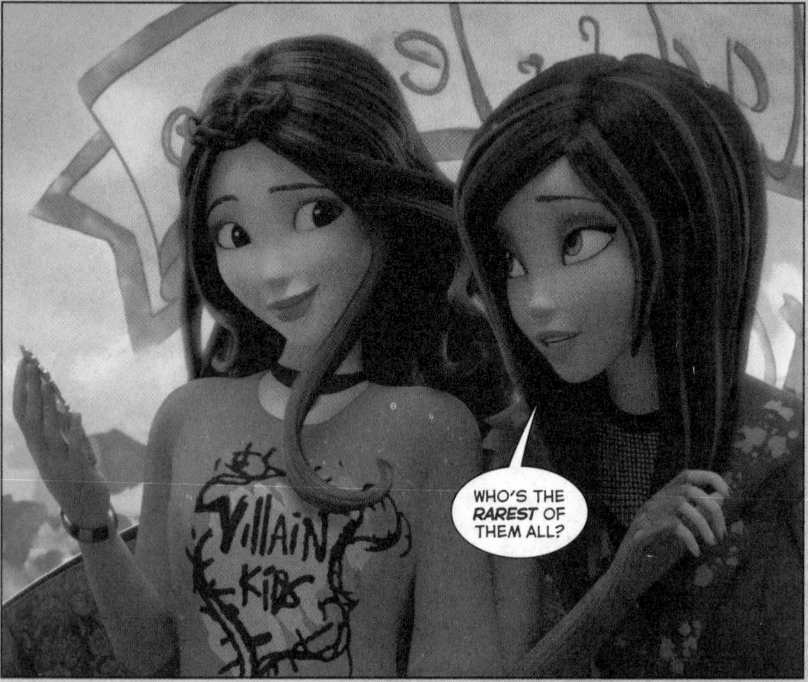
VILLAIN KIDS
WHO'S THE **RAREST** OF THEM ALL?

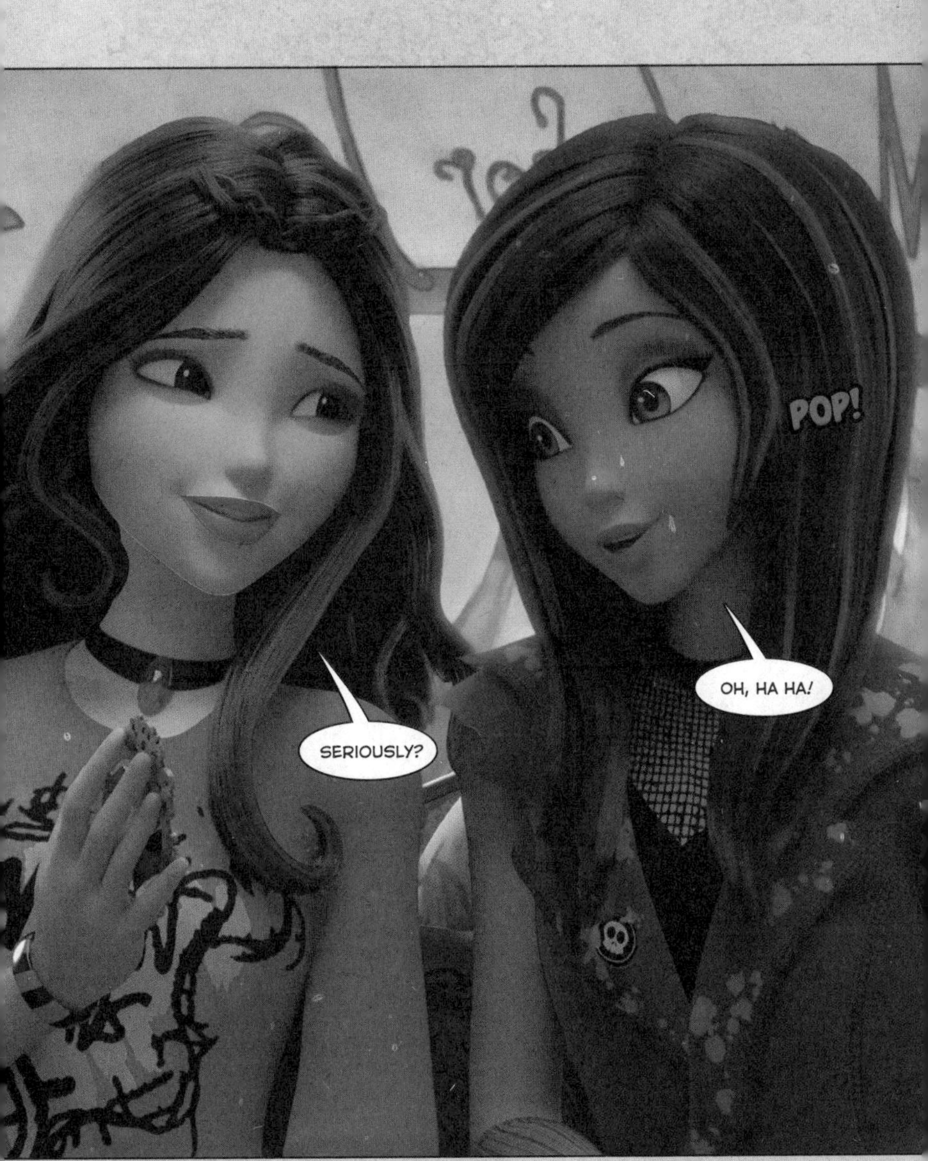
SERIOUSLY?
POP!
OH, HA HA!

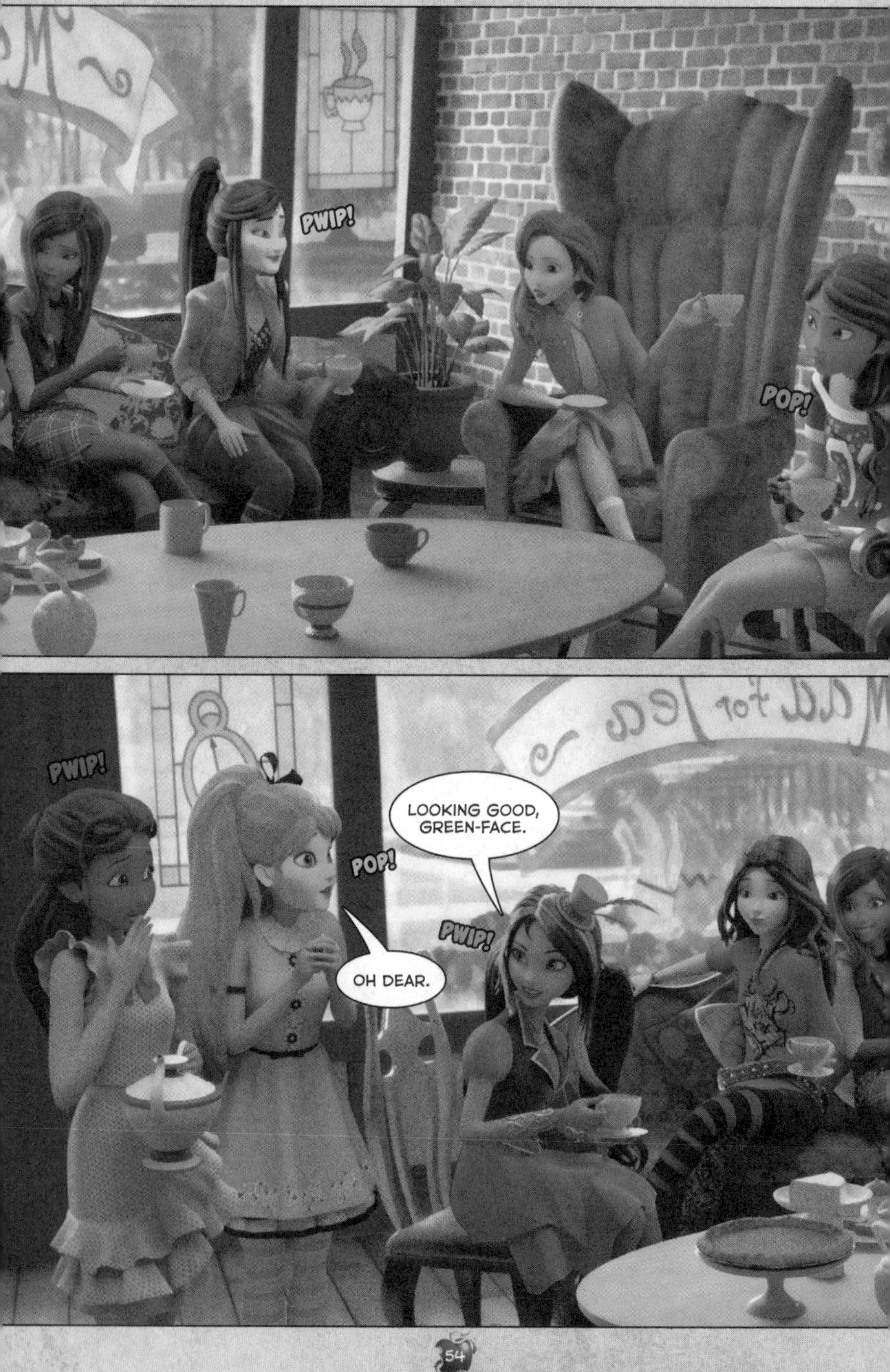
PWIP!
POP!
PWIP!
POP!
LOOKING GOOD, GREEN-FACE.
PWIP!
OH DEAR.

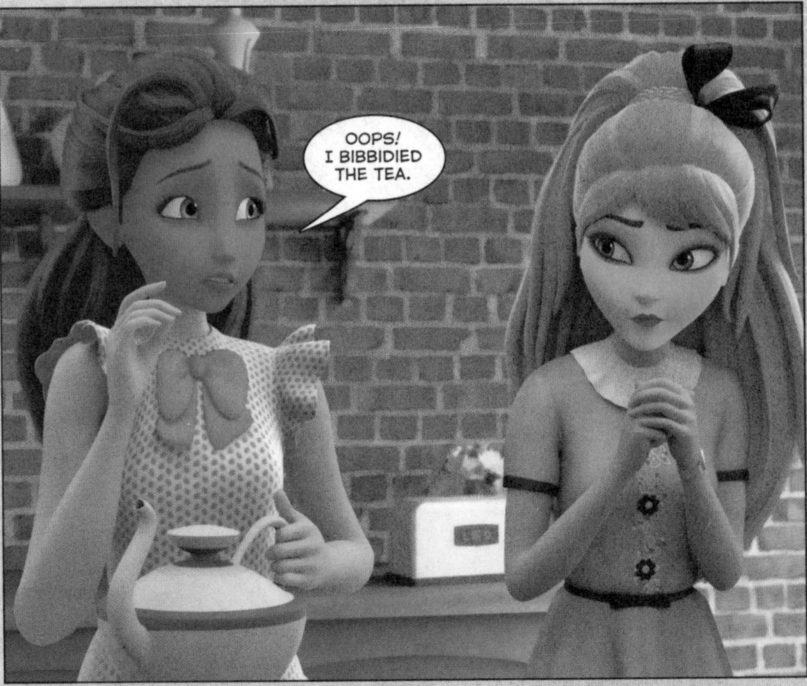
OOPS! I BIBBIDIED THE TEA.

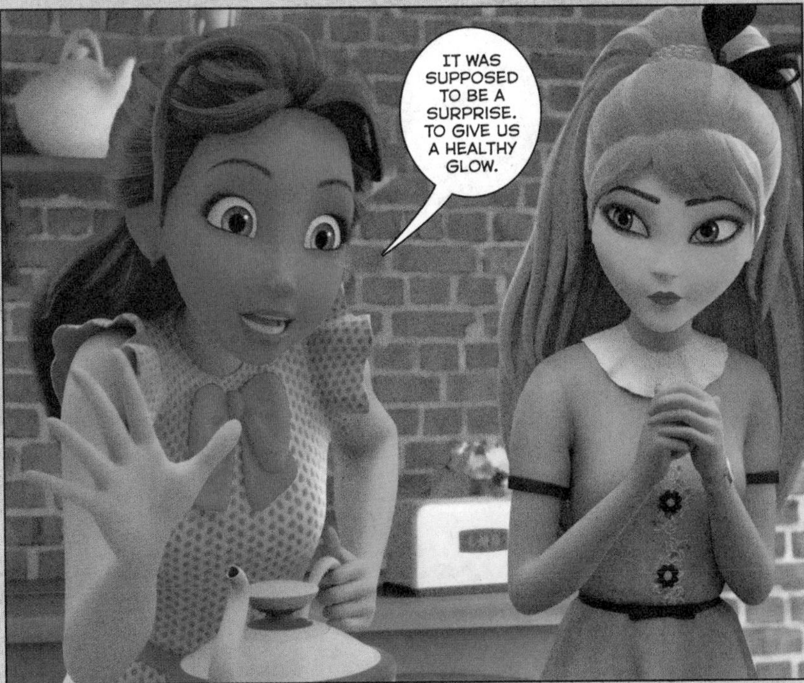
IT WAS SUPPOSED TO BE A SURPRISE. TO GIVE US A HEALTHY GLOW.

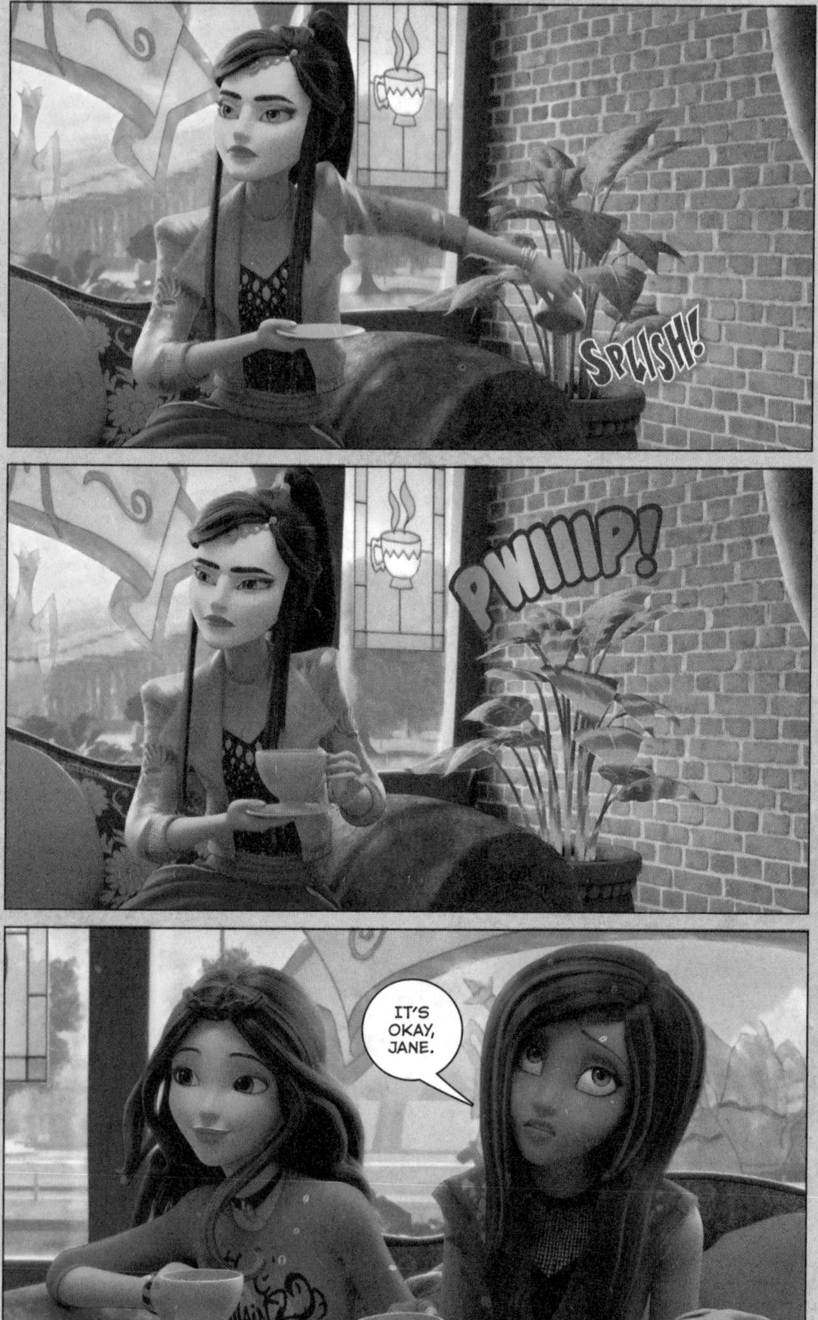
SPLISH!
PWIIIP!
IT'S OKAY, JANE.

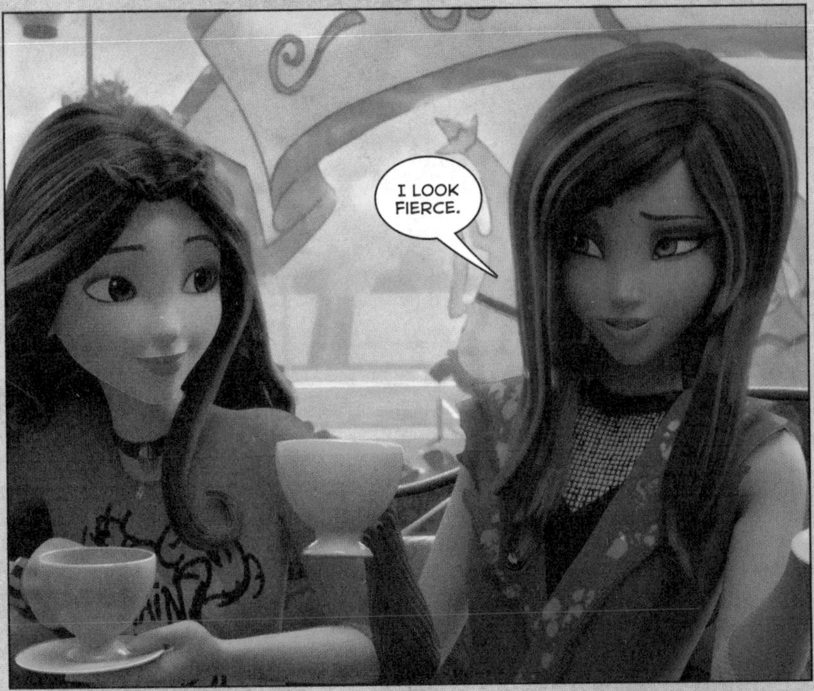
I LOOK FIERCE.

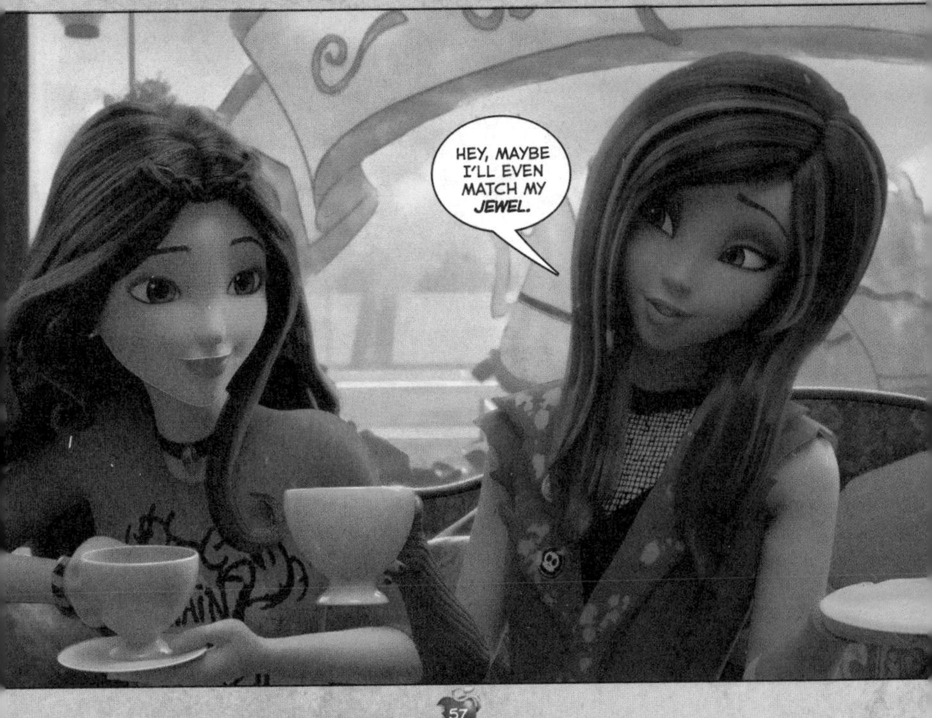
HEY, MAYBE I'LL EVEN MATCH MY **JEWEL.**

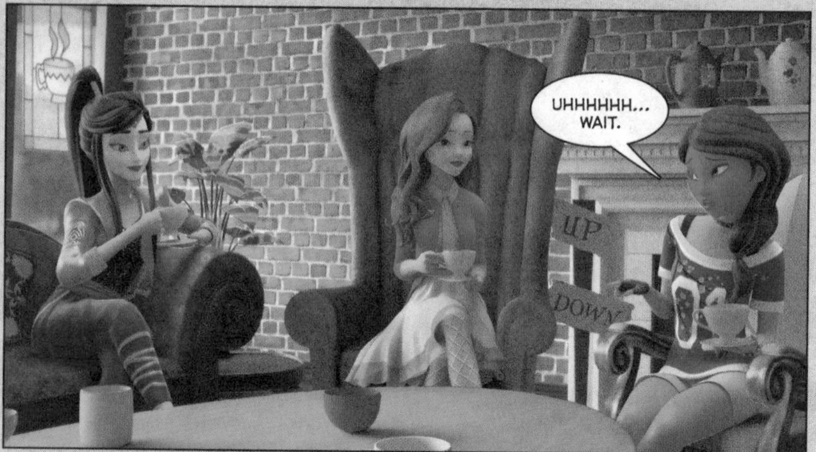
UHHHHHH... WAIT.

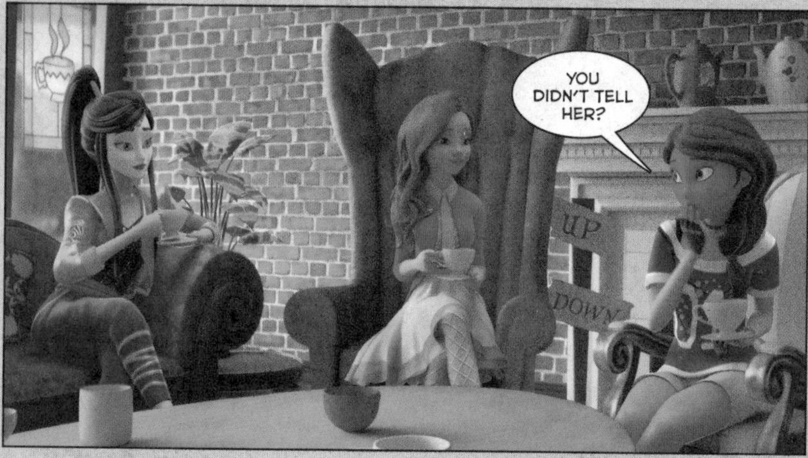
YOU DIDN'T TELL HER?

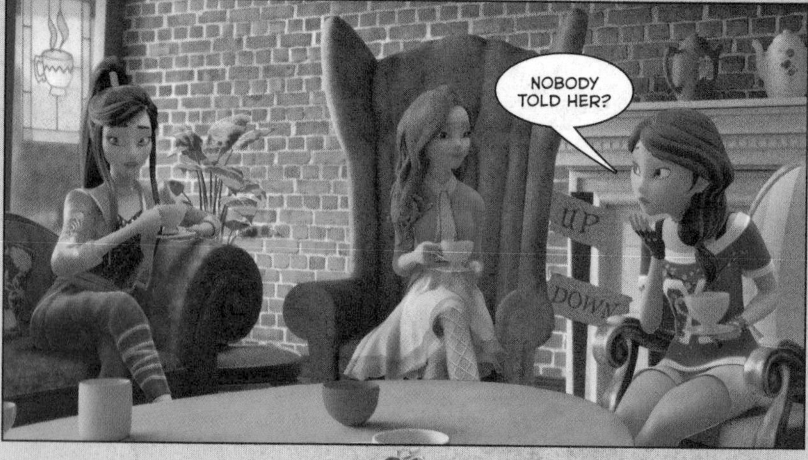
NOBODY TOLD HER?

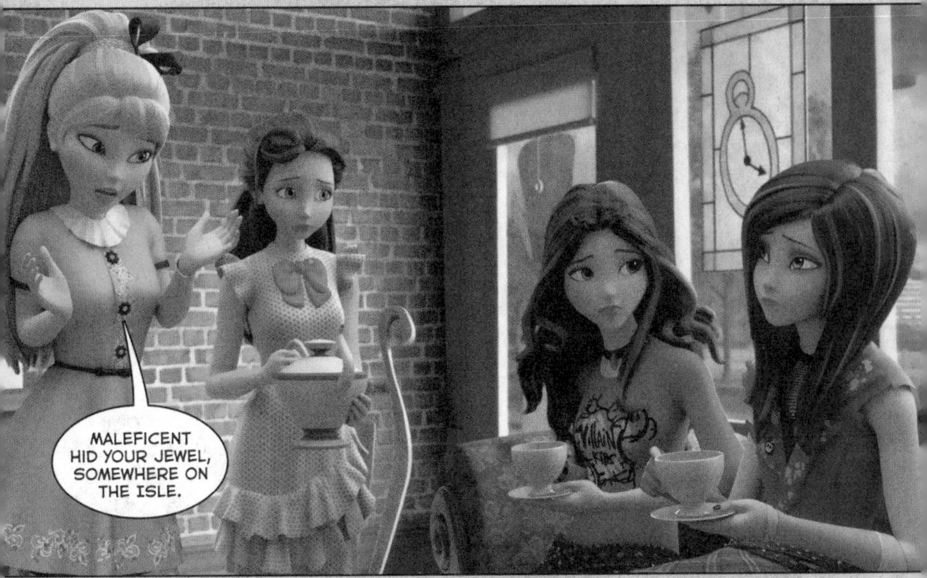
MALEFICENT HID YOUR JEWEL, SOMEWHERE ON THE ISLE.

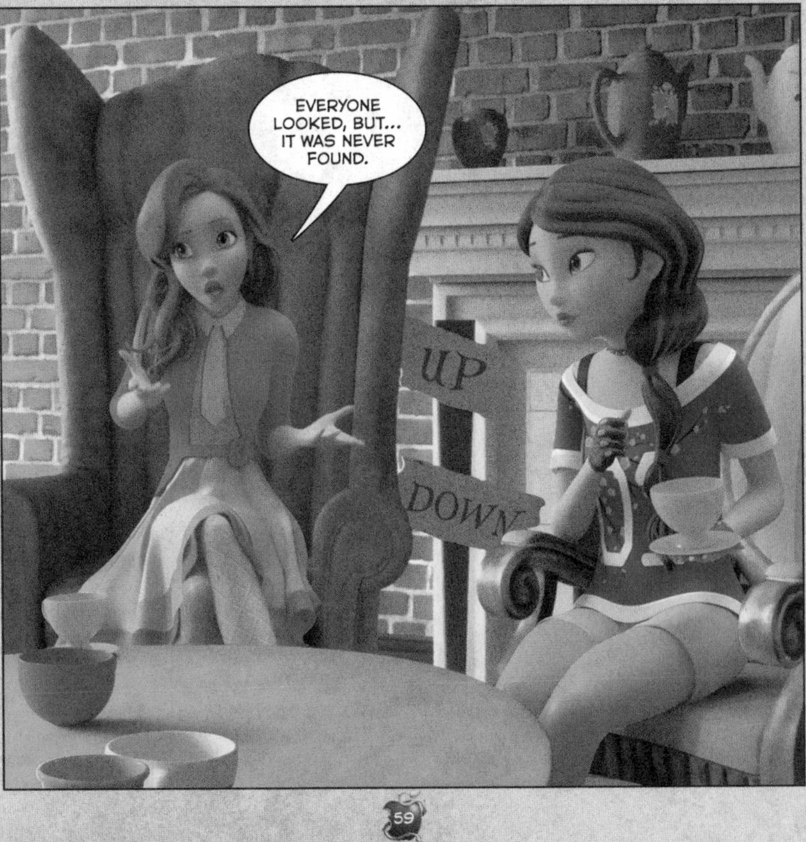
EVERYONE LOOKED, BUT... IT WAS NEVER FOUND.
UP
DOWN

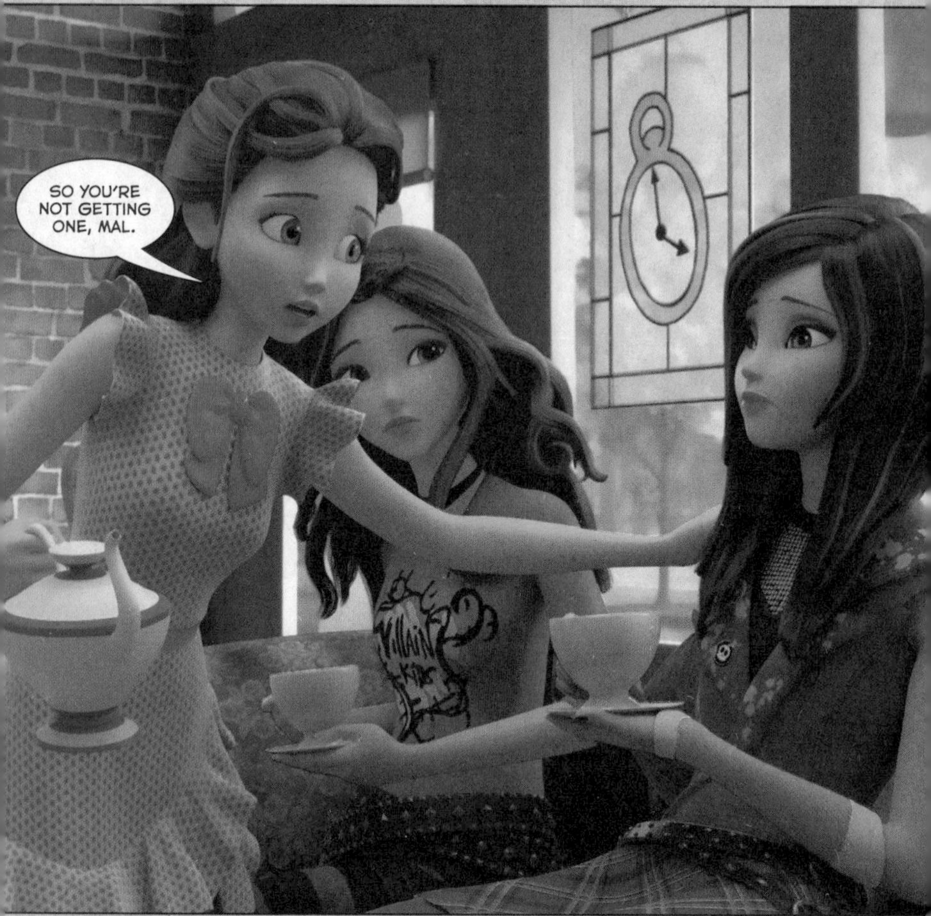
SO YOU'RE NOT GETTING ONE, MAL.

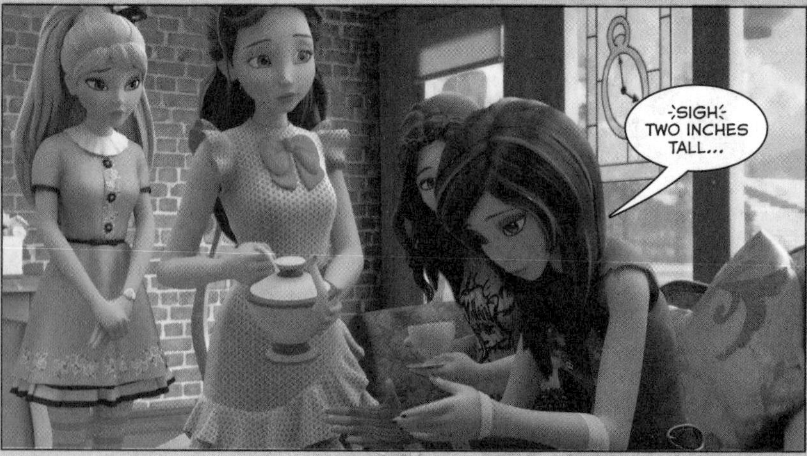
SIGH
TWO INCHES TALL...

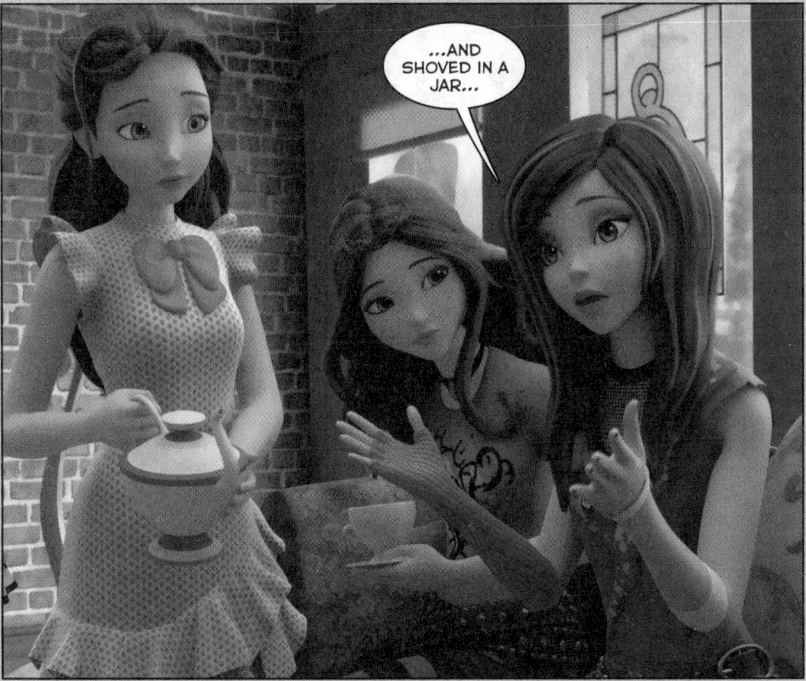
...AND SHOVED IN A JAR...

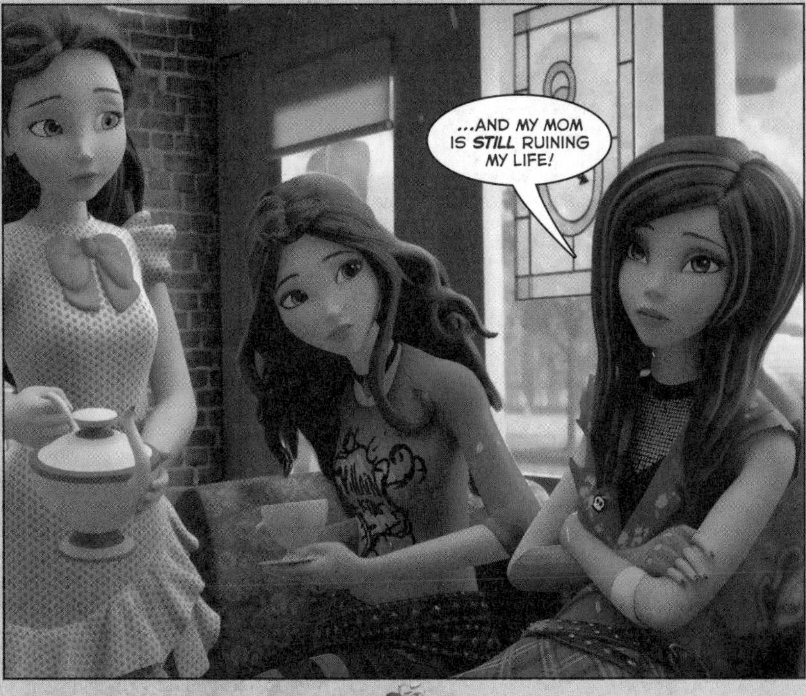
...AND MY MOM IS STILL RUINING MY LIFE!

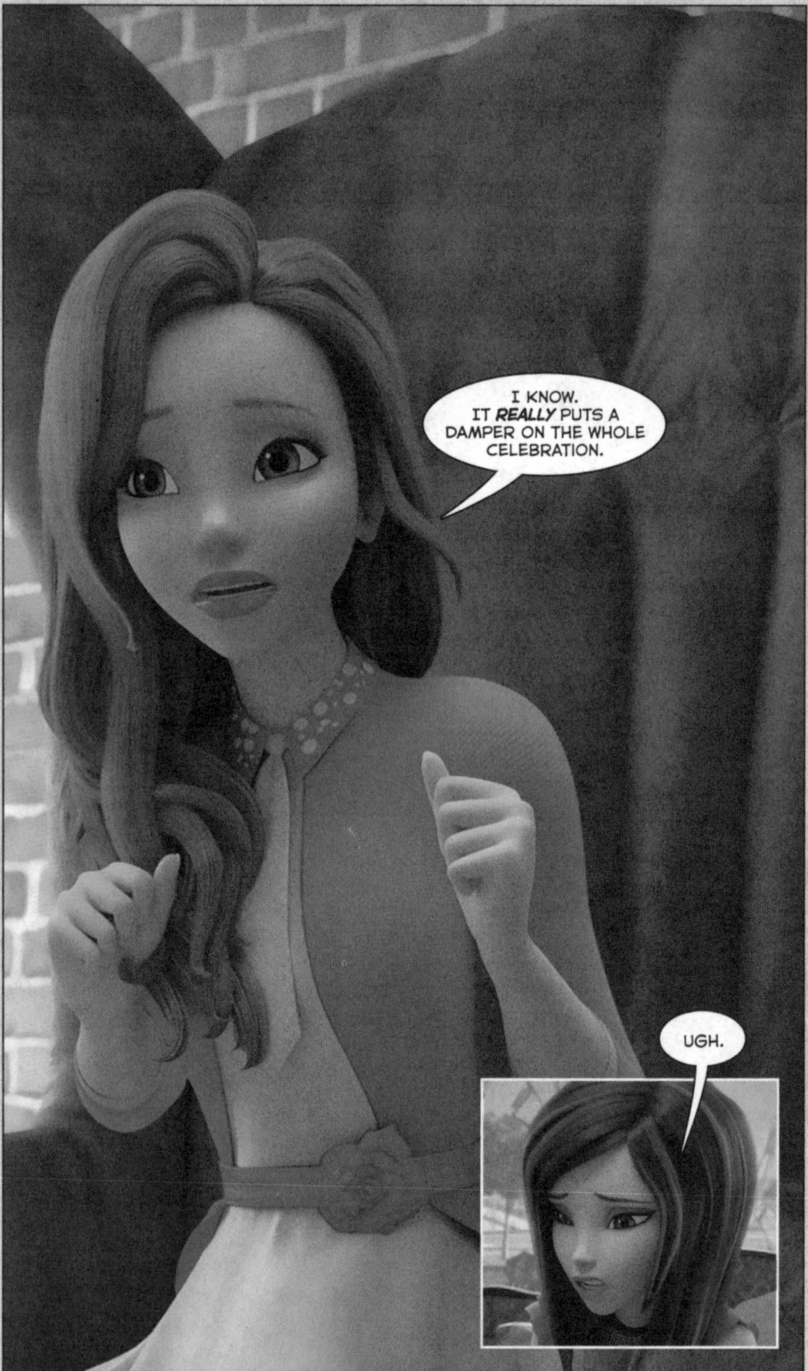
I KNOW. IT REALLY PUTS A DAMPER ON THE WHOLE CELEBRATION.
UGH.

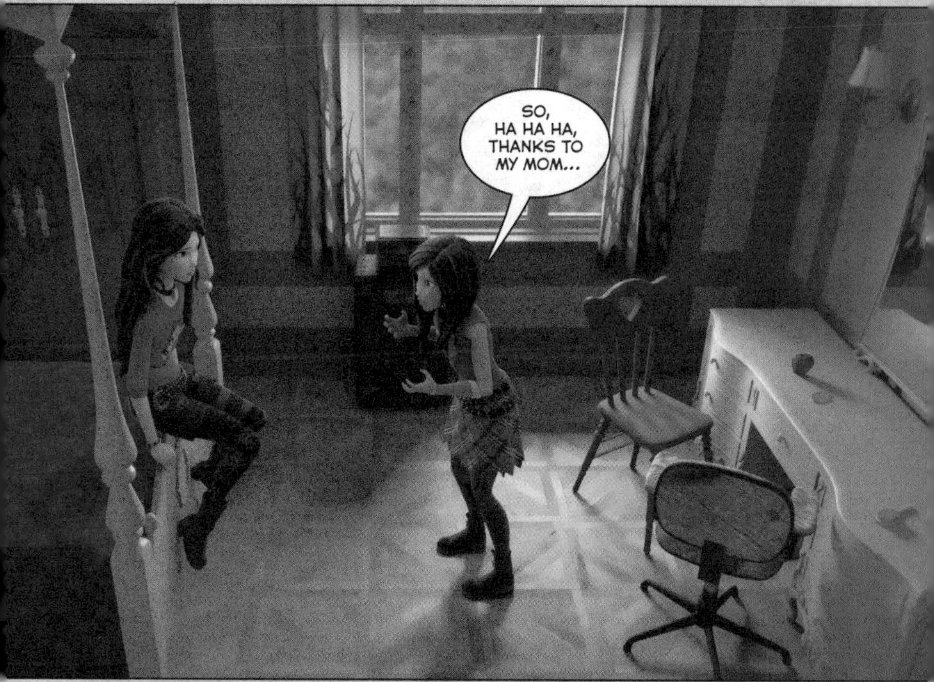
SO, HA HA HA, THANKS TO MY MOM...

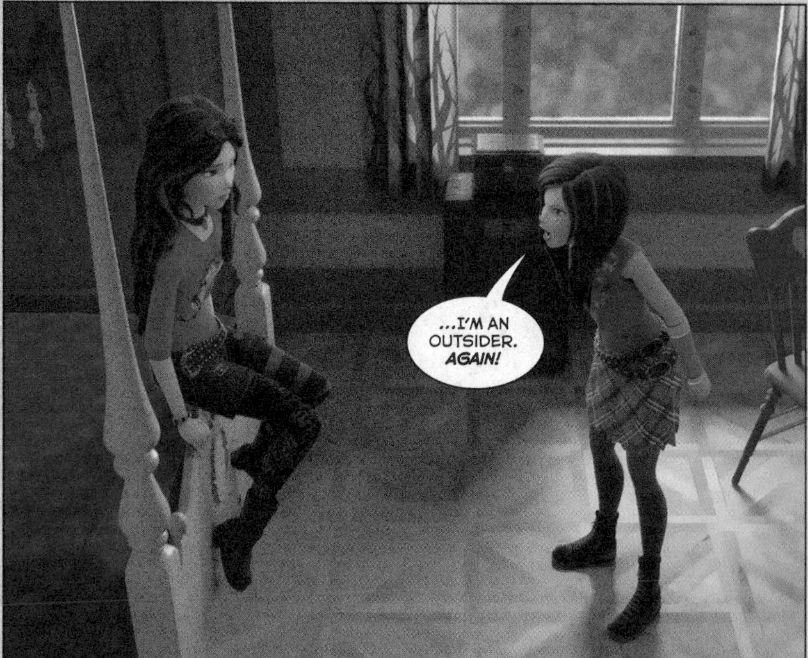
...I'M AN OUTSIDER. *AGAIN!*

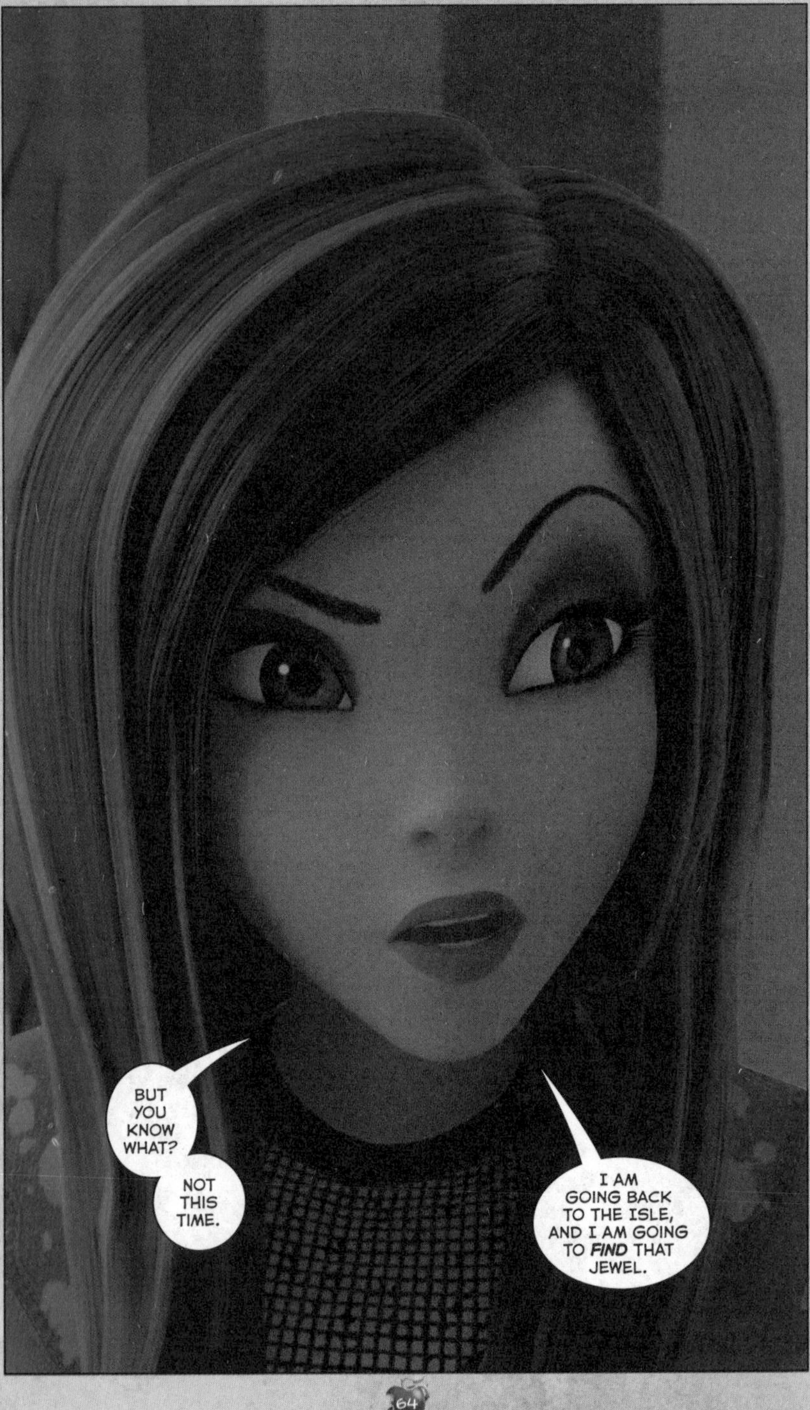
BUT YOU KNOW WHAT?
NOT THIS TIME.
I AM GOING BACK TO THE ISLE, AND I AM GOING TO *FIND* THAT JEWEL.

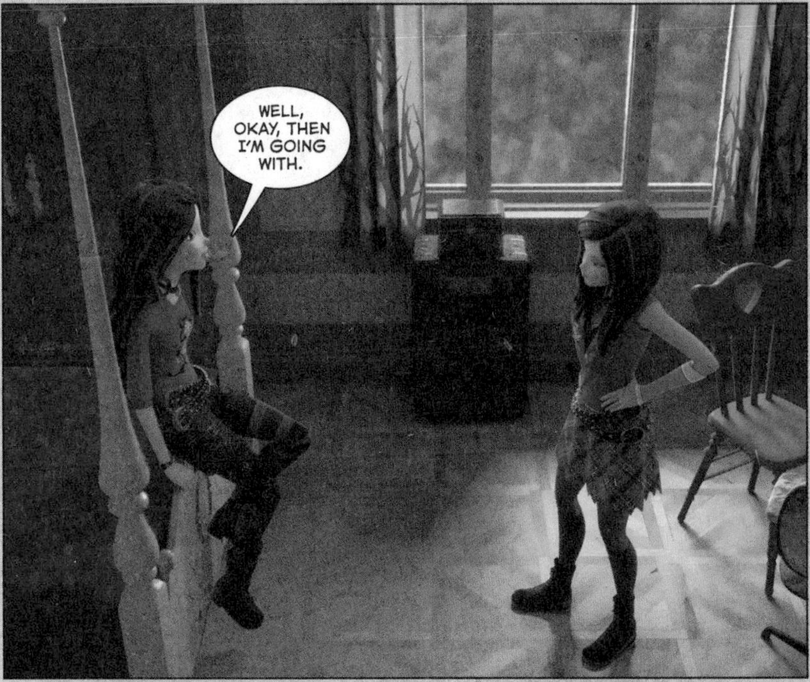
WELL, OKAY, THEN I'M GOING WITH.

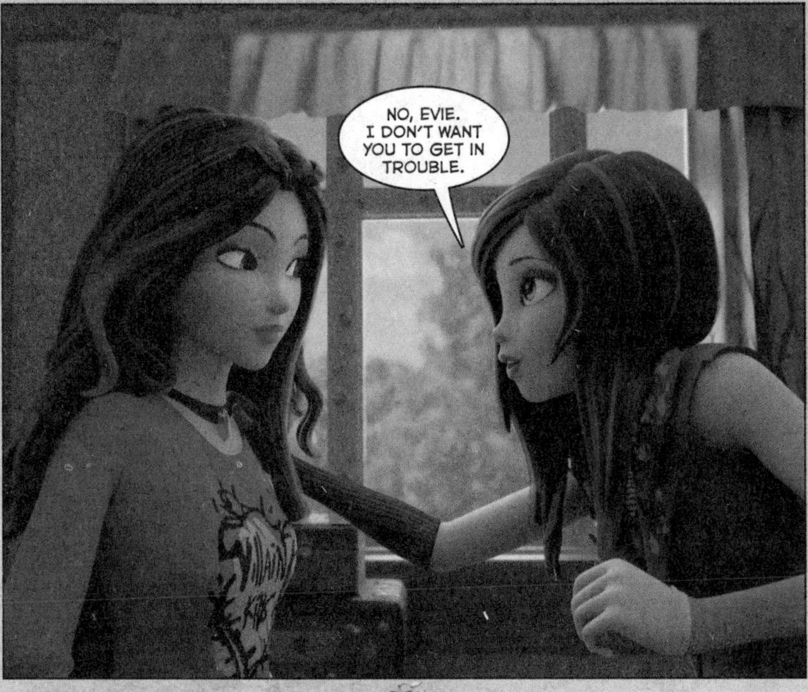
NO, EVIE. I DON'T WANT YOU TO GET IN TROUBLE.

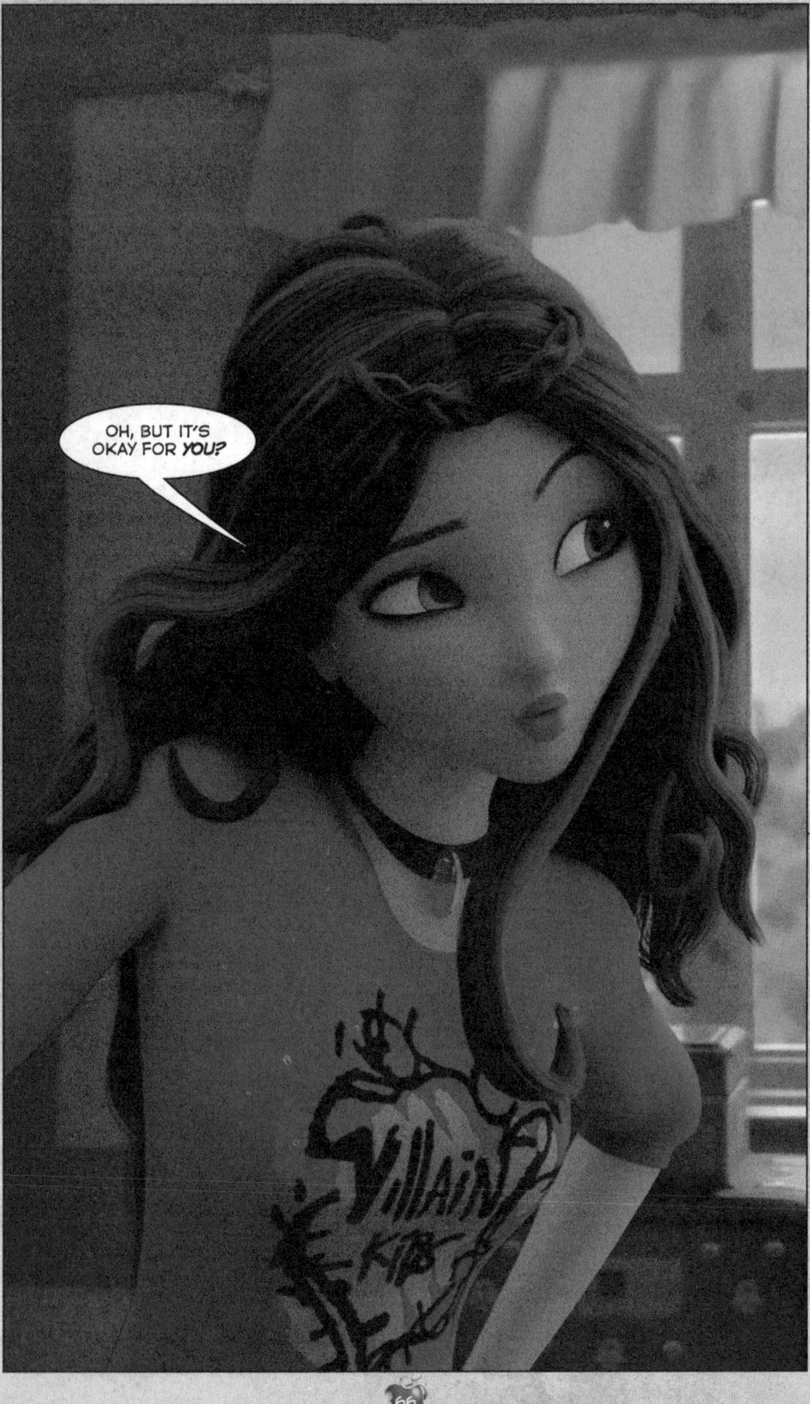
OH, BUT IT'S OKAY FOR *YOU?*

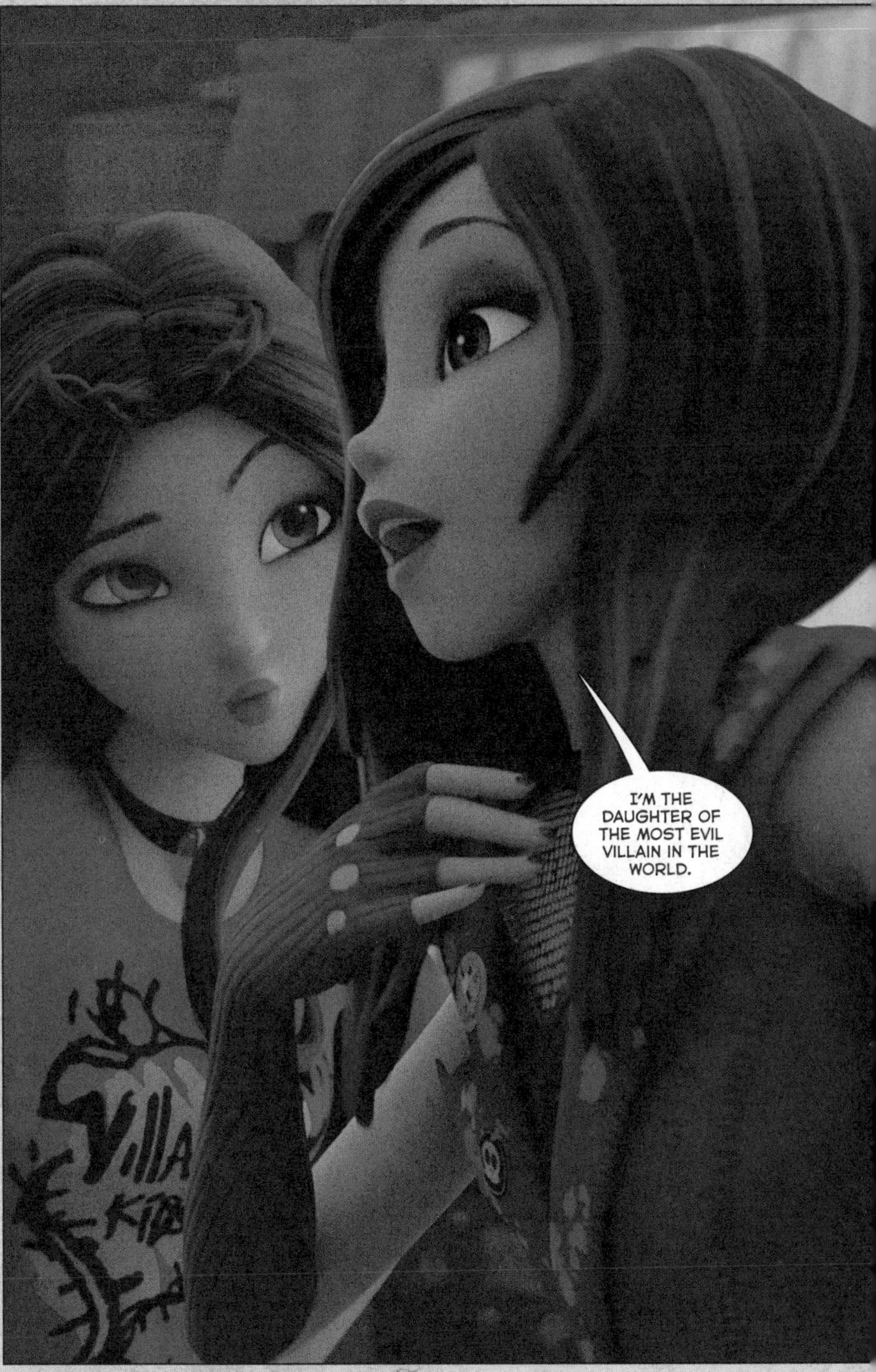
I'M THE DAUGHTER OF THE MOST EVIL VILLAIN IN THE WORLD.

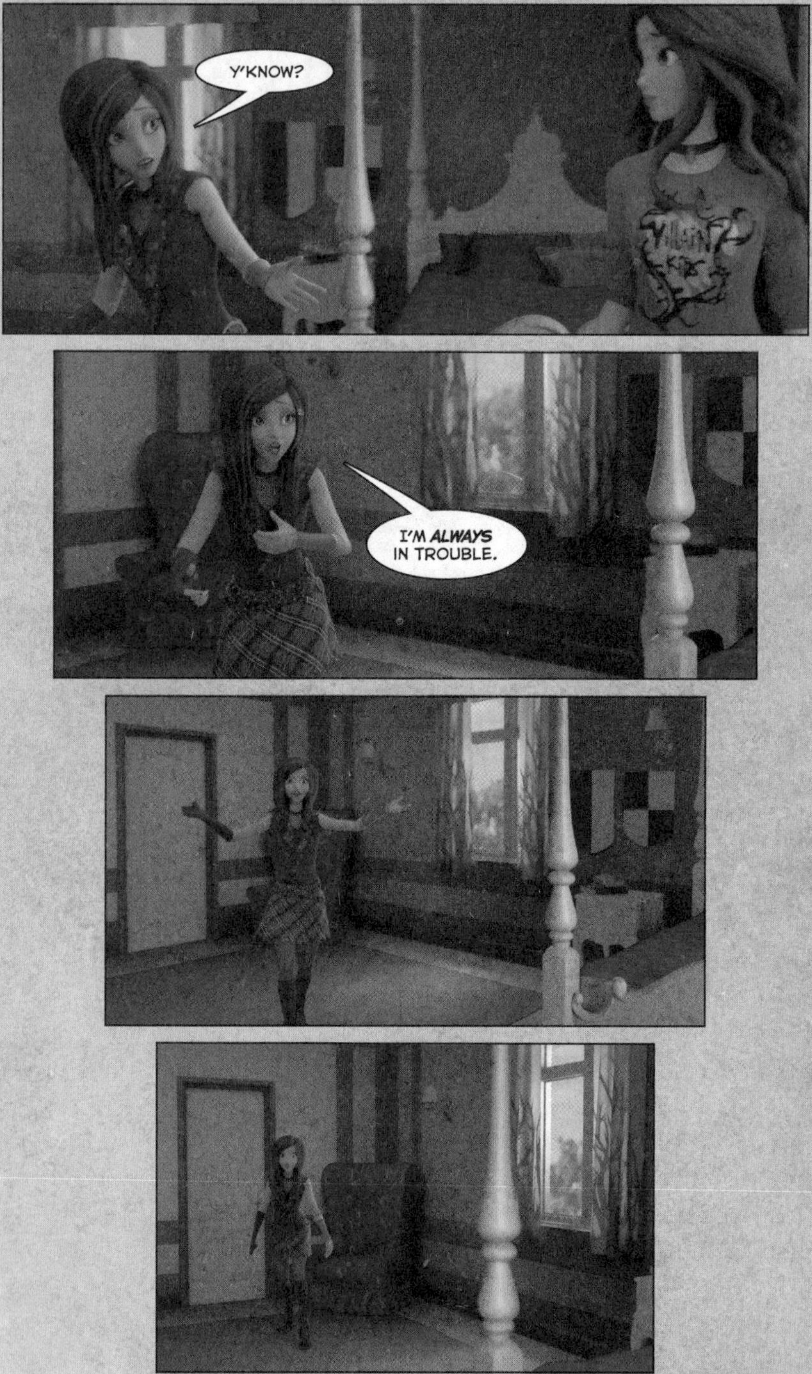
Y'KNOW?
I'M *ALWAYS* IN TROUBLE.

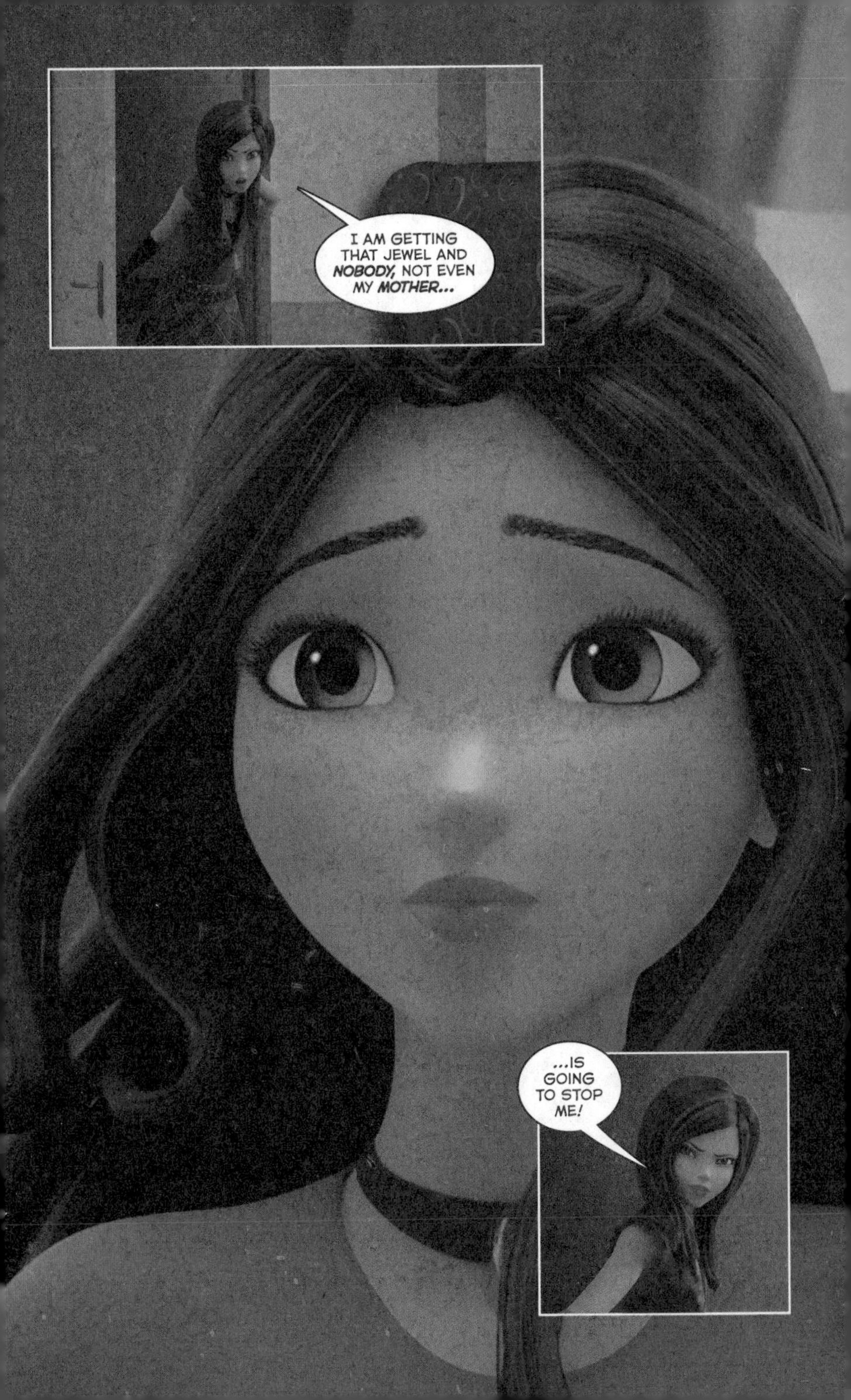
I AM GETTING THAT JEWEL AND *NOBODY,* NOT EVEN MY *MOTHER...*
...IS GOING TO STOP ME!

CHAPTER 21: PAIR OF SNEAKERS

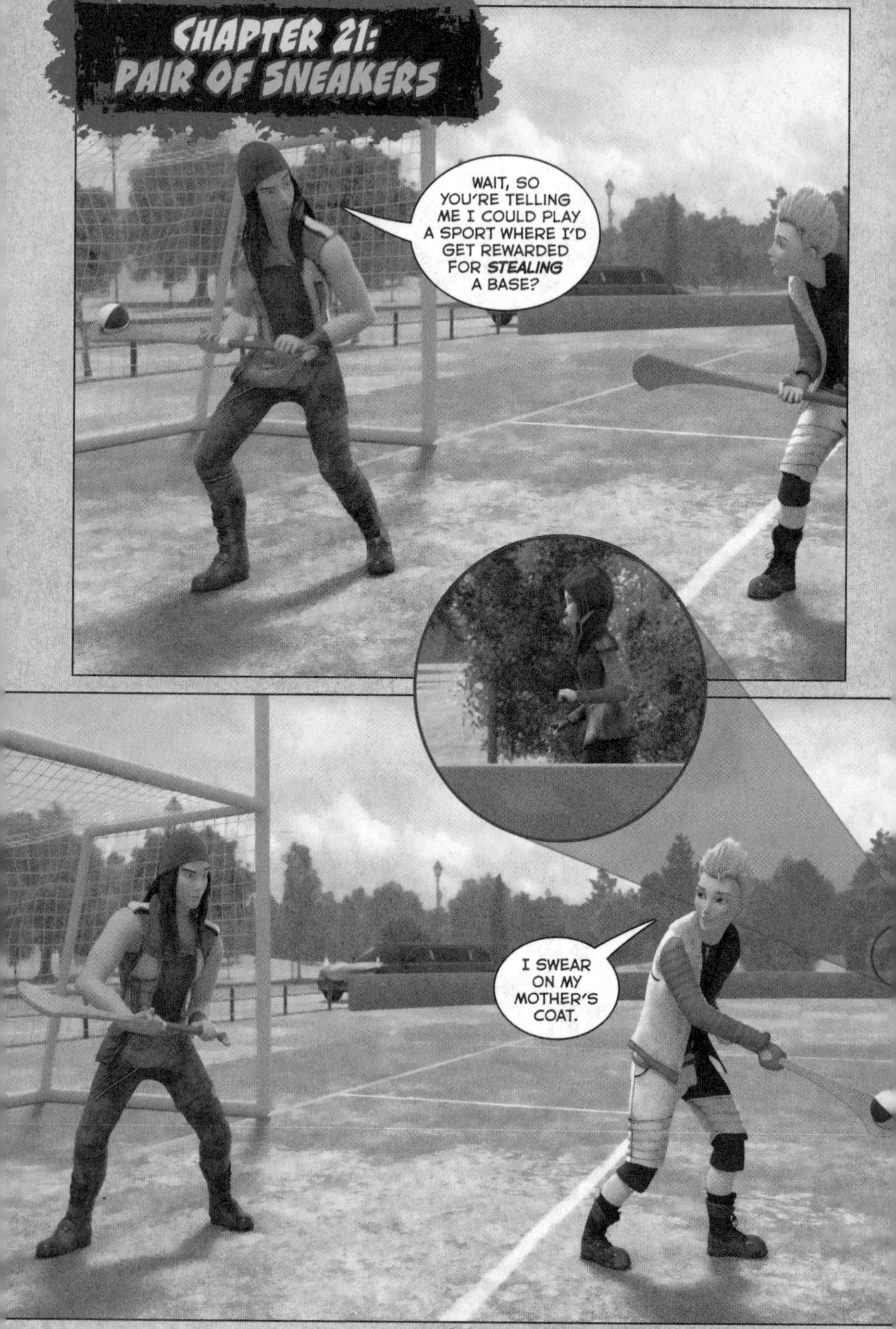

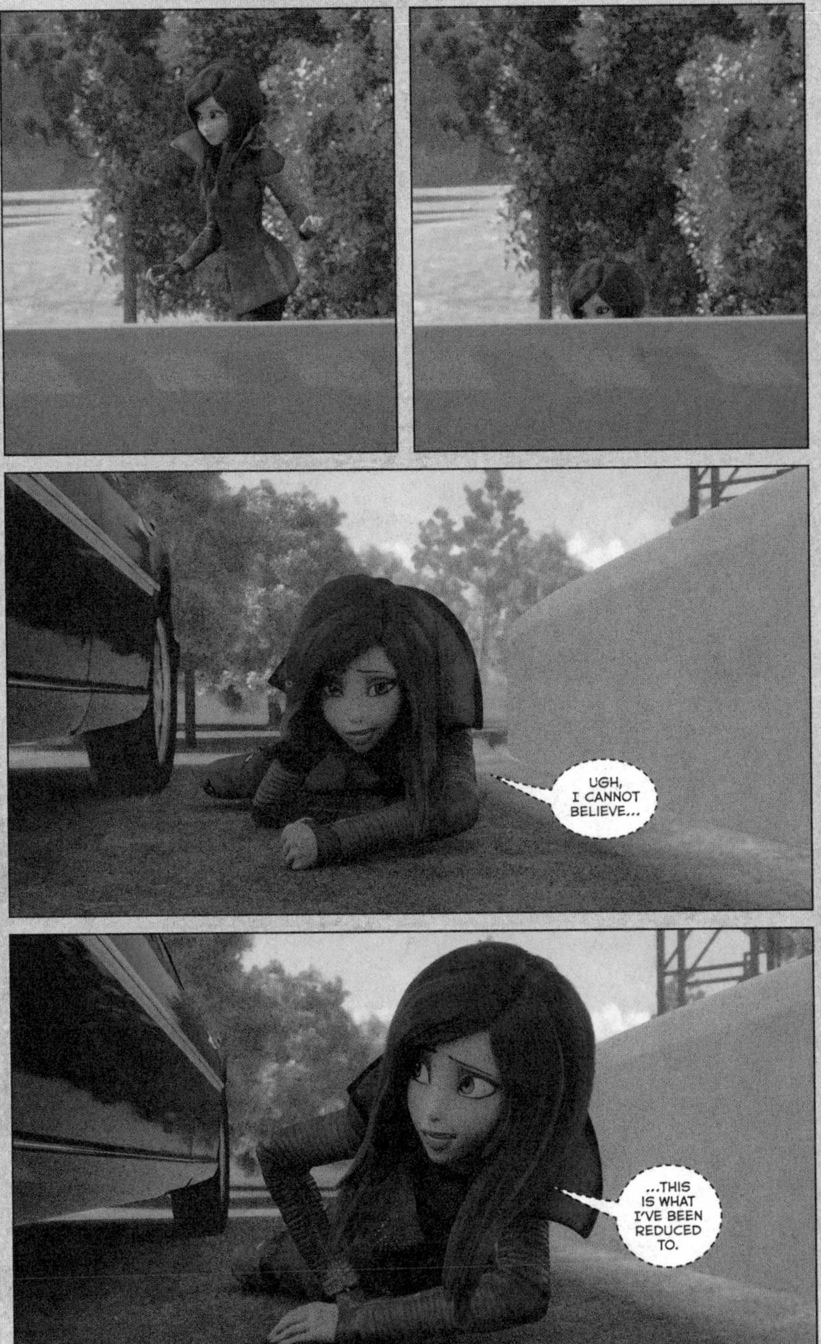
UGH, I CANNOT BELIEVE...
...THIS IS WHAT I'VE BEEN REDUCED TO.

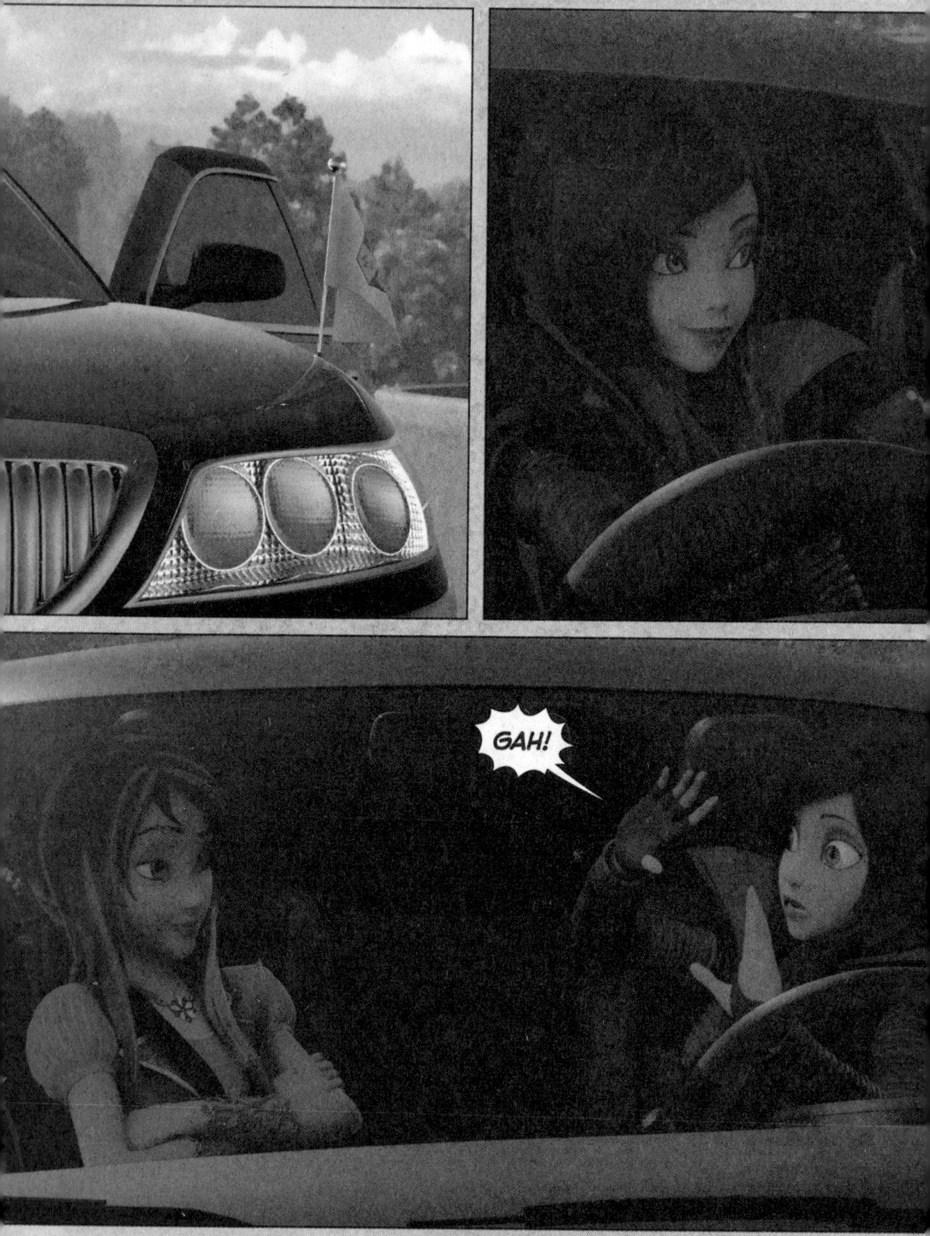
GAH!

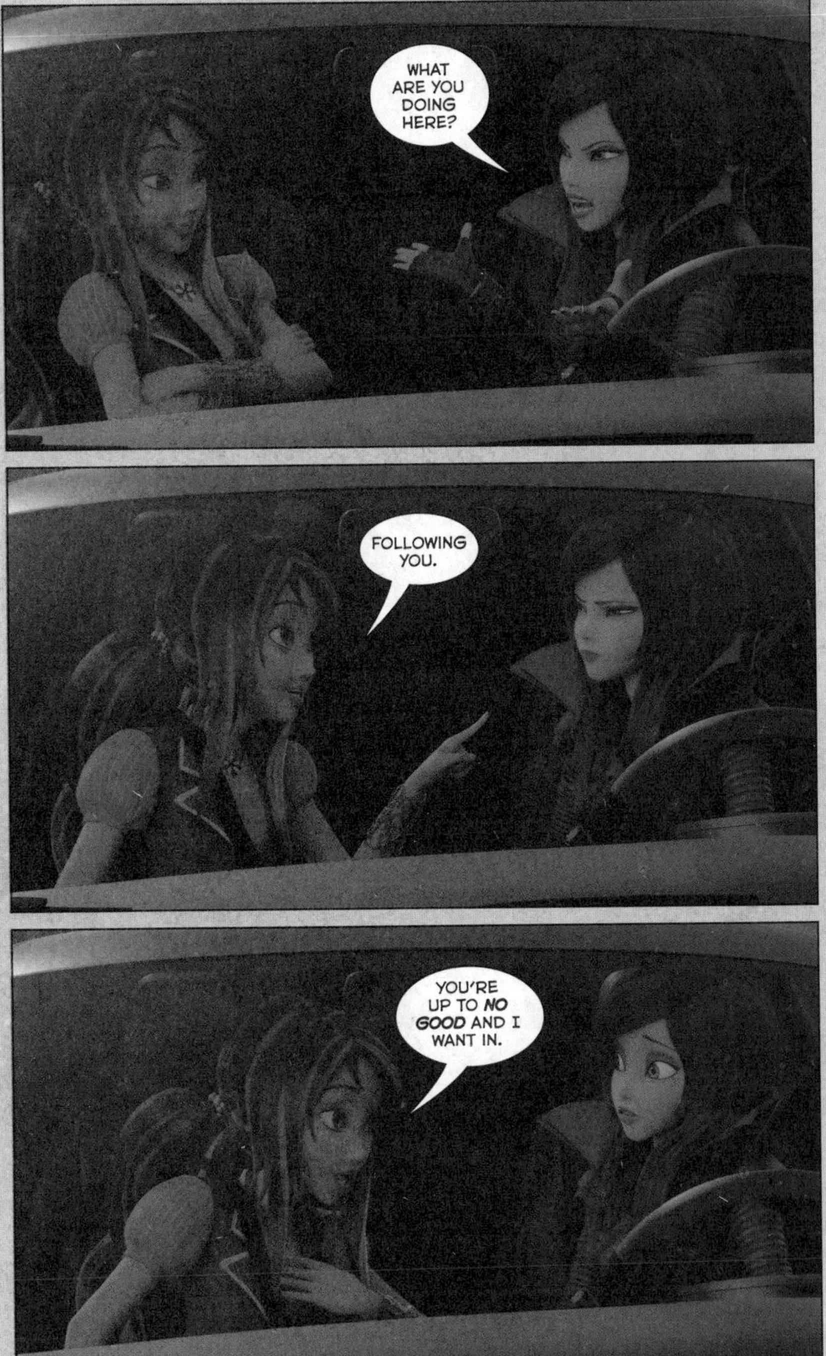
WHAT ARE YOU DOING HERE?
FOLLOWING YOU.
YOU'RE UP TO ***NO GOOD*** AND I WANT IN.

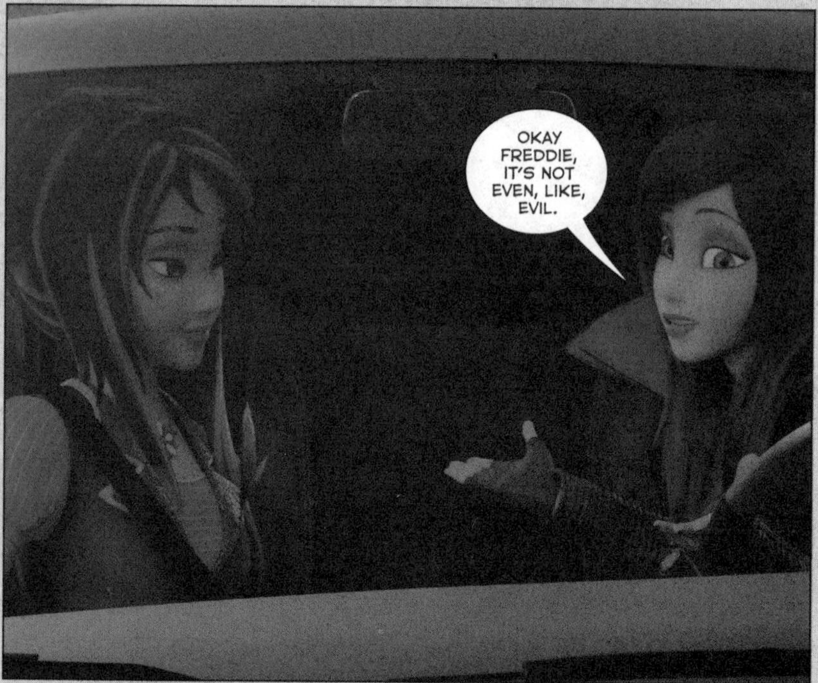
OKAY FREDDIE, IT'S NOT EVEN, LIKE, EVIL.

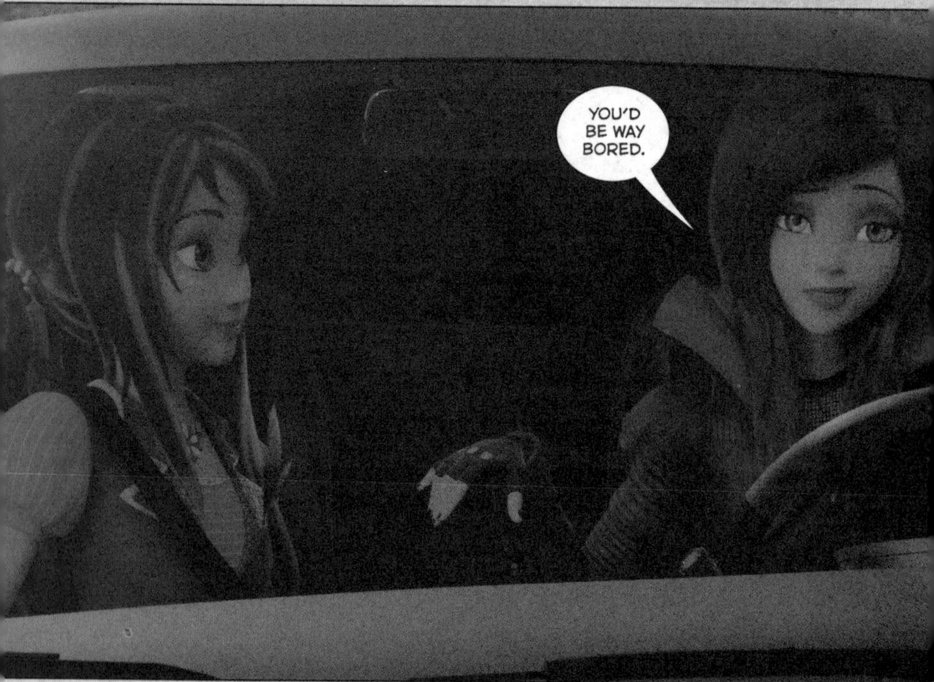
YOU'D BE WAY BORED.

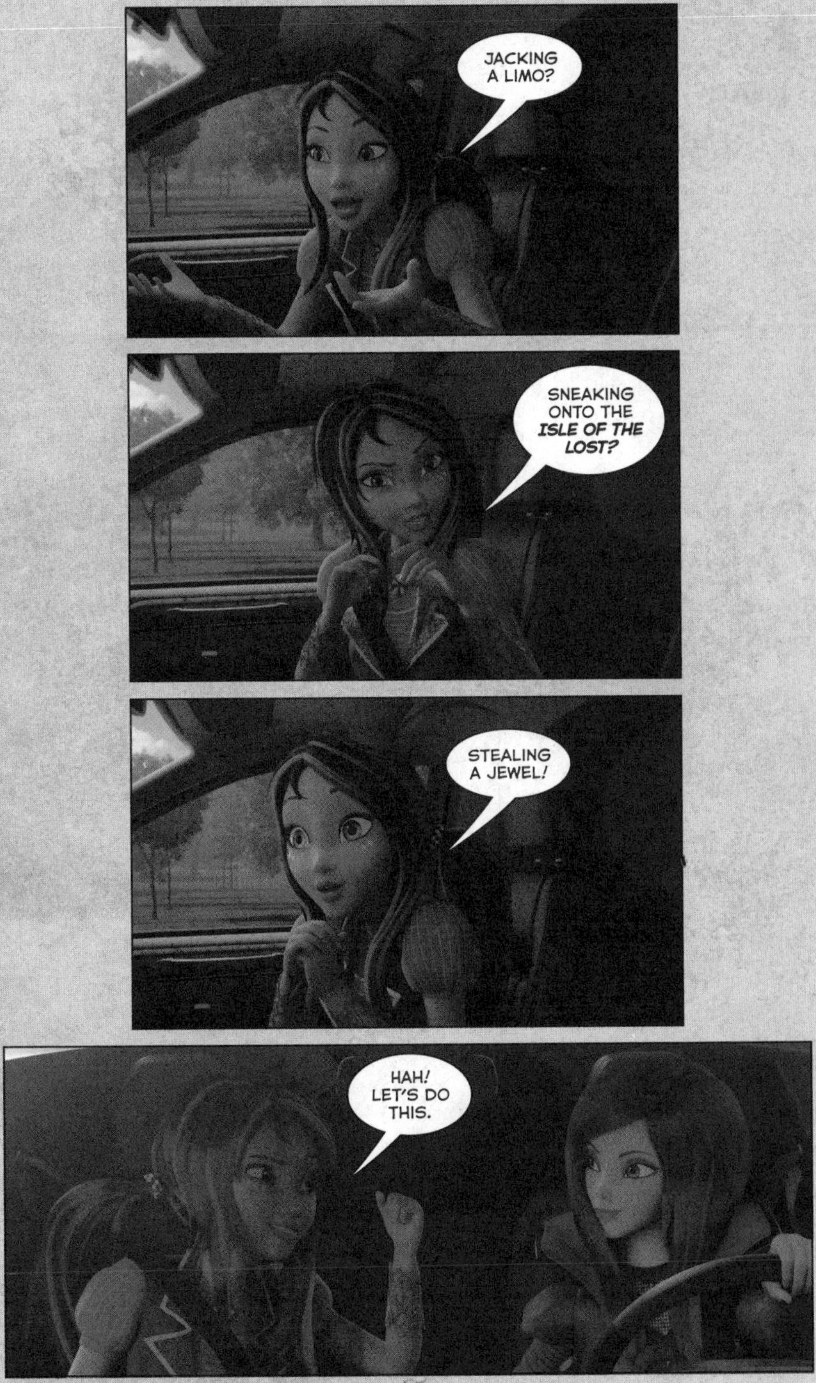
JACKING A LIMO?
SNEAKING ONTO THE *ISLE OF THE LOST?*
STEALING A JEWEL!
HAH! LET'S DO THIS.

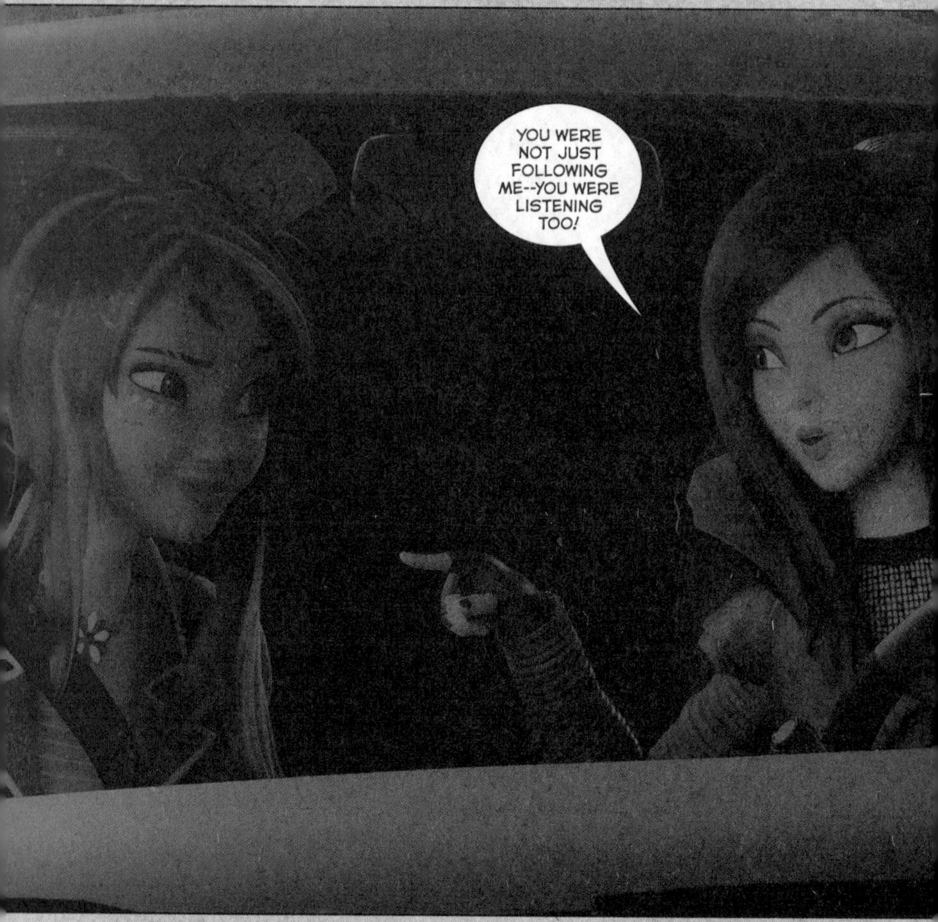
YOU WERE NOT JUST FOLLOWING ME--YOU WERE LISTENING TOO!

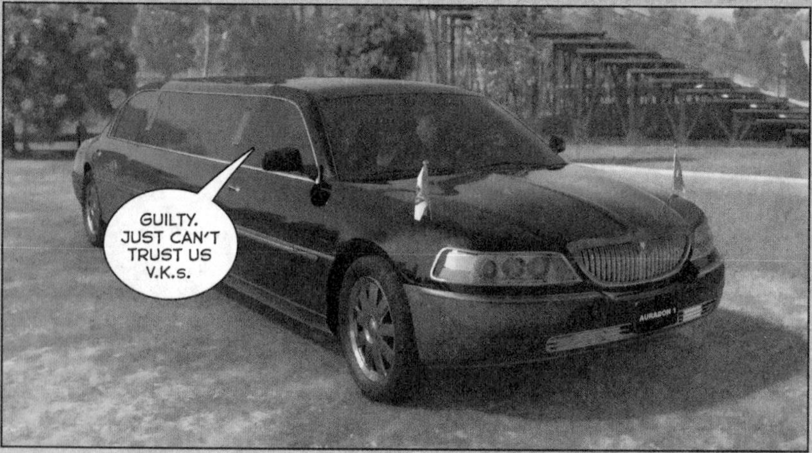
GUILTY. JUST CAN'T TRUST US V.K.s.
AURADON 1

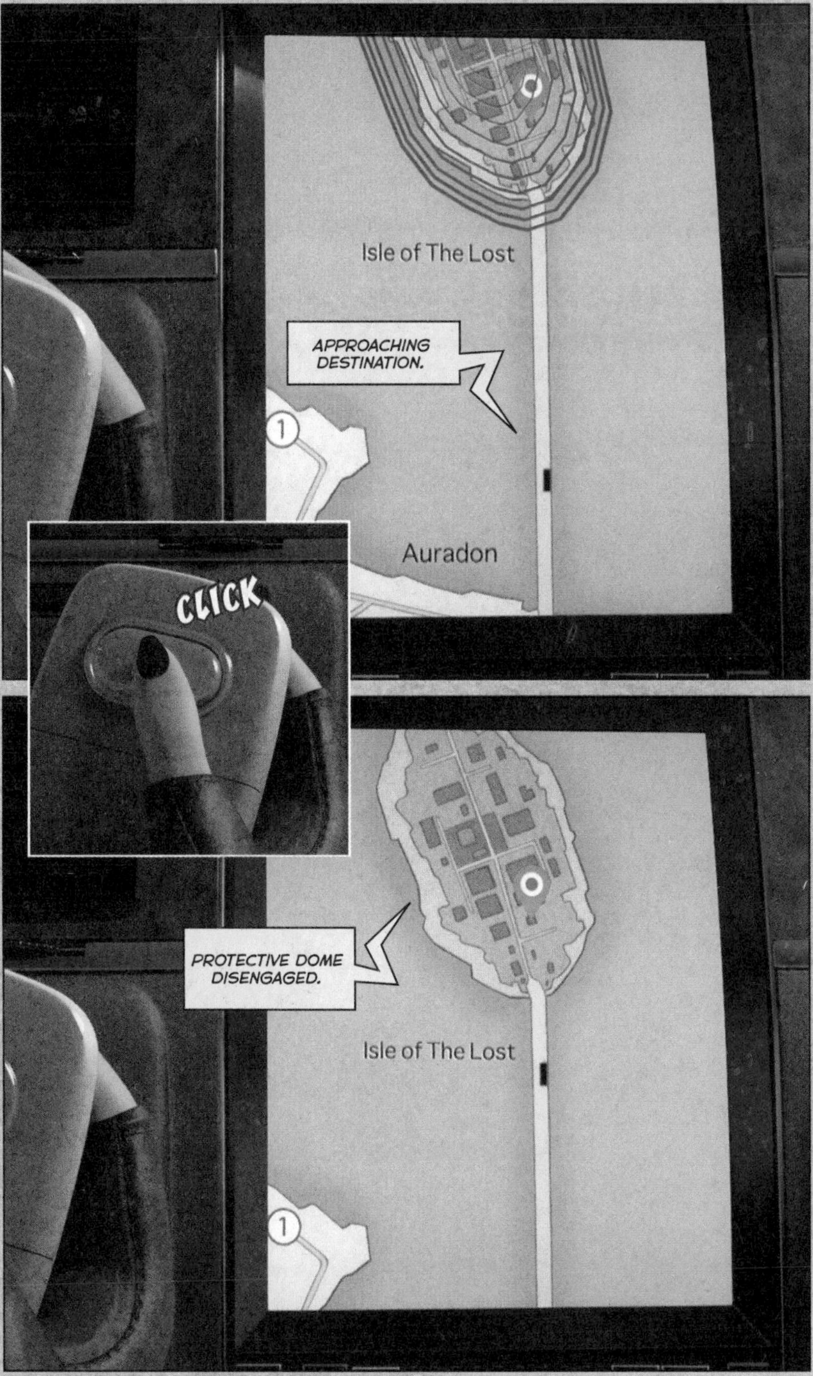
Isle of The Lost
APPROACHING DESTINATION.
1
Auradon
CLICK
PROTECTIVE DOME DISENGAGED.
Isle of The Lost
1

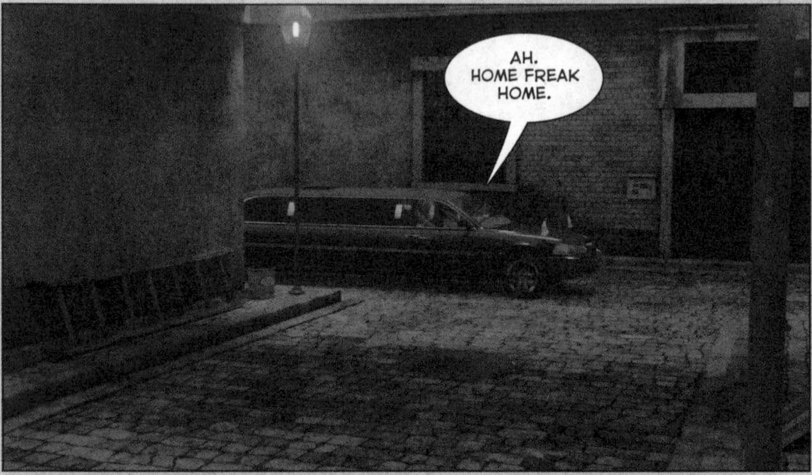
AH.
HOME FREAK
HOME.

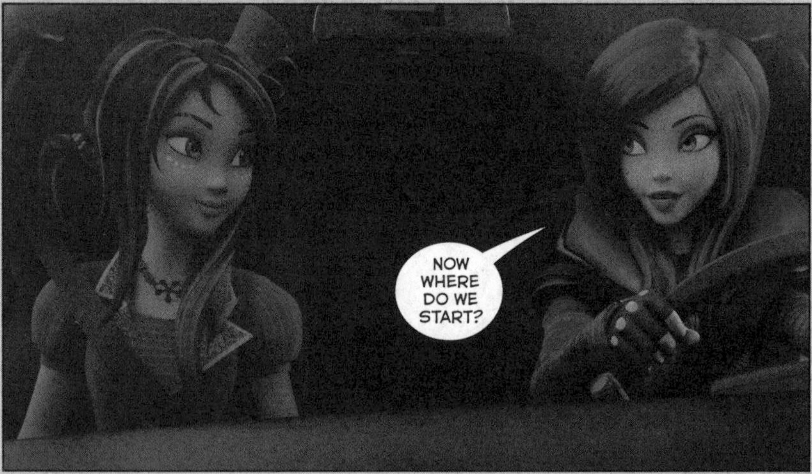
NOW
WHERE
DO WE
START?

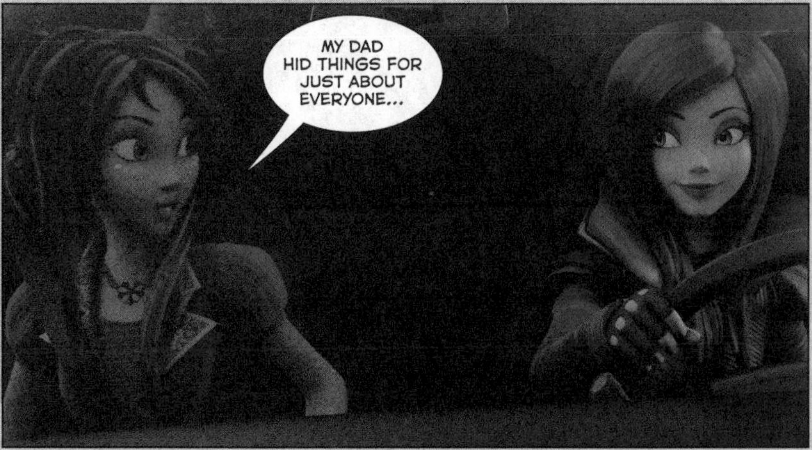
MY DAD HID THINGS FOR JUST ABOUT EVERYONE...

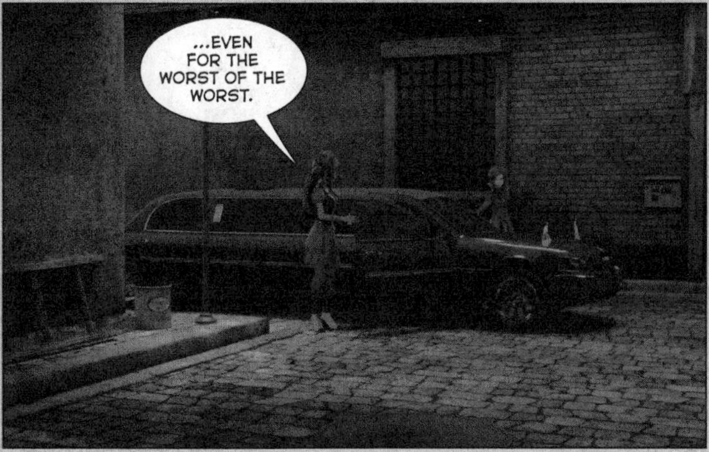
...EVEN FOR THE WORST OF THE WORST.

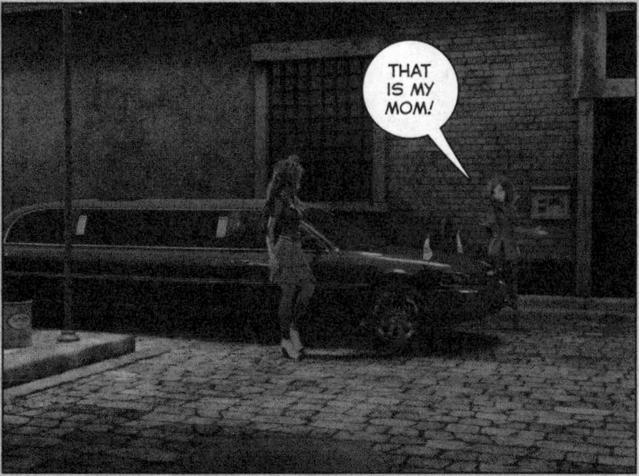
THAT IS MY MOM!

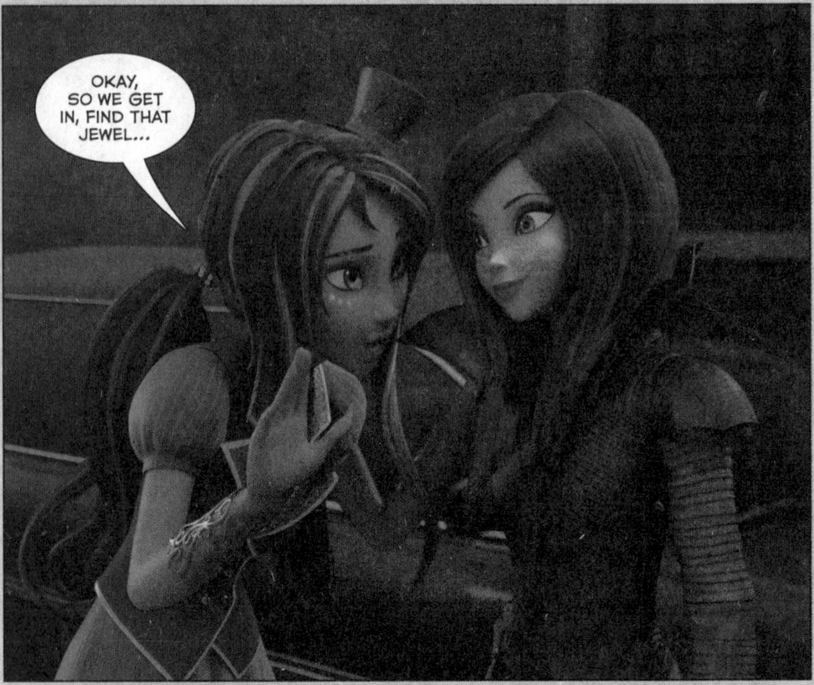
OKAY, SO WE GET IN, FIND THAT JEWEL...

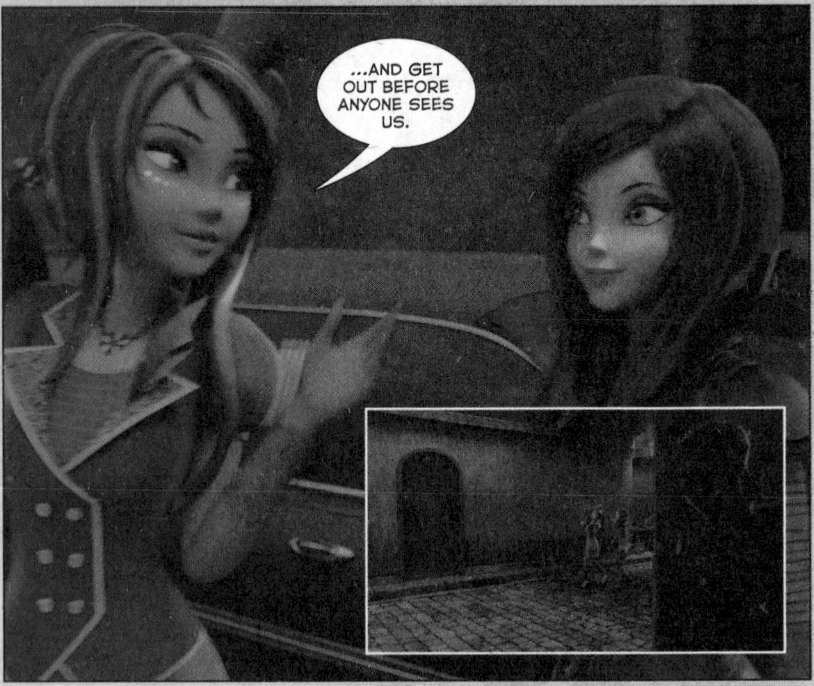
...AND GET OUT BEFORE ANYONE SEES US.

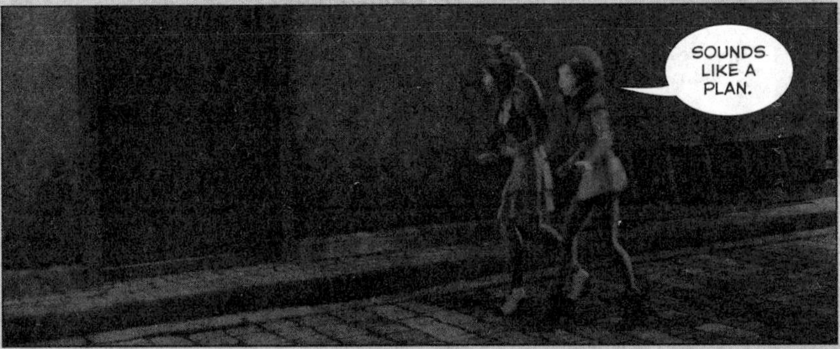
SOUNDS LIKE A PLAN.

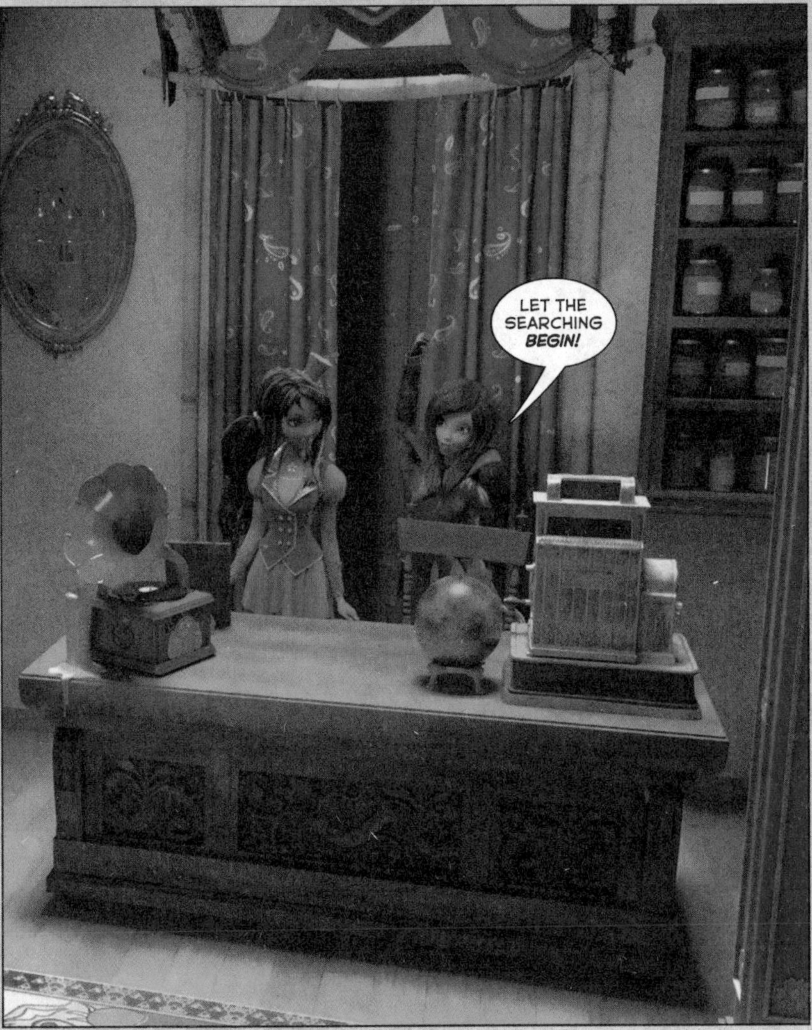
LET THE SEARCHING *BEGIN!*

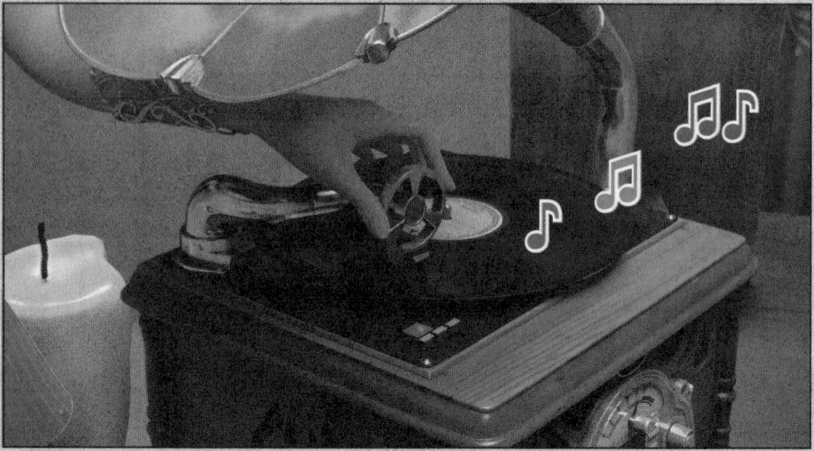

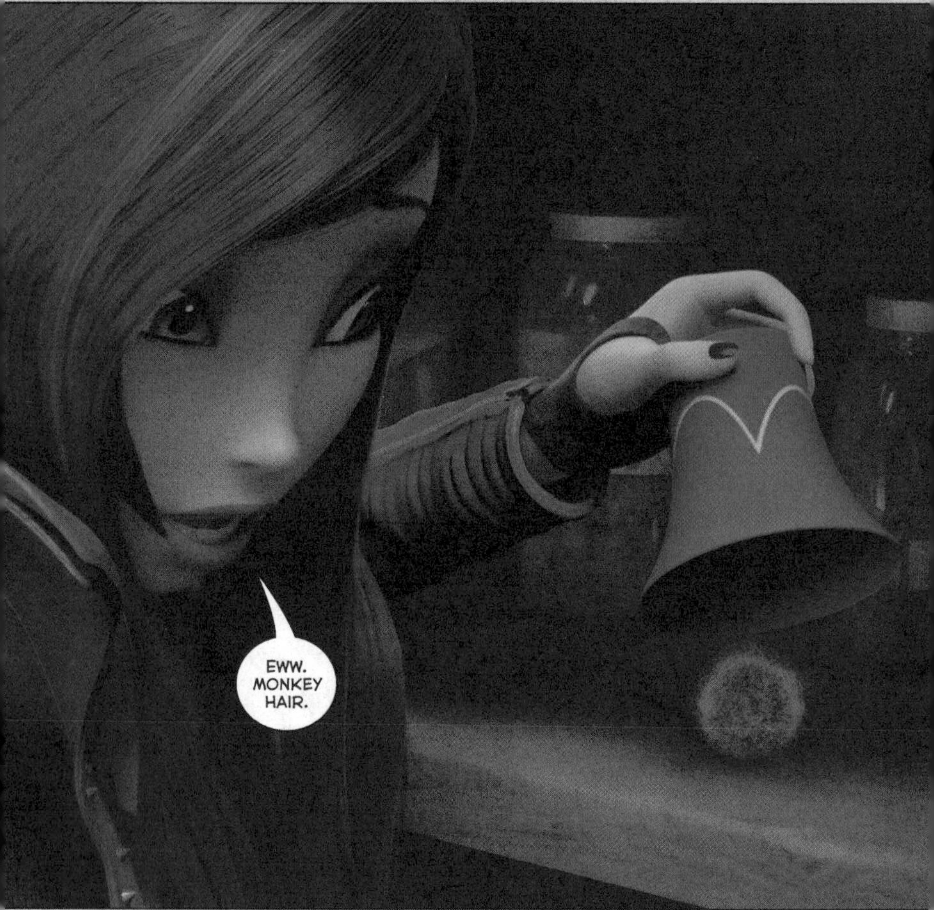
EWW. MONKEY HAIR.

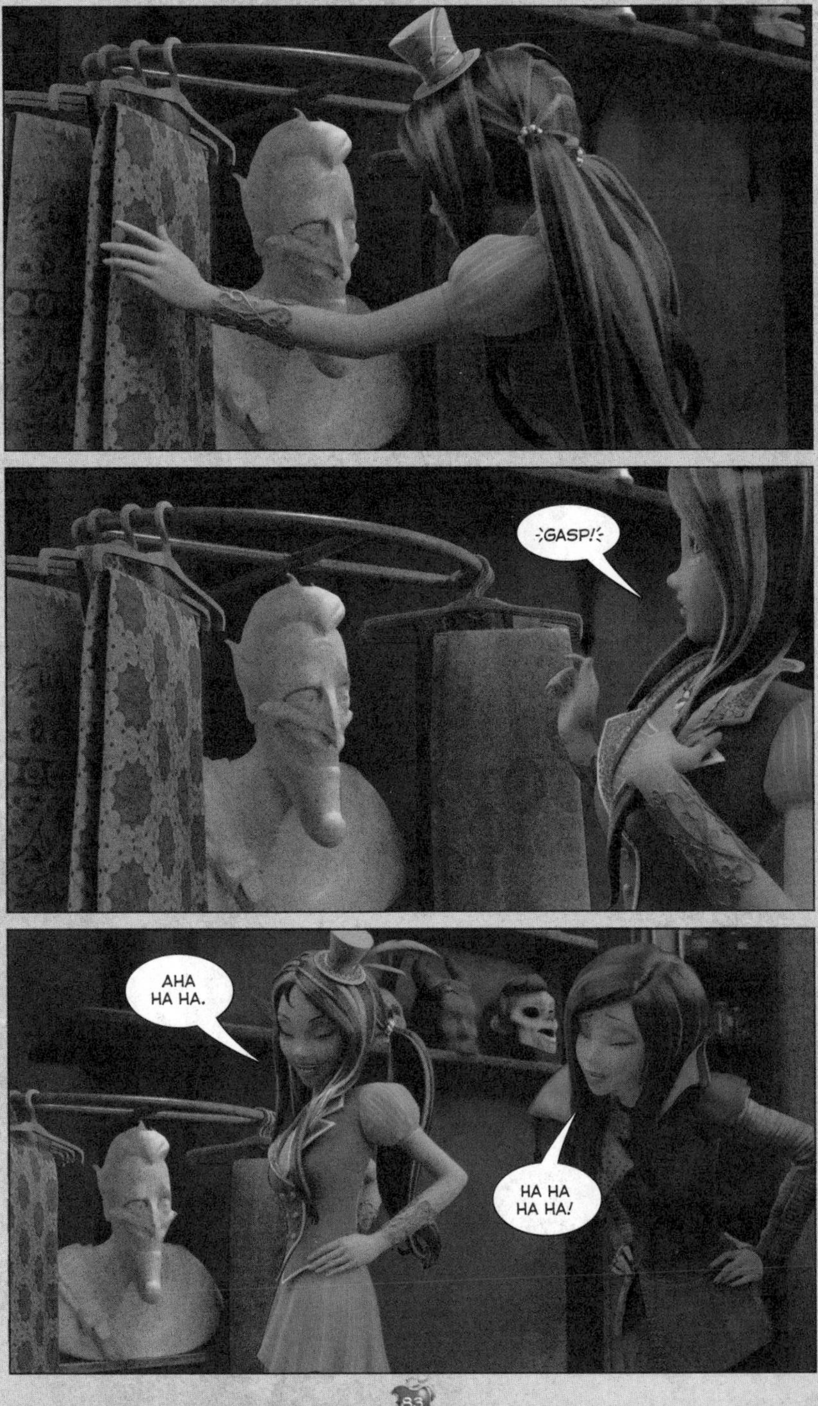
GASP!
AHA
HA HA.
HA HA
HA HA!

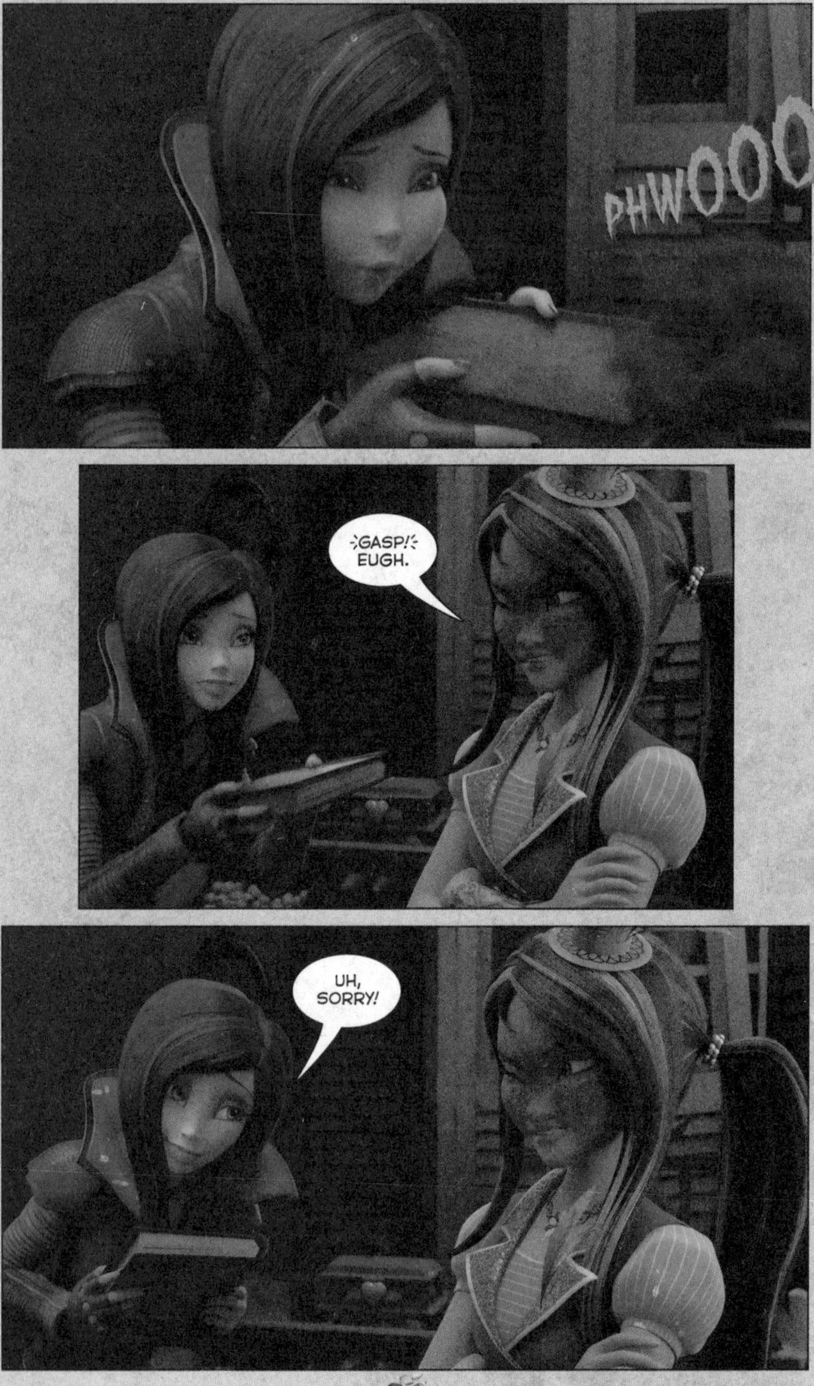
PHWOOO
GASP! EUGH.
UH, SORRY!

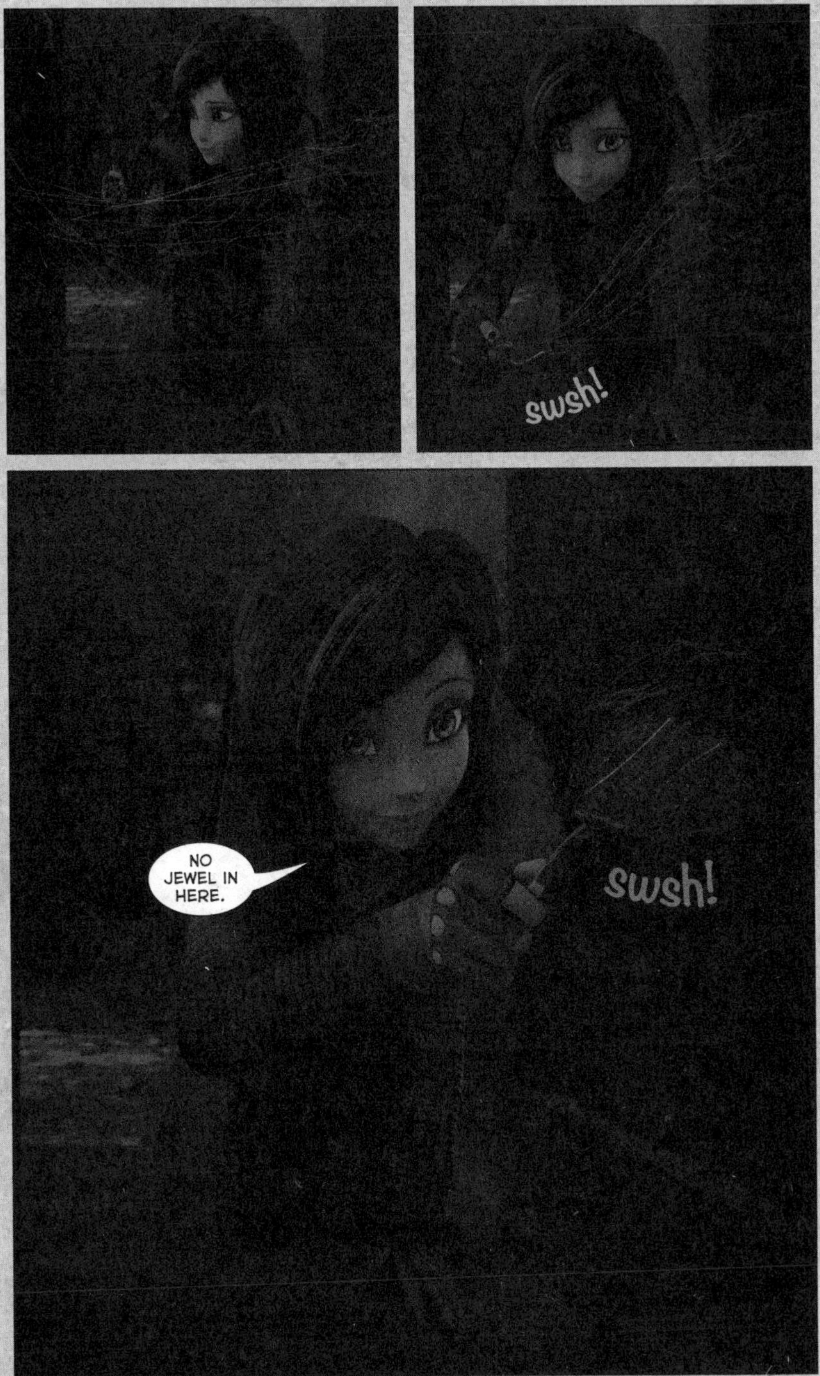
swsh!
NO JEWEL IN HERE.
swsh!

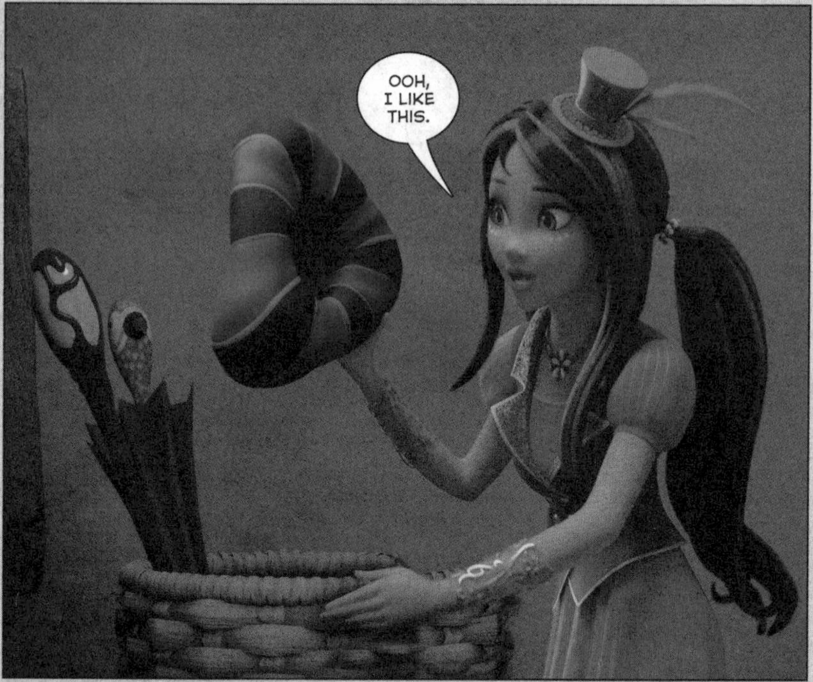
OOH, I LIKE THIS.

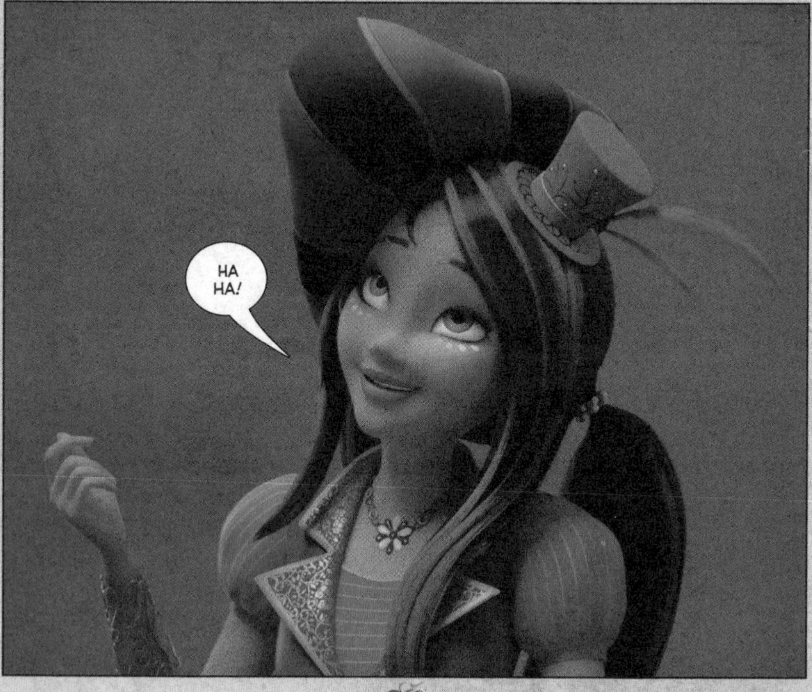
HA HA!

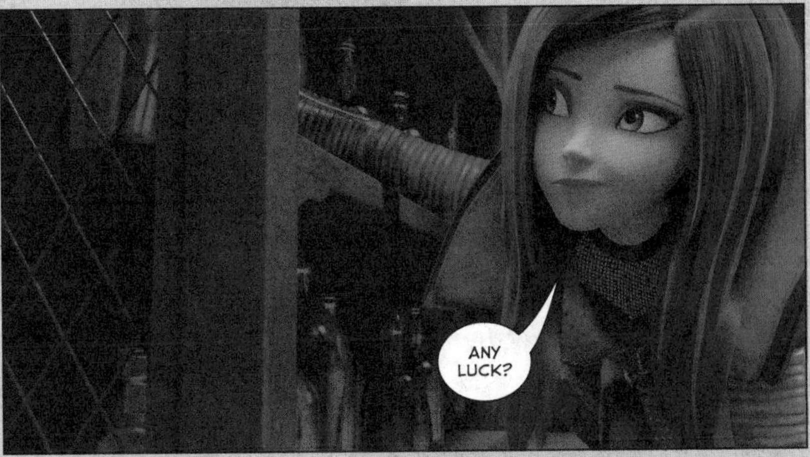
ANY LUCK?

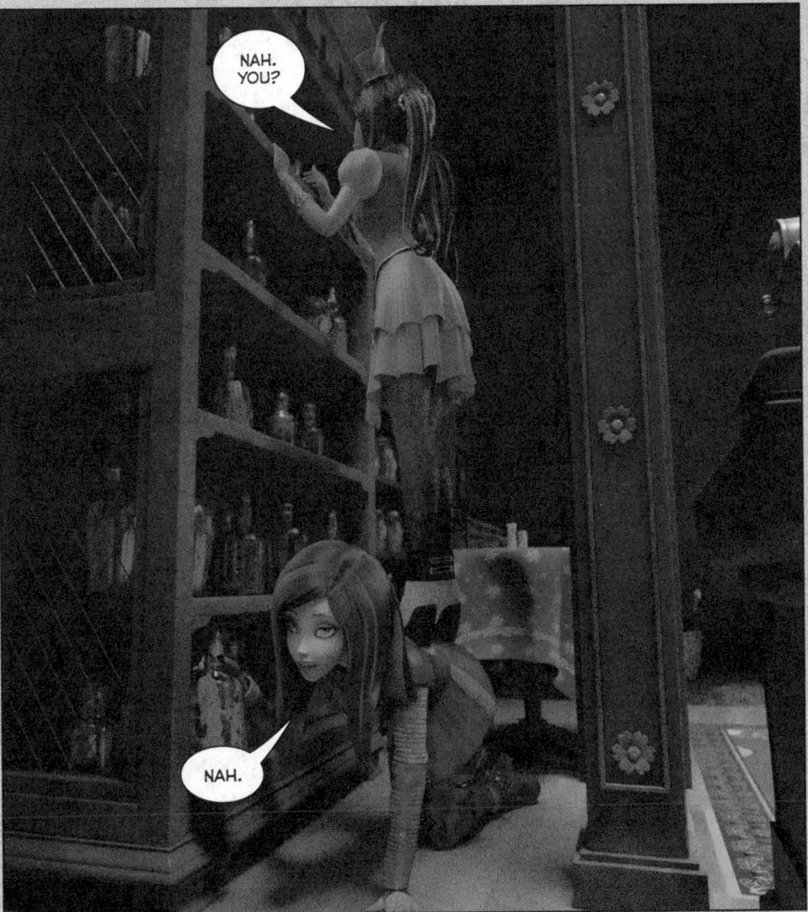
NAH. YOU?
NAH.

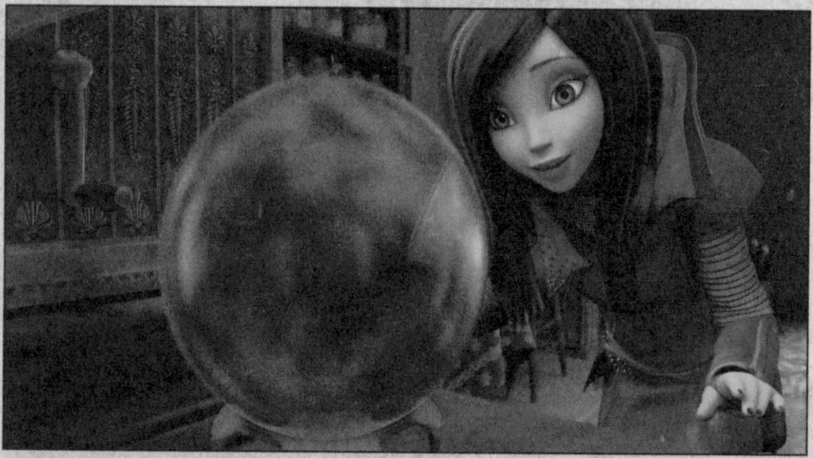

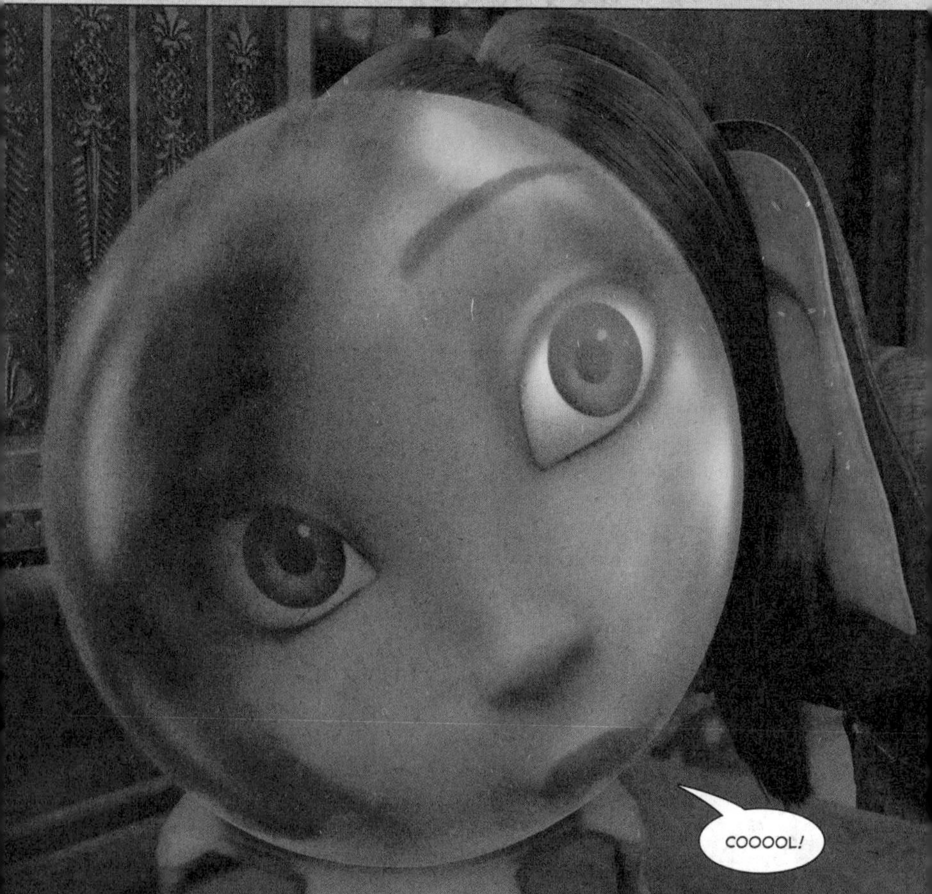
COOOOL!

SWOOSH!
WOAH!
TA-DAH! HA HA HA.
OH-KAY.
CRASH!

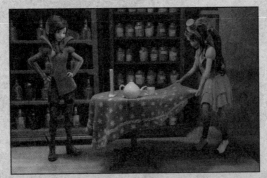

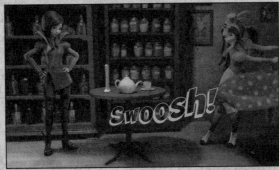

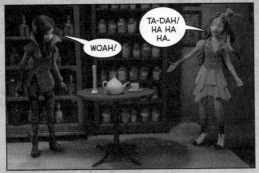

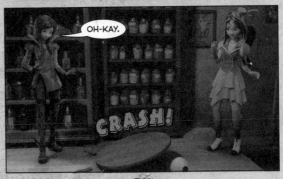

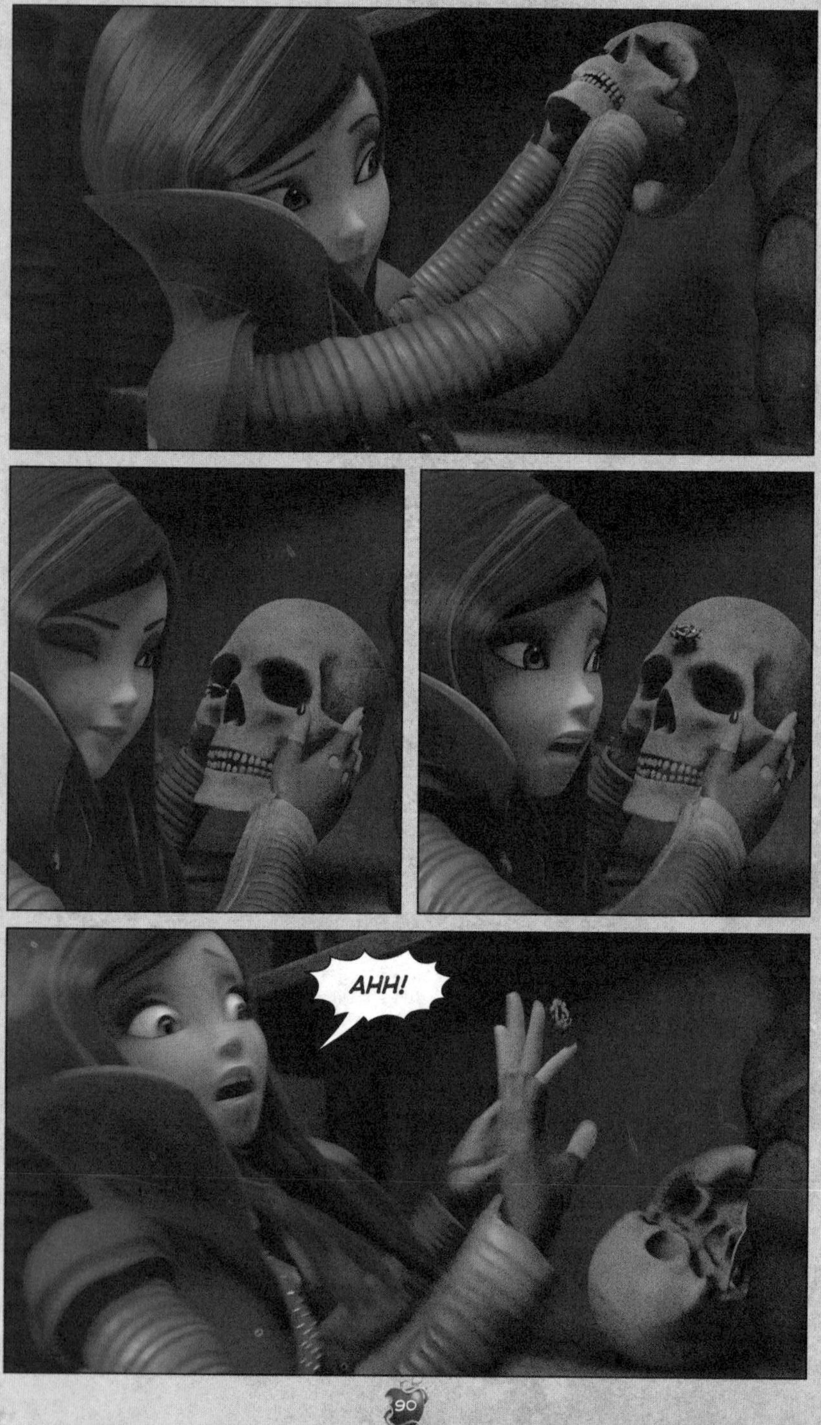
AHH!

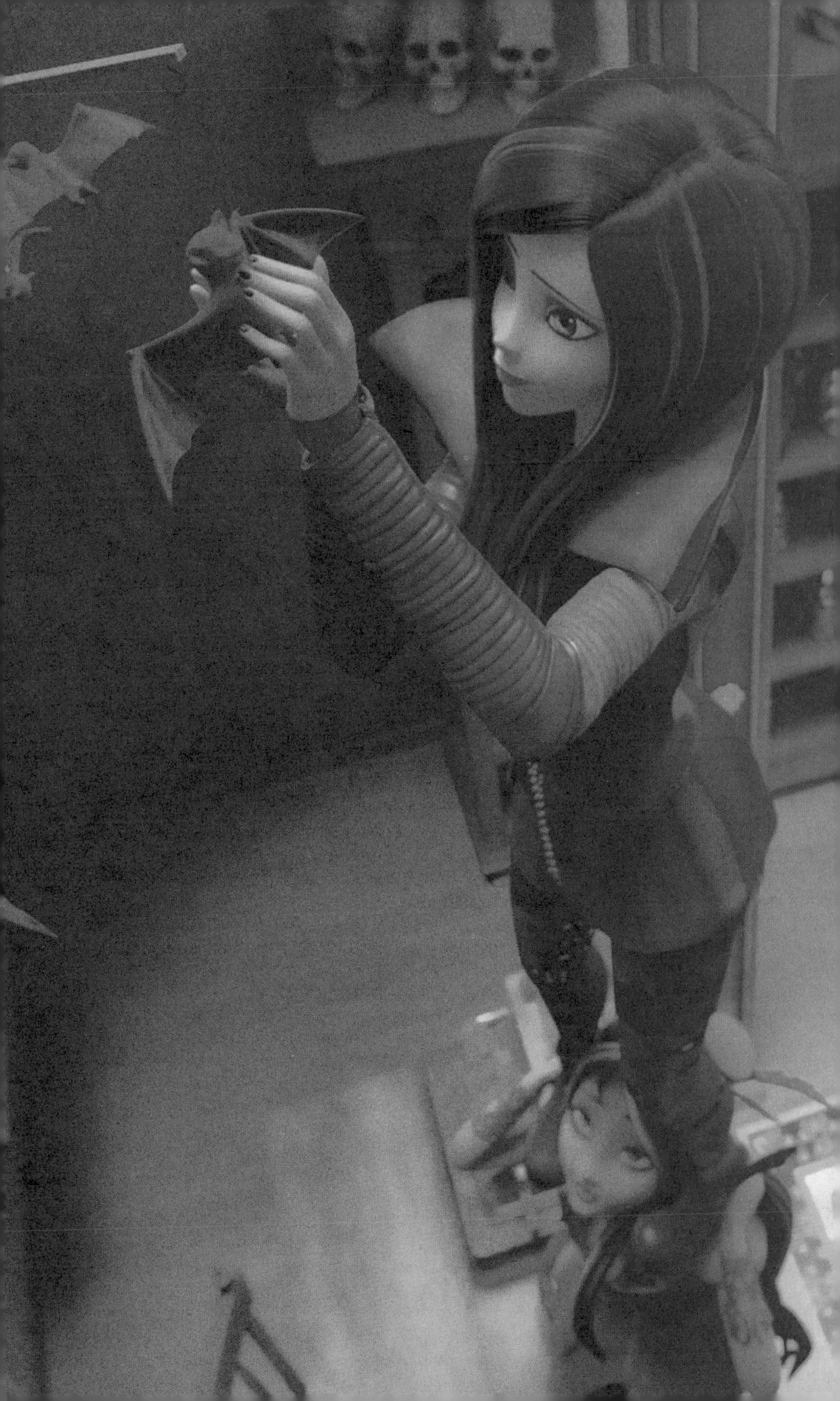

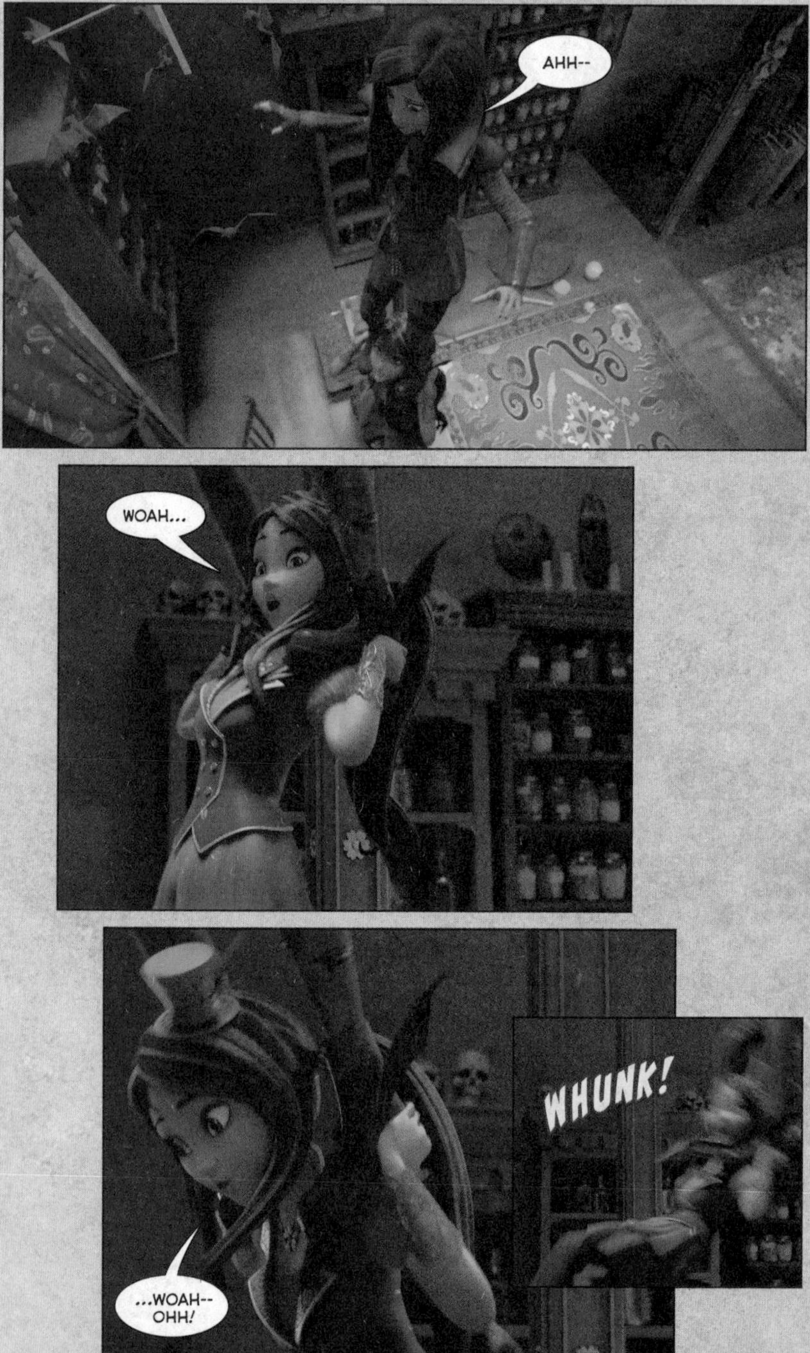
AHH--
WOAH...
...WOAH--
OHH!
WHUNK!

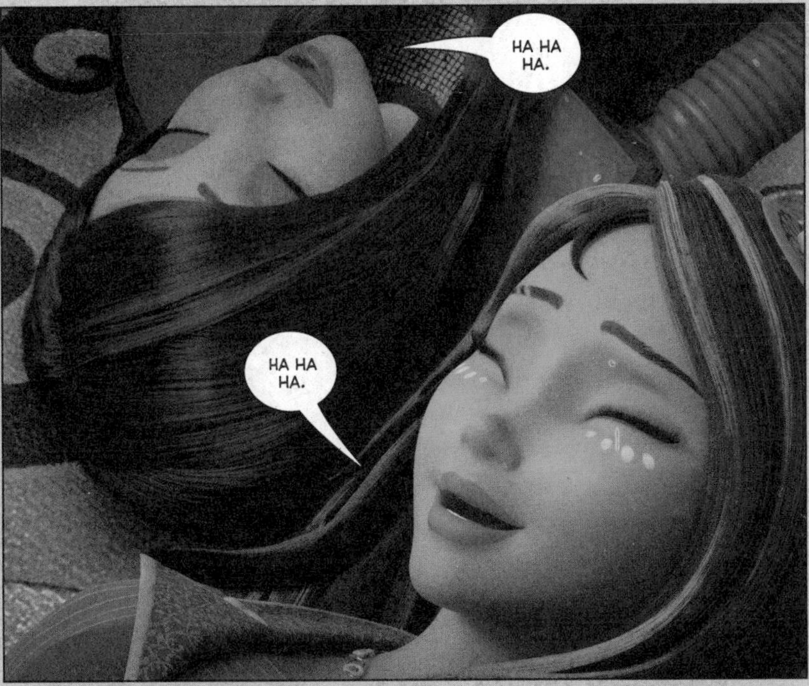
HA HA HA.
HA HA HA.

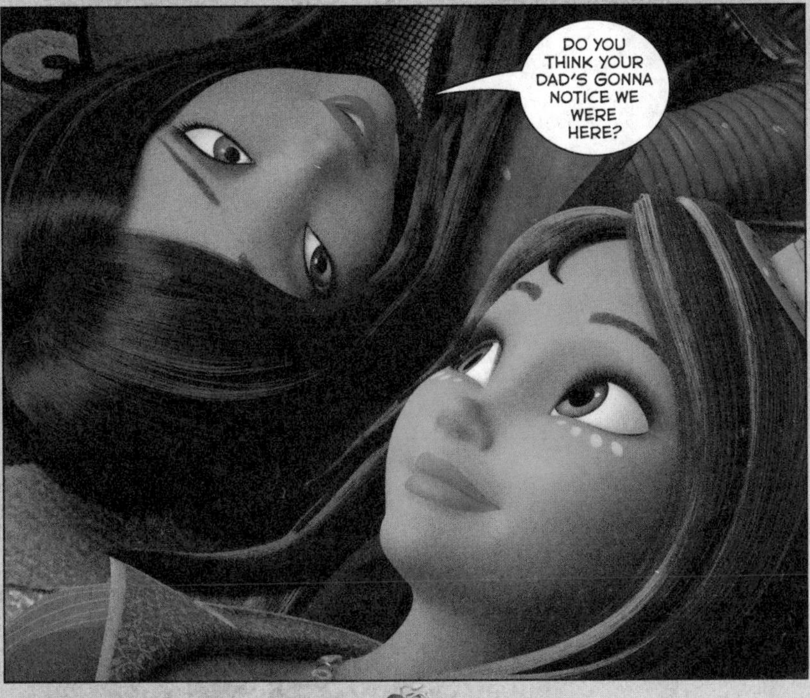
DO YOU THINK YOUR DAD'S GONNA NOTICE WE WERE HERE?

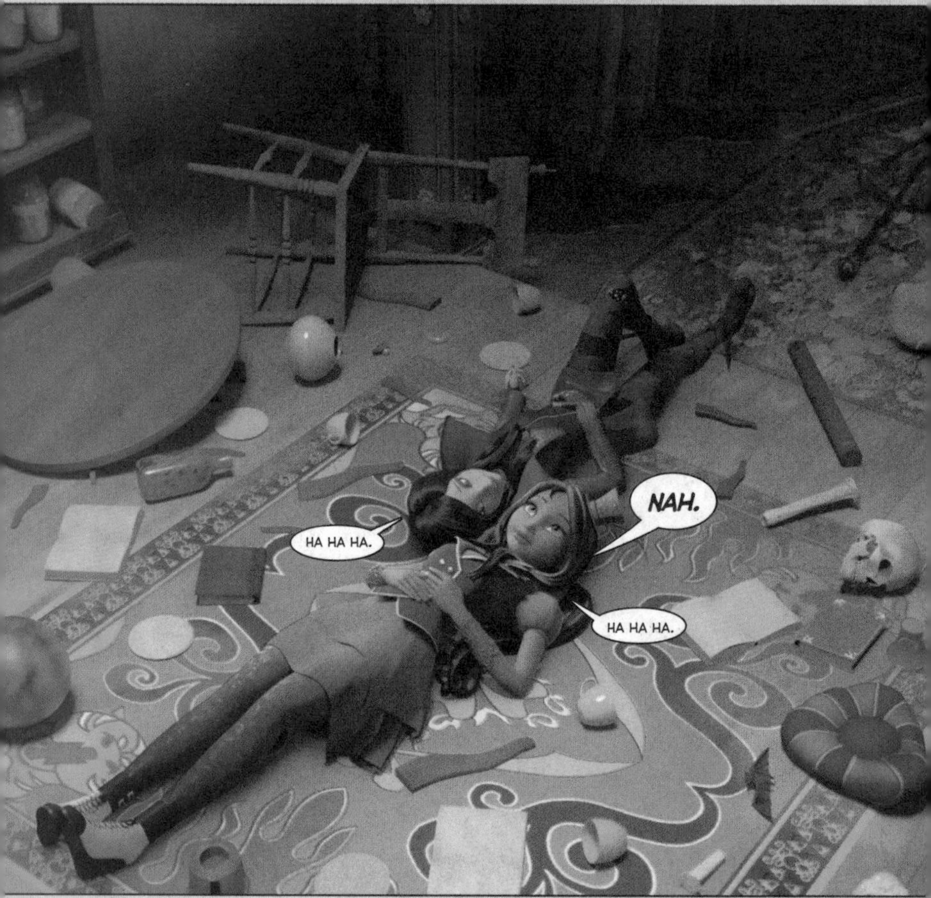

NAH.
HA HA HA.
HA HA HA.

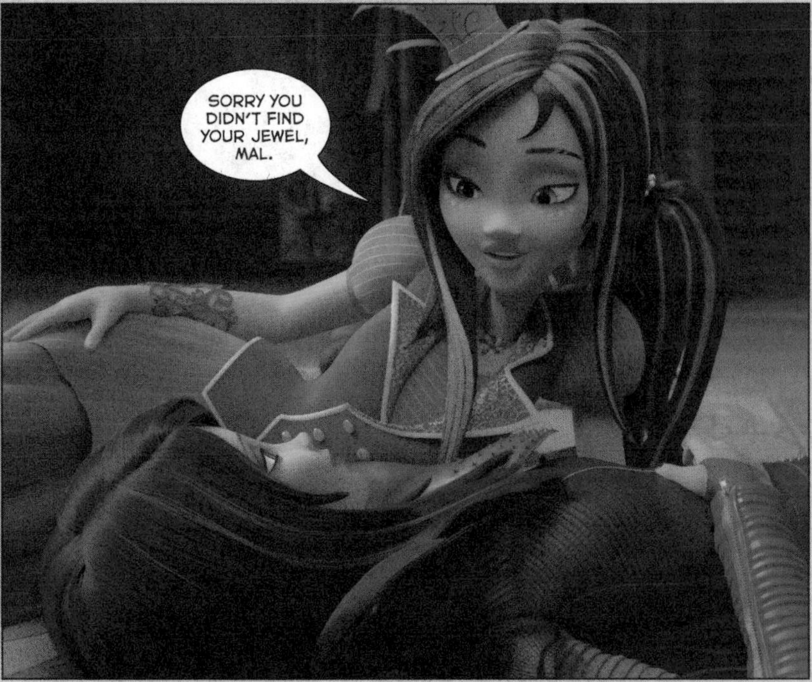
SORRY YOU DIDN'T FIND YOUR JEWEL, MAL.

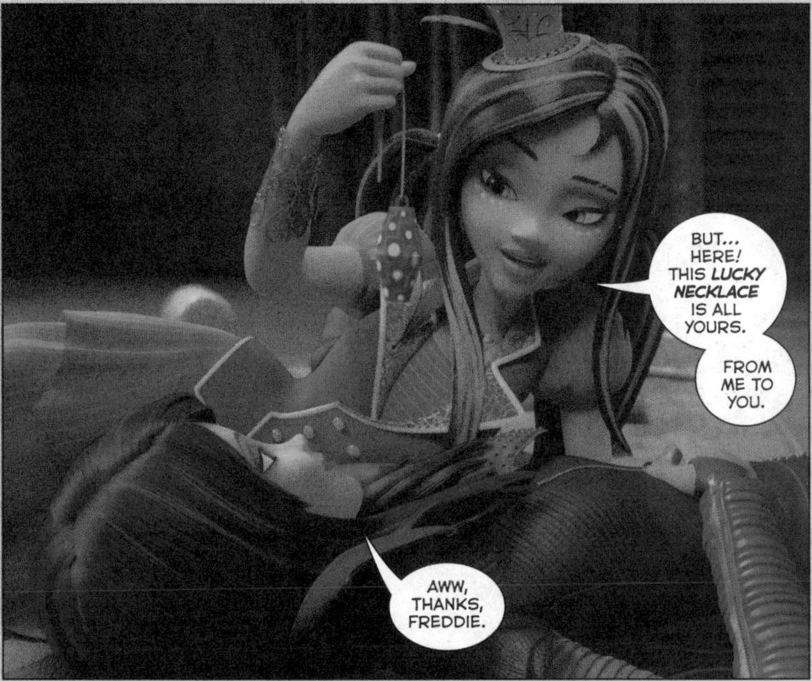
BUT... HERE! THIS ***LUCKY NECKLACE*** IS ALL YOURS.
FROM ME TO YOU.
AWW, THANKS, FREDDIE.

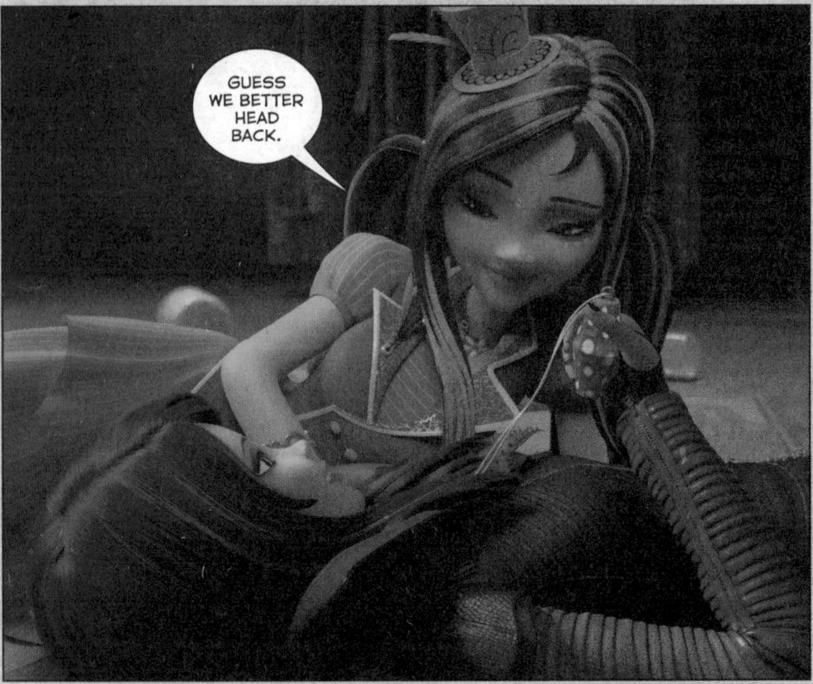
GUESS WE BETTER HEAD BACK.

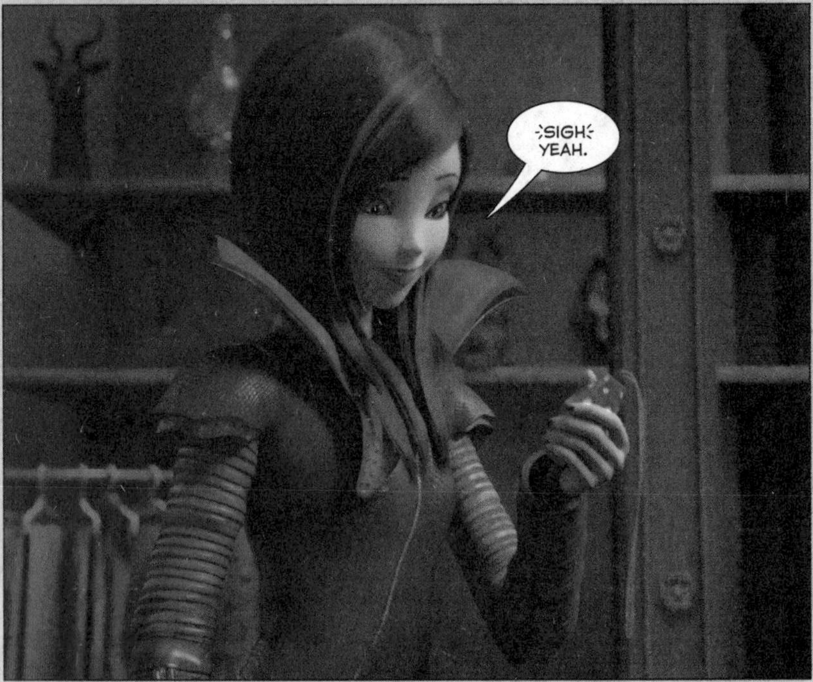
SIGH YEAH.

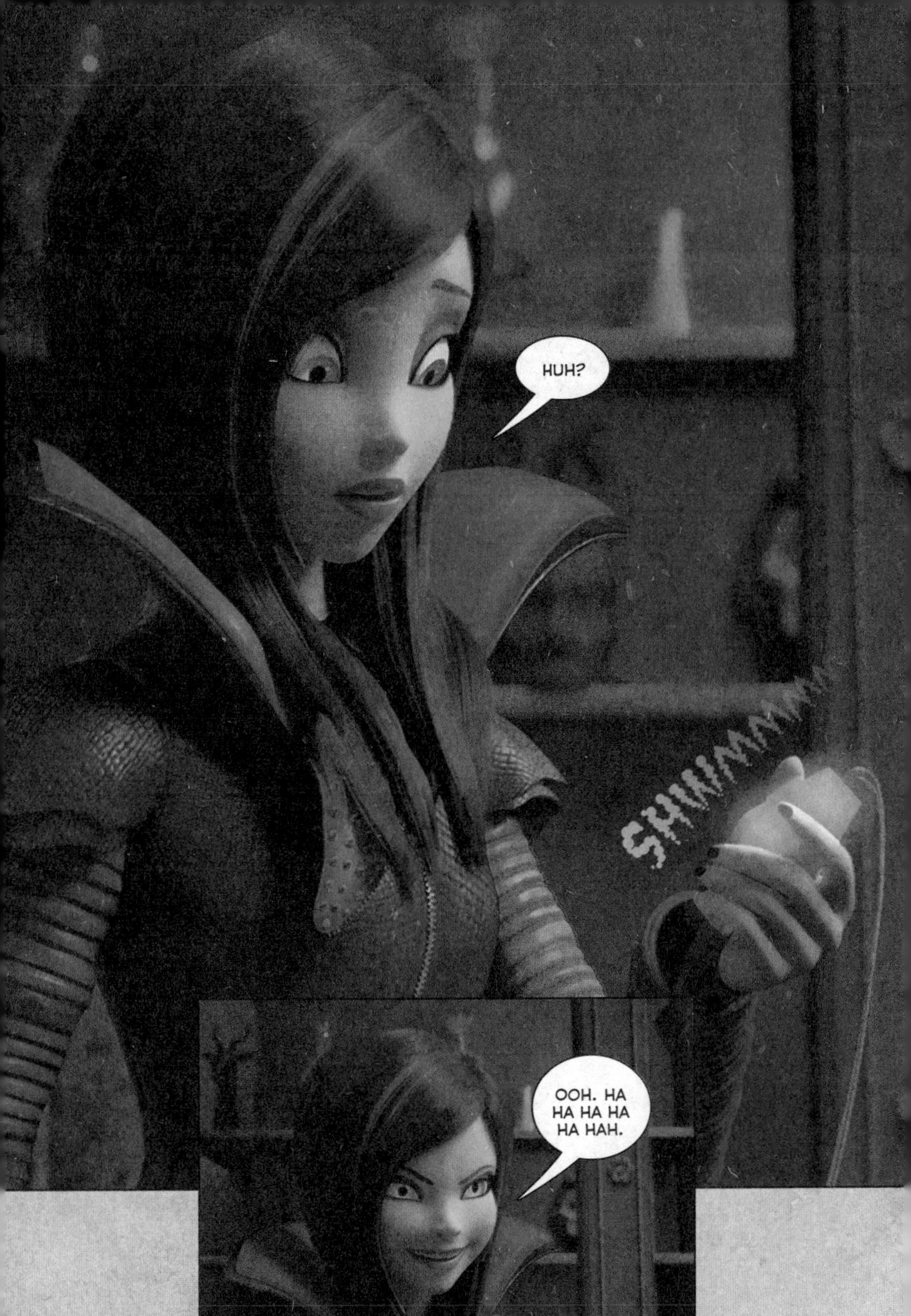
HUH?
SHIMMMM
OOH. HA HA HA HA HA HAH.

CHAPTER 22: A WILD REHEARSAL

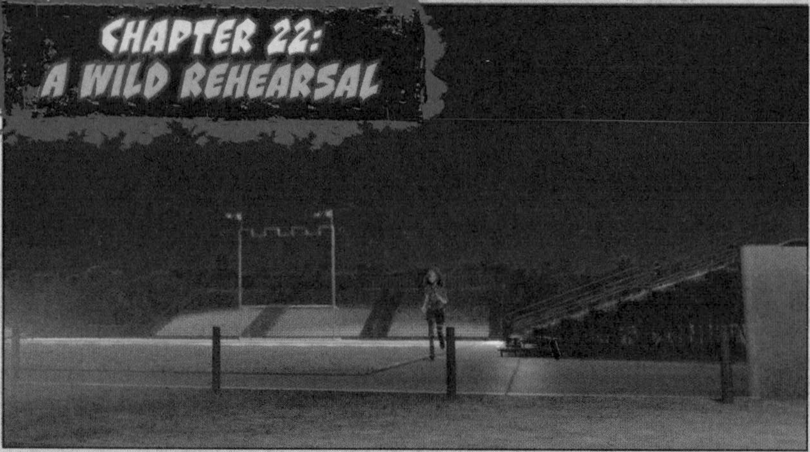

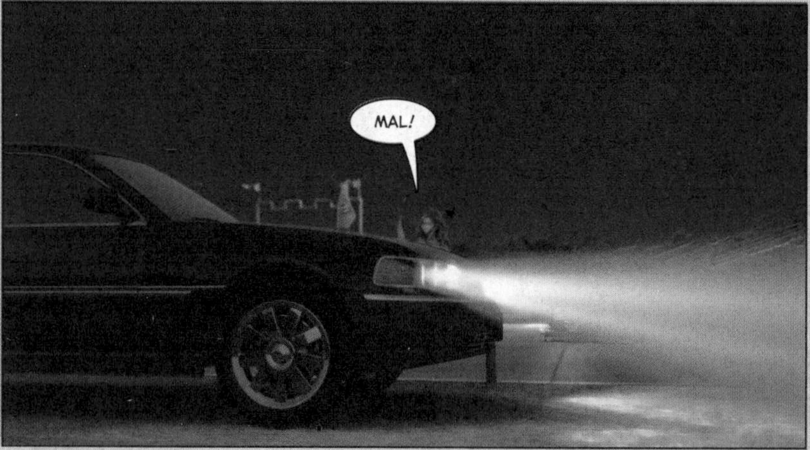
MAL!

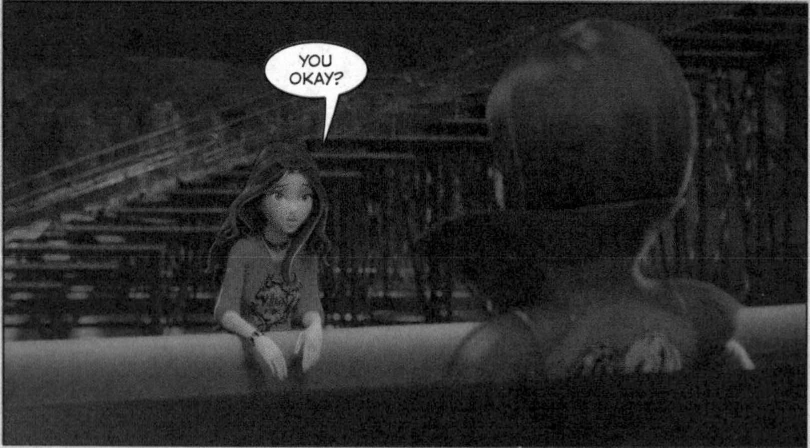
YOU OKAY?

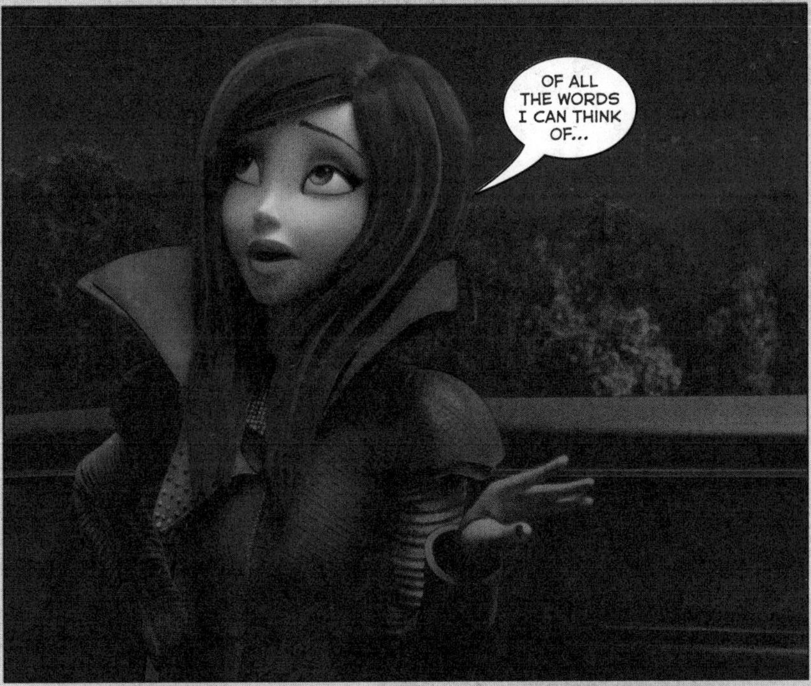
OF ALL THE WORDS I CAN THINK OF...

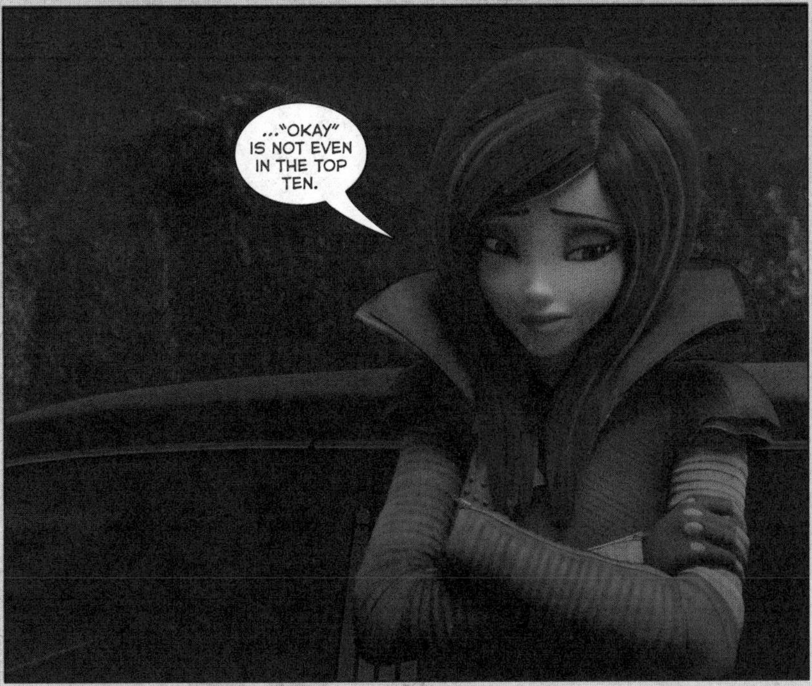
..."OKAY" IS NOT EVEN IN THE TOP TEN.

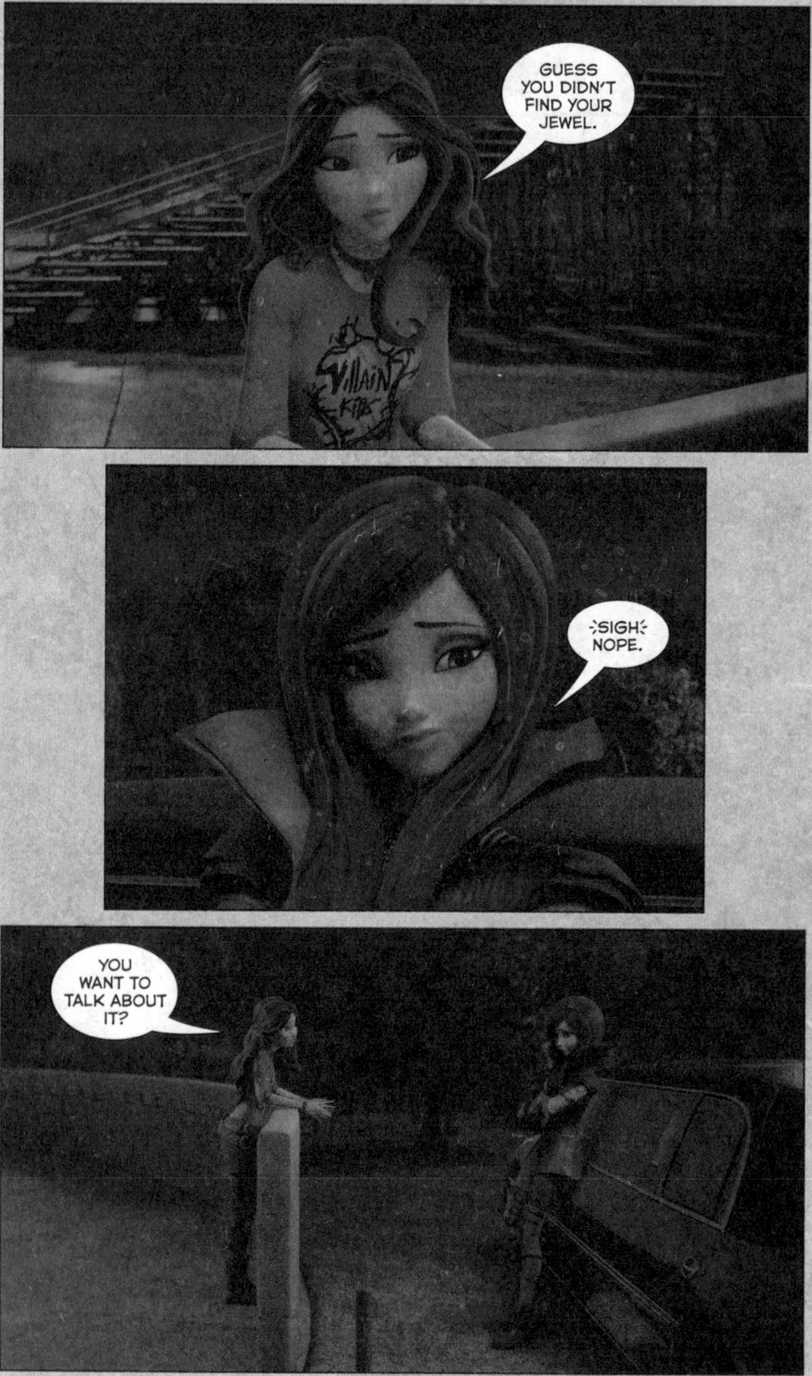
GUESS YOU DIDN'T FIND YOUR JEWEL.
SIGH
NOPE.
YOU WANT TO TALK ABOUT IT?

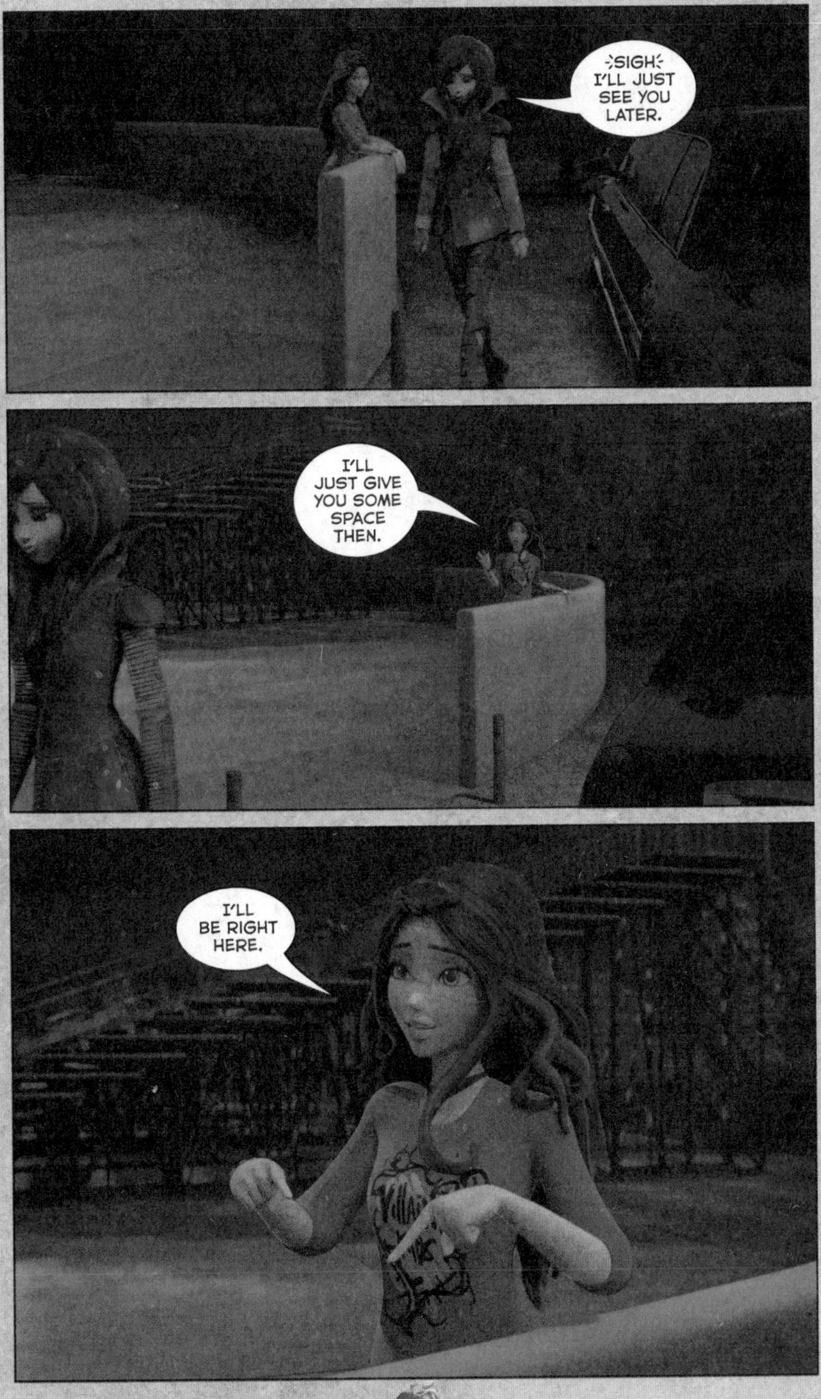
SIGH
I'LL JUST SEE YOU LATER.
I'LL JUST GIVE YOU SOME SPACE THEN.
I'LL BE RIGHT HERE.

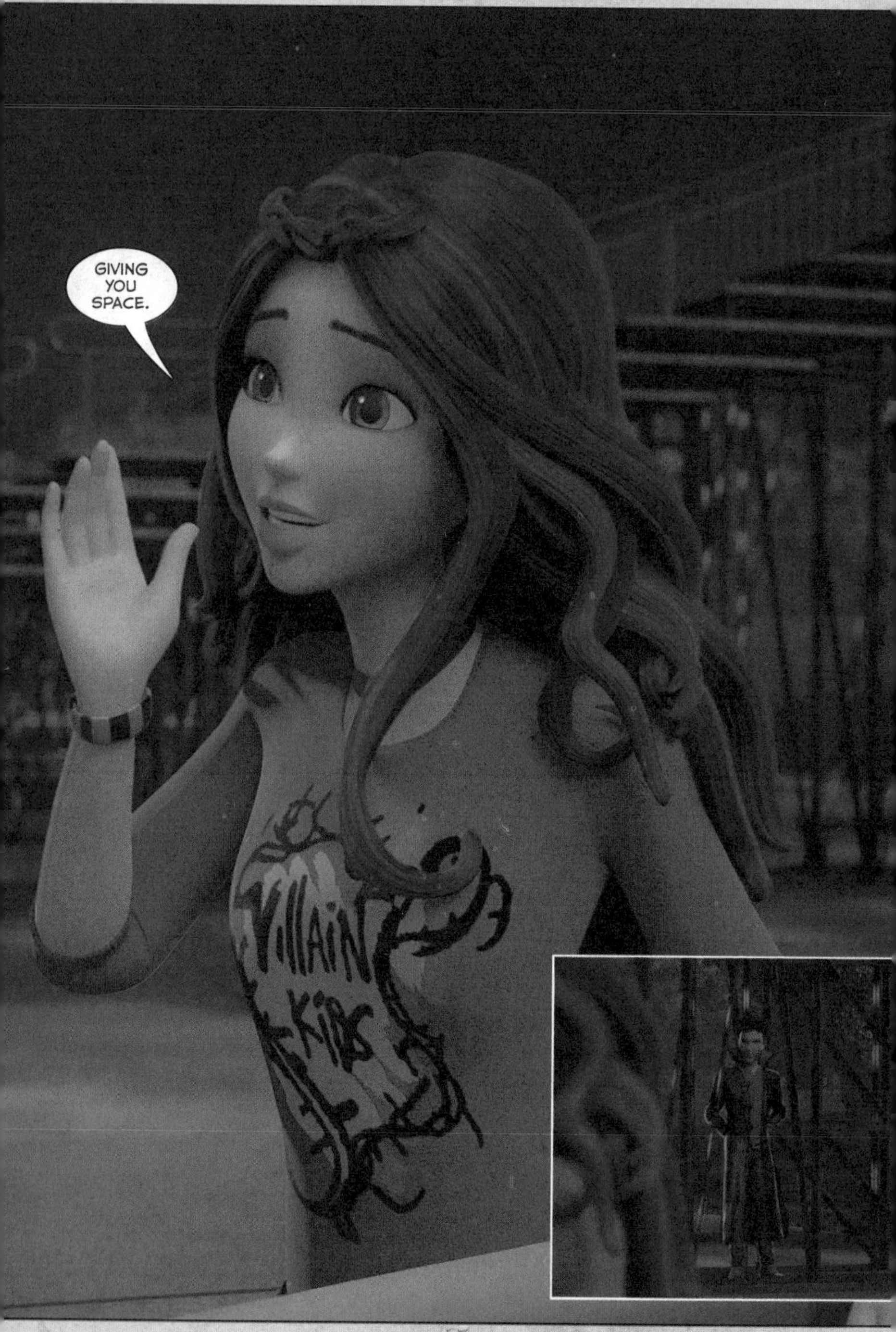
GIVING YOU SPACE.

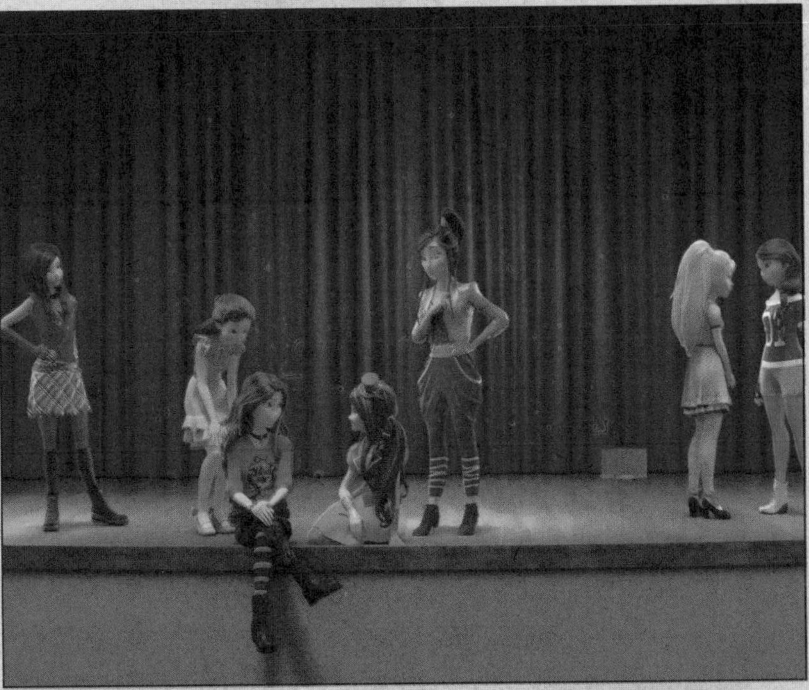

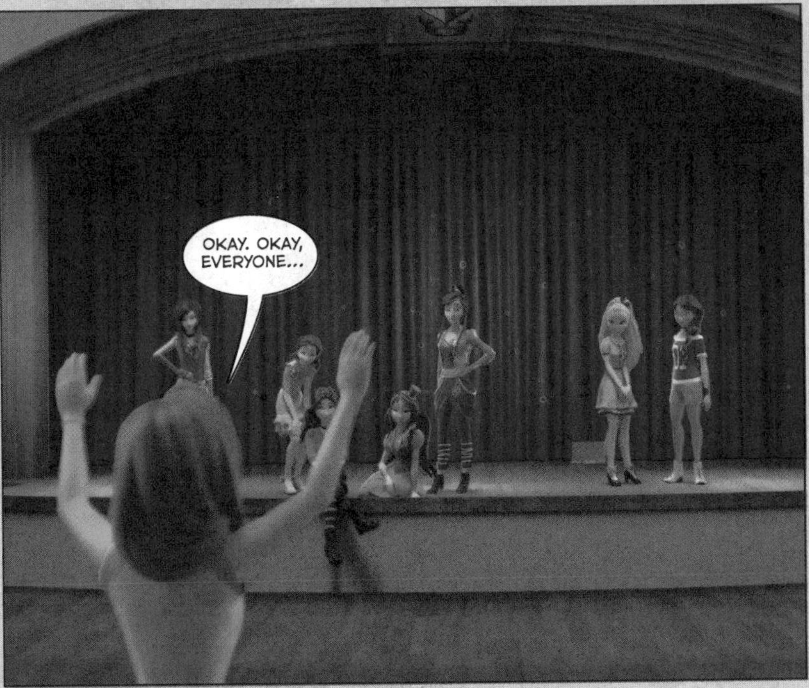
OKAY. OKAY, EVERYONE...

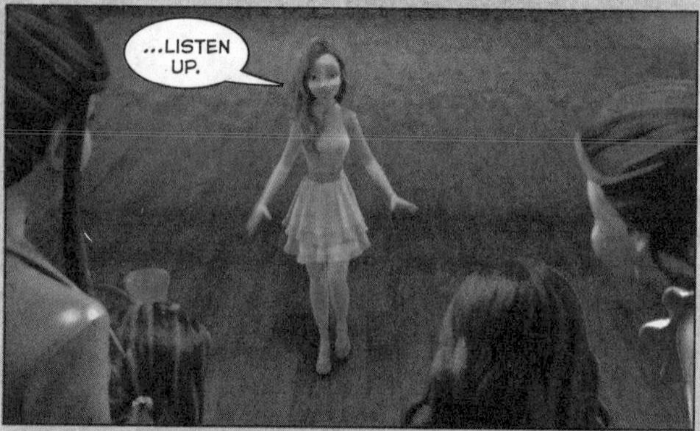
...LISTEN UP.

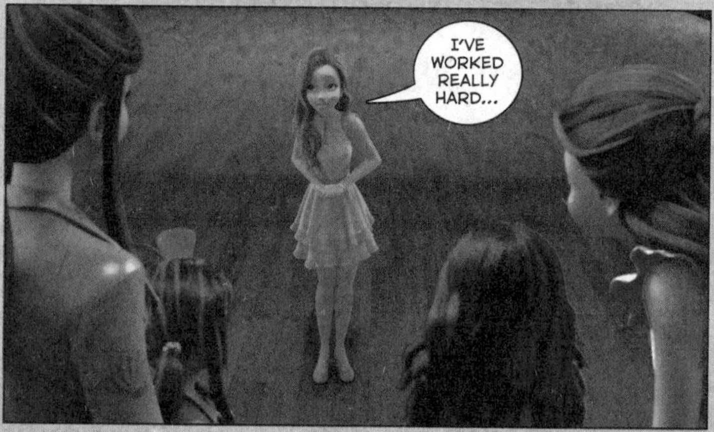
I'VE WORKED REALLY HARD...

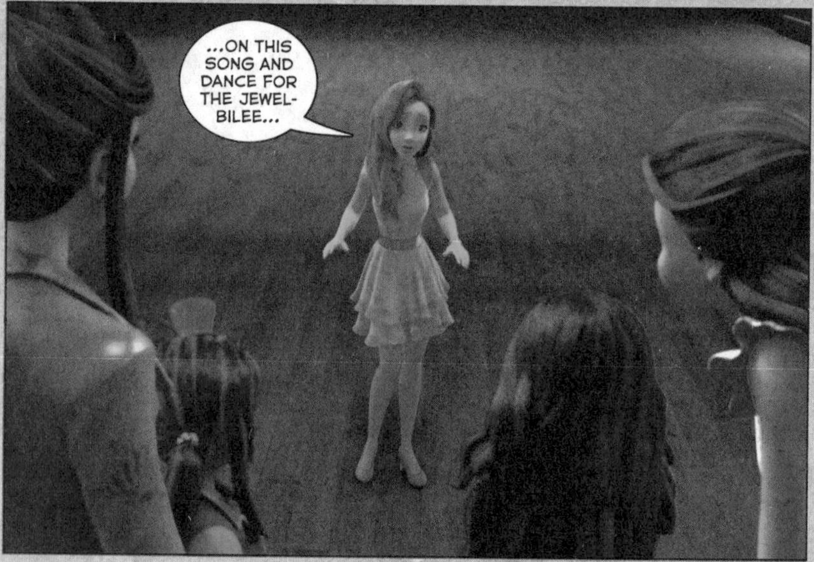
...ON THIS SONG AND DANCE FOR THE JEWEL-BILEE...

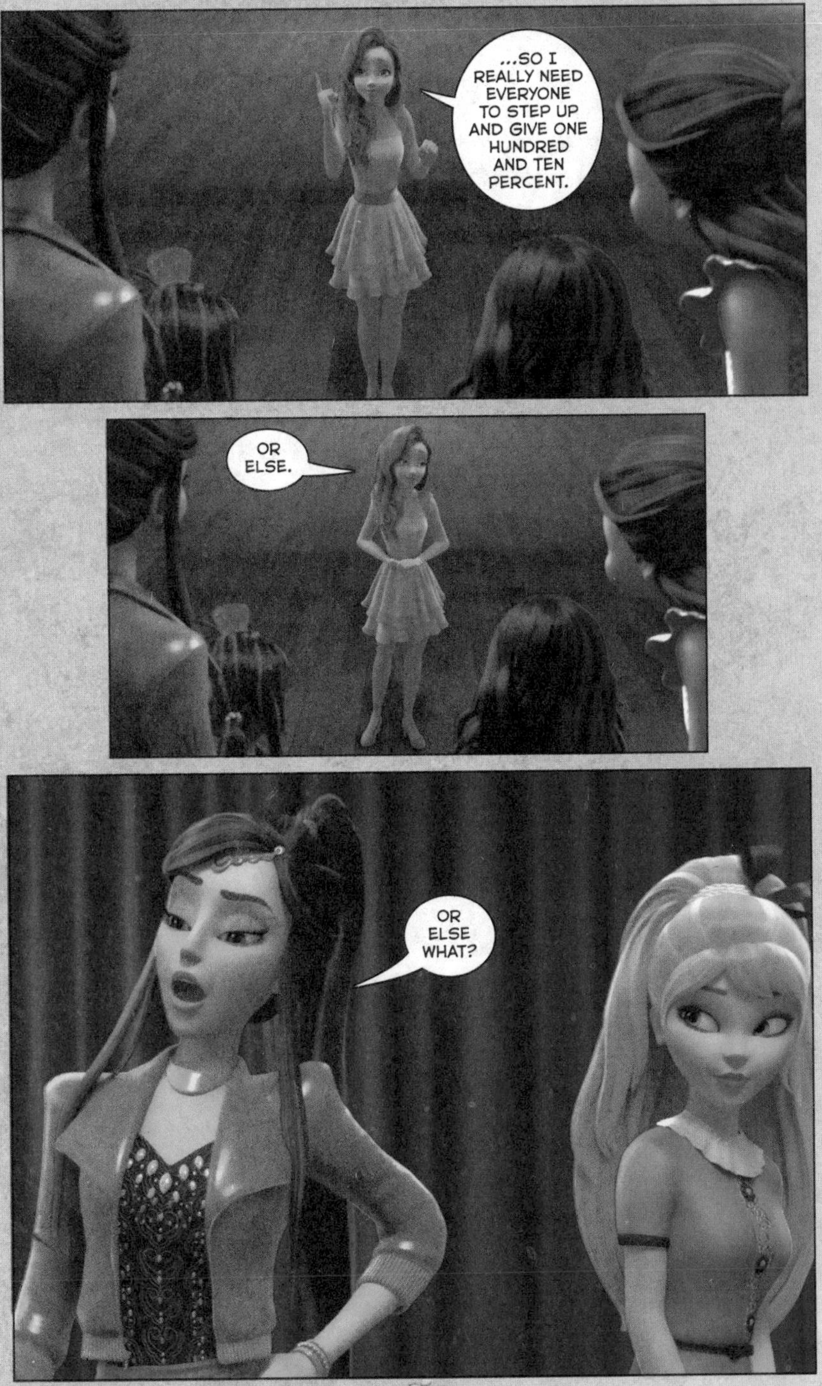
...SO I REALLY NEED EVERYONE TO STEP UP AND GIVE ONE HUNDRED AND TEN PERCENT.
OR ELSE.
OR ELSE WHAT?

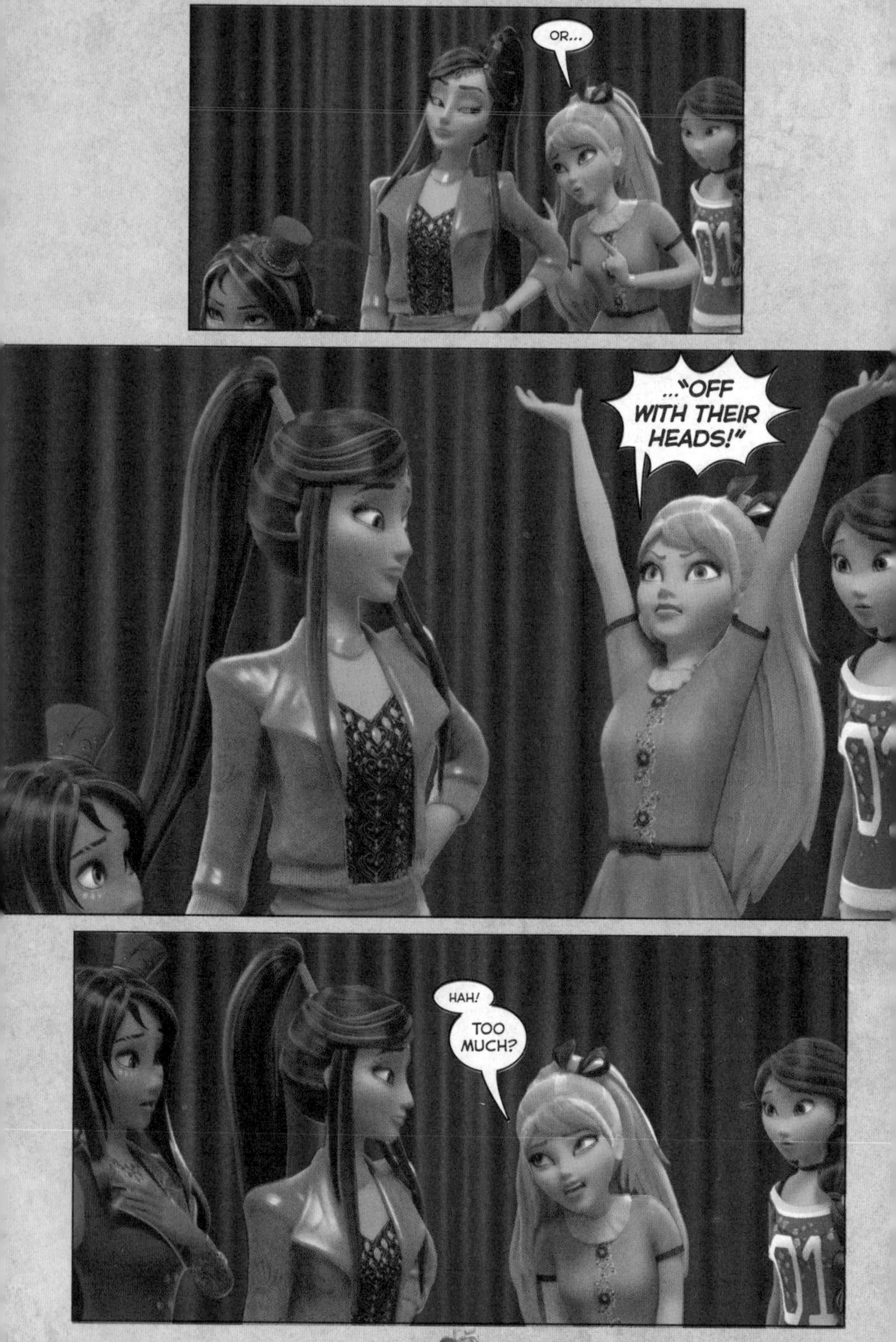
OR...
..."OFF WITH THEIR HEADS!"
HAH!
TOO MUCH?

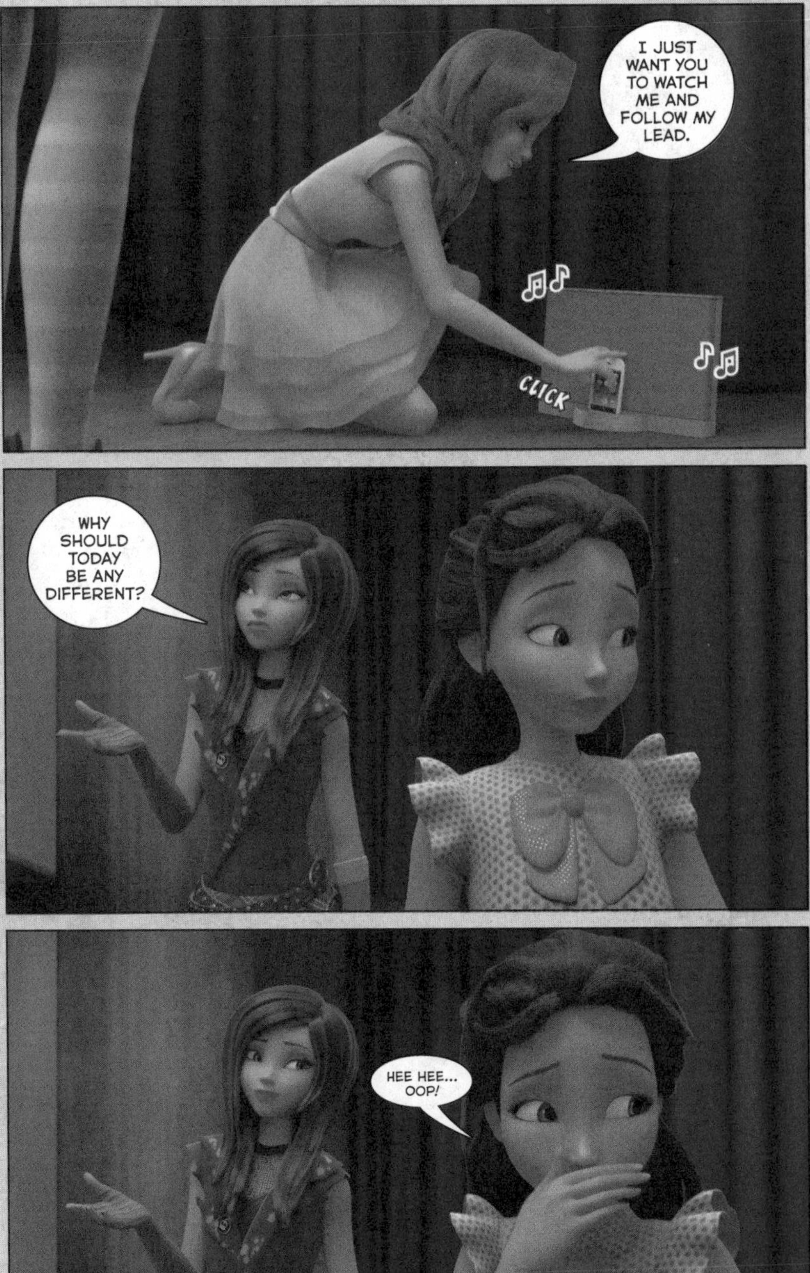
I JUST WANT YOU TO WATCH ME AND FOLLOW MY LEAD.
CLICK
WHY SHOULD TODAY BE ANY DIFFERENT?
HEE HEE... OOP!

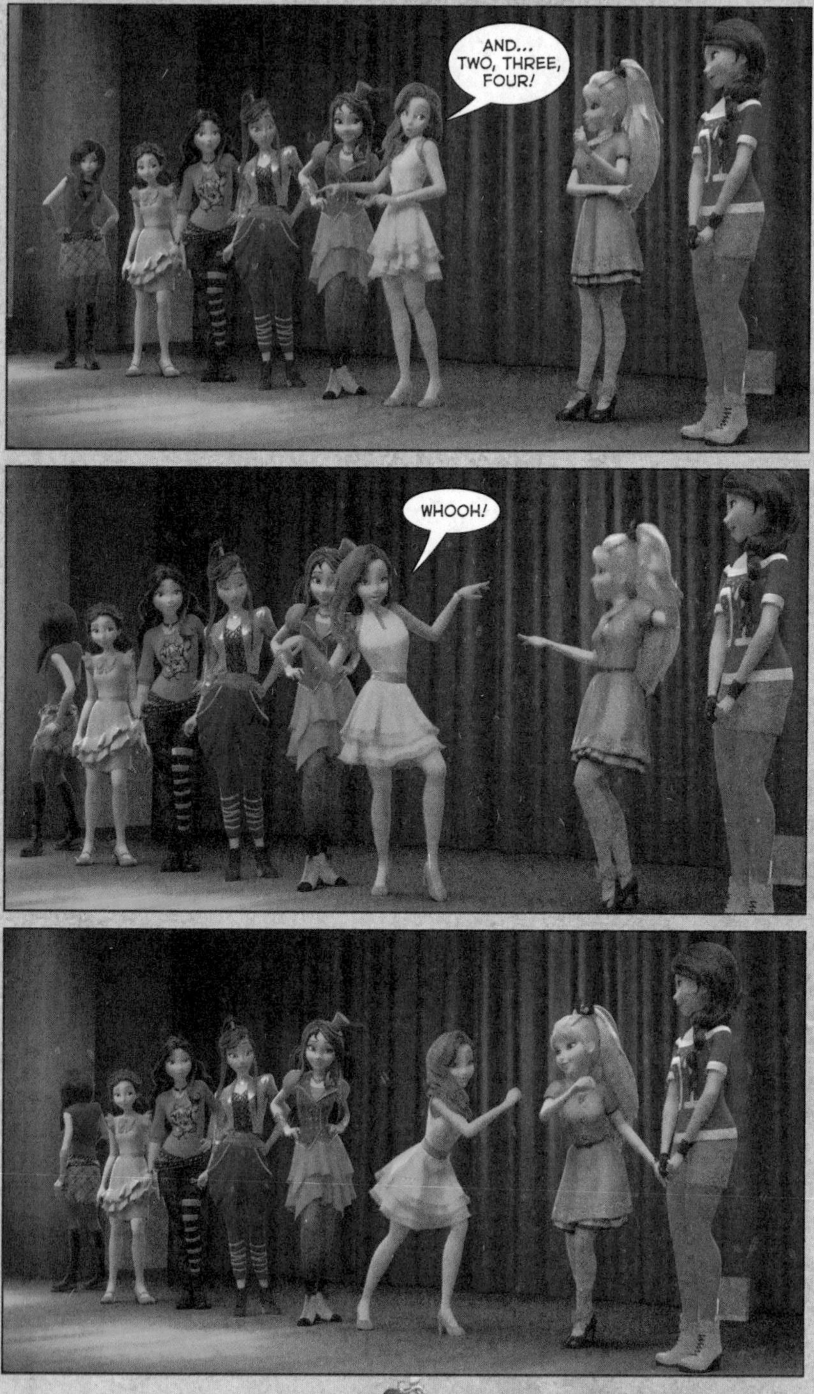
AND...
TWO, THREE,
FOUR!
WHOOH!

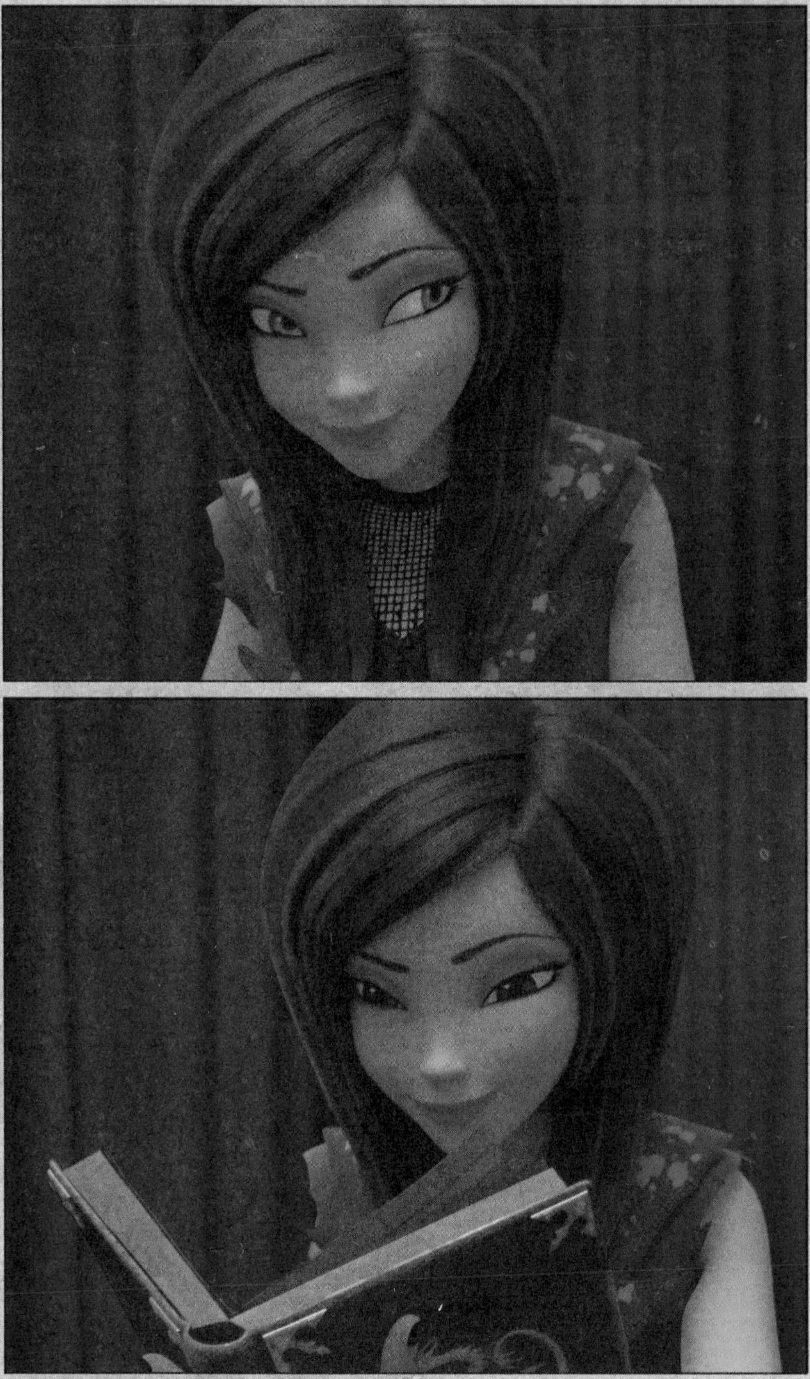

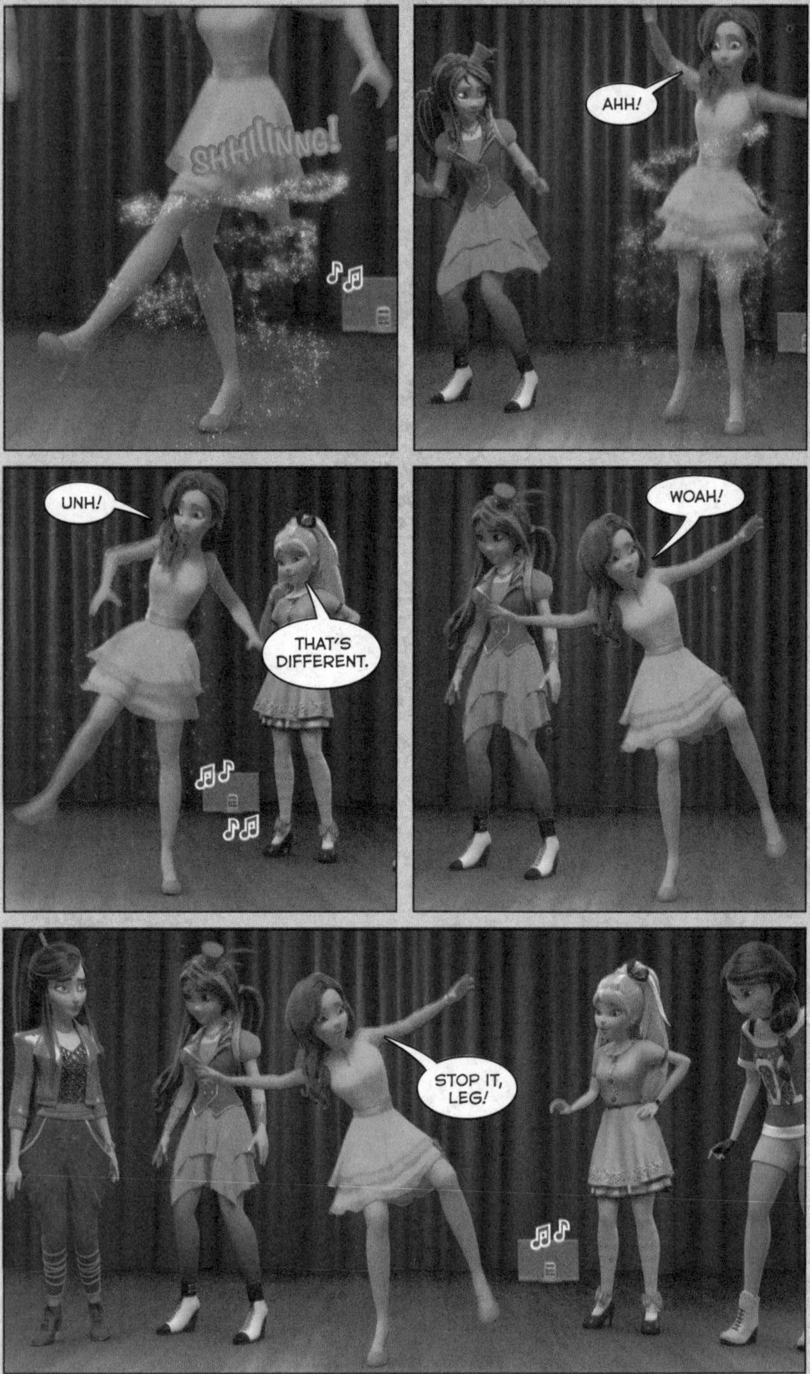
SHHIIINNG!
AHH!
UNH!
THAT'S DIFFERENT.
WOAH!
STOP IT, LEG!

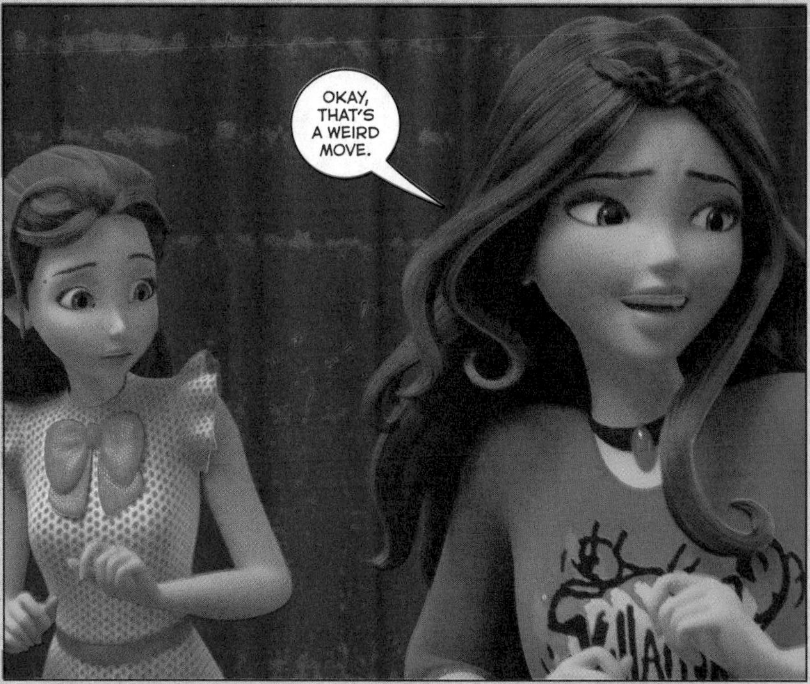
OKAY, THAT'S A WEIRD MOVE.

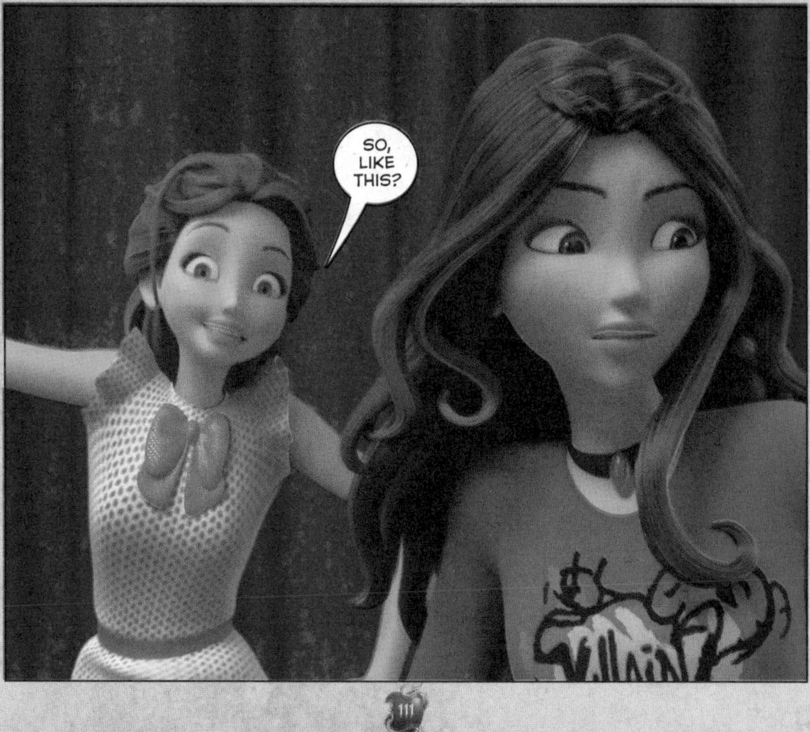
SO, LIKE THIS?

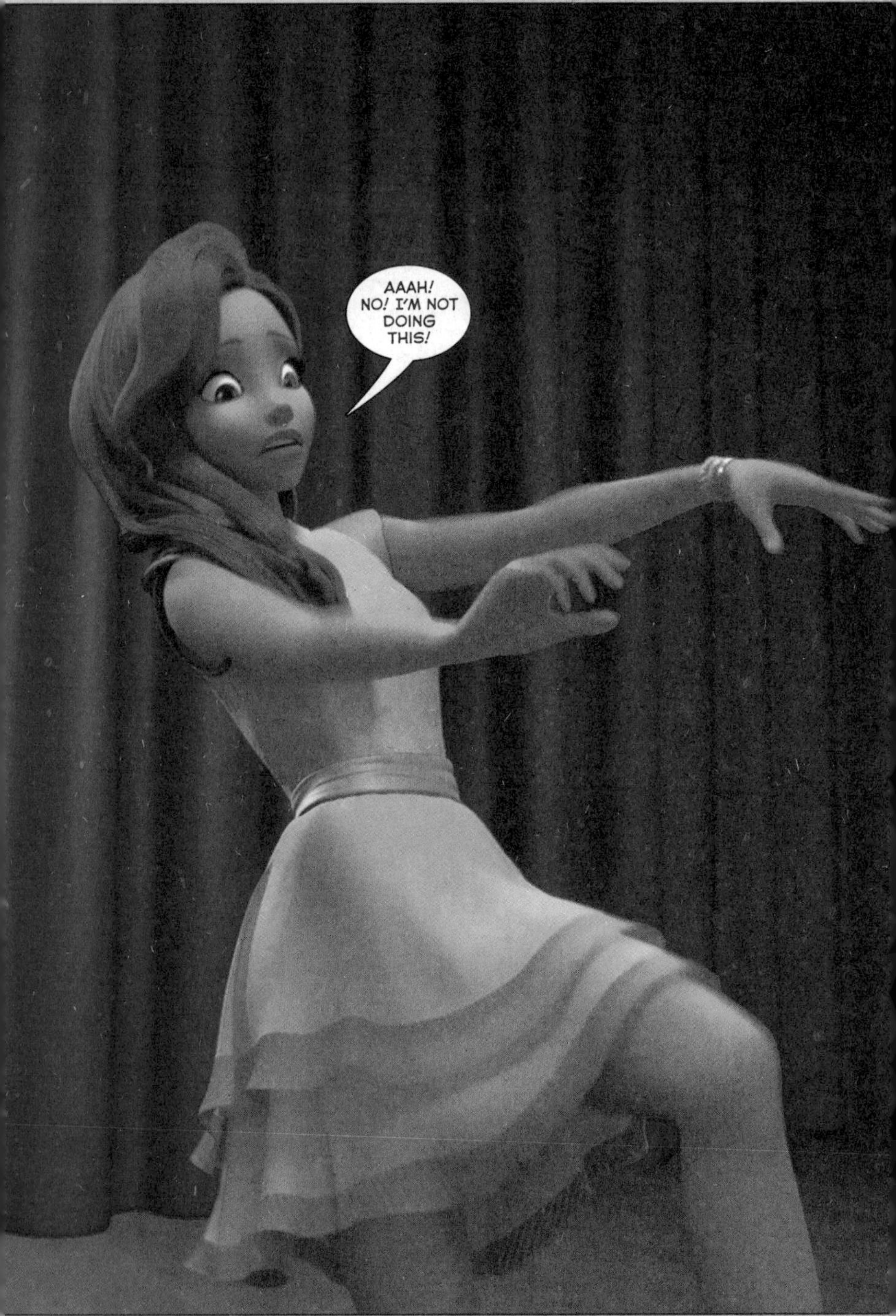
AAAH! NO! I'M NOT DOING THIS!

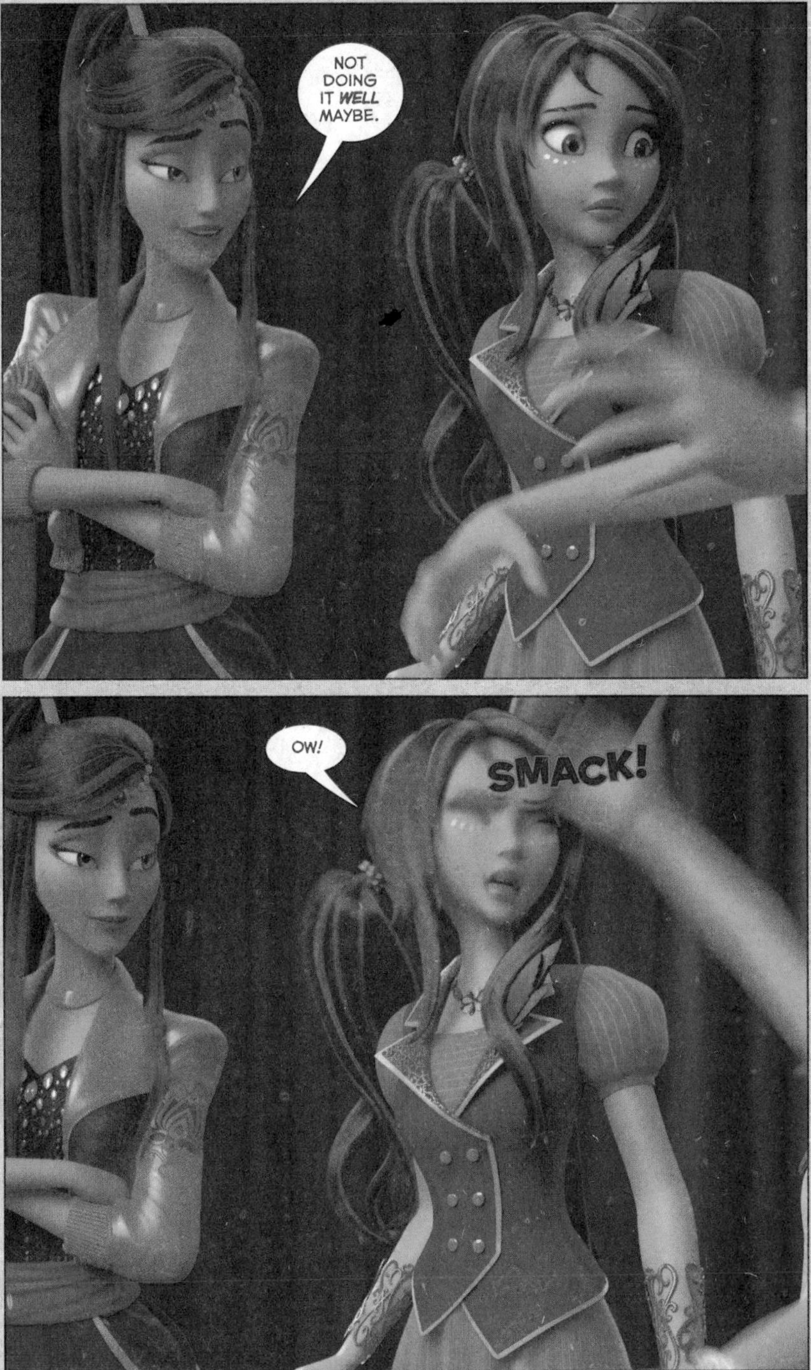
NOT DOING IT WELL MAYBE.
OW!
SMACK!

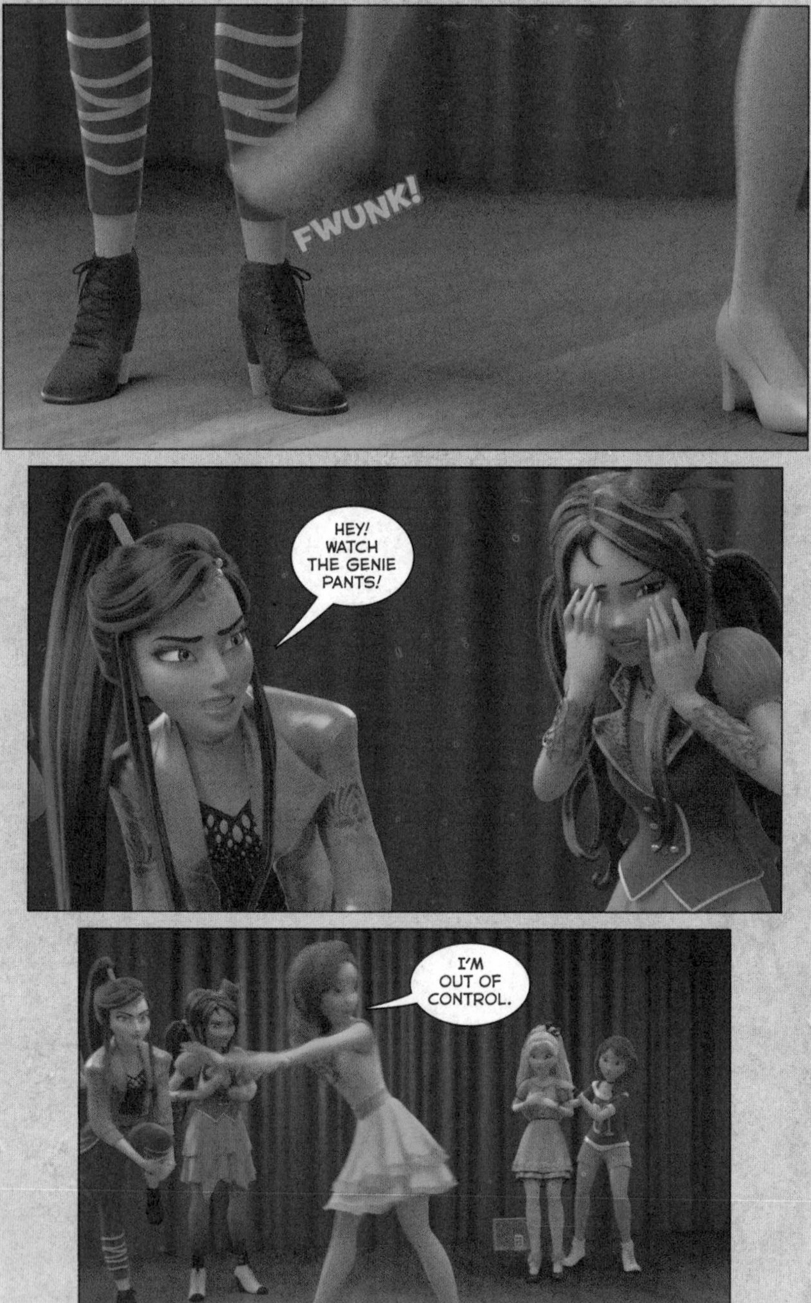
FWUNK!
HEY! WATCH THE GENIE PANTS!
I'M OUT OF CONTROL.

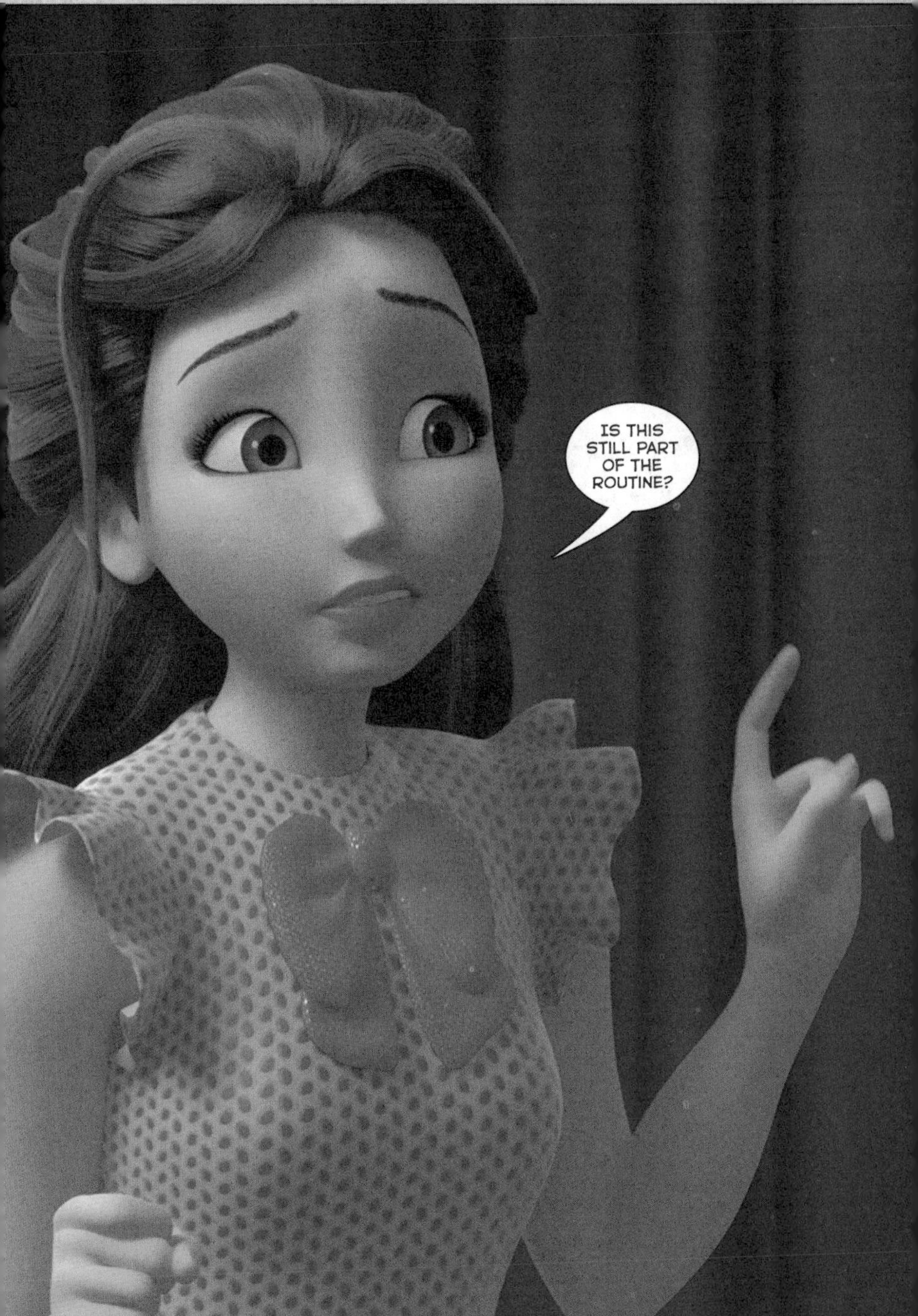
IS THIS STILL PART OF THE ROUTINE?

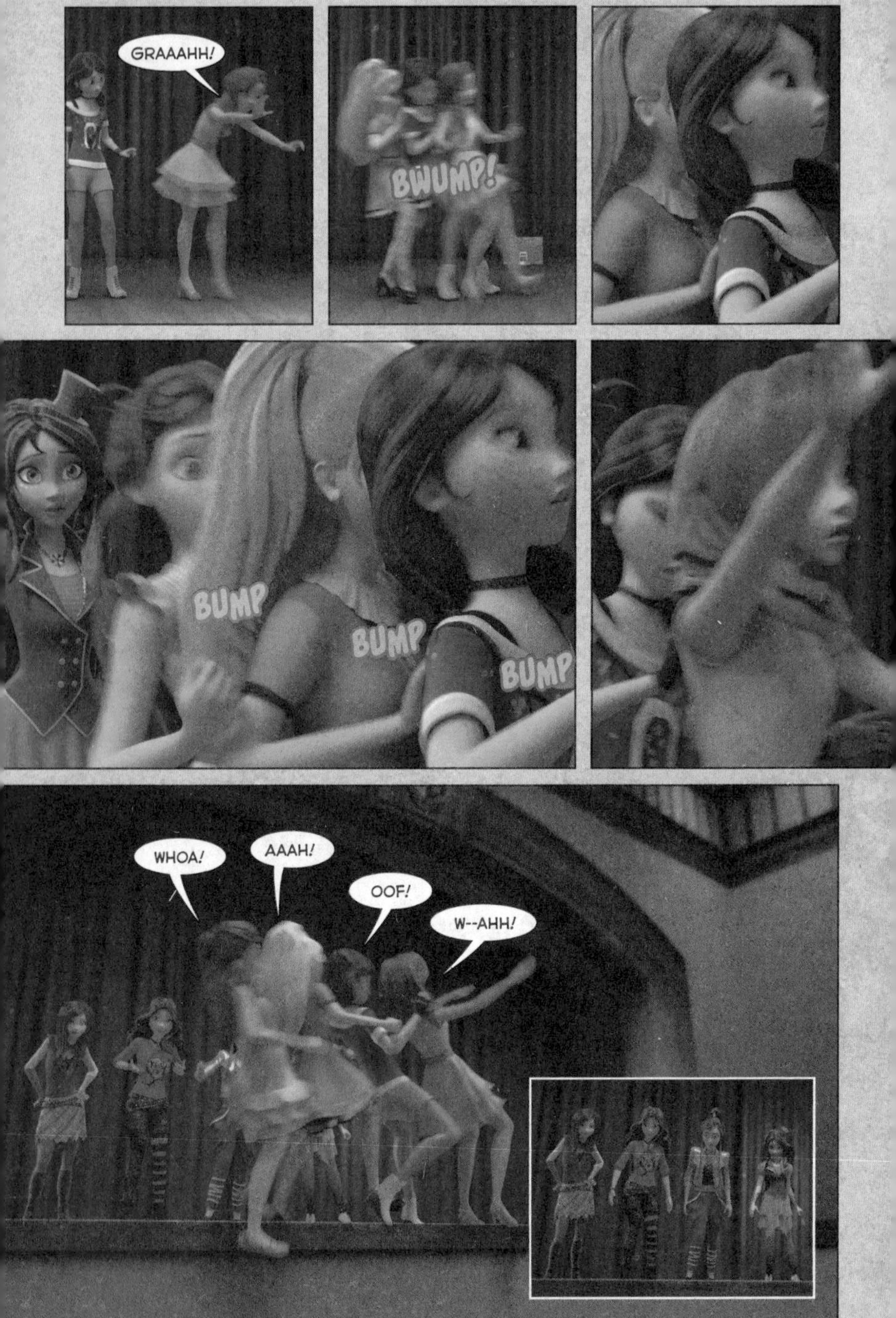
GRAAAHH!
BWUMP!
BUMP
BUMP
BUMP
WHOA!
AAAH!
OOF!
W--AHH!

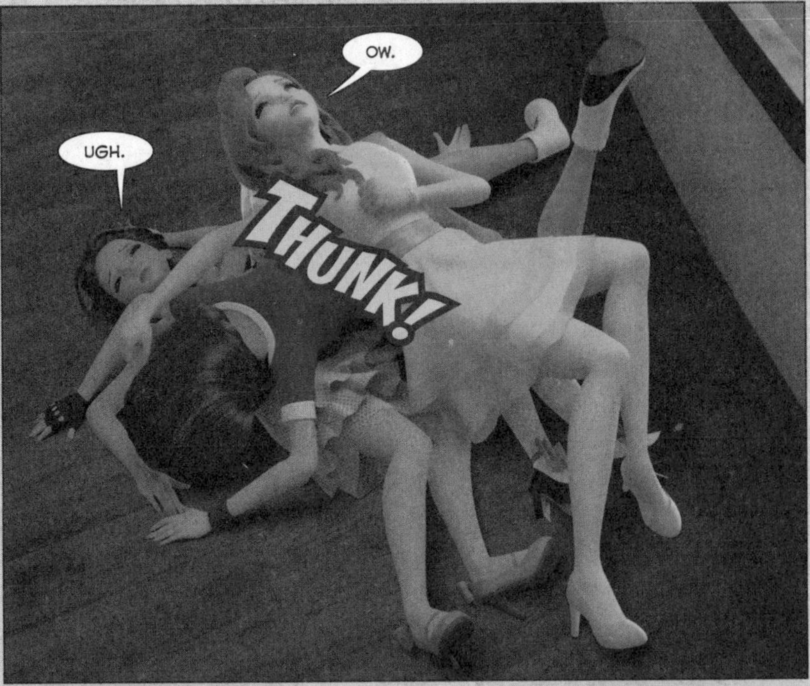
OW.
UGH.
THUNK!

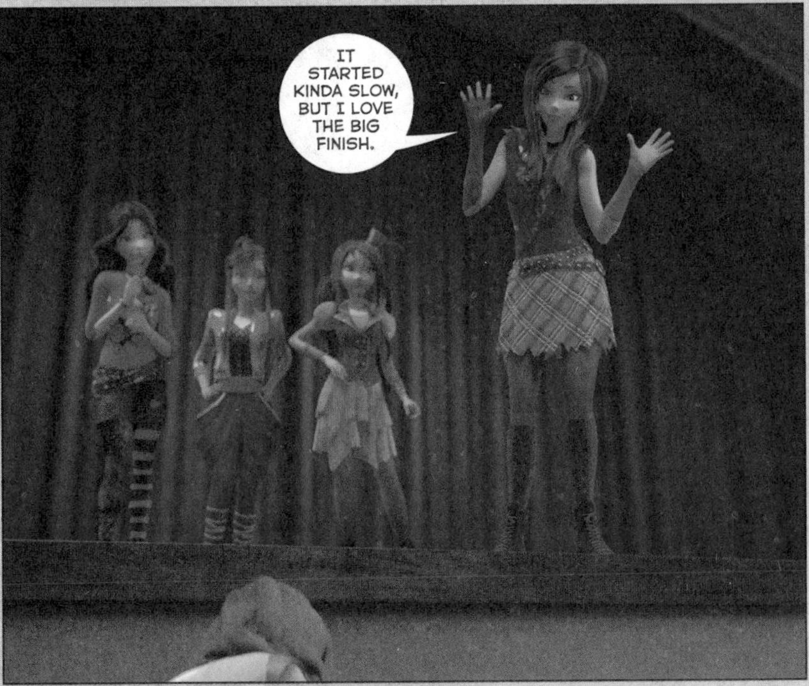
IT STARTED KINDA SLOW, BUT I LOVE THE BIG FINISH.

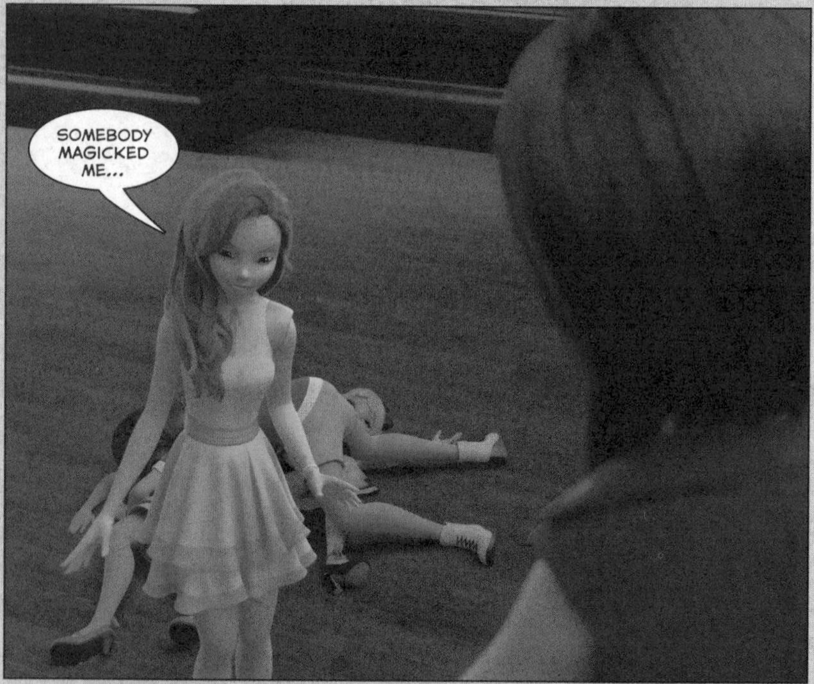
SOMEBODY MAGICKED ME...

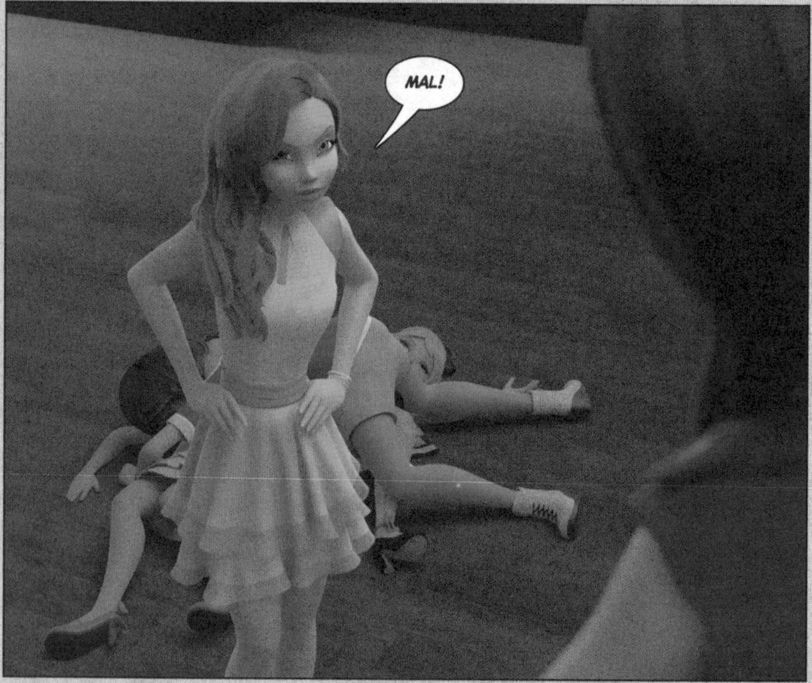
MAL!

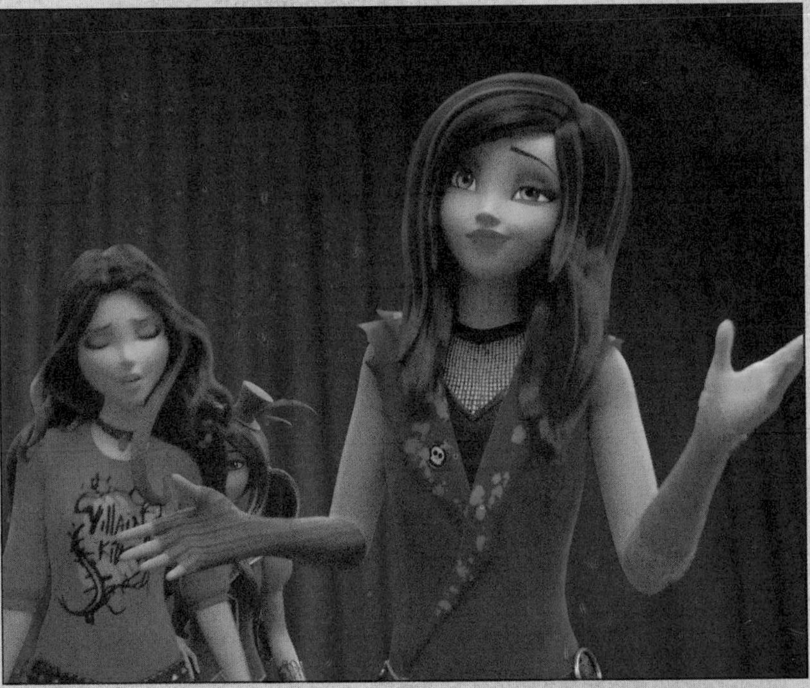
Villain Kids

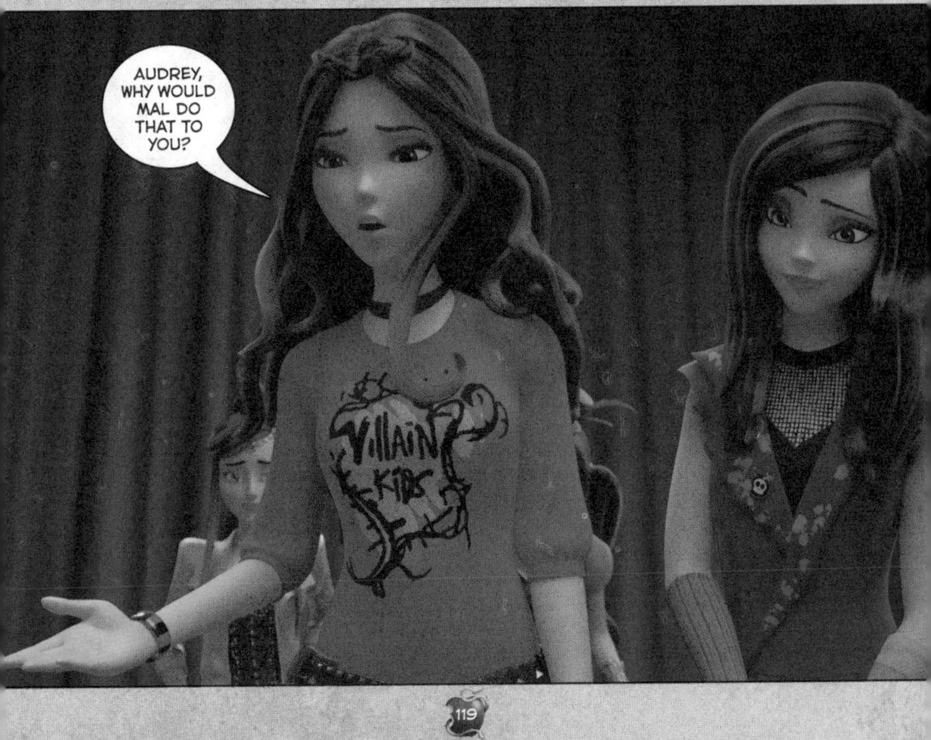
AUDREY, WHY WOULD MAL DO THAT TO YOU?
Villain Kids

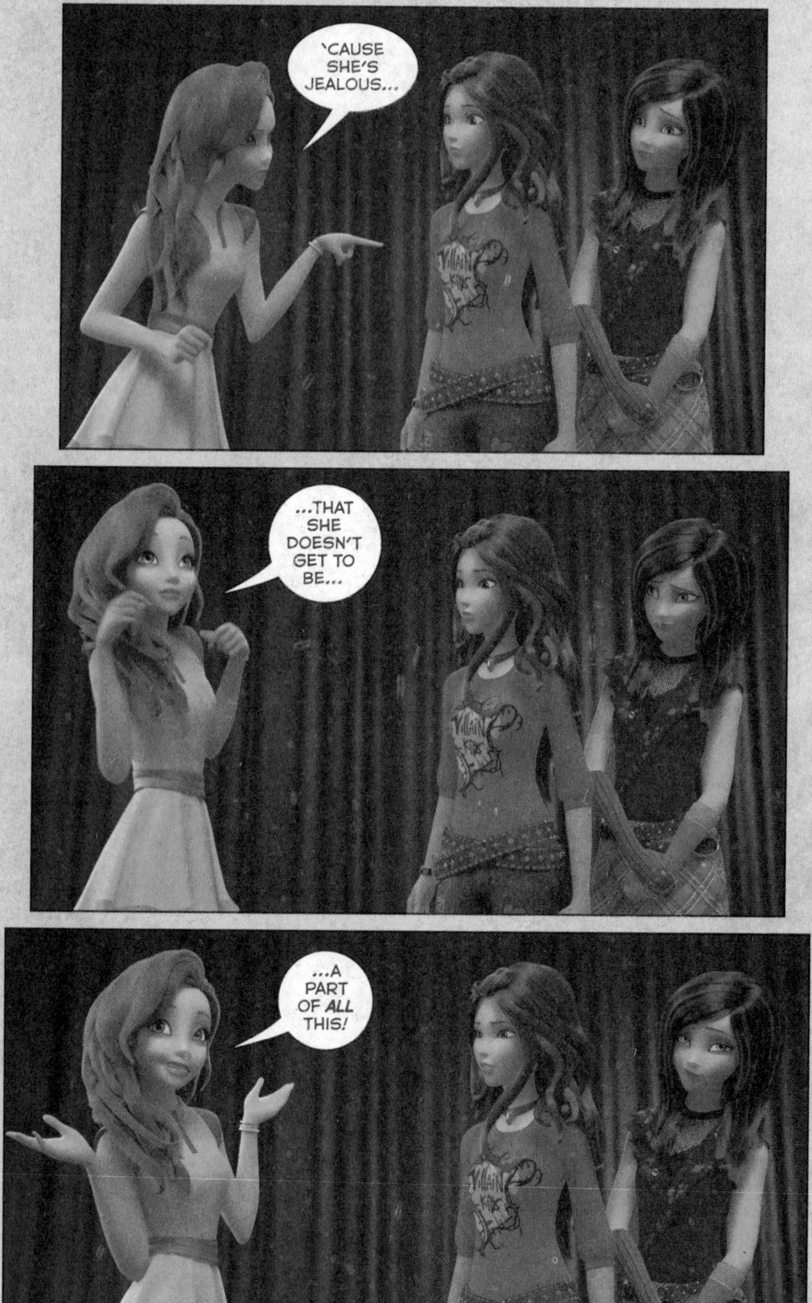
'CAUSE SHE'S JEALOUS...
...THAT SHE DOESN'T GET TO BE...
...A PART OF *ALL* THIS!

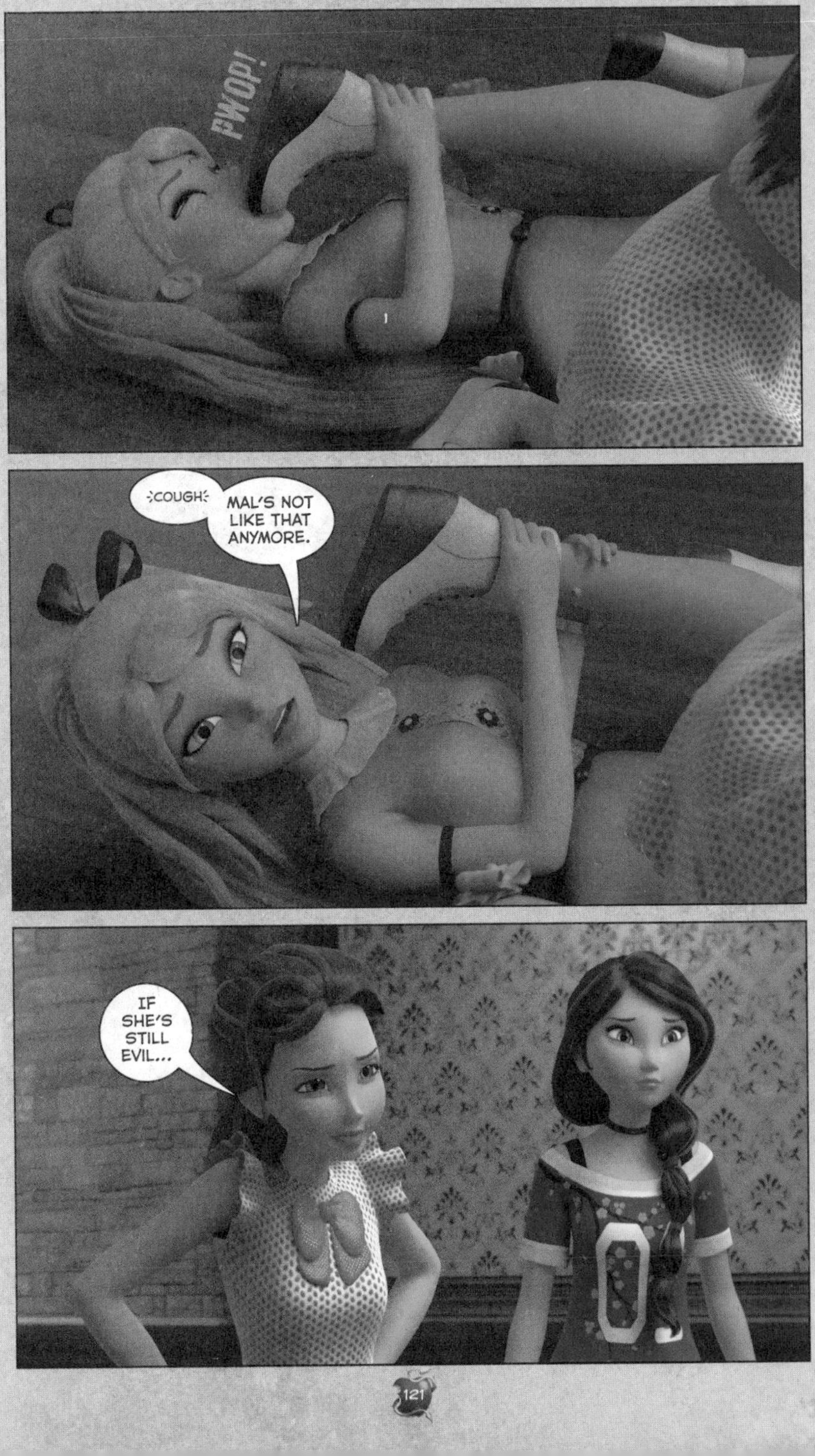
PWOP!
COUGH
MAL'S NOT LIKE THAT ANYMORE.
IF SHE'S STILL EVIL...

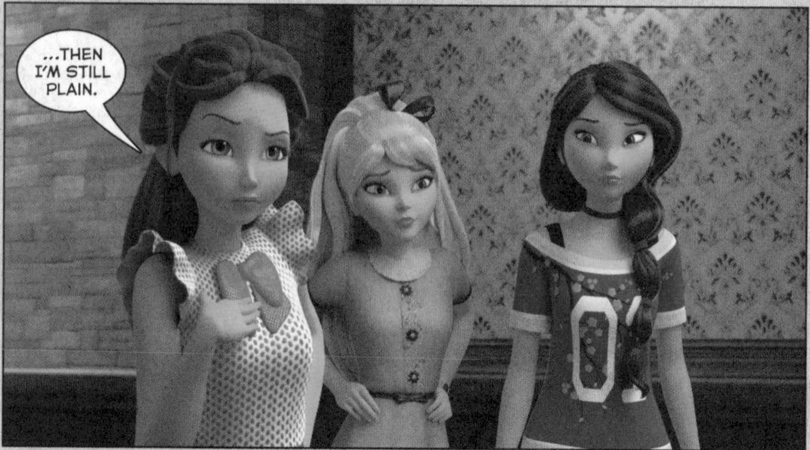
...THEN I'M STILL PLAIN.

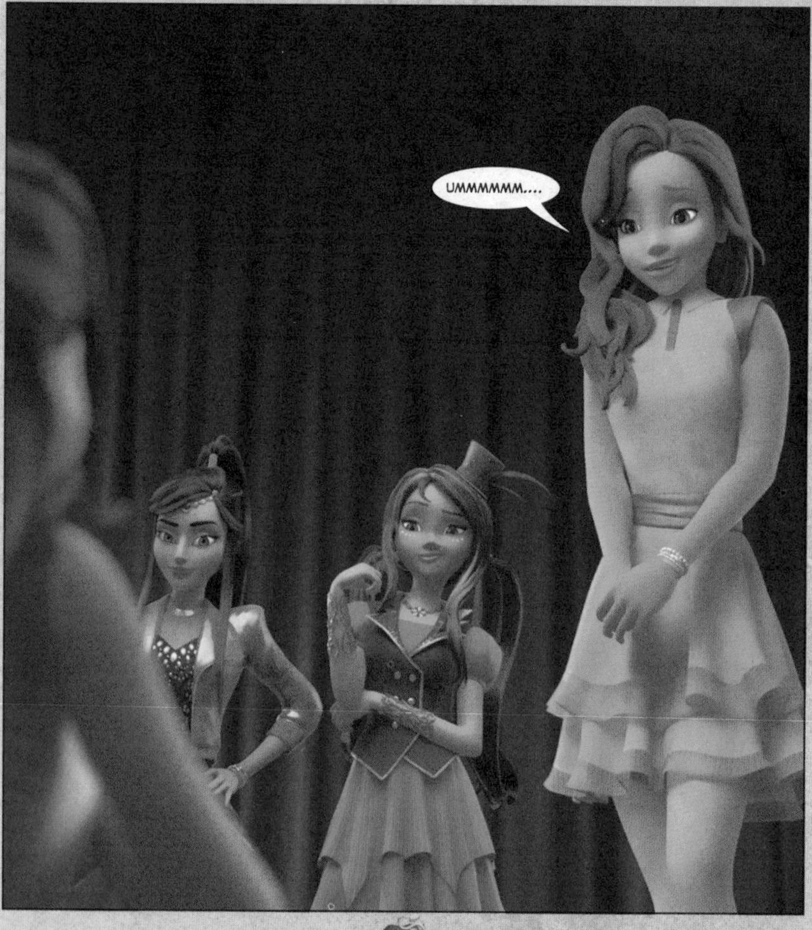
UMMMMMM....

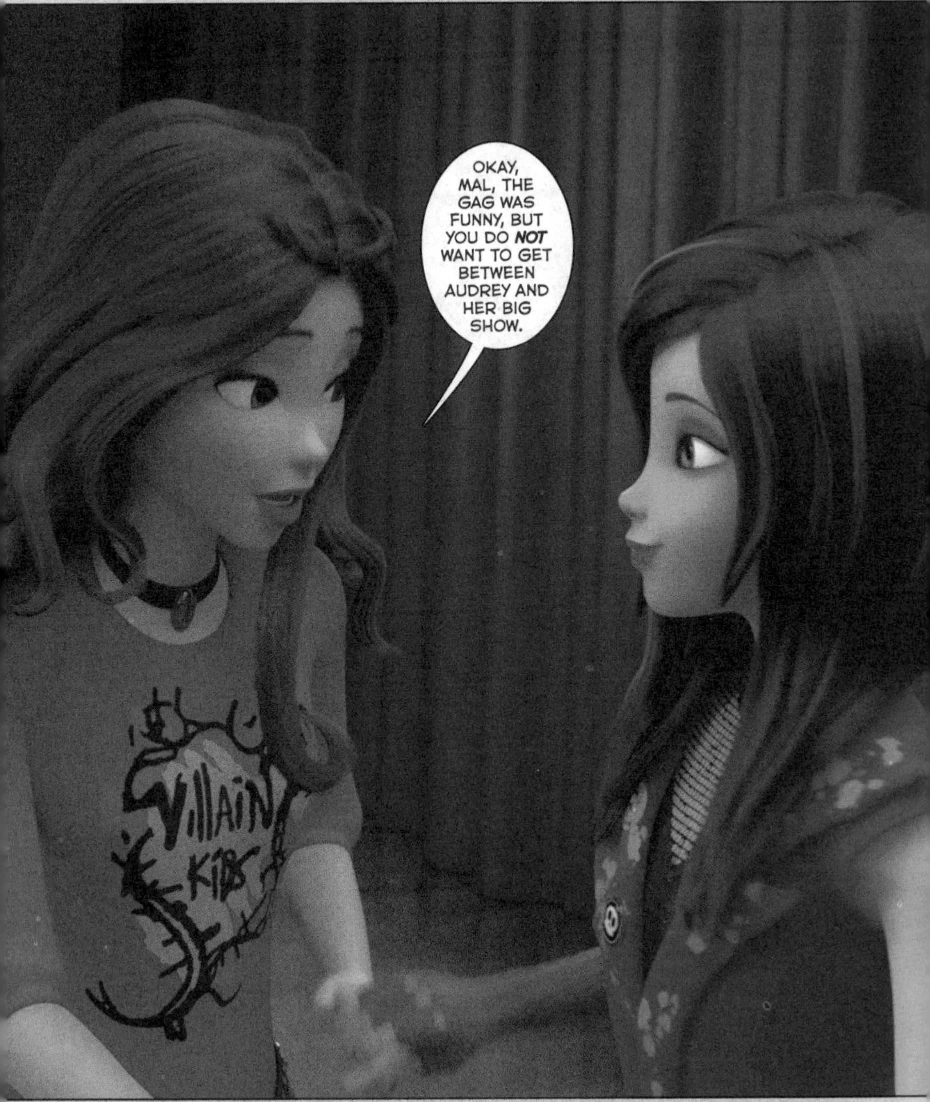
OKAY, MAL, THE GAG WAS FUNNY, BUT YOU DO ***NOT*** WANT TO GET BETWEEN AUDREY AND HER BIG SHOW.

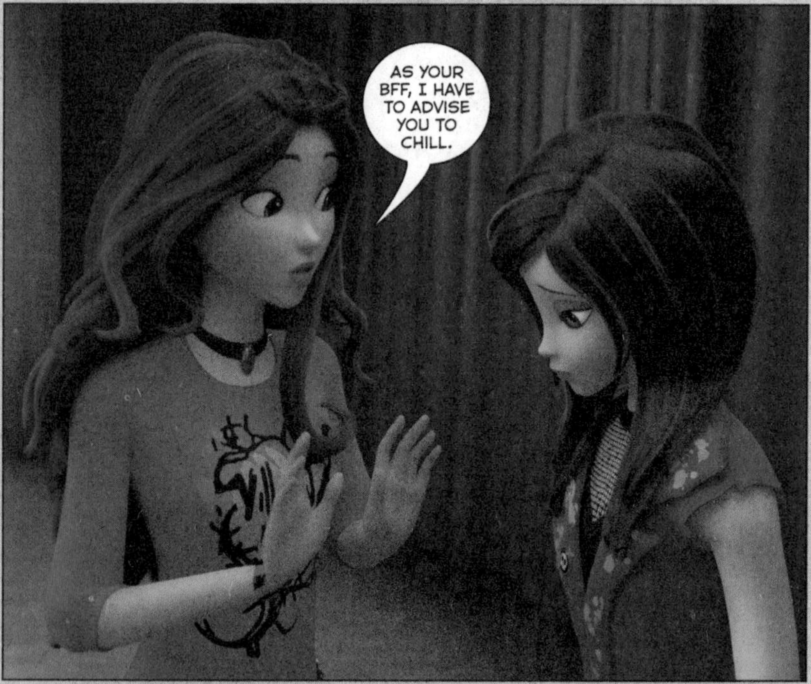
AS YOUR BFF, I HAVE TO ADVISE YOU TO CHILL.

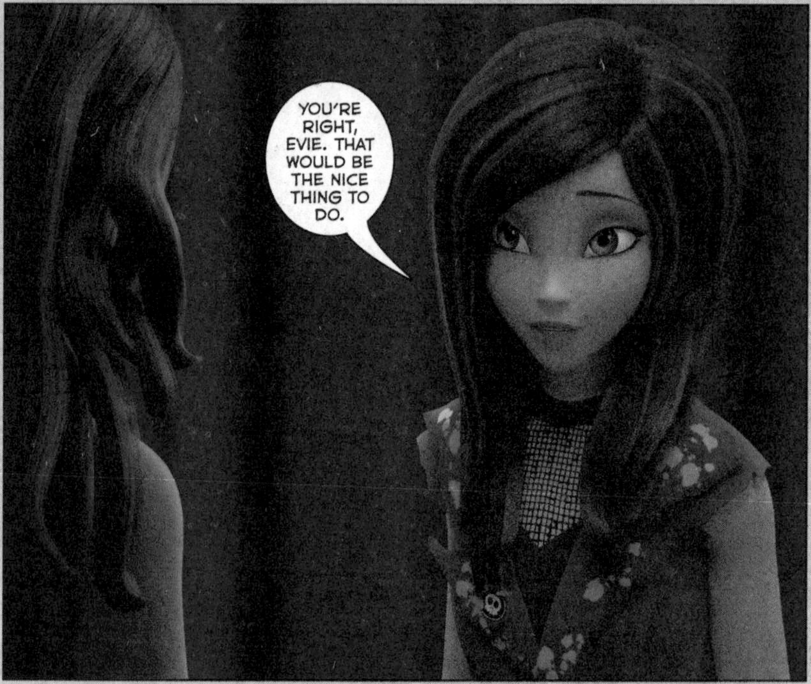
YOU'RE RIGHT, EVIE. THAT WOULD BE THE NICE THING TO DO.

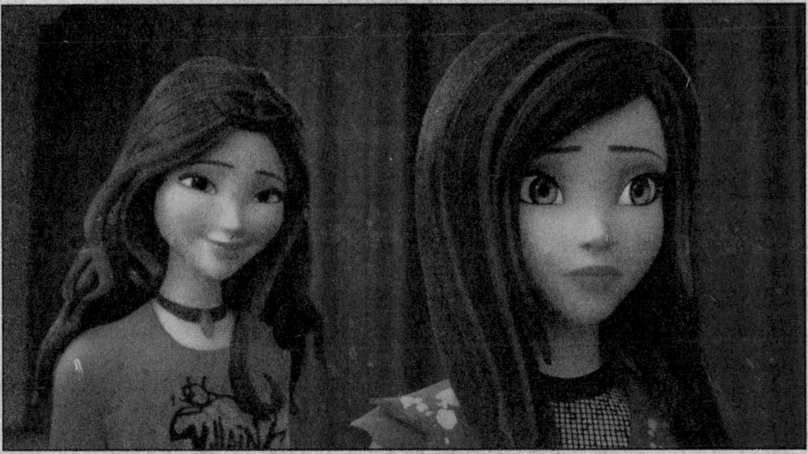

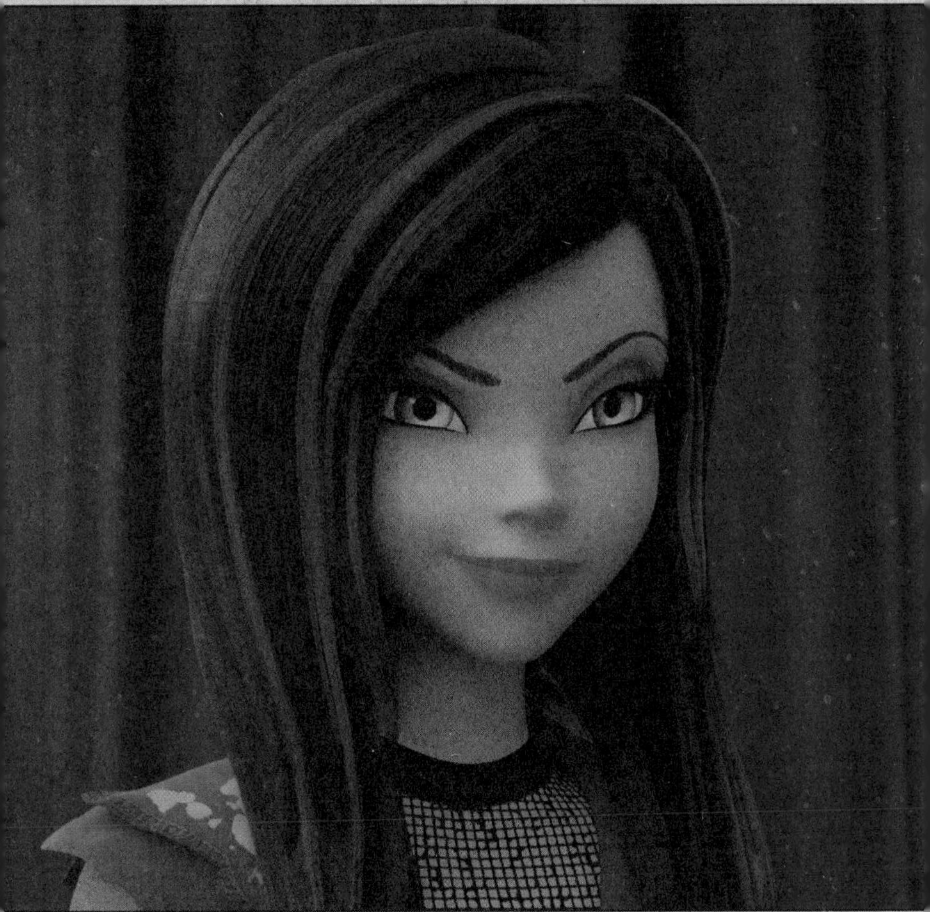

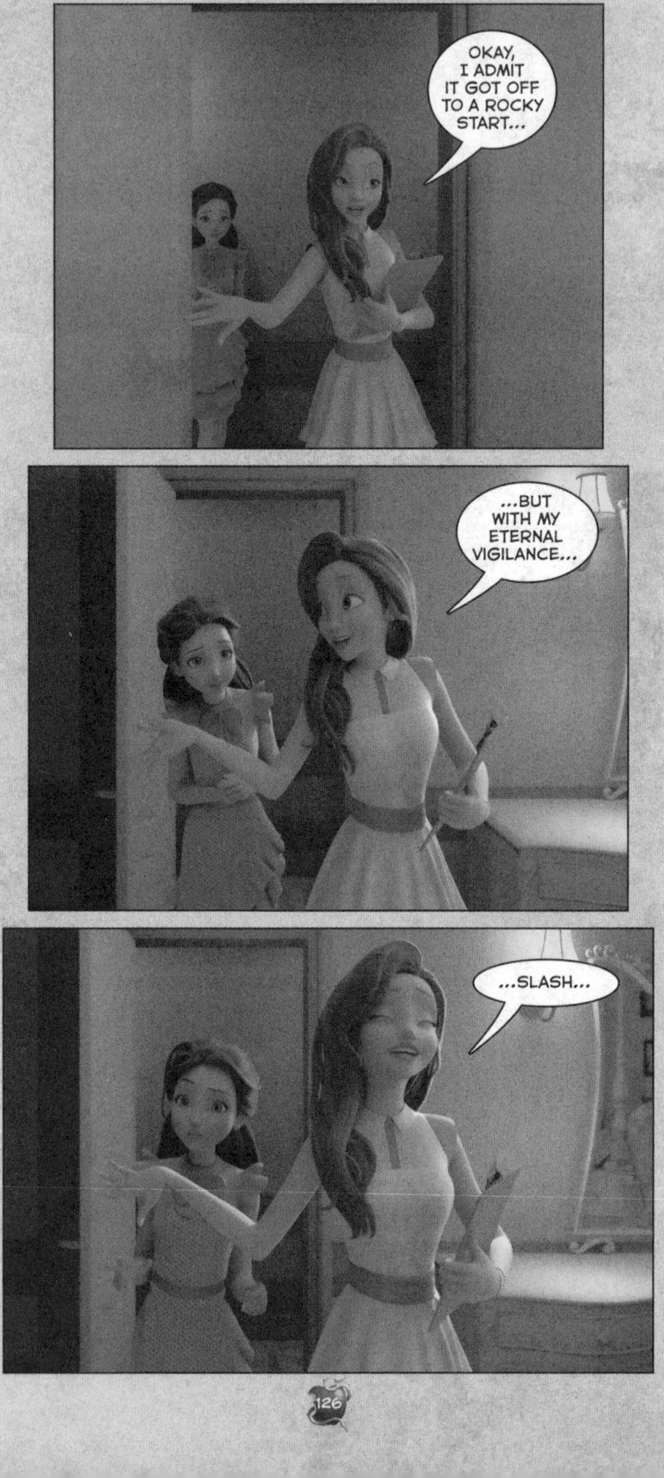
OKAY, I ADMIT IT GOT OFF TO A ROCKY START...
...BUT WITH MY ETERNAL VIGILANCE...
...SLASH...

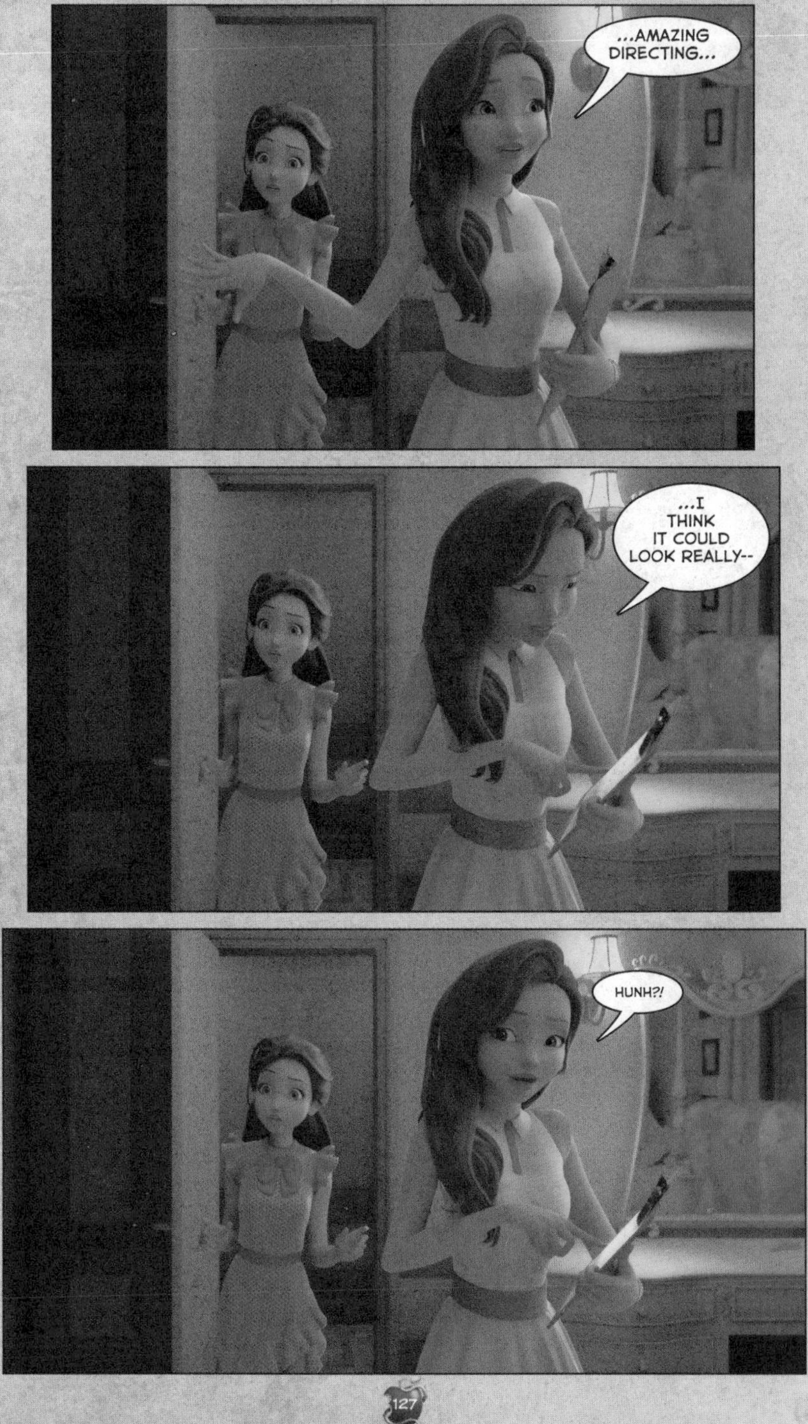
...AMAZING DIRECTING...
...I THINK IT COULD LOOK REALLY--
HUNH?!

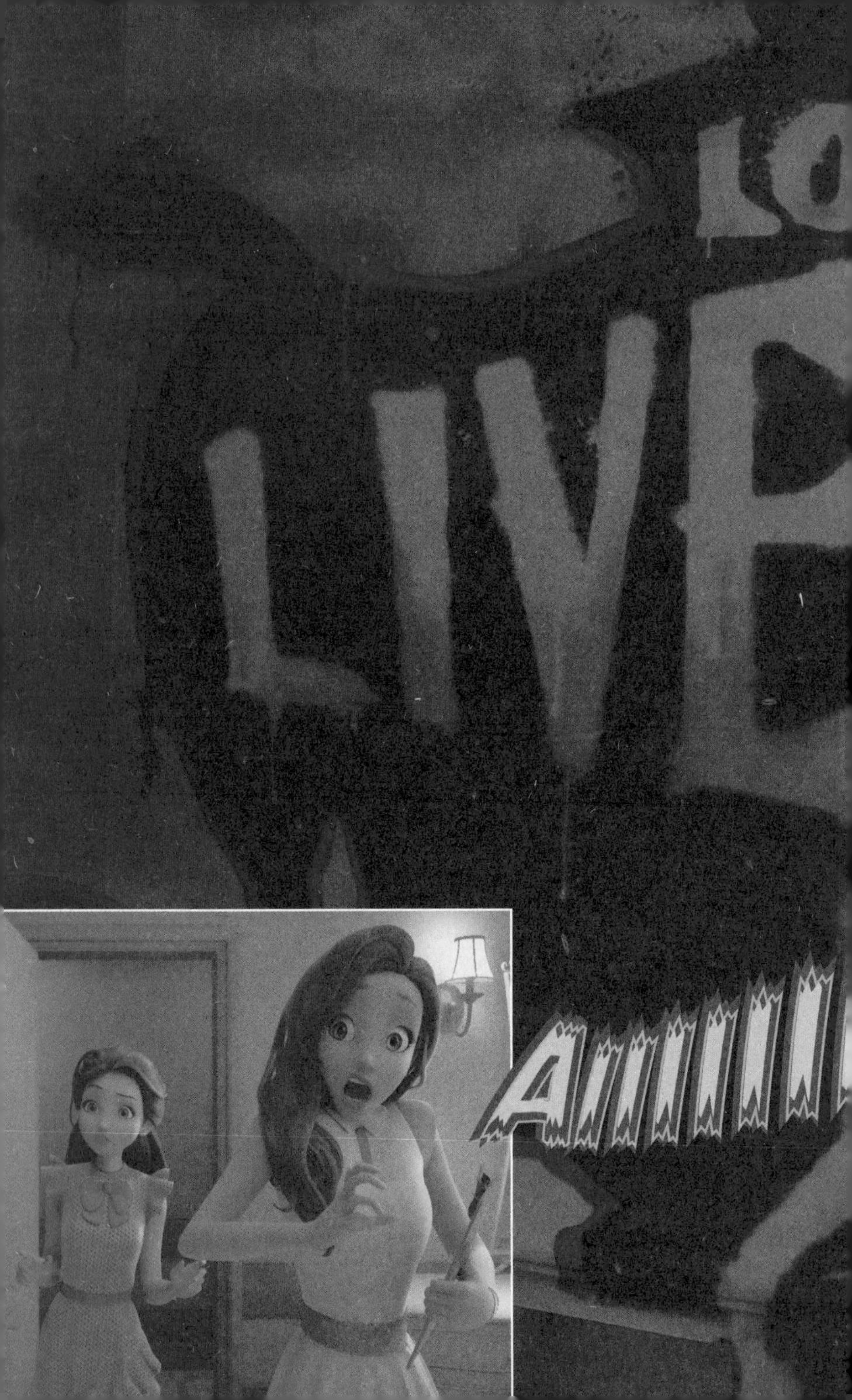
AIIIIII

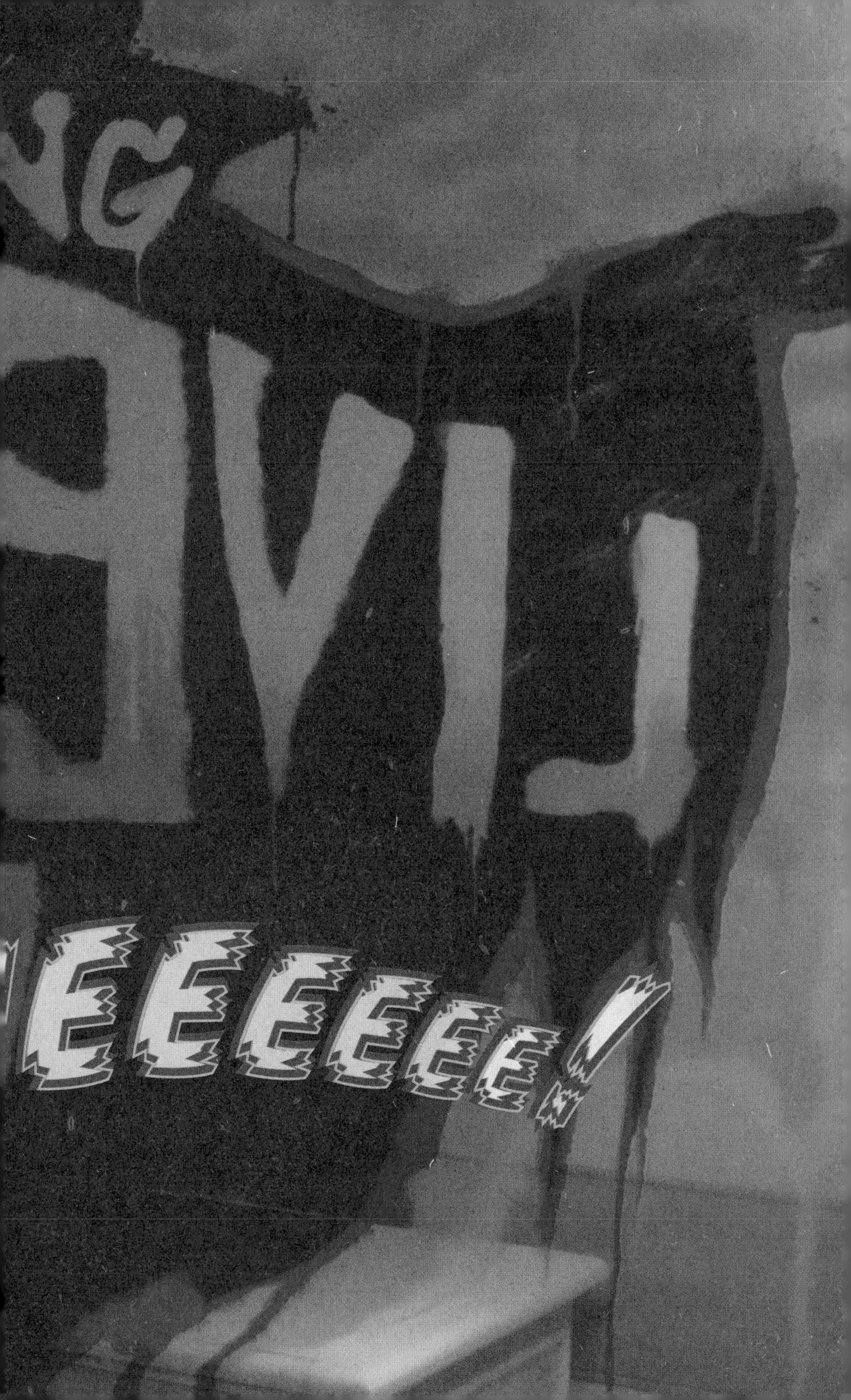
EEEEEE!

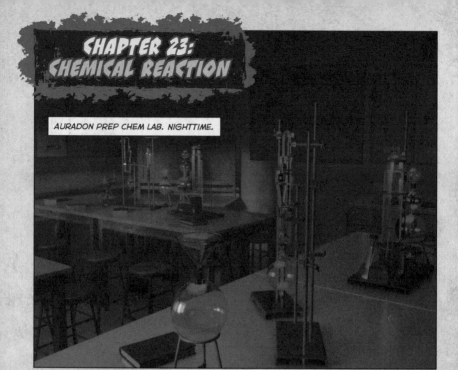

CHAPTER 23: CHEMICAL REACTION

AURADON PREP CHEM LAB. NIGHTTIME.

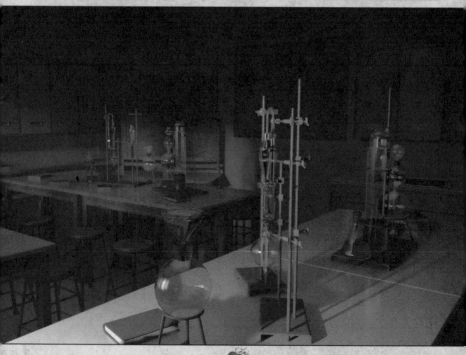

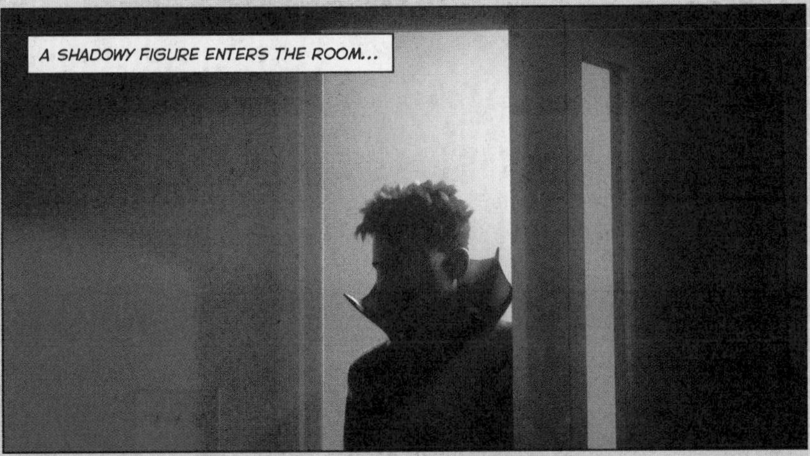
A SHADOWY FIGURE ENTERS THE ROOM...

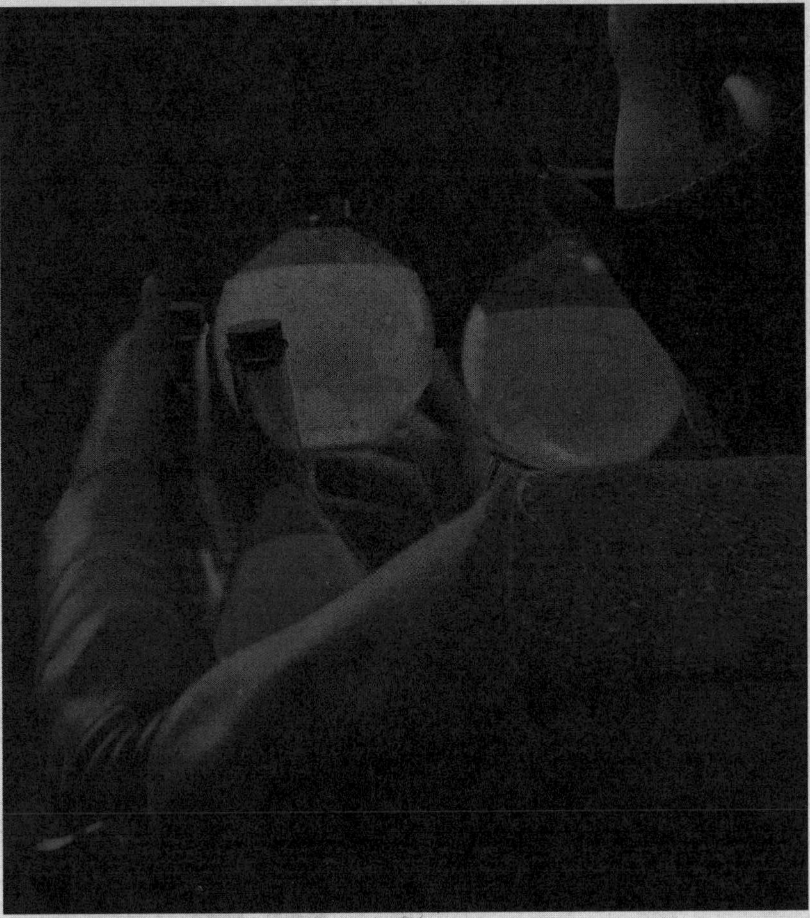

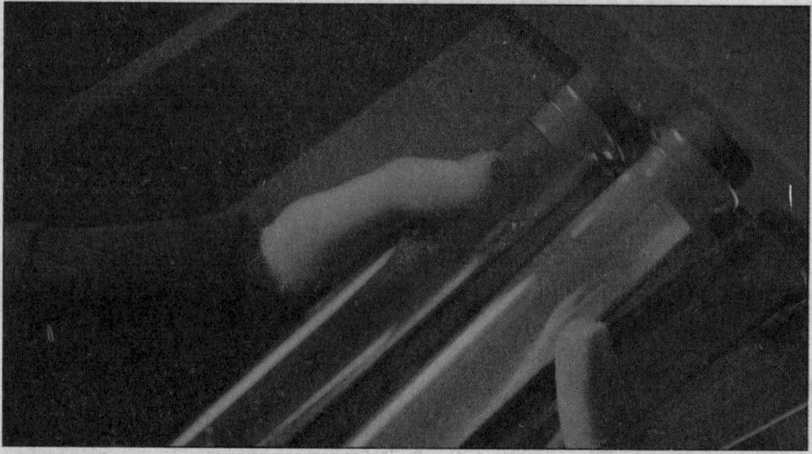

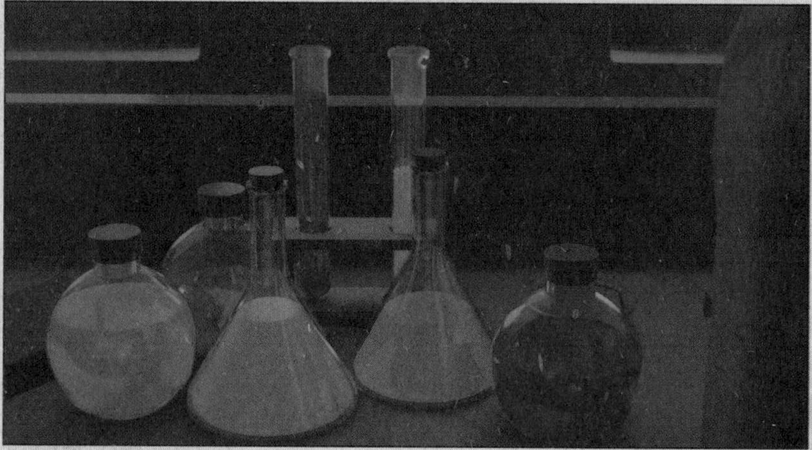

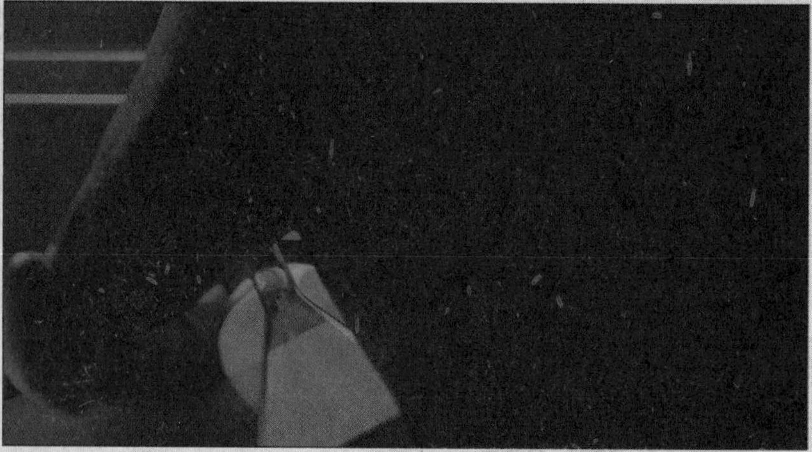

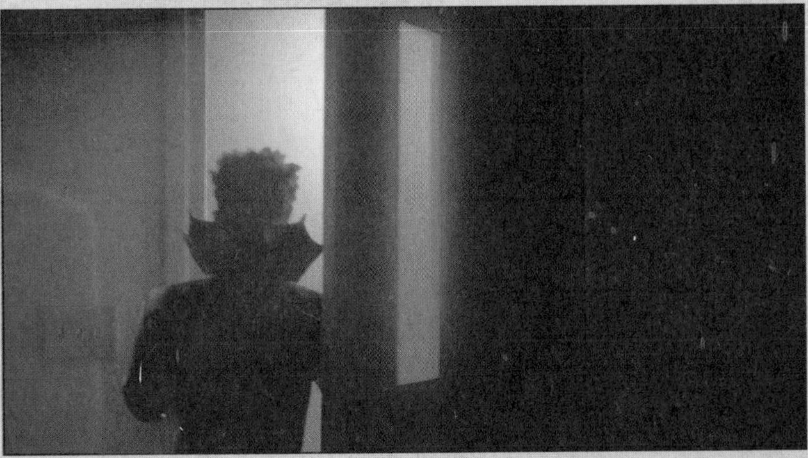

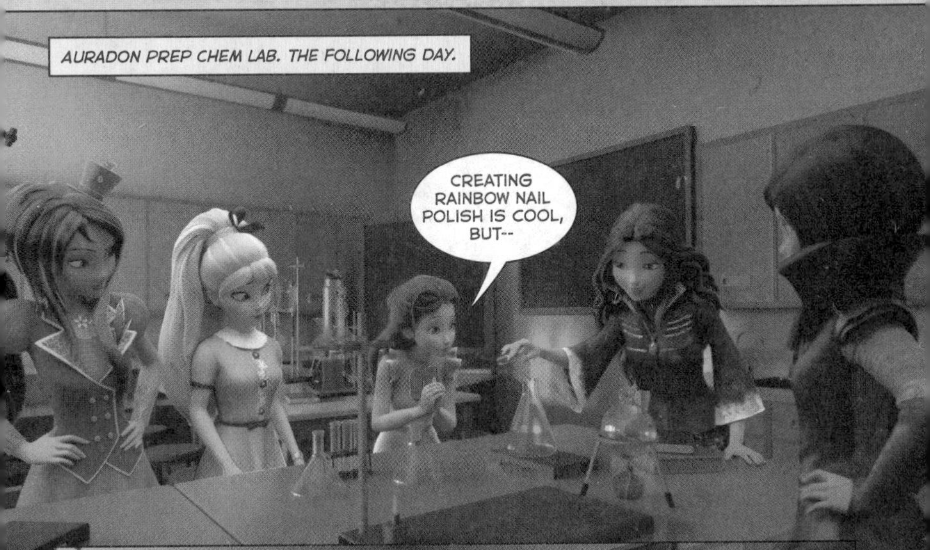
AURADON PREP CHEM LAB. THE FOLLOWING DAY.
CREATING RAINBOW NAIL POLISH IS COOL, BUT--

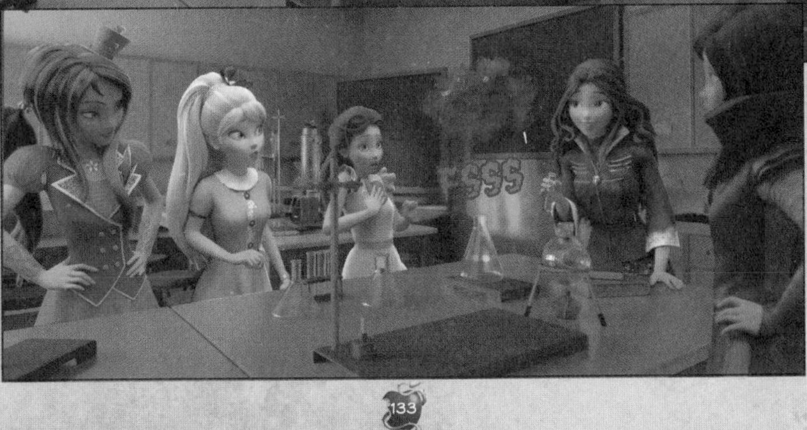

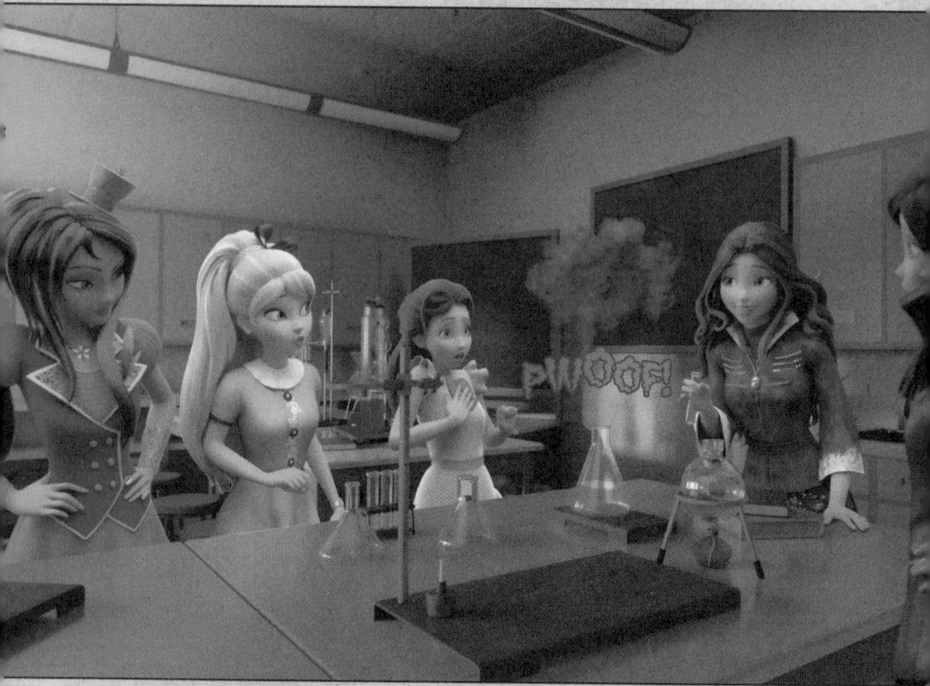
PWOOF!

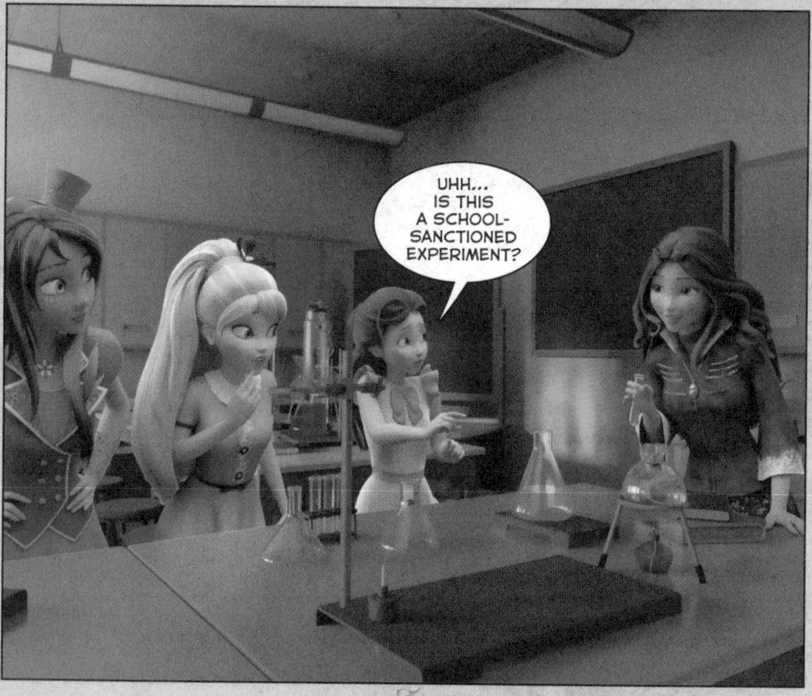
UHH... IS THIS A SCHOOL-SANCTIONED EXPERIMENT?

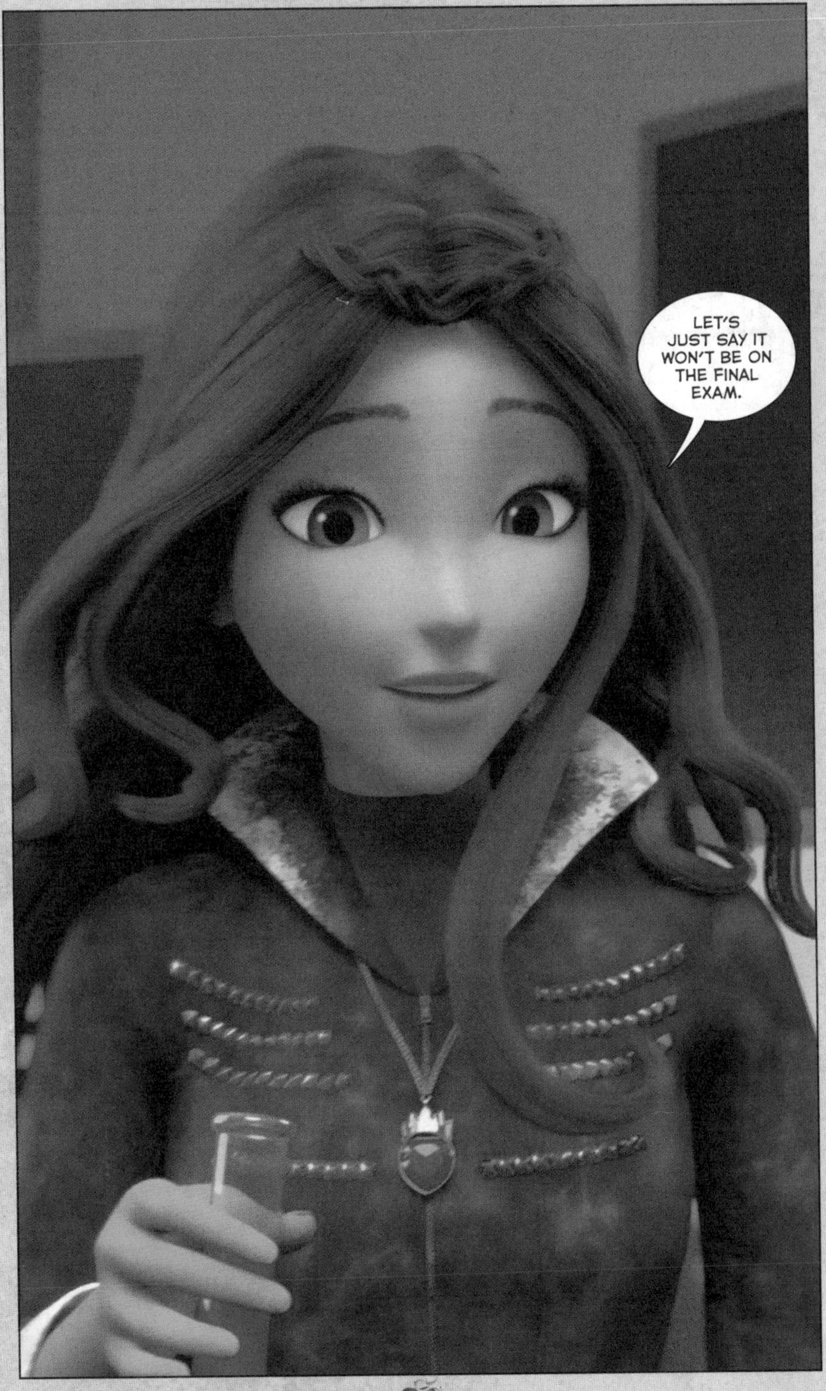
LET'S JUST SAY IT WON'T BE ON THE FINAL EXAM.

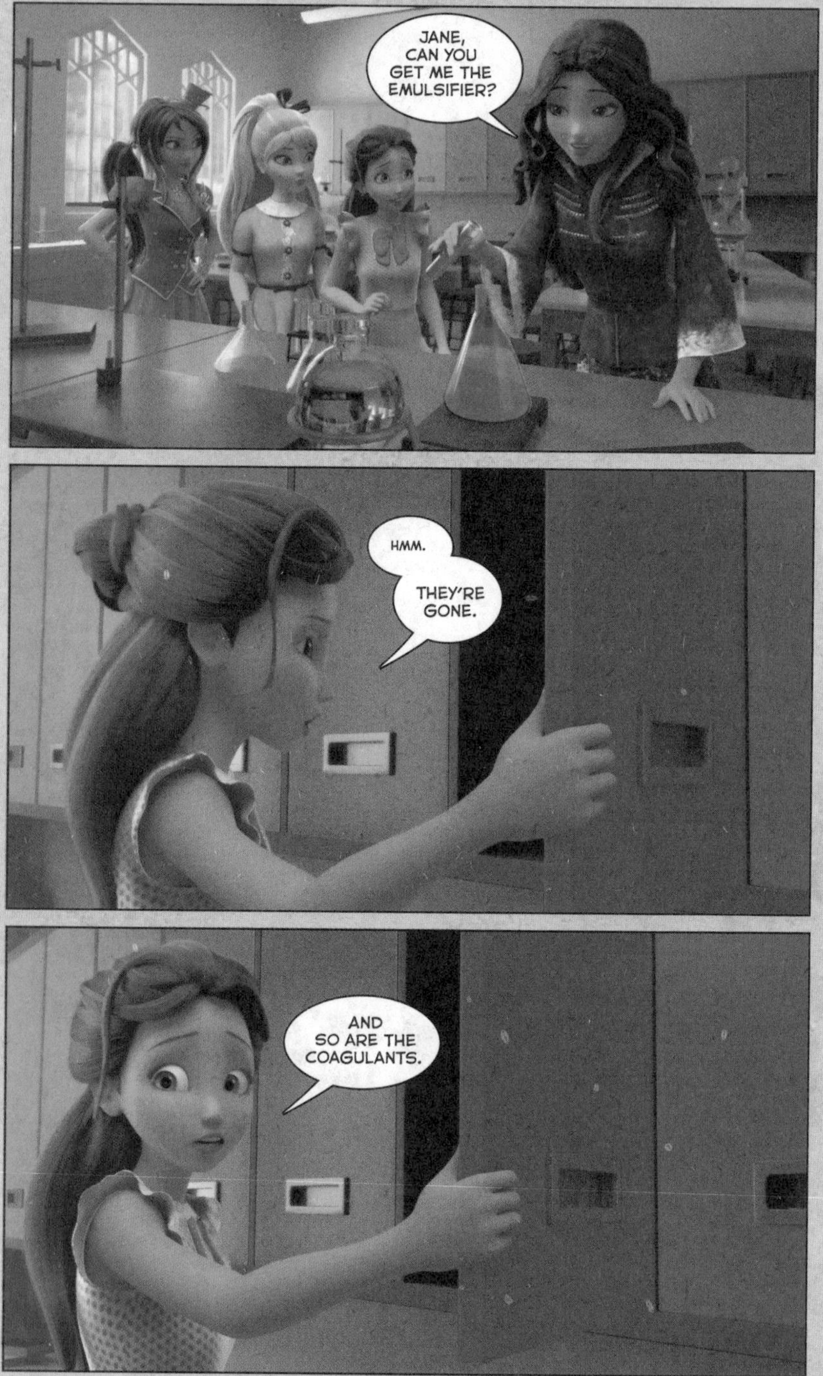
JANE, CAN YOU GET ME THE EMULSIFIER?
HMM.
THEY'RE GONE.
AND SO ARE THE COAGULANTS.

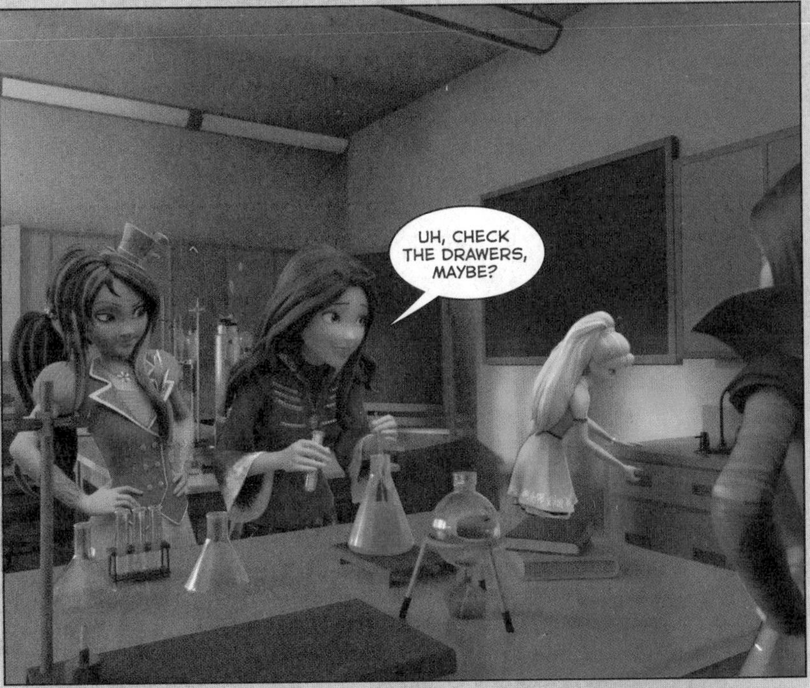
UH, CHECK THE DRAWERS, MAYBE?

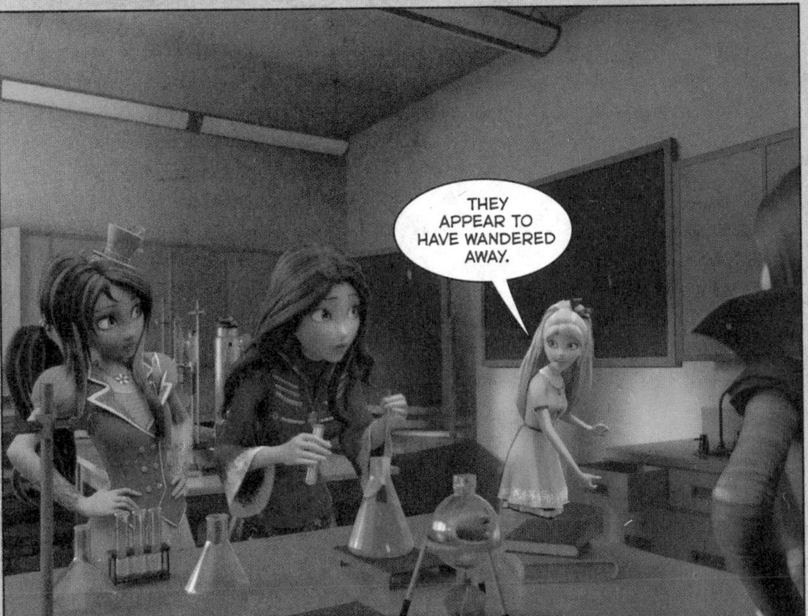
THEY APPEAR TO HAVE WANDERED AWAY.

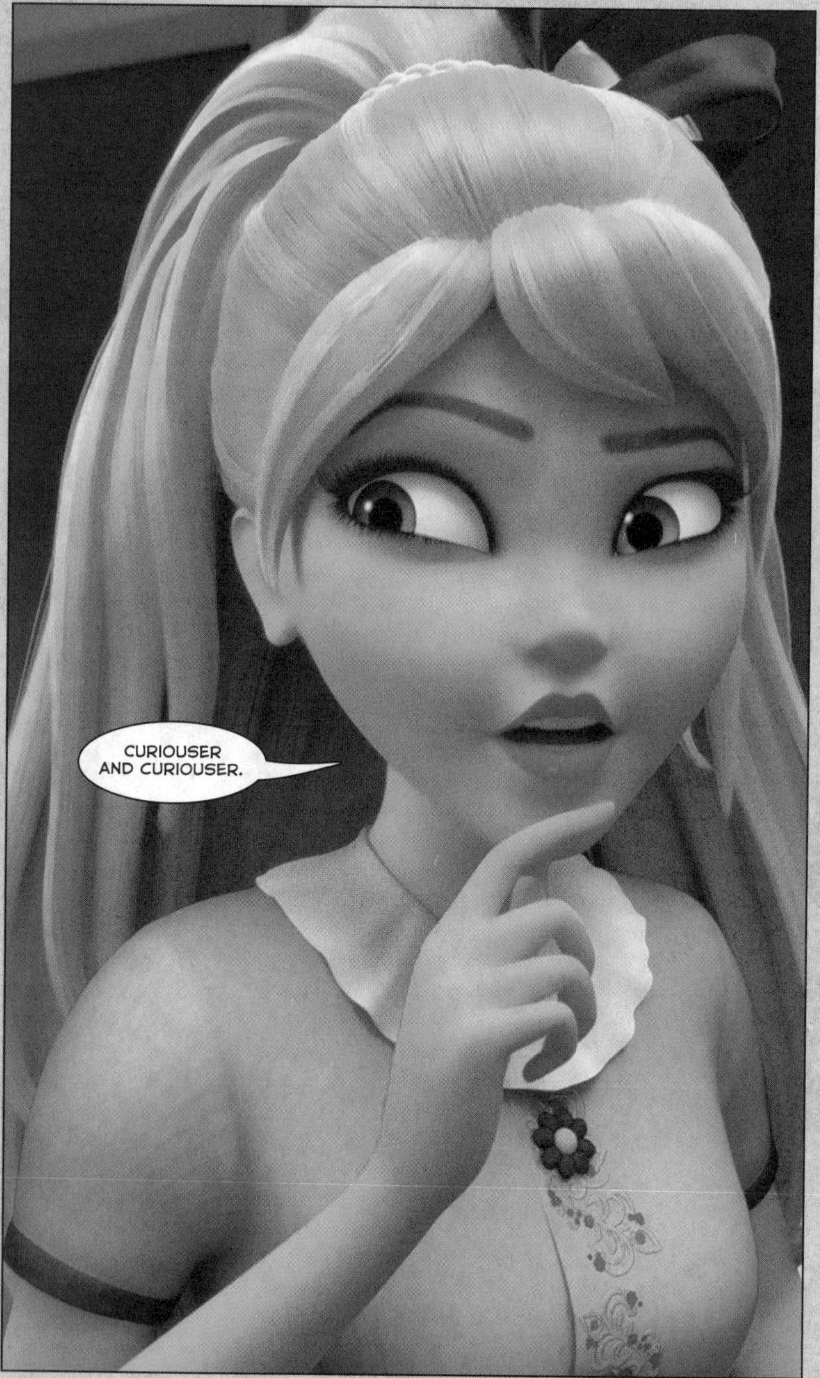
CURIOUSER AND CURIOUSER.

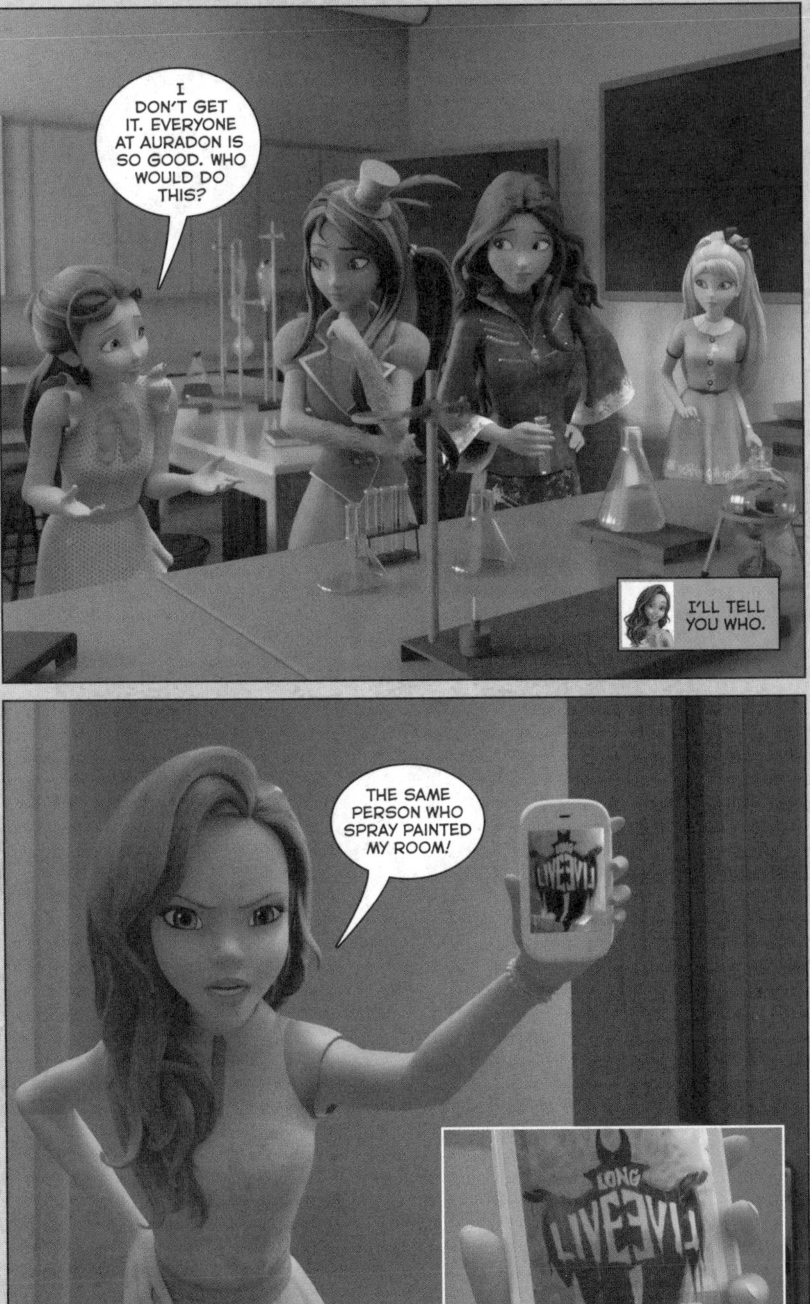
I DON'T GET IT. EVERYONE AT AURADON IS SO GOOD. WHO WOULD DO THIS?
I'LL TELL YOU WHO.
THE SAME PERSON WHO SPRAY PAINTED MY ROOM!
LONG LIVE EVIL

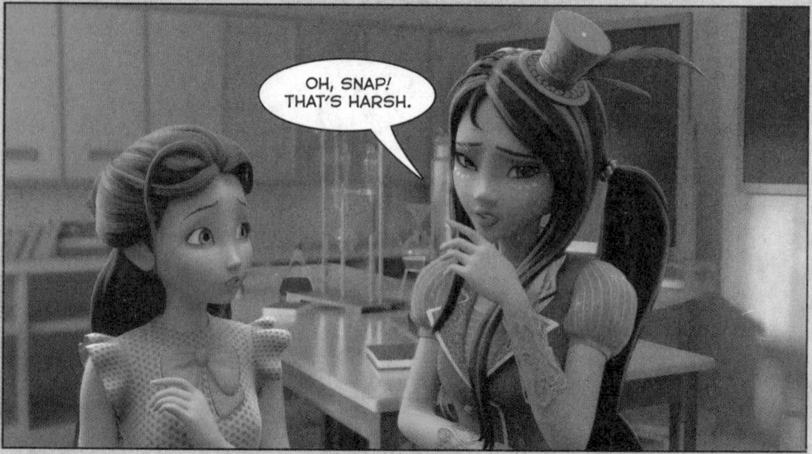
OH, SNAP! THAT'S HARSH.

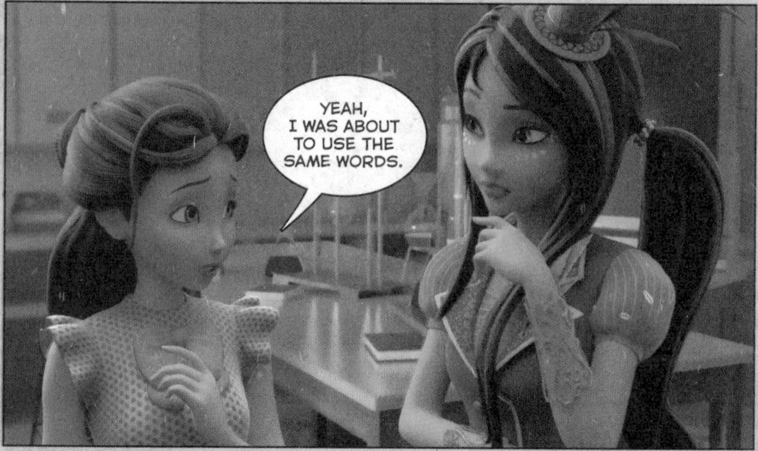
YEAH, I WAS ABOUT TO USE THE SAME WORDS.

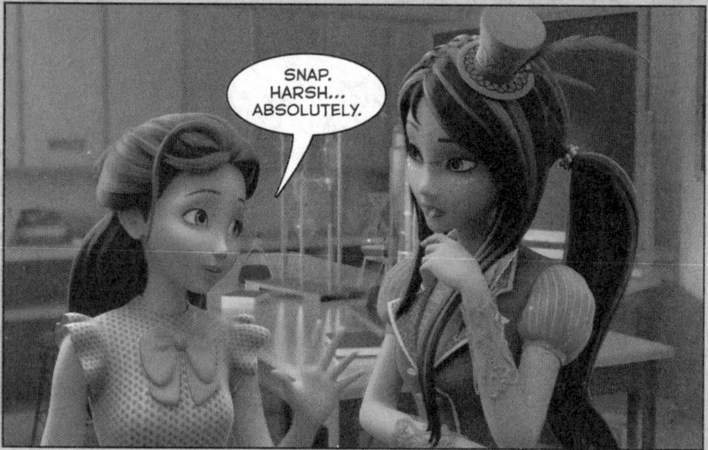
SNAP. HARSH... ABSOLUTELY.

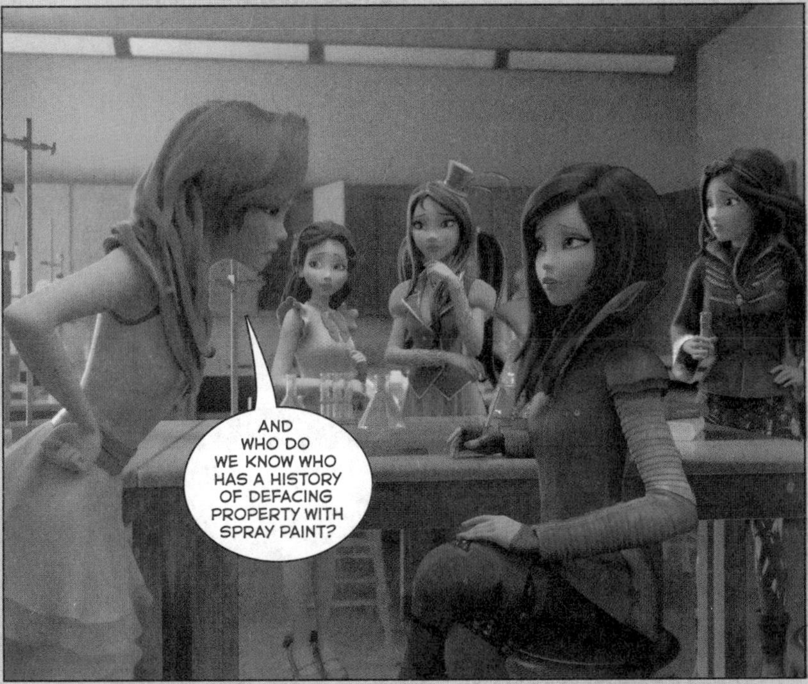
AND WHO DO WE KNOW WHO HAS A HISTORY OF DEFACING PROPERTY WITH SPRAY PAINT?

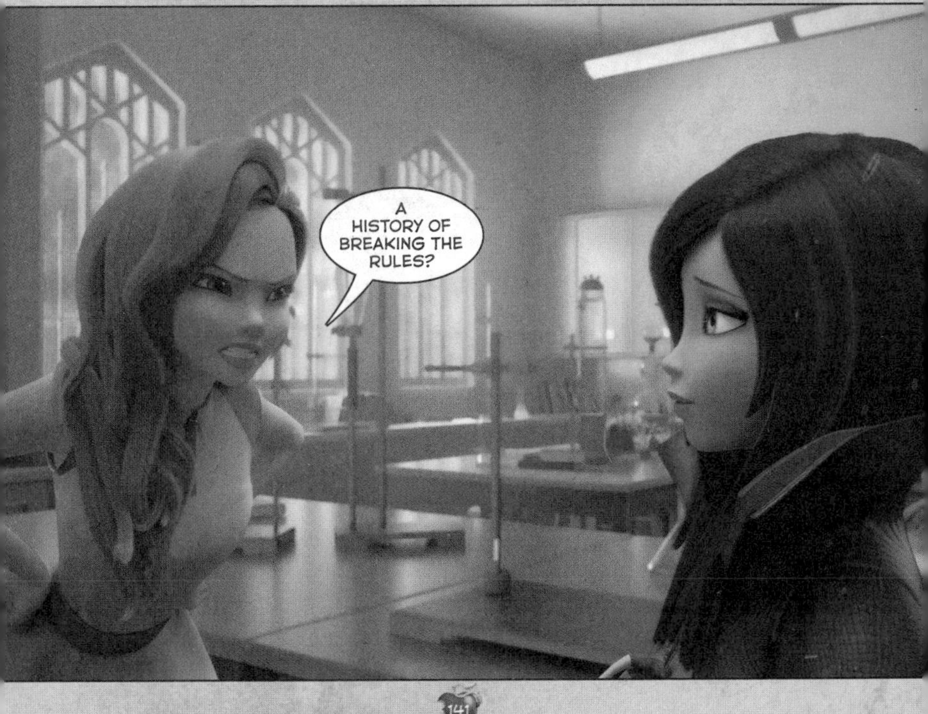
A HISTORY OF BREAKING THE RULES?

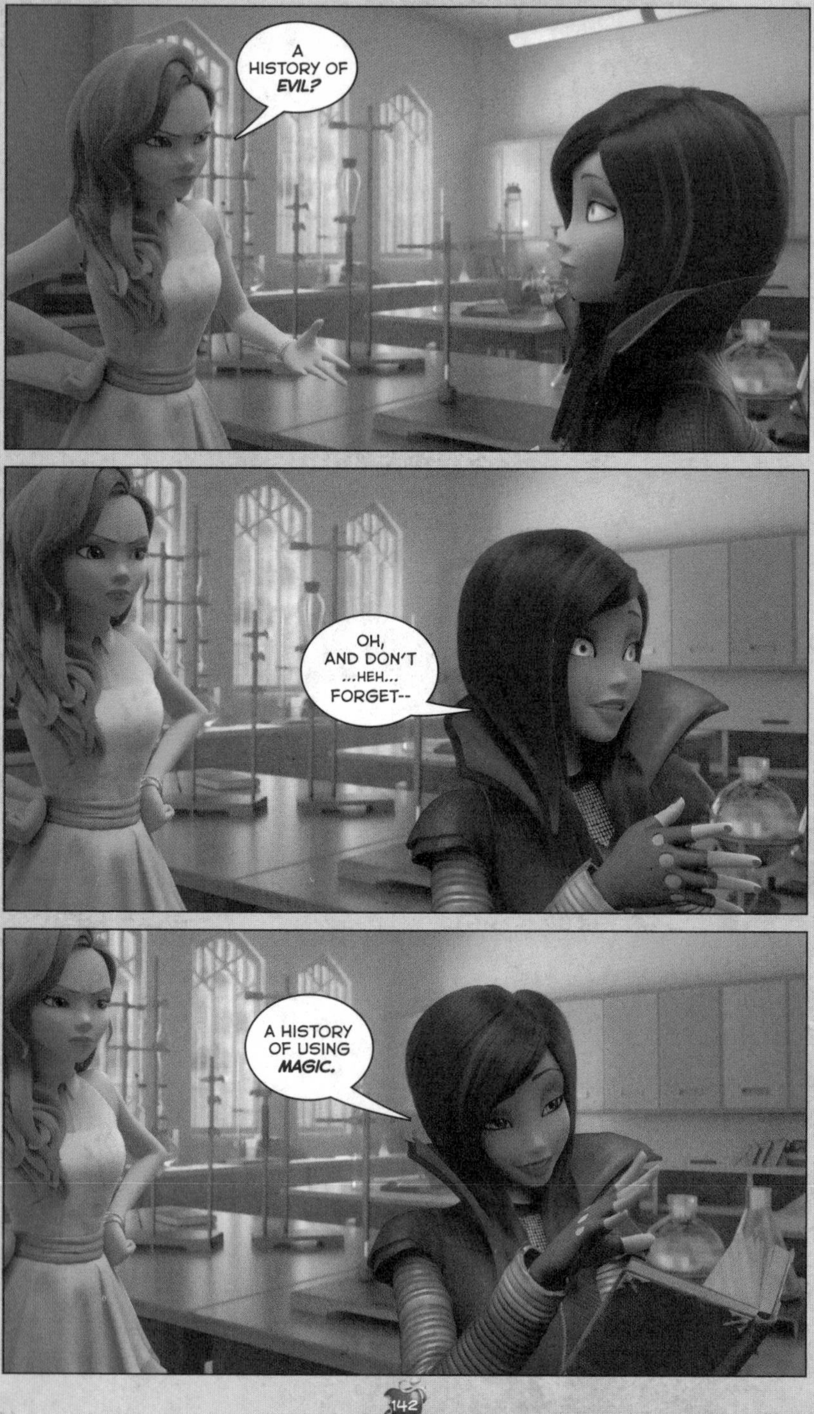
A HISTORY OF ***EVIL?***
OH, AND DON'T ...HEH... FORGET--
A HISTORY OF USING ***MAGIC.***

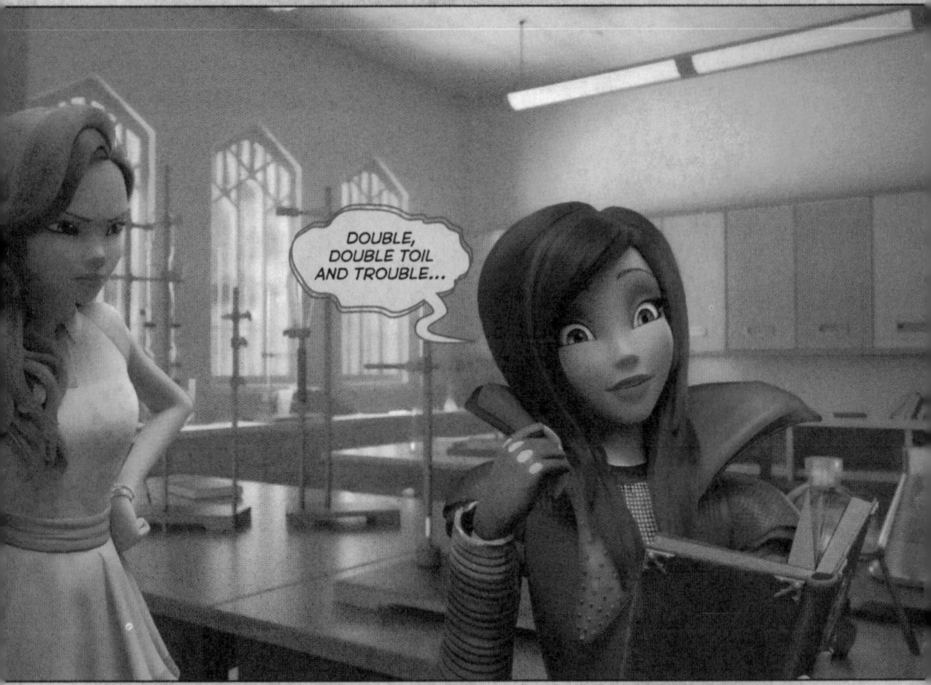
DOUBLE, DOUBLE TOIL AND TROUBLE...

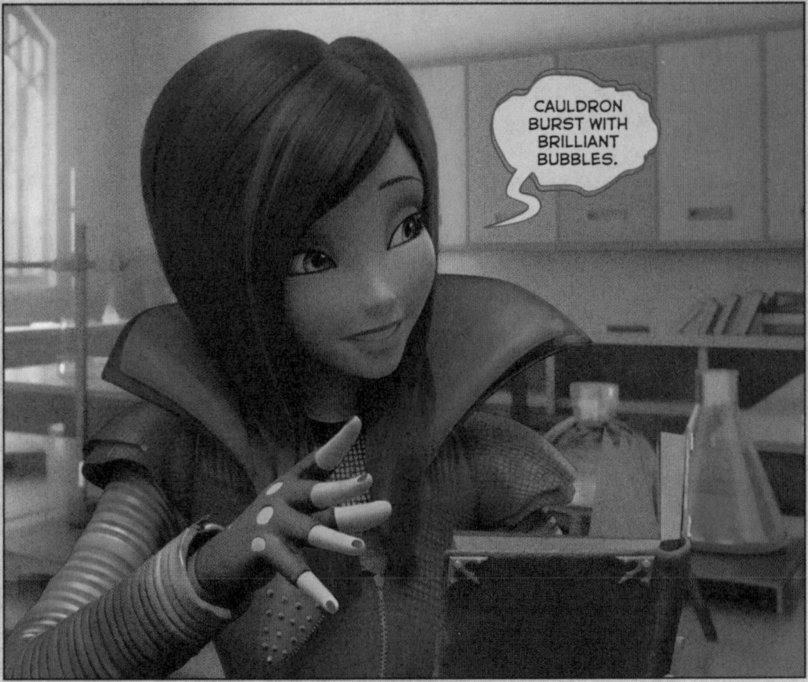
CAULDRON BURST WITH BRILLIANT BUBBLES.

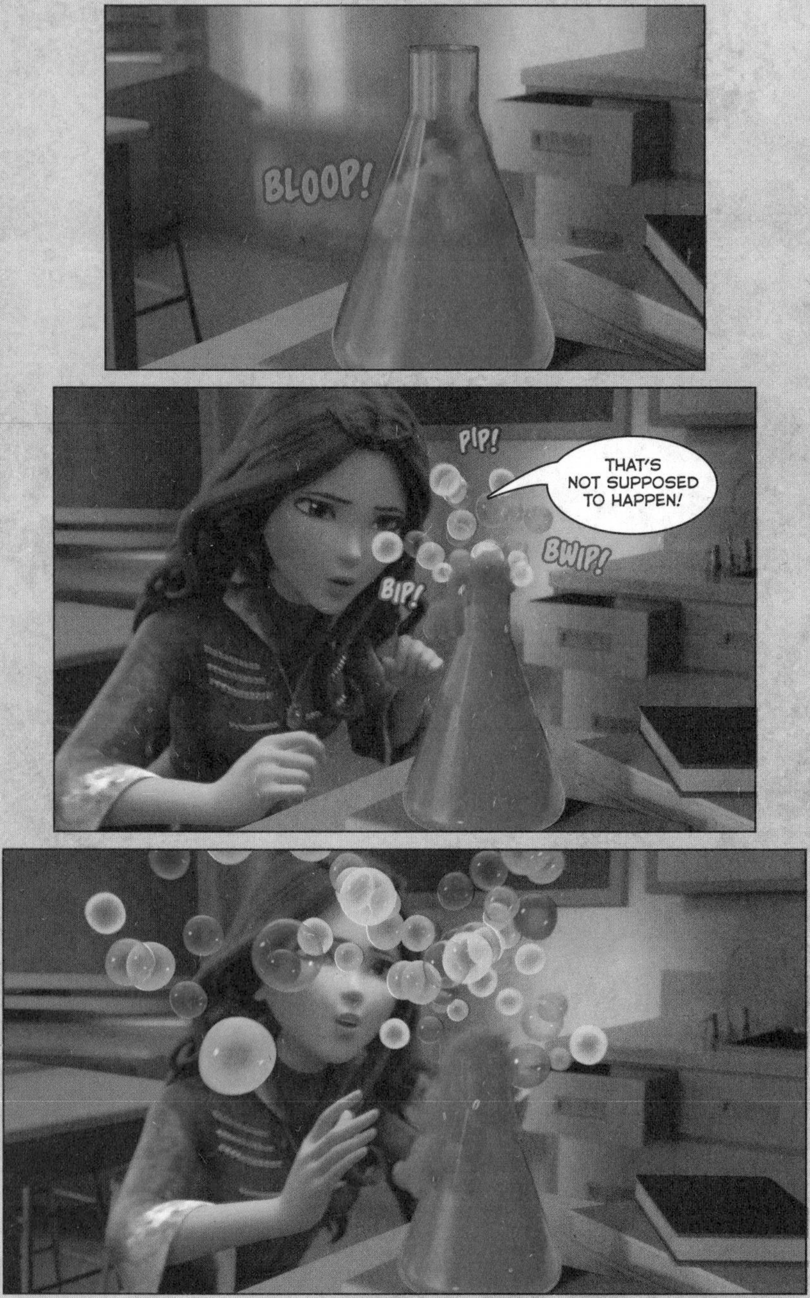
BLOOP!
PIP!
THAT'S NOT SUPPOSED TO HAPPEN!
BWIP!
BIP!

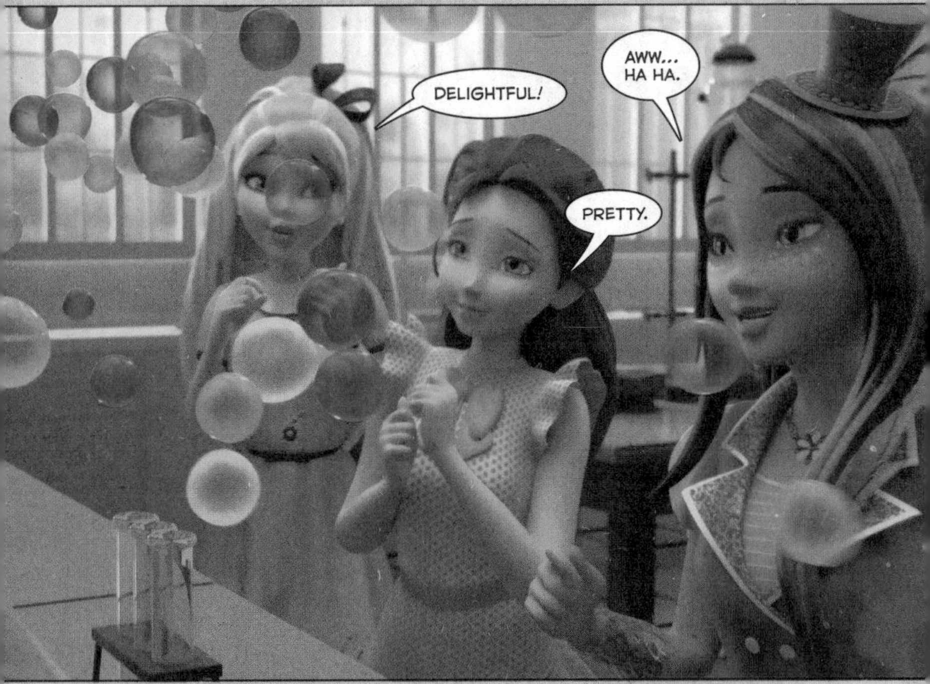
DELIGHTFUL!
AWW... HA HA.
PRETTY.

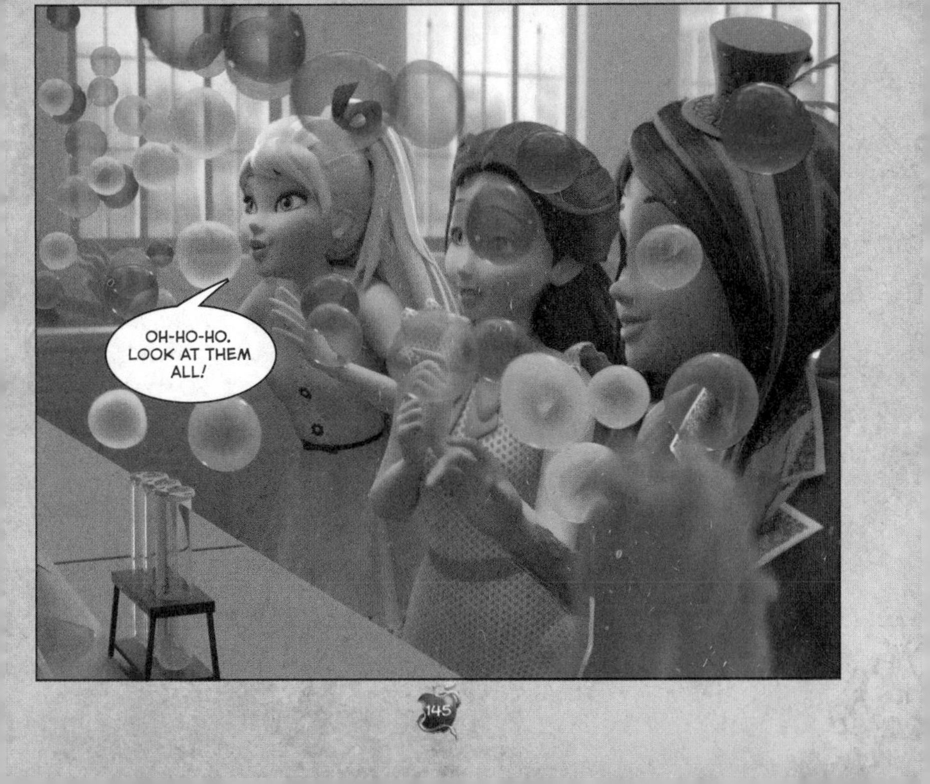
OH-HO-HO. LOOK AT THEM ALL!

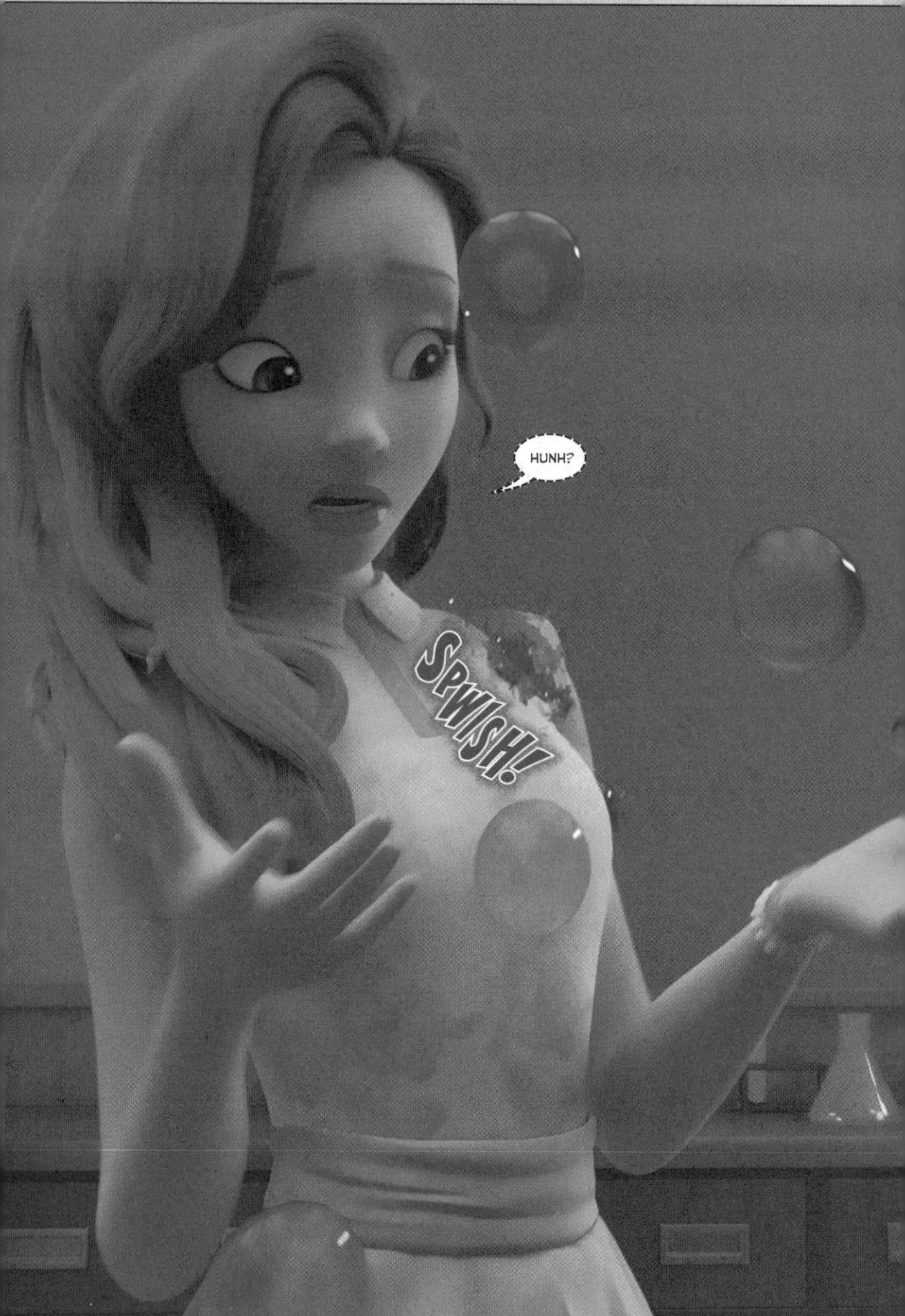
HUNH?
SPWISH!

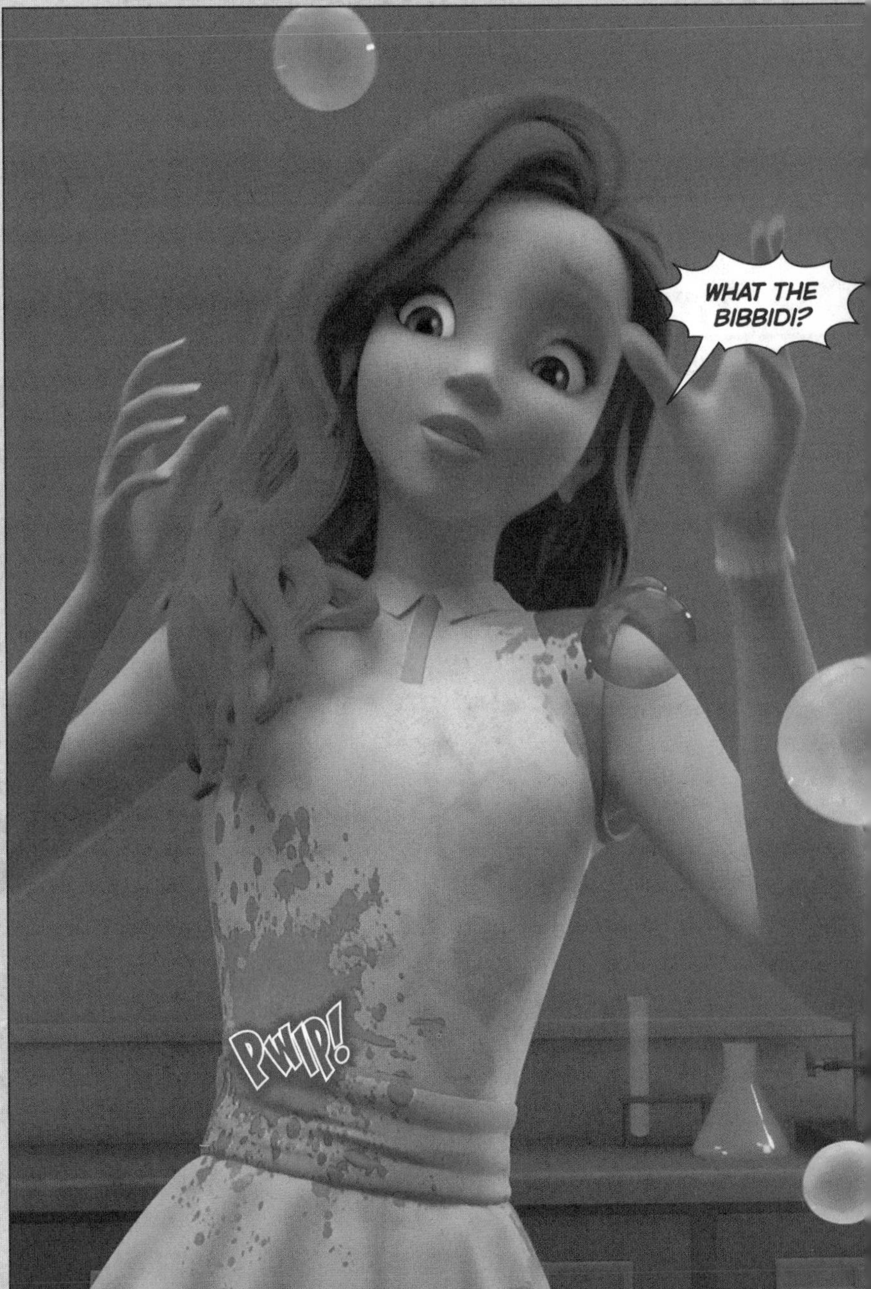
WHAT THE BIBBIDI?
PWIP!

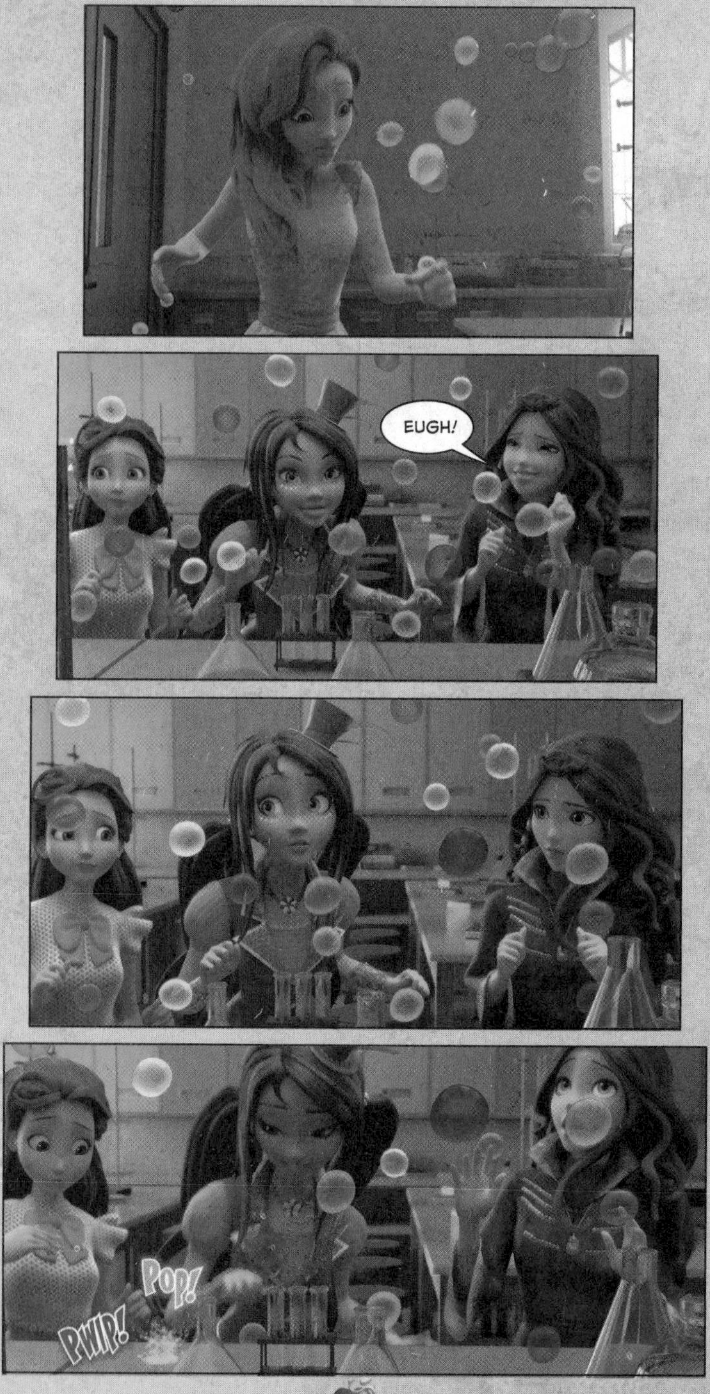
EUGH!
Pop!
PWIP!

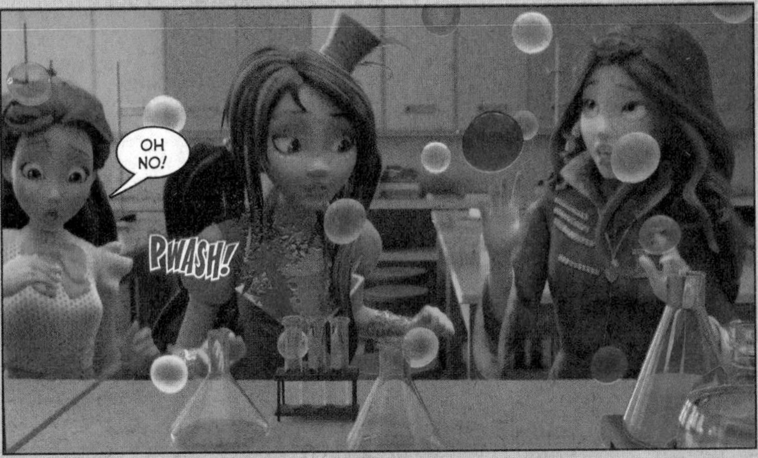
OH NO!
PWASH!

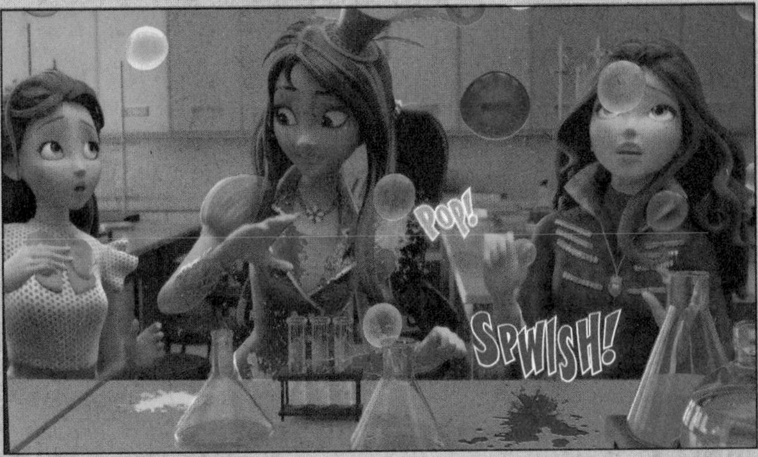
POP!
SPWISH!

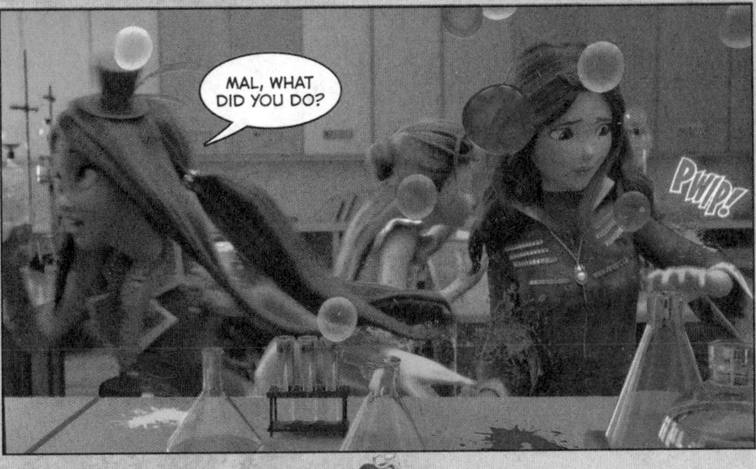
MAL, WHAT DID YOU DO?
PWIP!

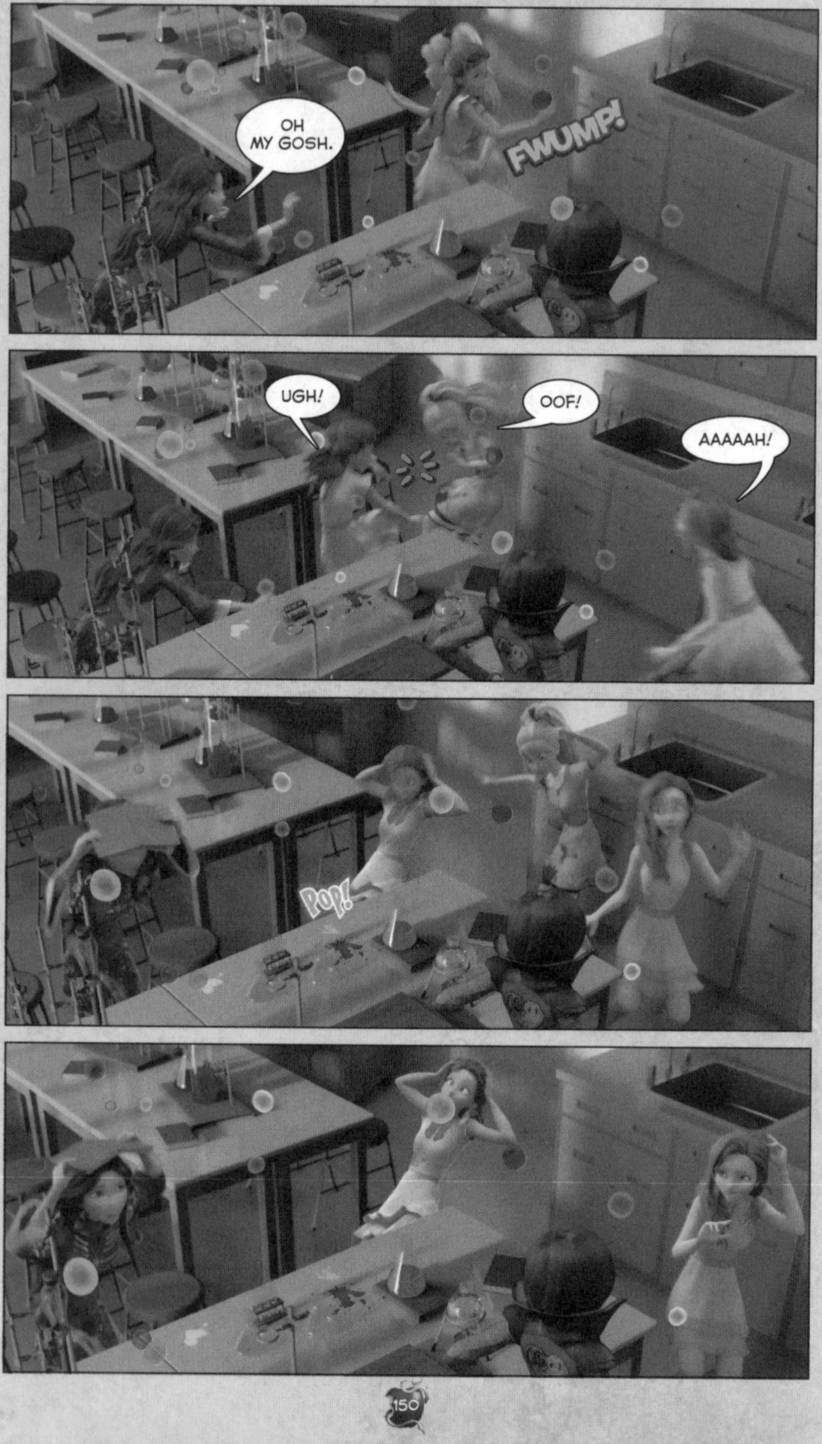
OH
MY GOSH.
FWUMP!
UGH!
OOF!
AAAAAH!
POP!

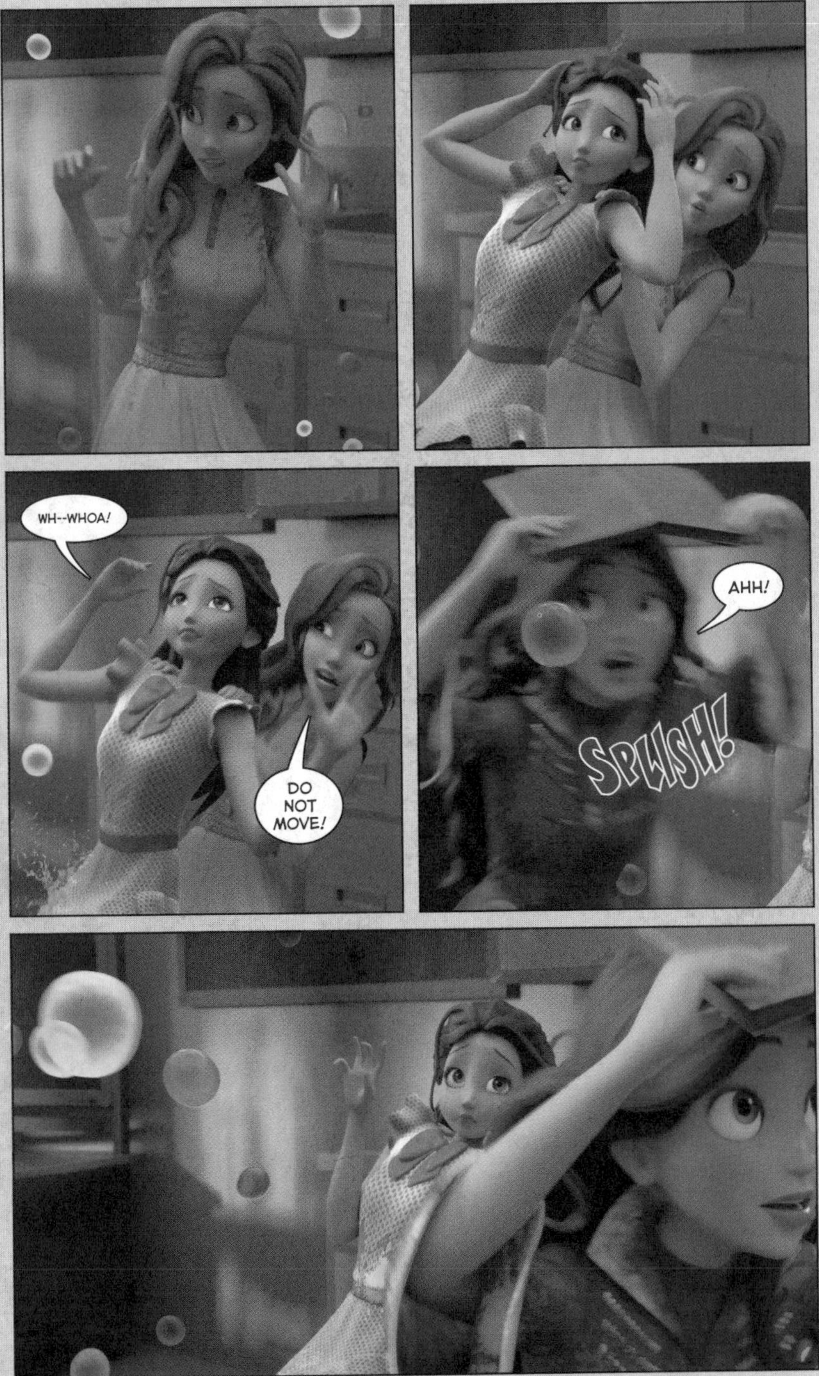
WH--WHOA!
DO NOT MOVE!
AHH!
SPLISH!

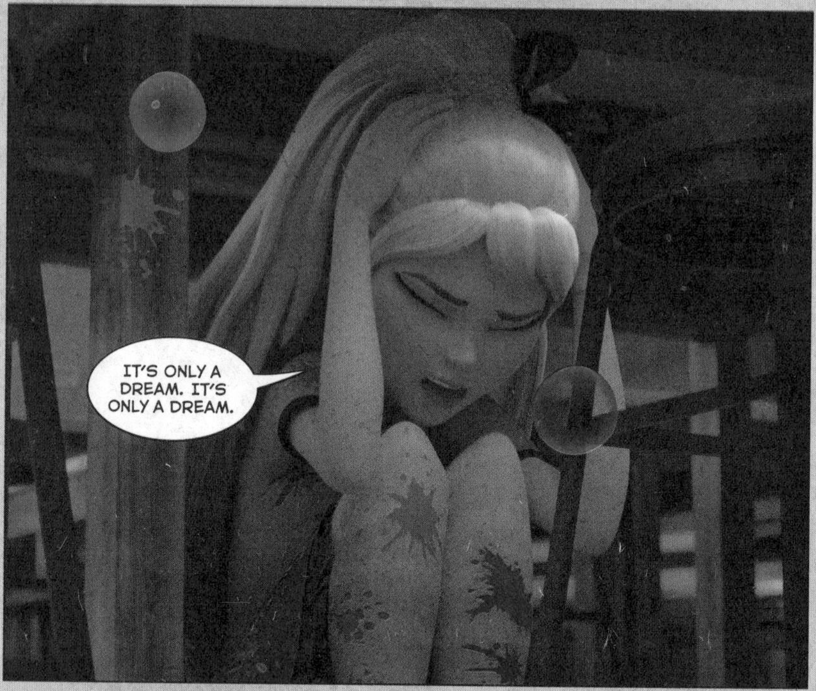
IT'S ONLY A DREAM. IT'S ONLY A DREAM.

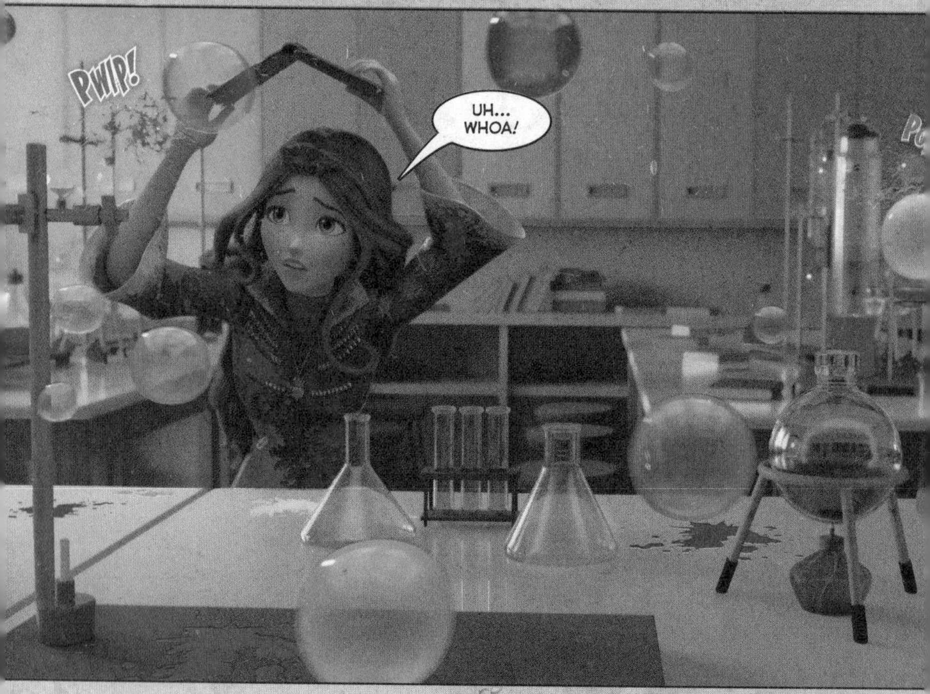
PWIP!
UH... WHOA!

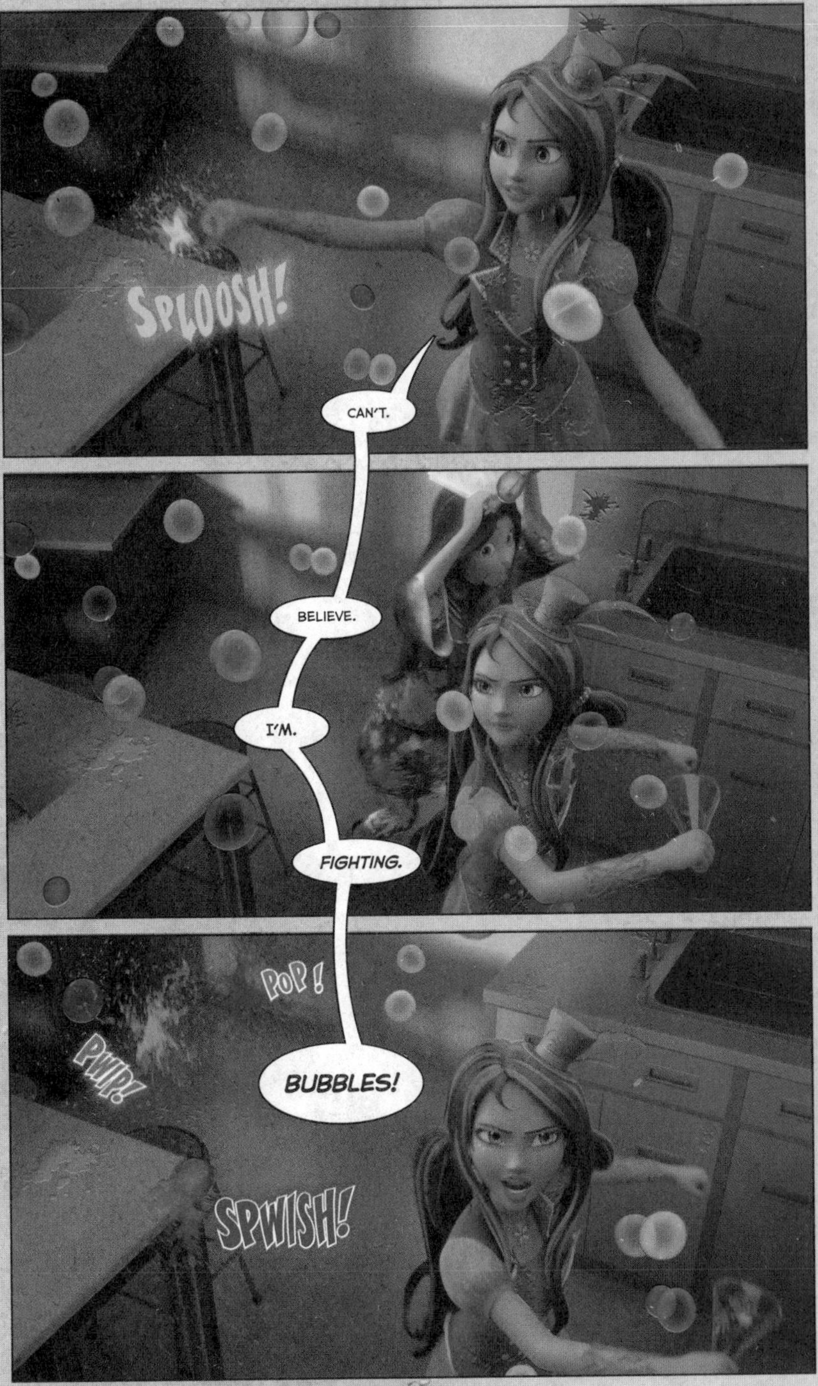
SPLOOSH!
CAN'T.
BELIEVE.
I'M.
FIGHTING.
POP!
PWIP!
BUBBLES!
SPWISH!

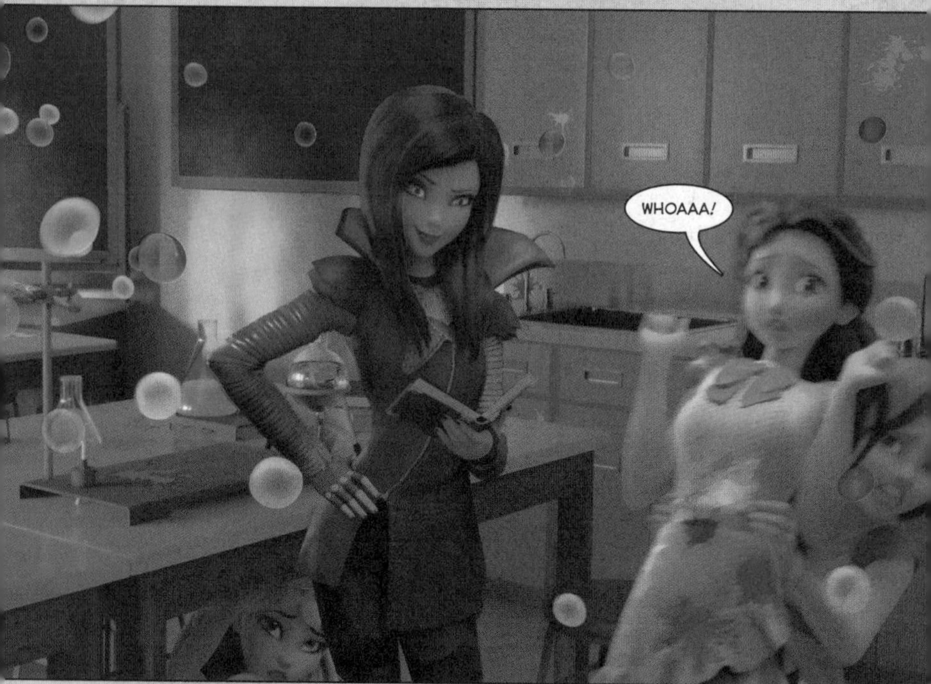
WHOAAA!

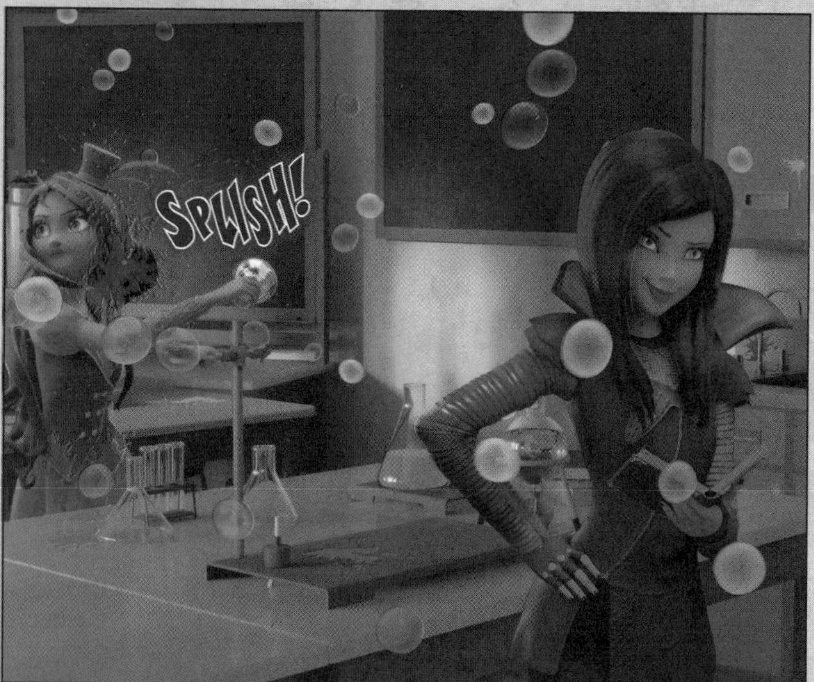
SPLISH!

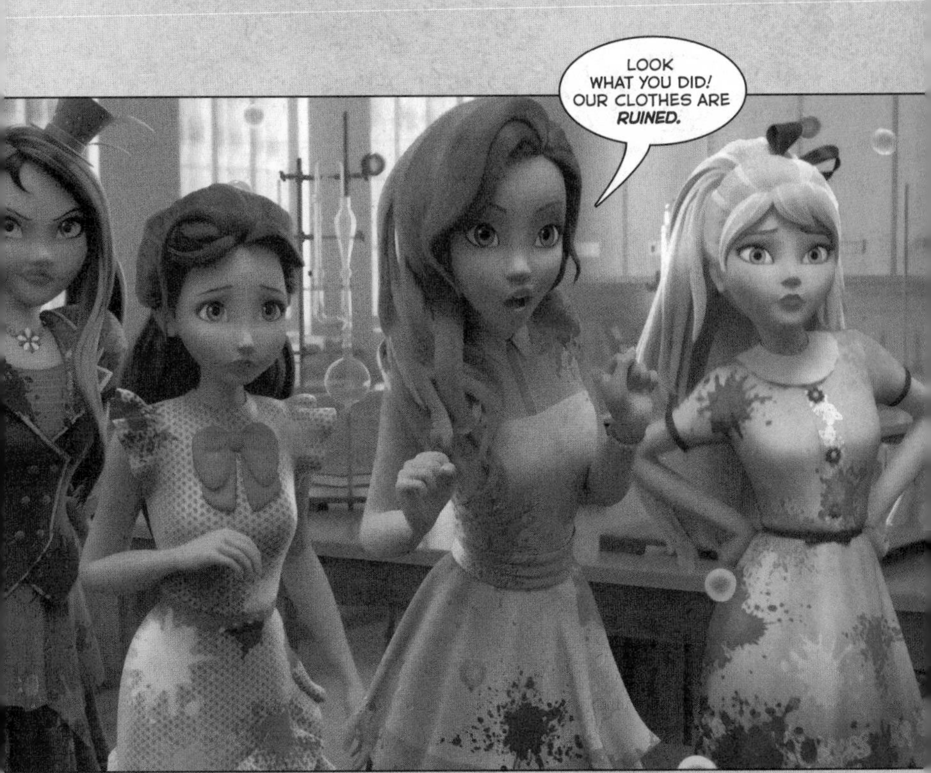
LOOK WHAT YOU DID! OUR CLOTHES ARE *RUINED.*

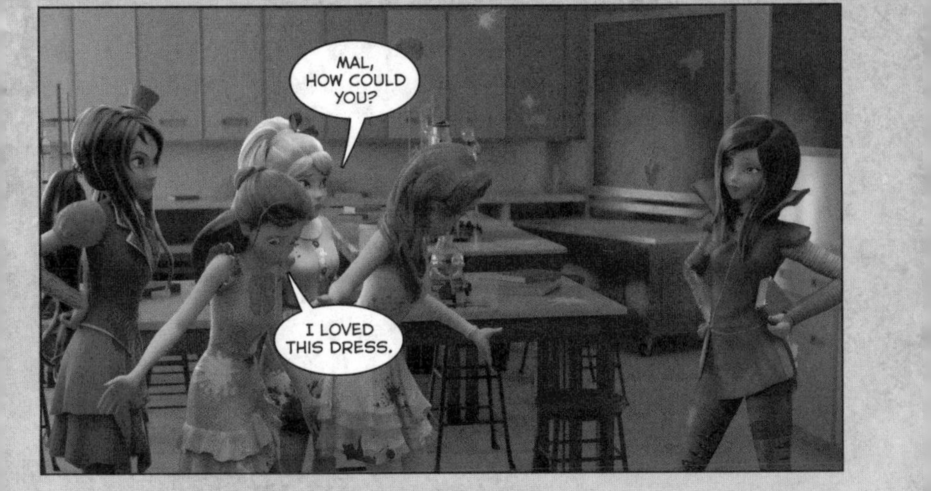
MAL, HOW COULD YOU?
I LOVED THIS DRESS.

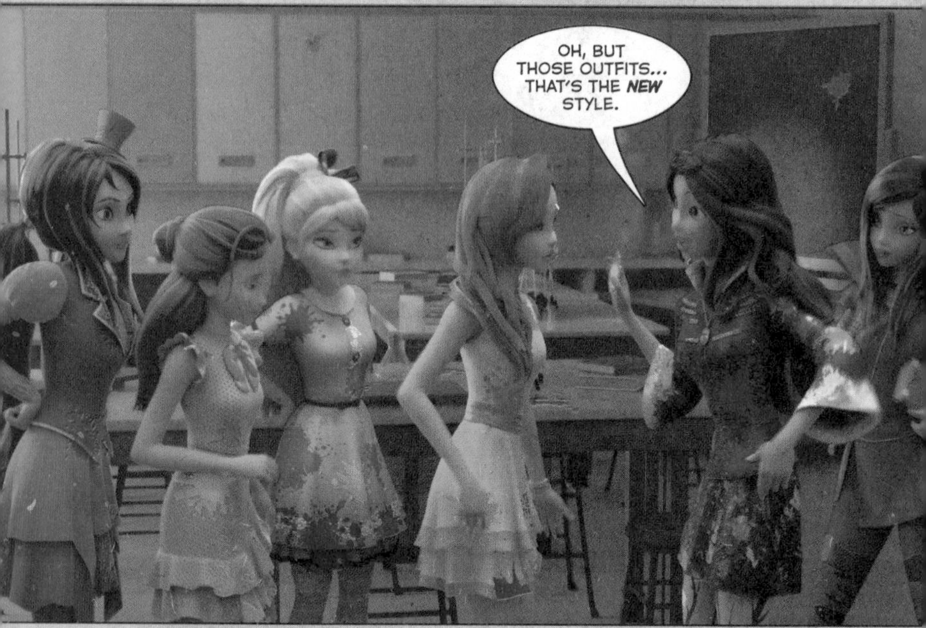
OH, BUT THOSE OUTFITS... THAT'S THE *NEW* STYLE.

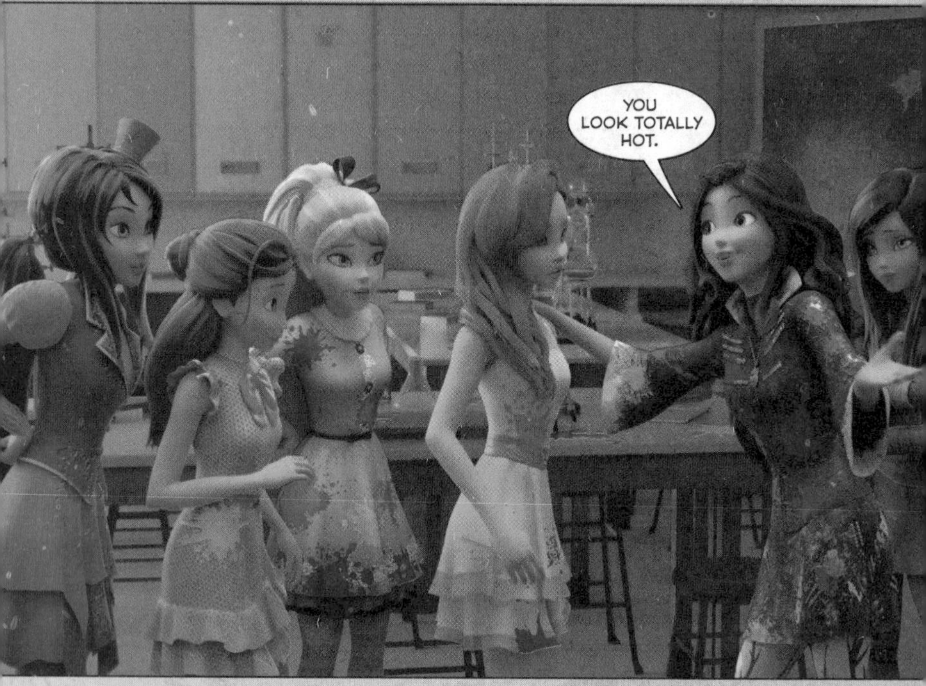
YOU LOOK TOTALLY HOT.

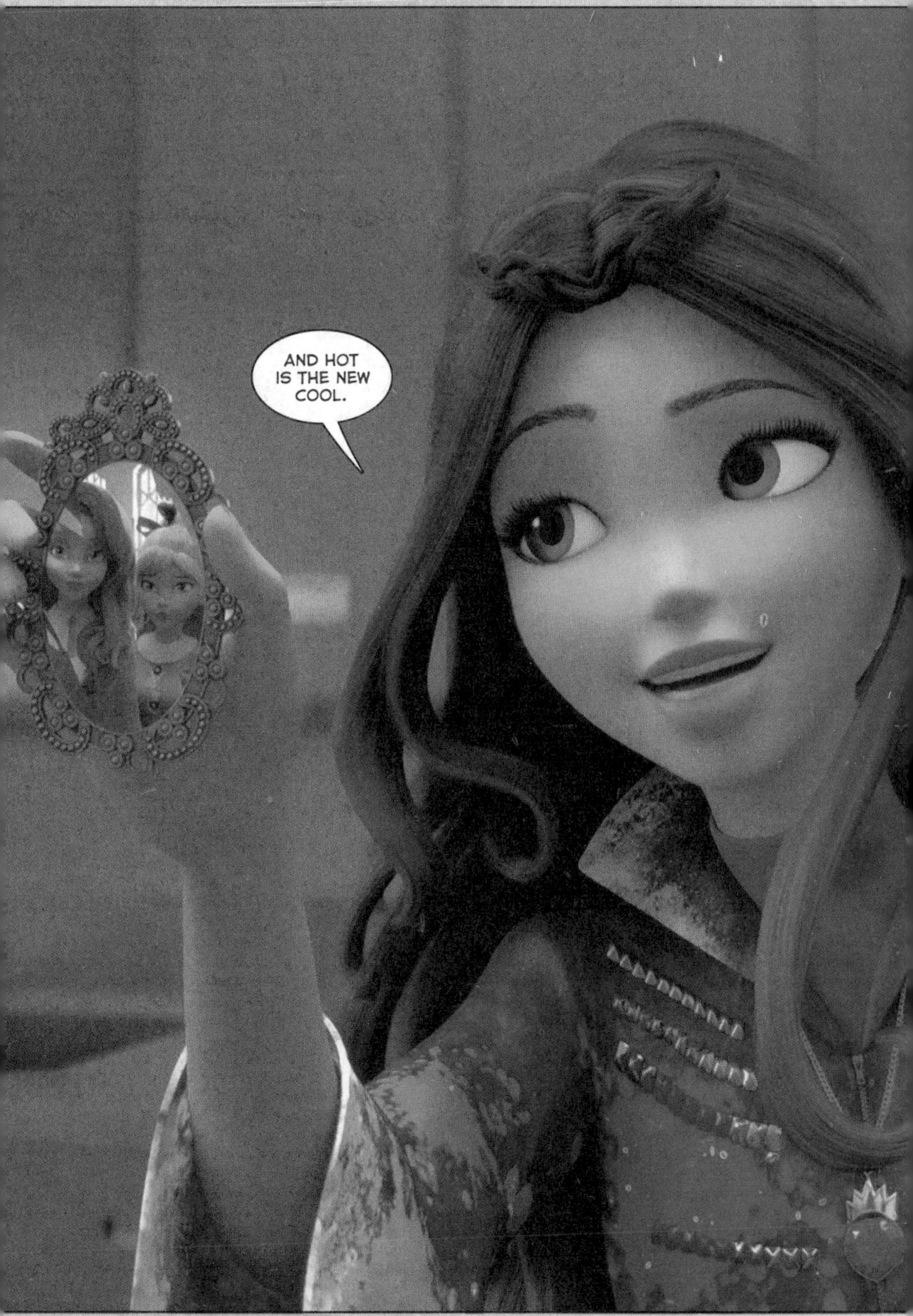
AND HOT IS THE NEW COOL.

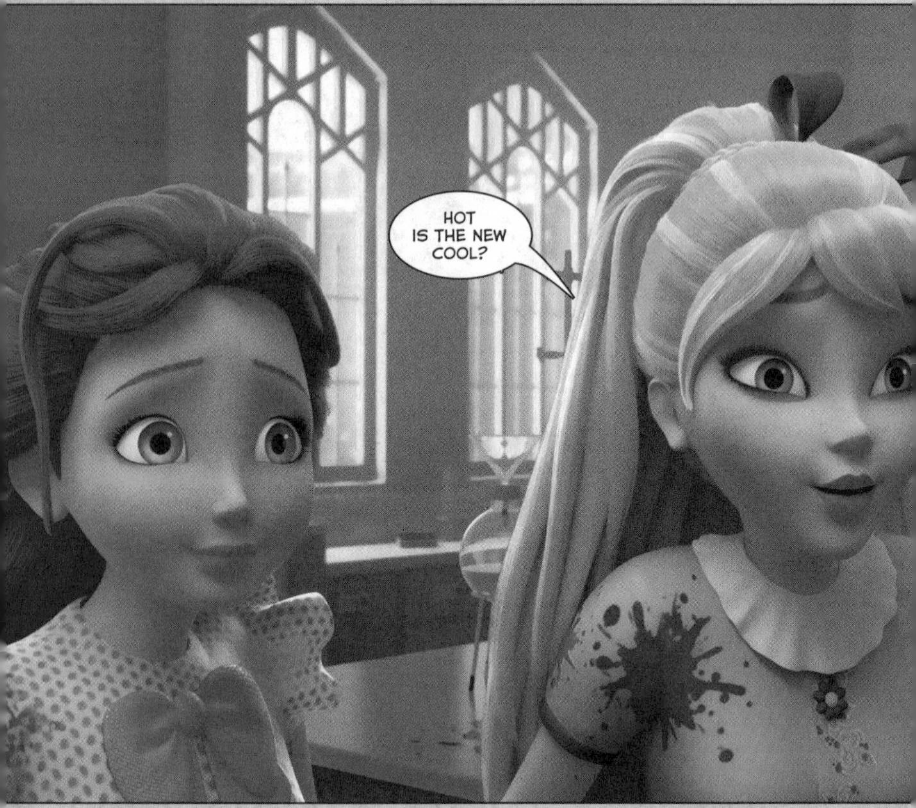
HOT
IS THE NEW
COOL?

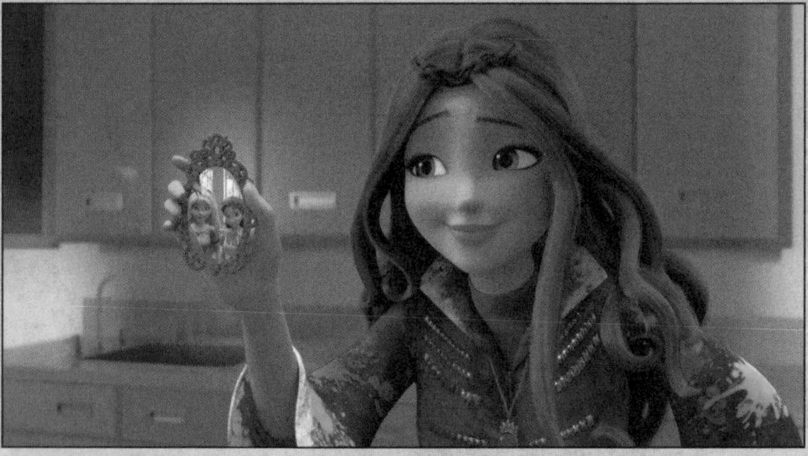

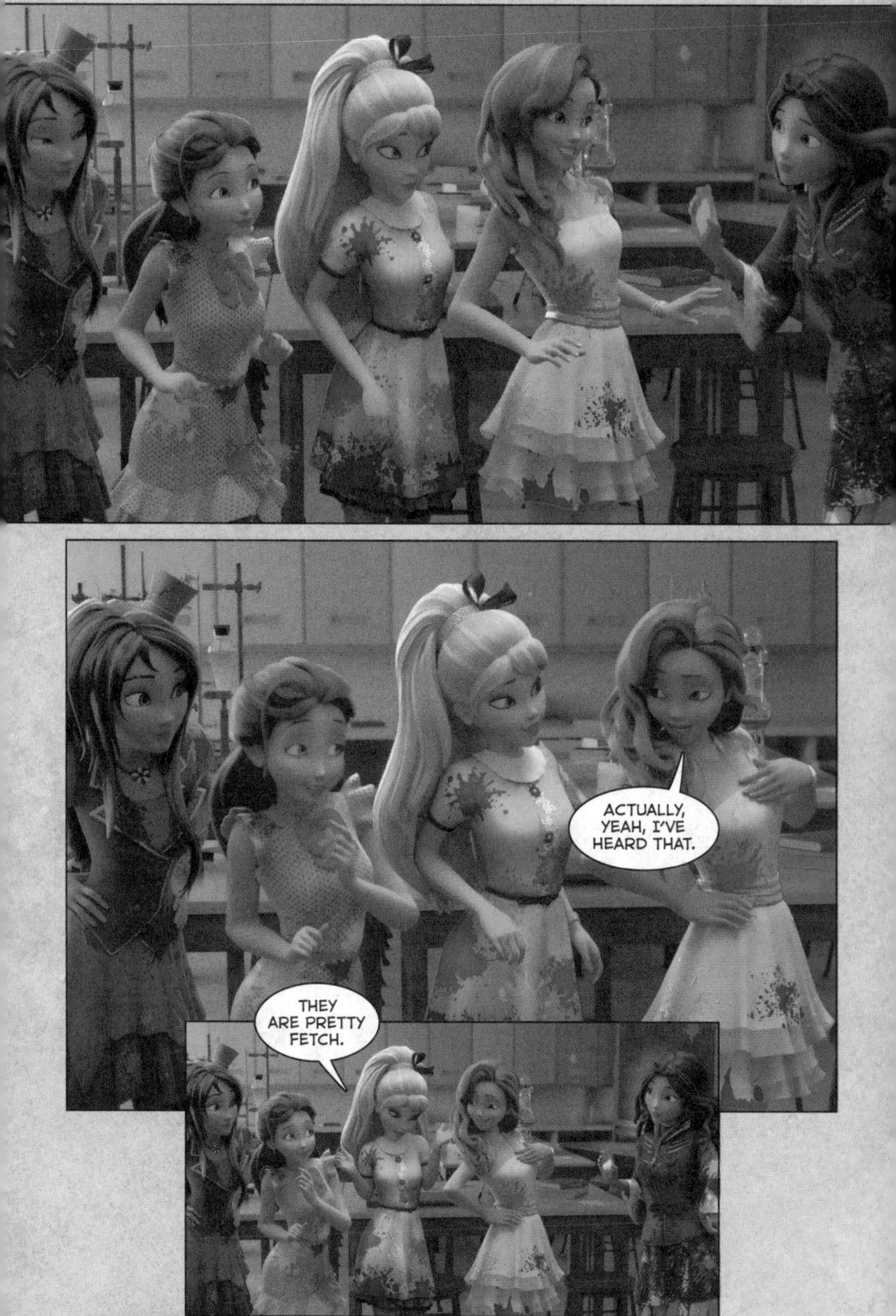
ACTUALLY, YEAH, I'VE HEARD THAT.
THEY ARE PRETTY FETCH.

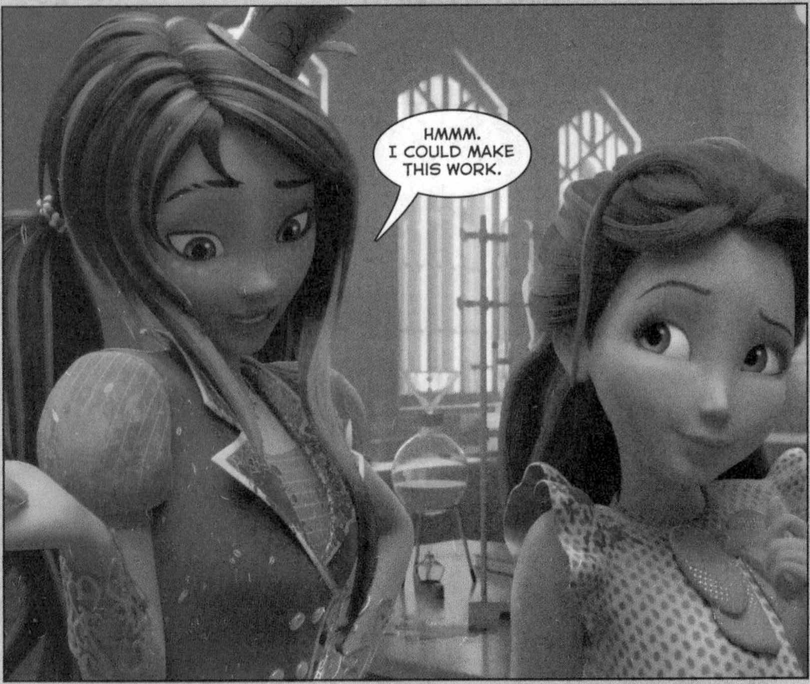
HMMM. I COULD MAKE THIS WORK.

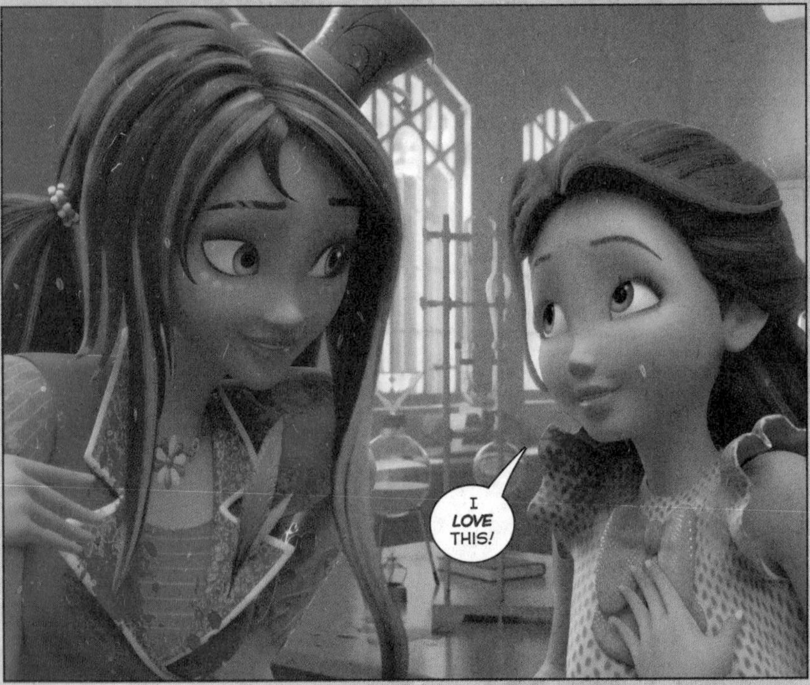
I LOVE THIS!

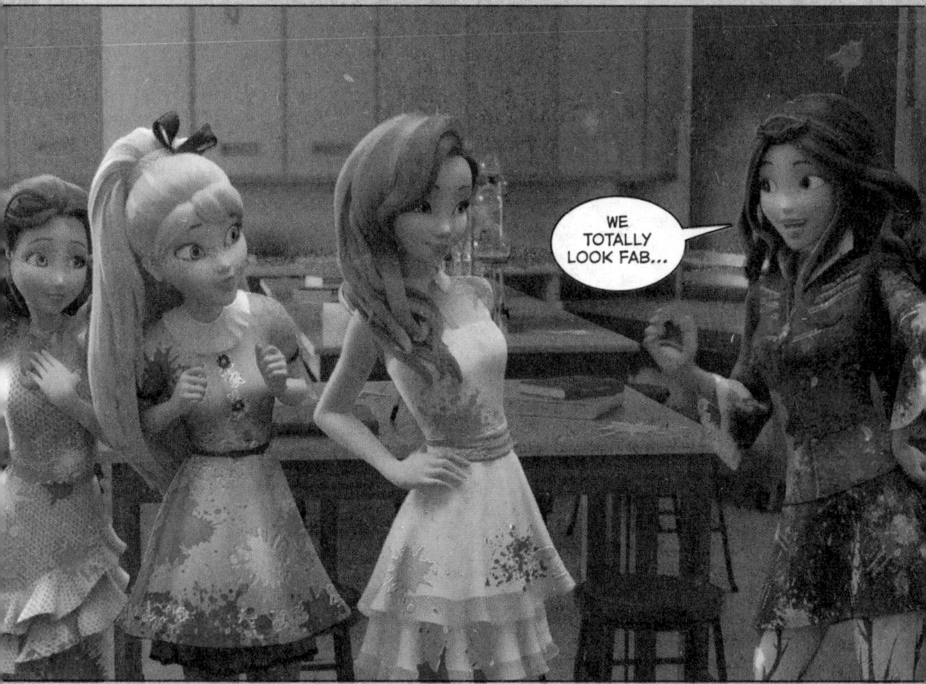
WE TOTALLY LOOK FAB...

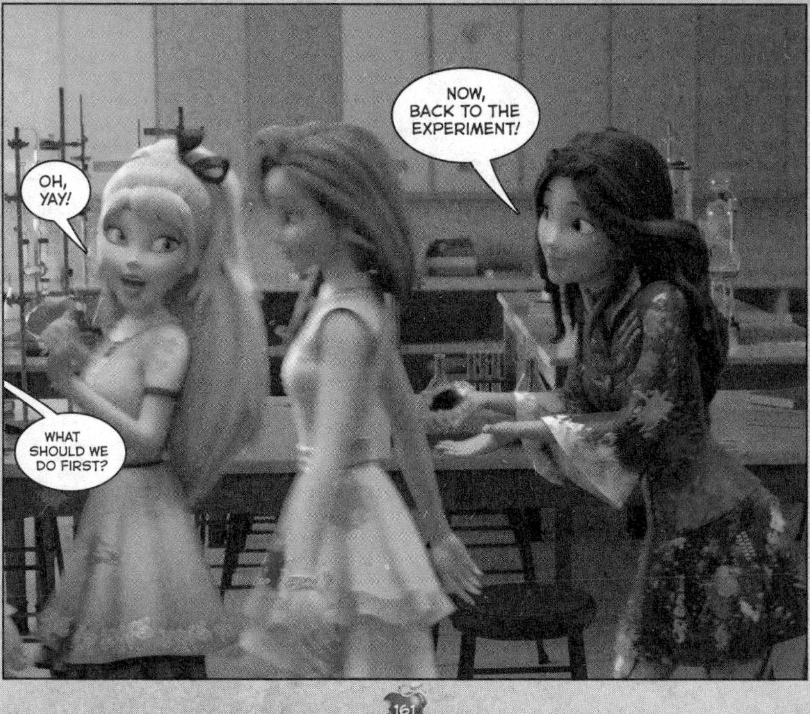
NOW, BACK TO THE EXPERIMENT!
OH, YAY!
WHAT SHOULD WE DO FIRST?

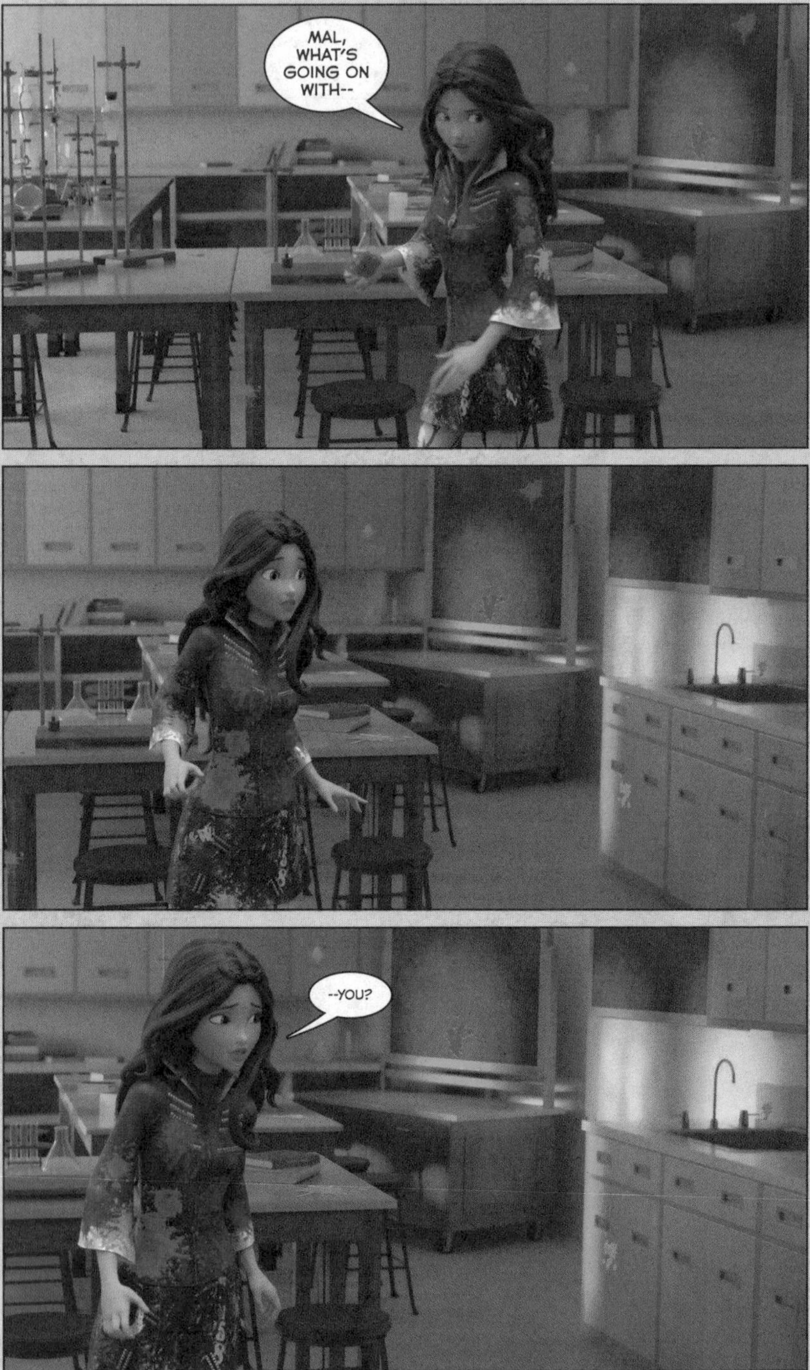
MAL, WHAT'S GOING ON WITH--
--YOU?

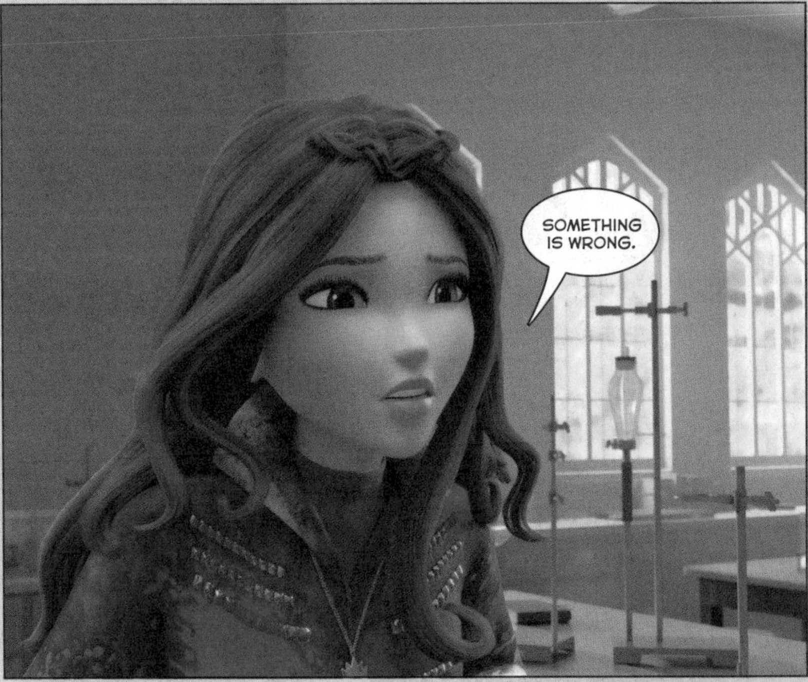
SOMETHING IS WRONG.

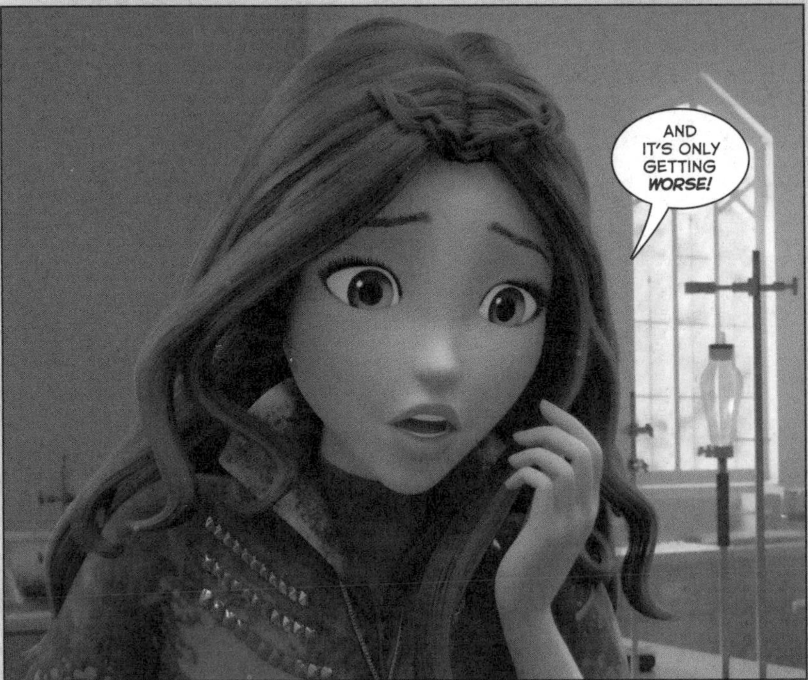
AND IT'S ONLY GETTING **WORSE!**

CHAPTER 24: TALKING HEADS

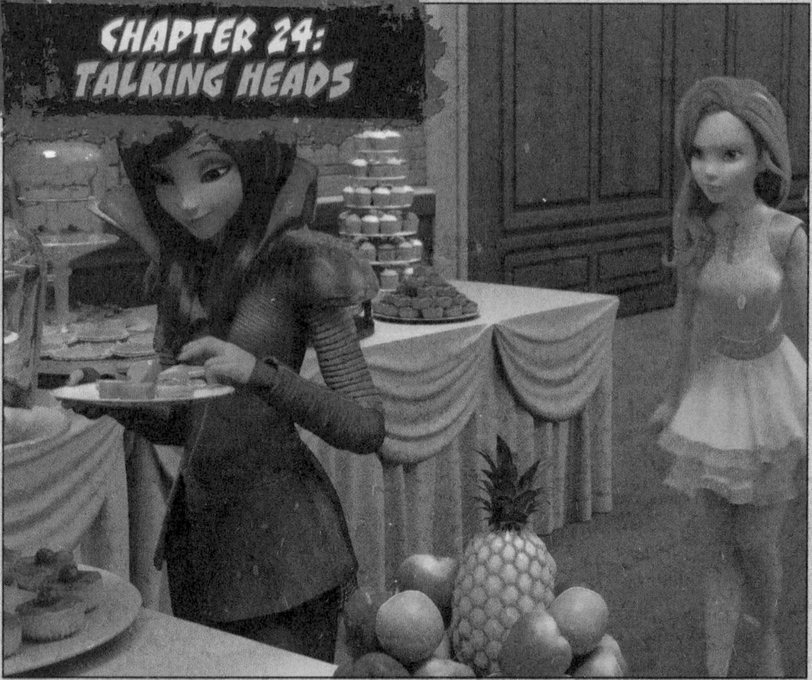

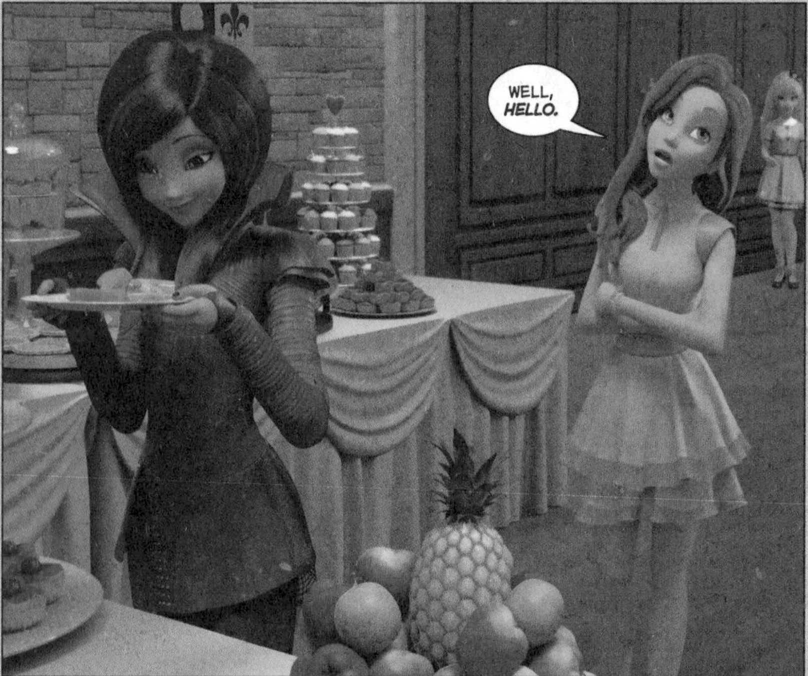
WELL, HELLO.

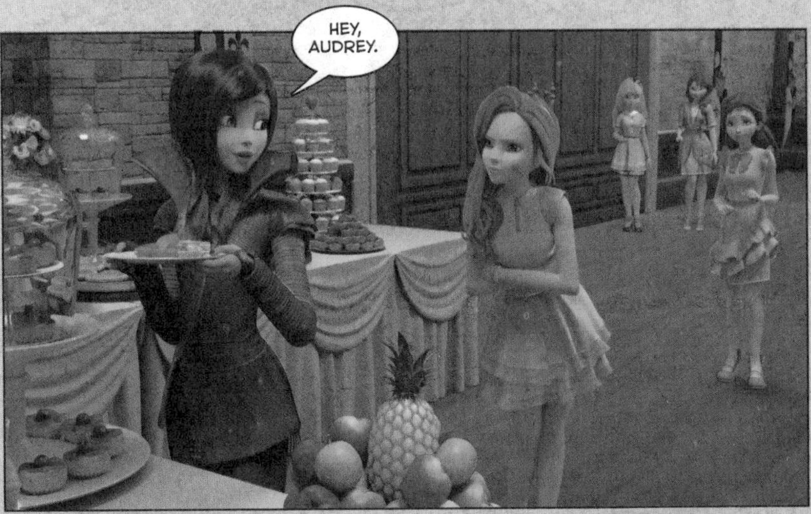
HEY, AUDREY.

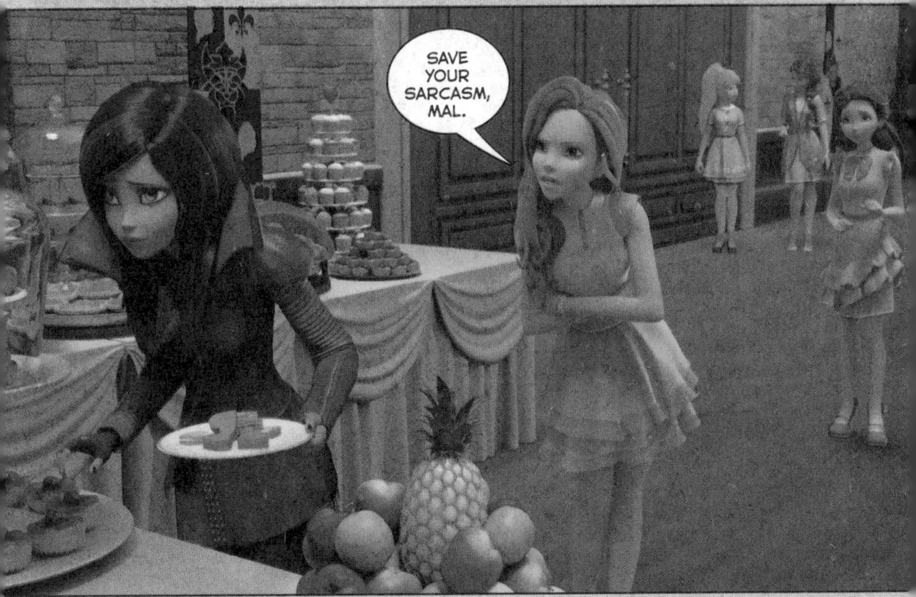
SAVE YOUR SARCASM, MAL.

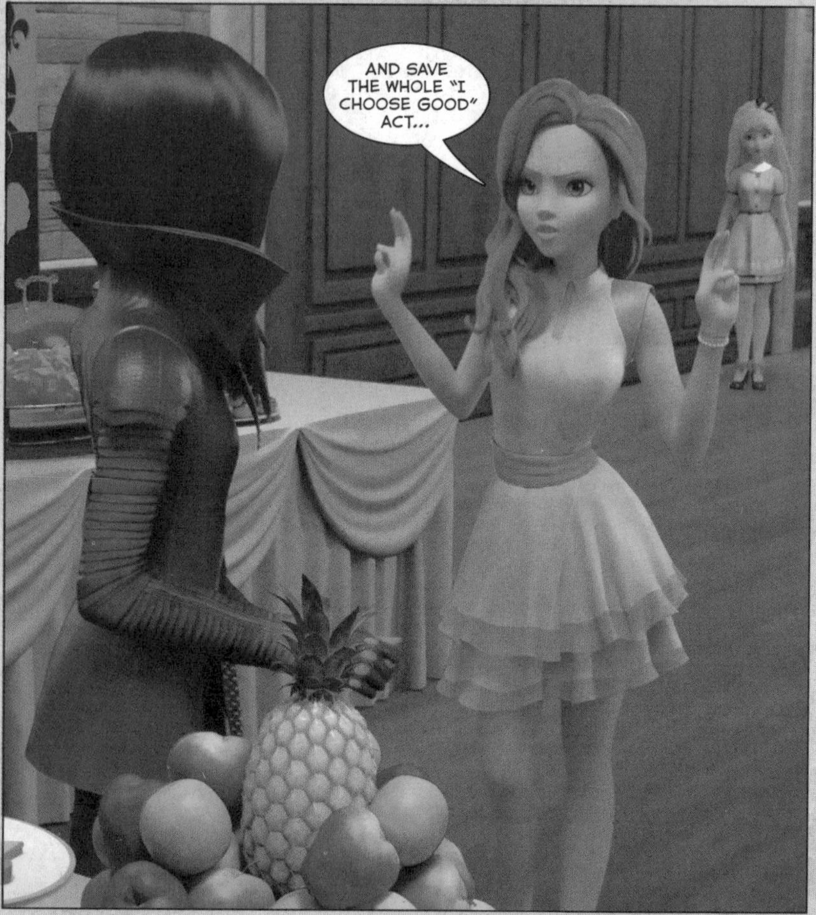
AND SAVE THE WHOLE "I CHOOSE GOOD" ACT...

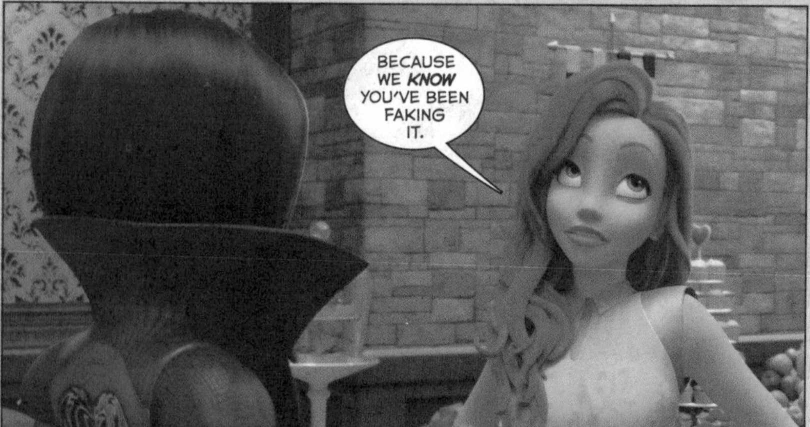
BECAUSE WE *KNOW* YOU'VE BEEN FAKING IT.

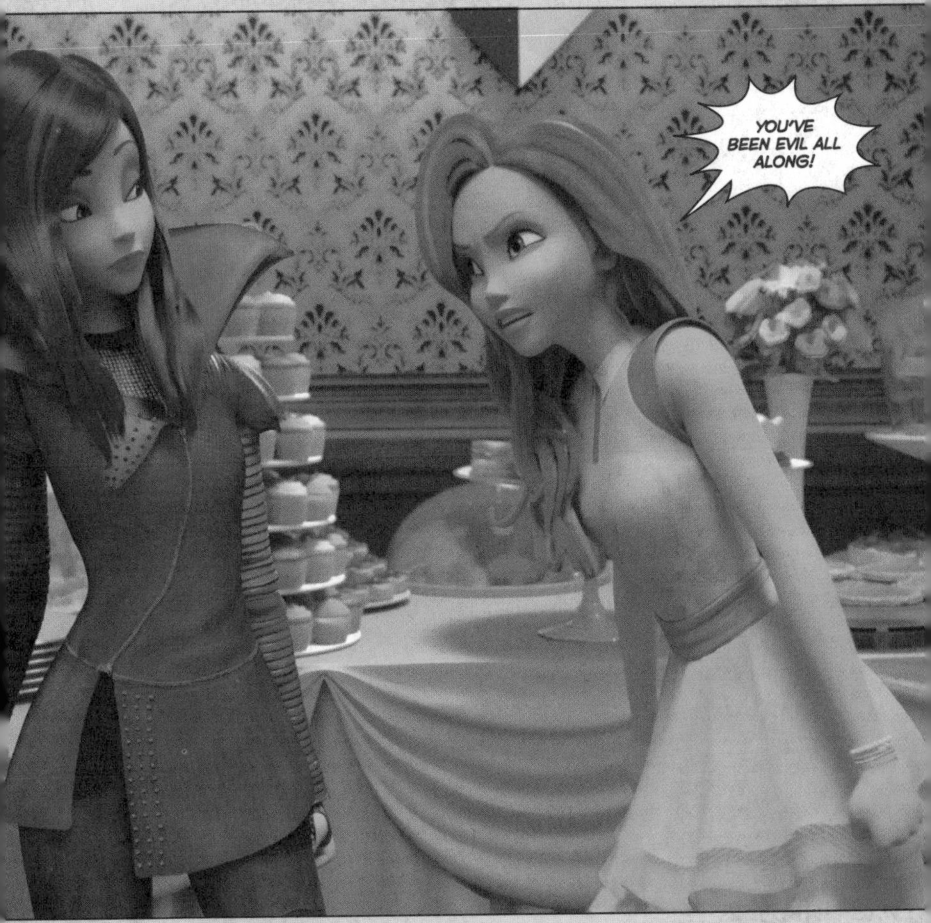
YOU'VE BEEN EVIL ALL ALONG!

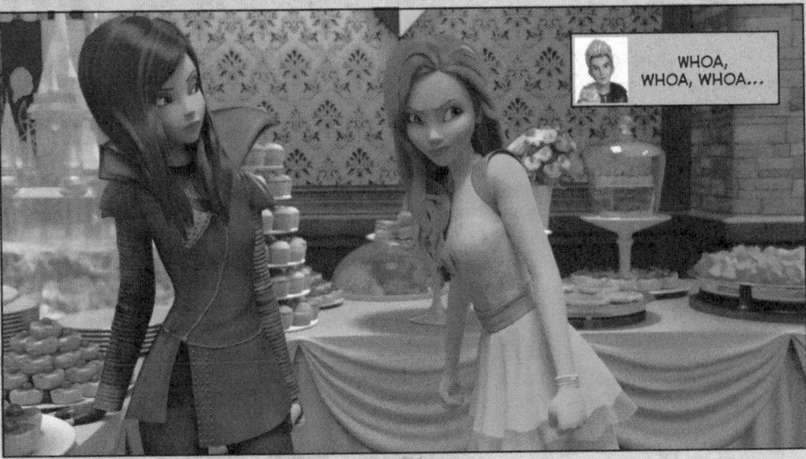
WHOA, WHOA, WHOA...

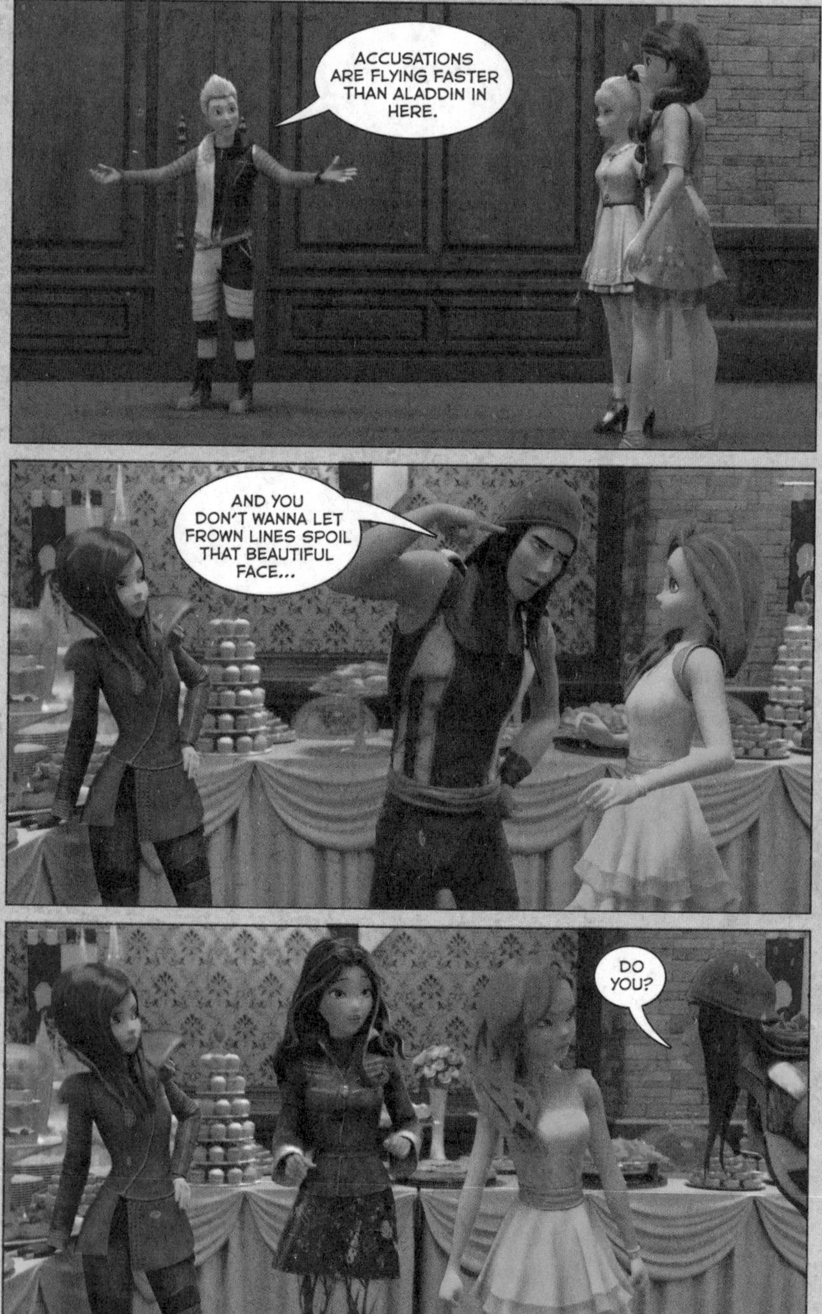
ACCUSATIONS ARE FLYING FASTER THAN ALADDIN IN HERE.
AND YOU DON'T WANNA LET FROWN LINES SPOIL THAT BEAUTIFUL FACE...
DO YOU?

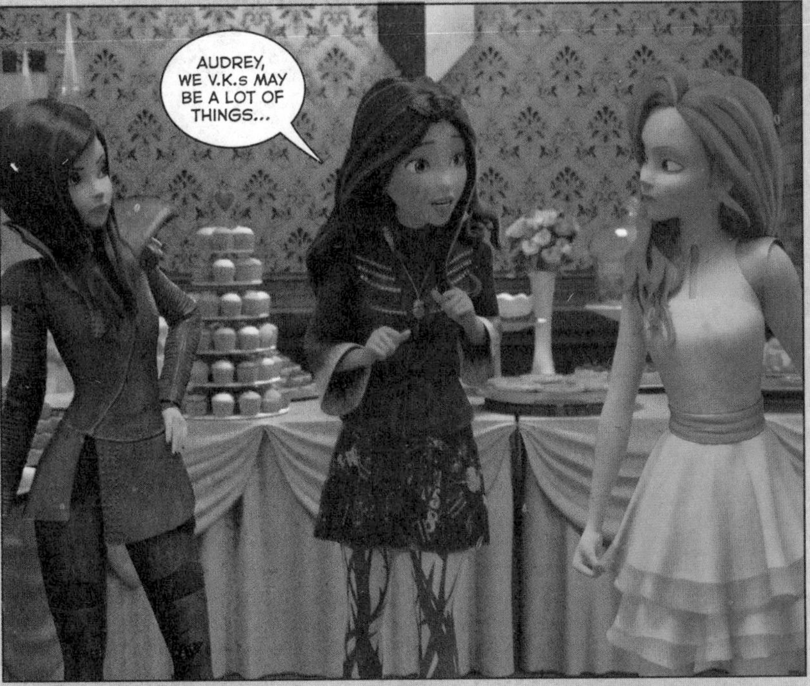
AUDREY, WE V.K.s MAY BE A LOT OF THINGS...

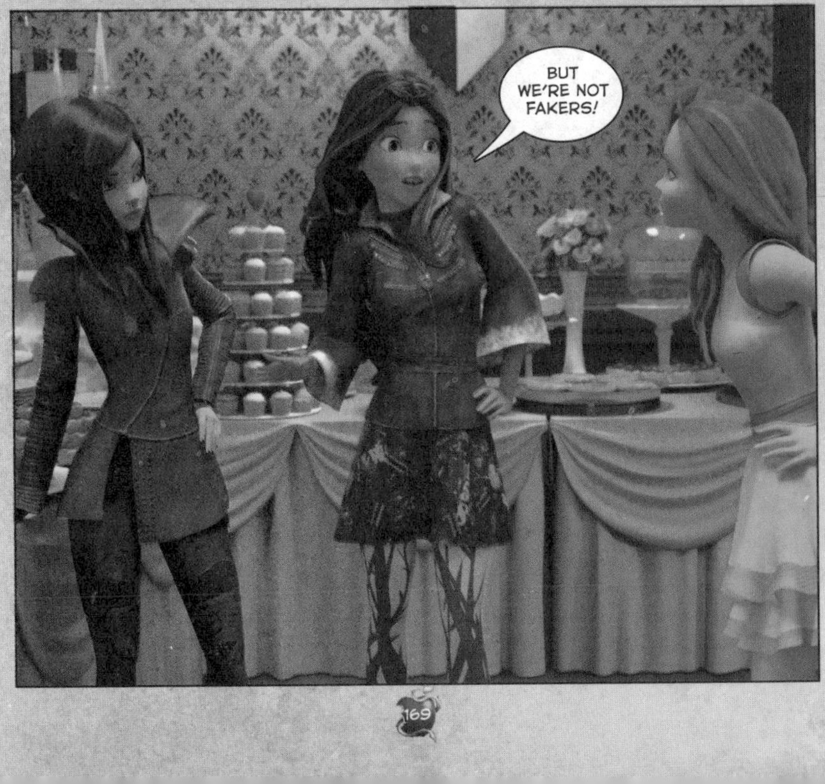
BUT WE'RE NOT FAKERS!

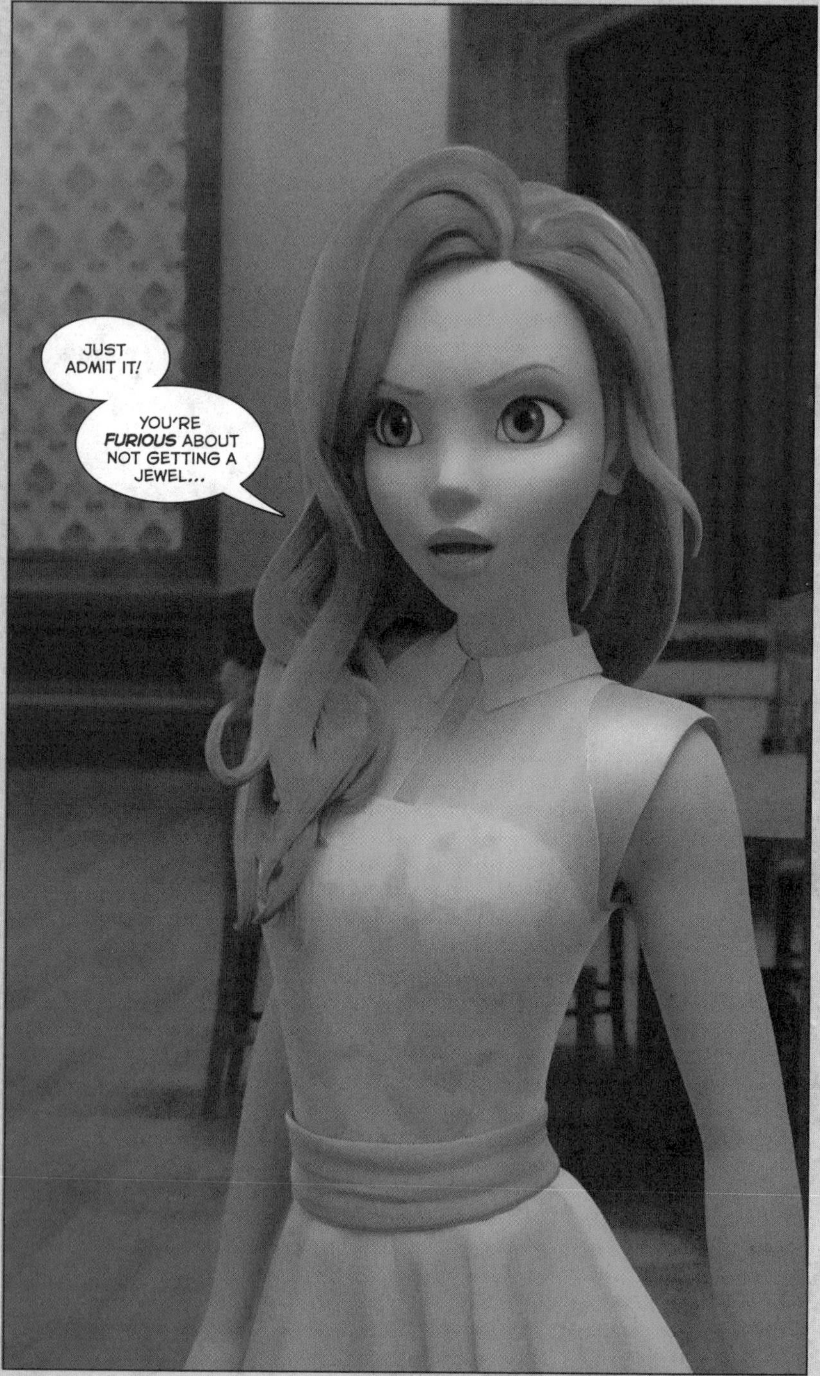
JUST ADMIT IT!
YOU'RE *FURIOUS* ABOUT NOT GETTING A JEWEL...

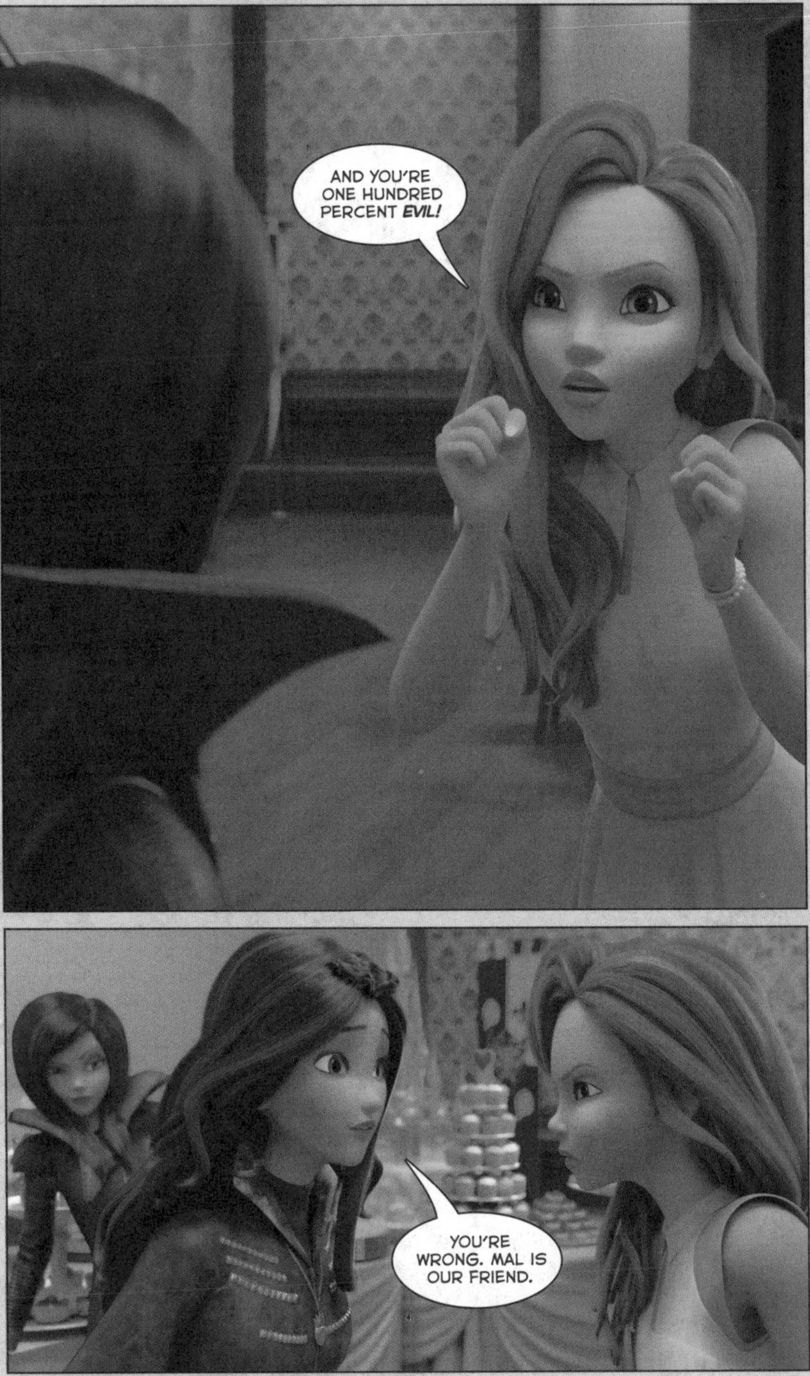
AND YOU'RE ONE HUNDRED PERCENT EVIL!
YOU'RE WRONG. MAL IS OUR FRIEND.

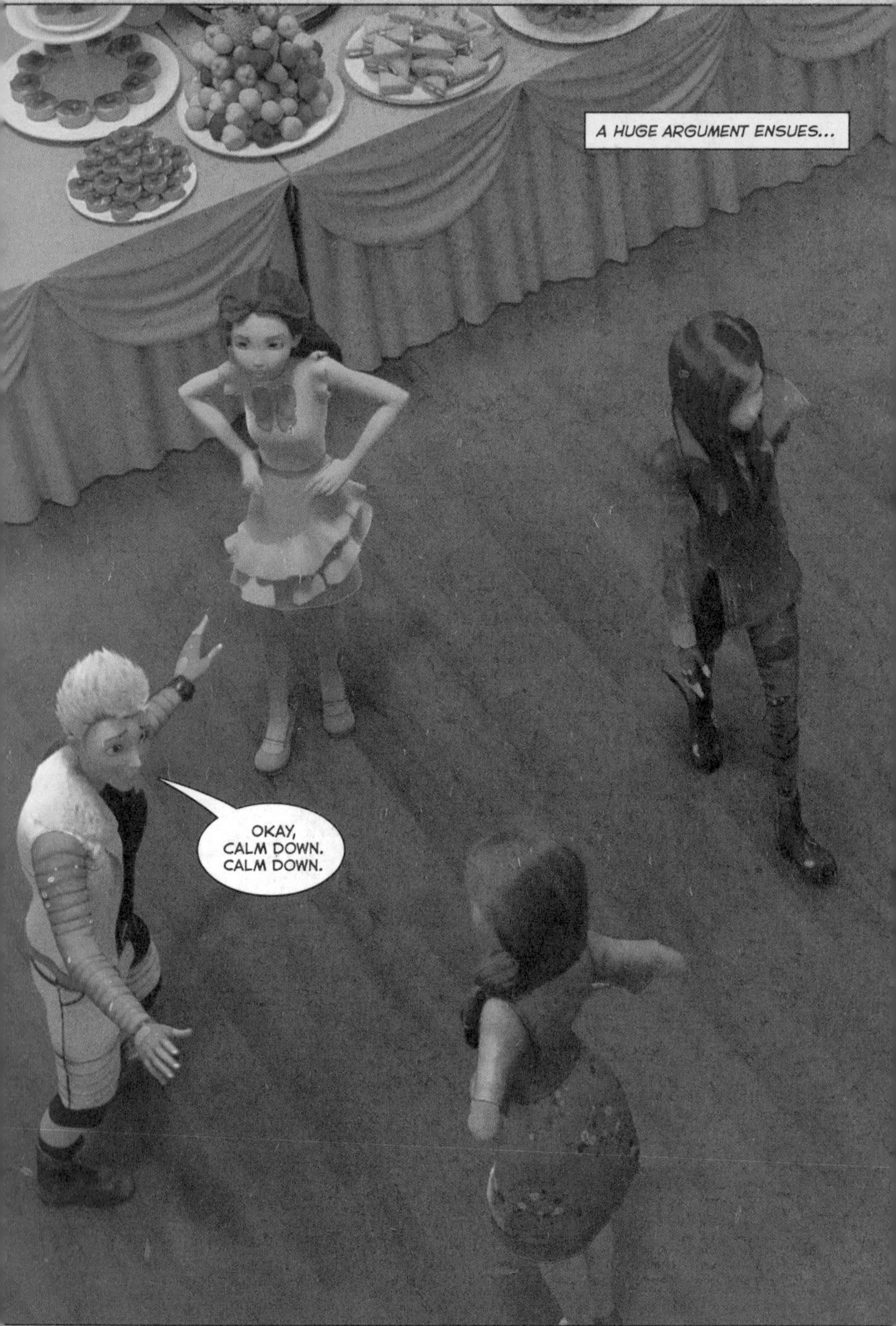
A HUGE ARGUMENT ENSUES...
OKAY, CALM DOWN. CALM DOWN.

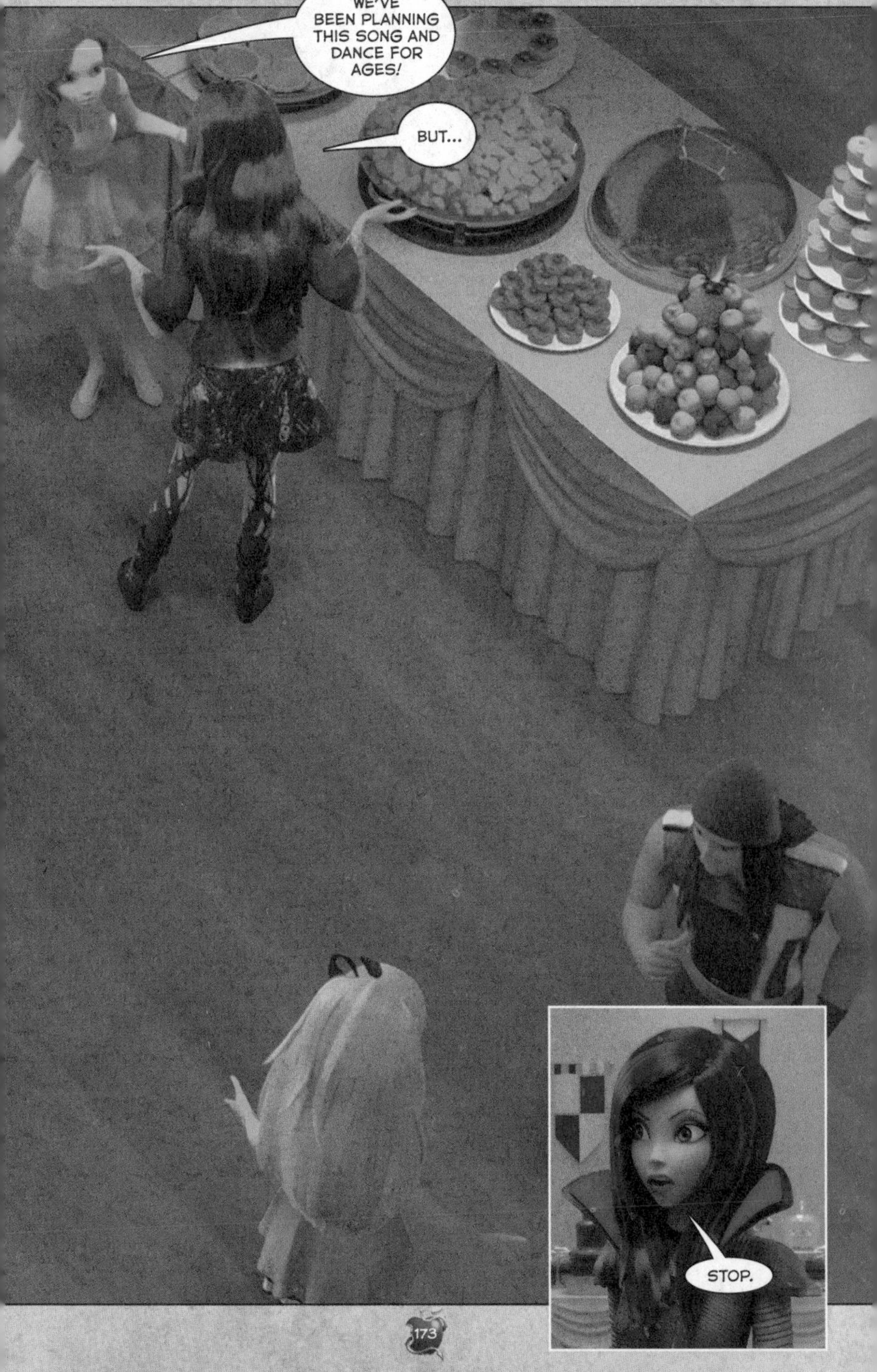
WE'VE BEEN PLANNING THIS SONG AND DANCE FOR AGES!
BUT...
STOP.

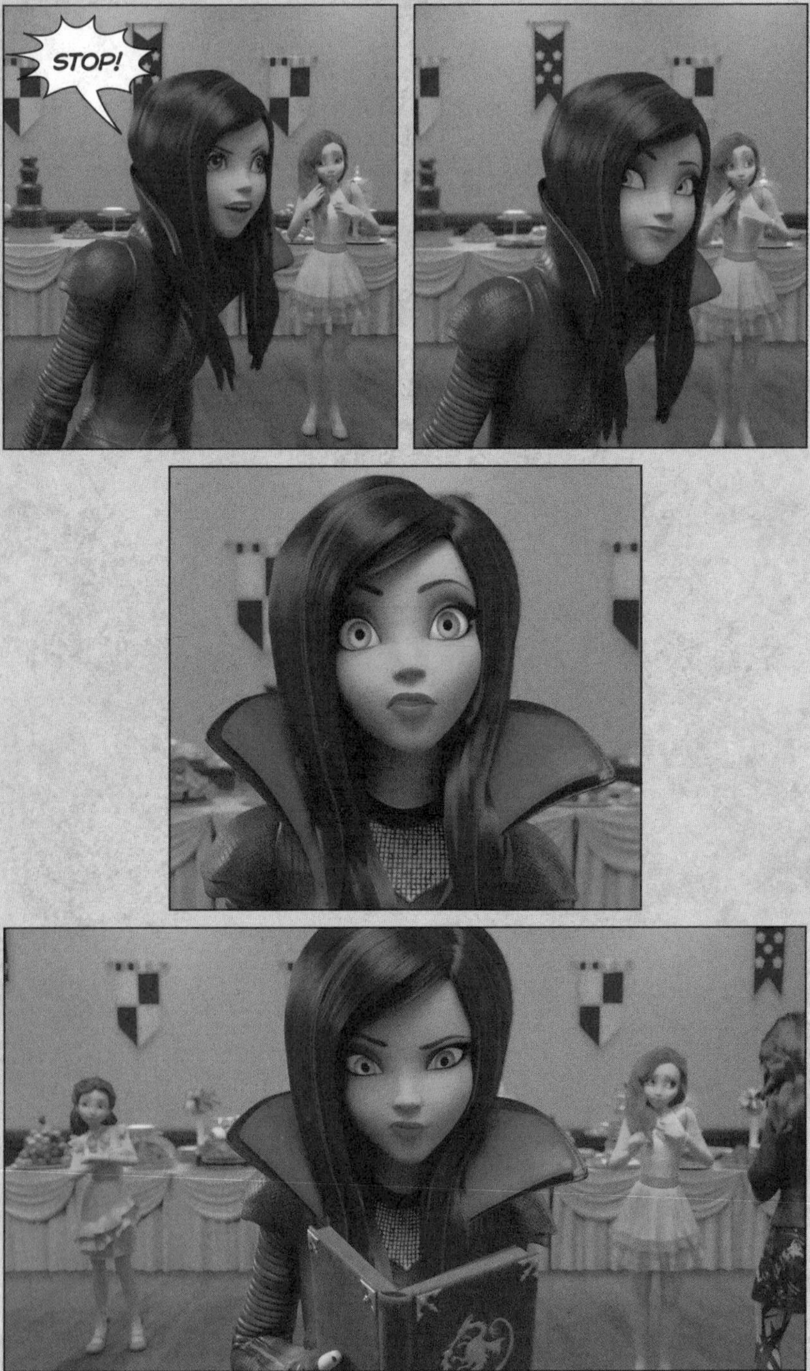
STOP!

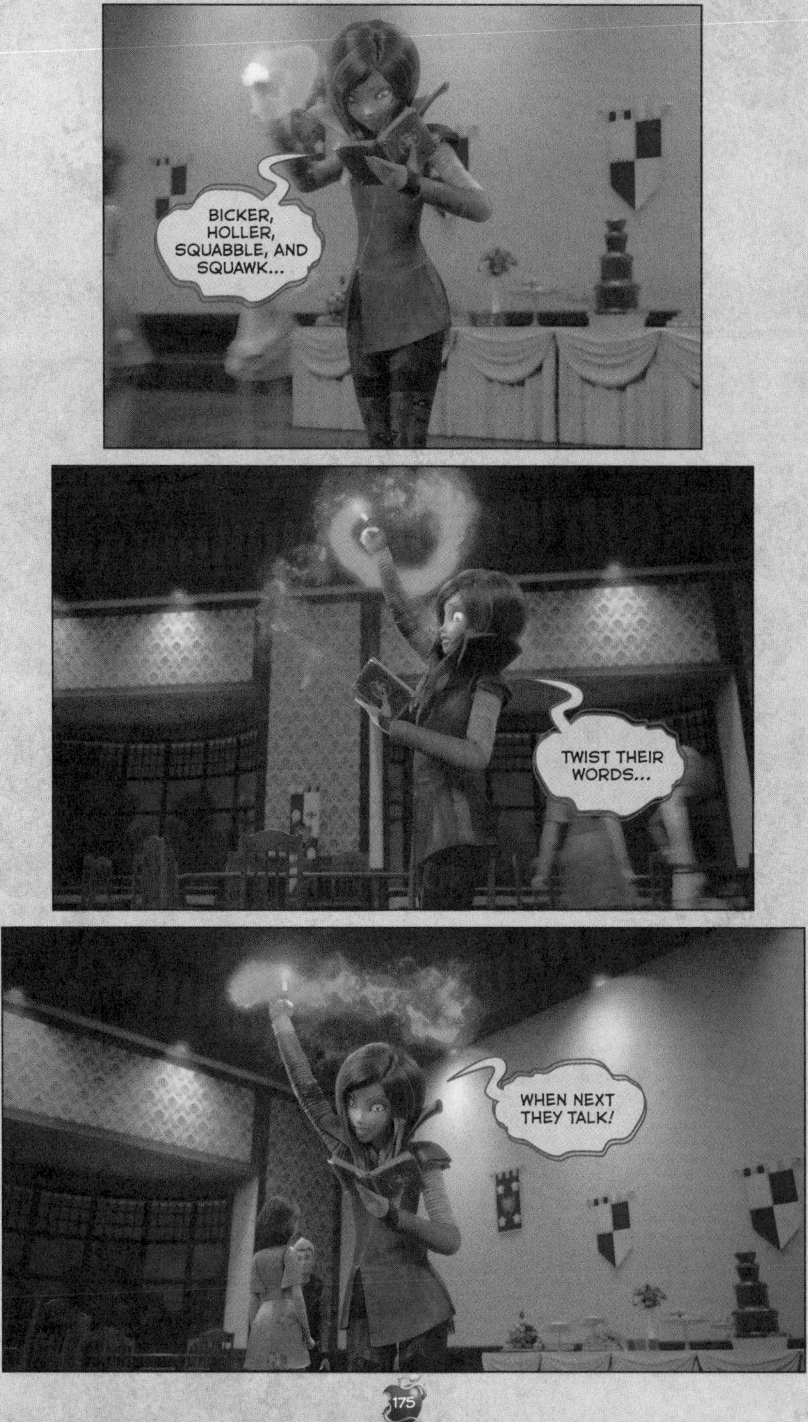
BICKER, HOLLER, SQUABBLE, AND SQUAWK...
TWIST THEIR WORDS...
WHEN NEXT THEY TALK!

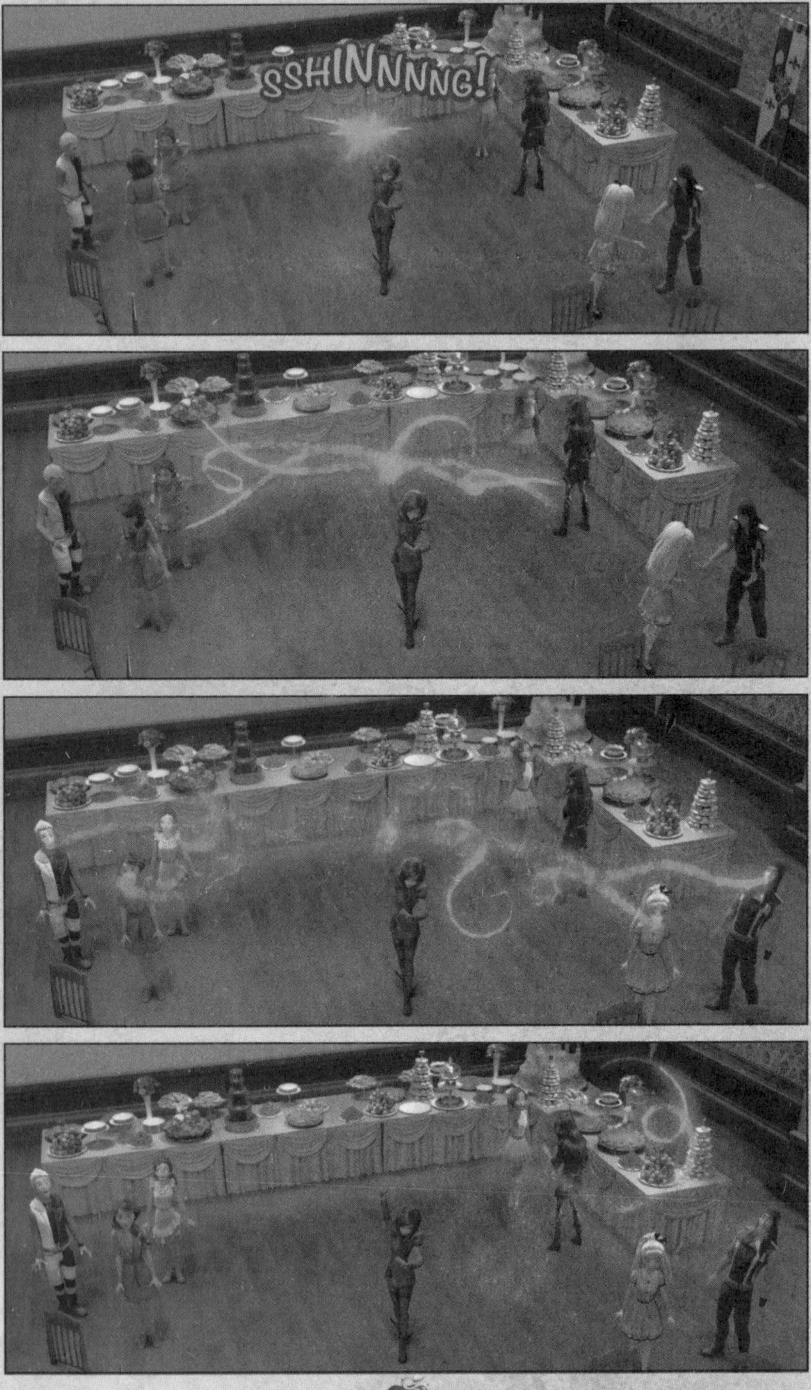
SSHINNNNG!

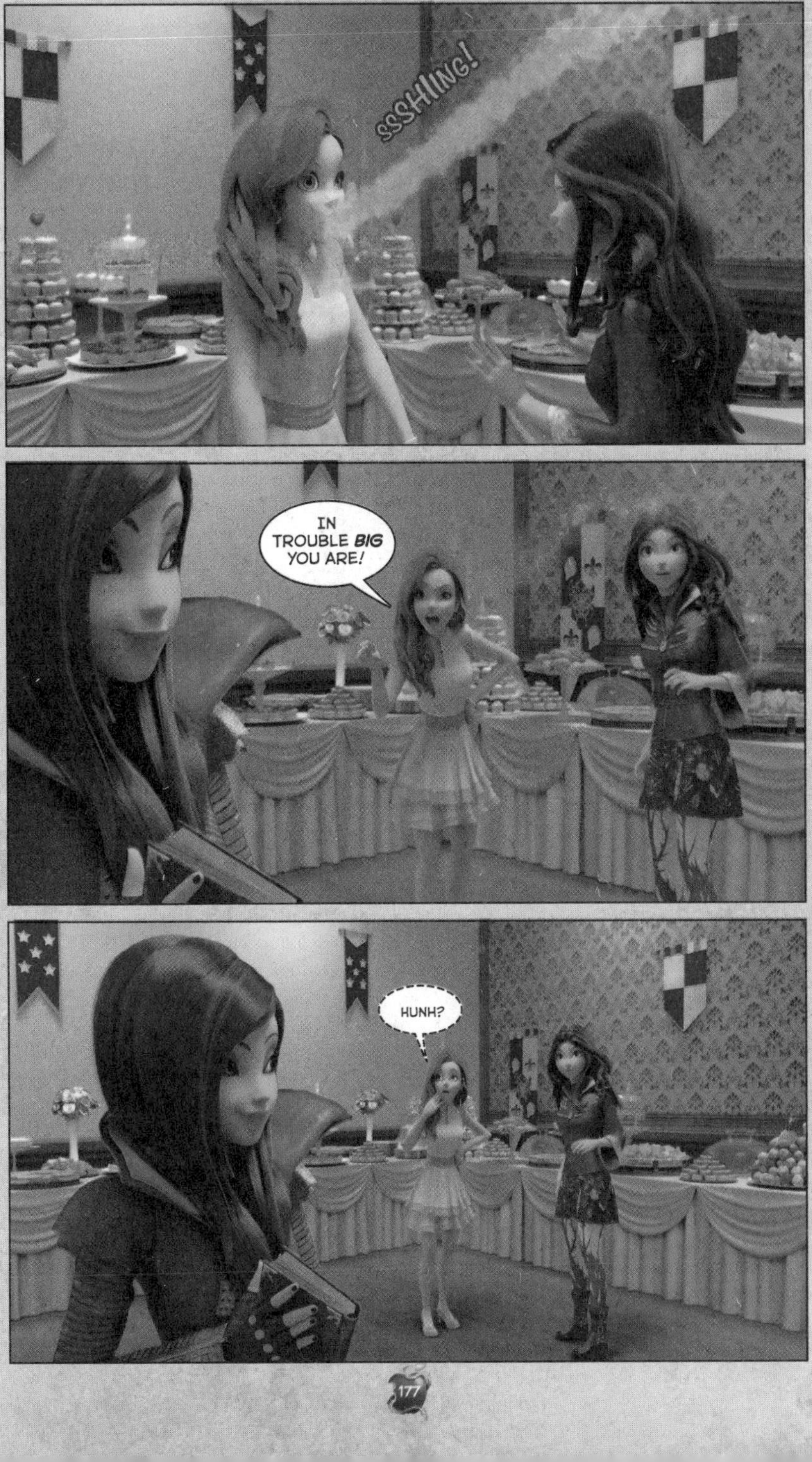
SSSHIING!
IN TROUBLE *BIG* YOU ARE!
HUNH?

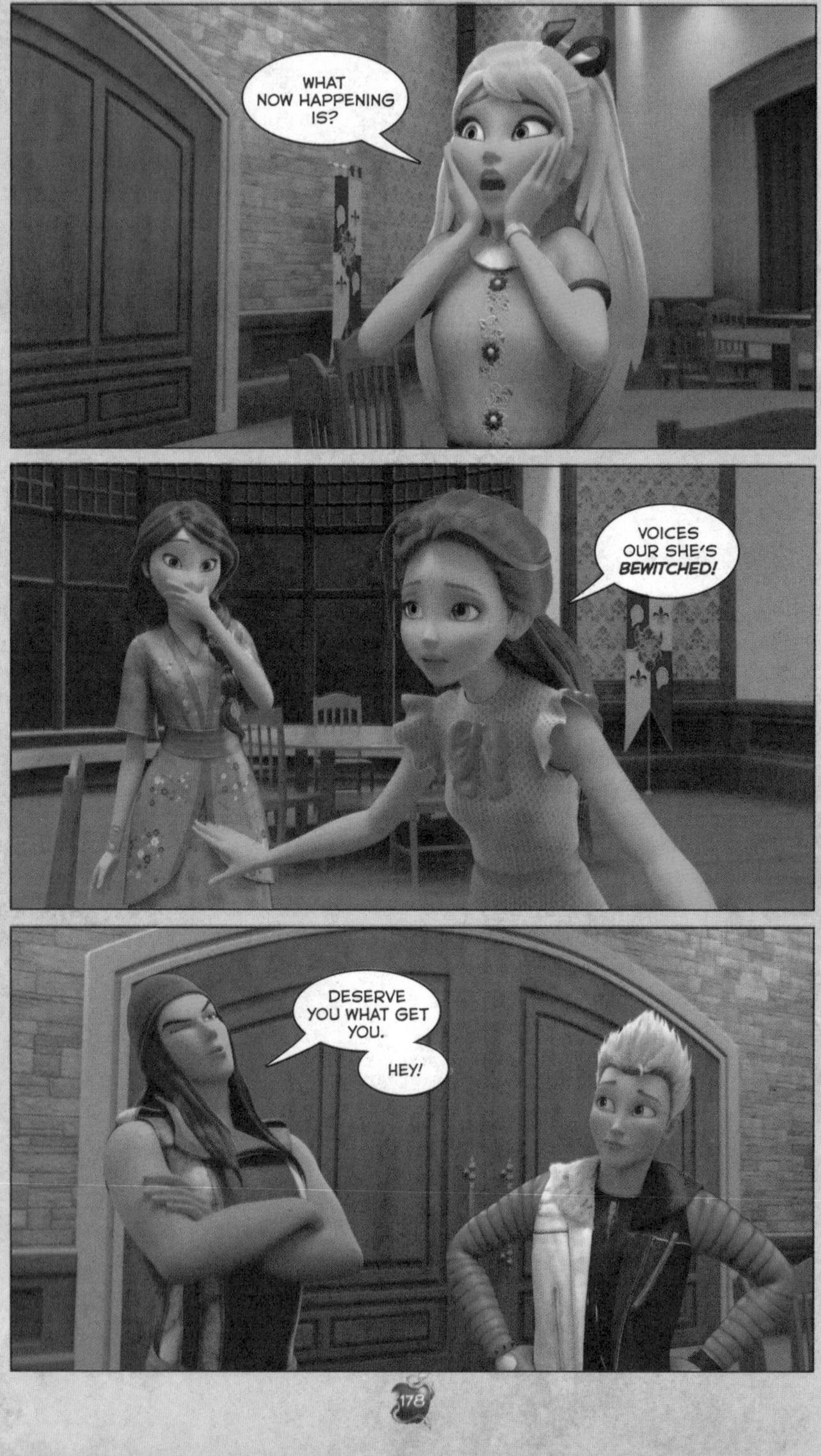
WHAT NOW HAPPENING IS?
VOICES OUR SHE'S *BEWITCHED!*
DESERVE YOU WHAT GET YOU.
HEY!

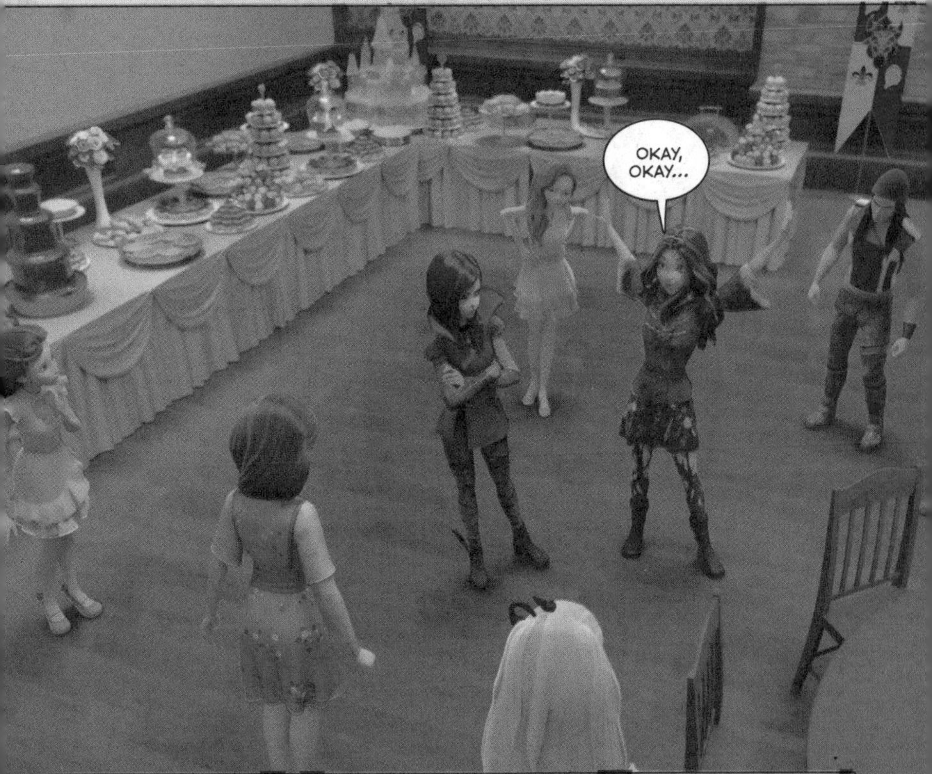
OKAY, OKAY...

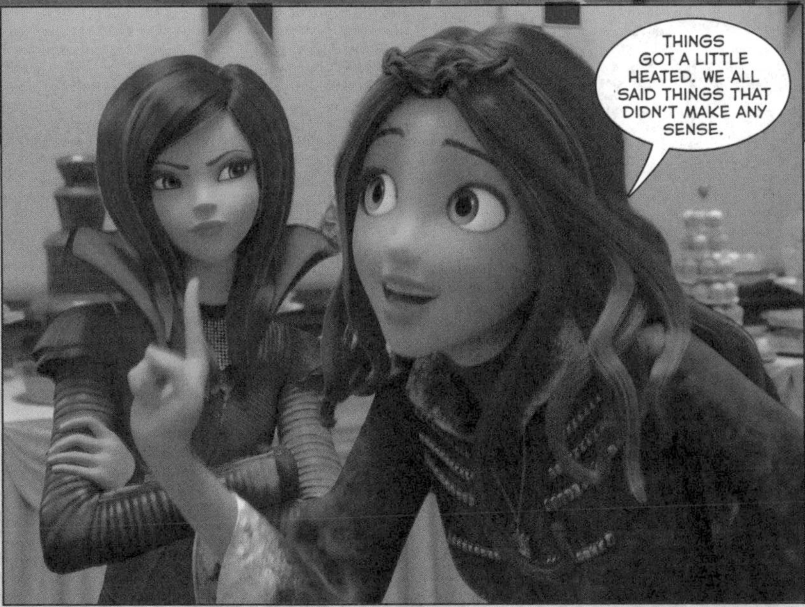
THINGS GOT A LITTLE HEATED. WE ALL SAID THINGS THAT DIDN'T MAKE ANY SENSE.

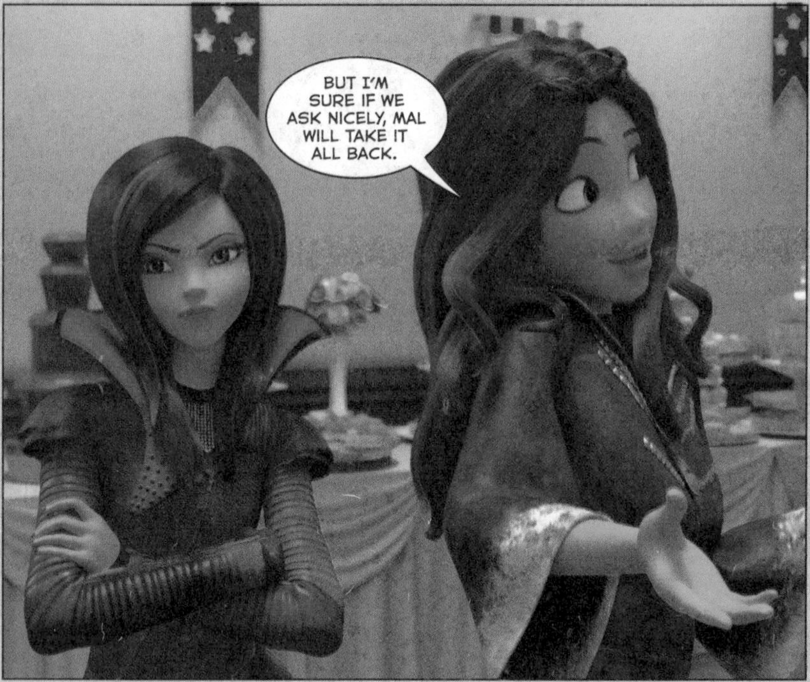
BUT I'M SURE IF WE ASK NICELY, MAL WILL TAKE IT ALL BACK.

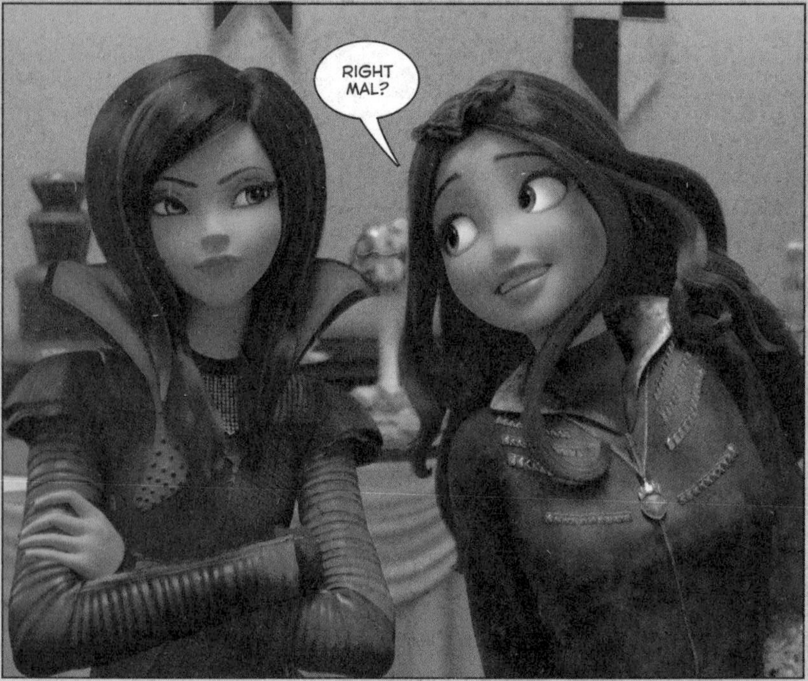
RIGHT MAL?

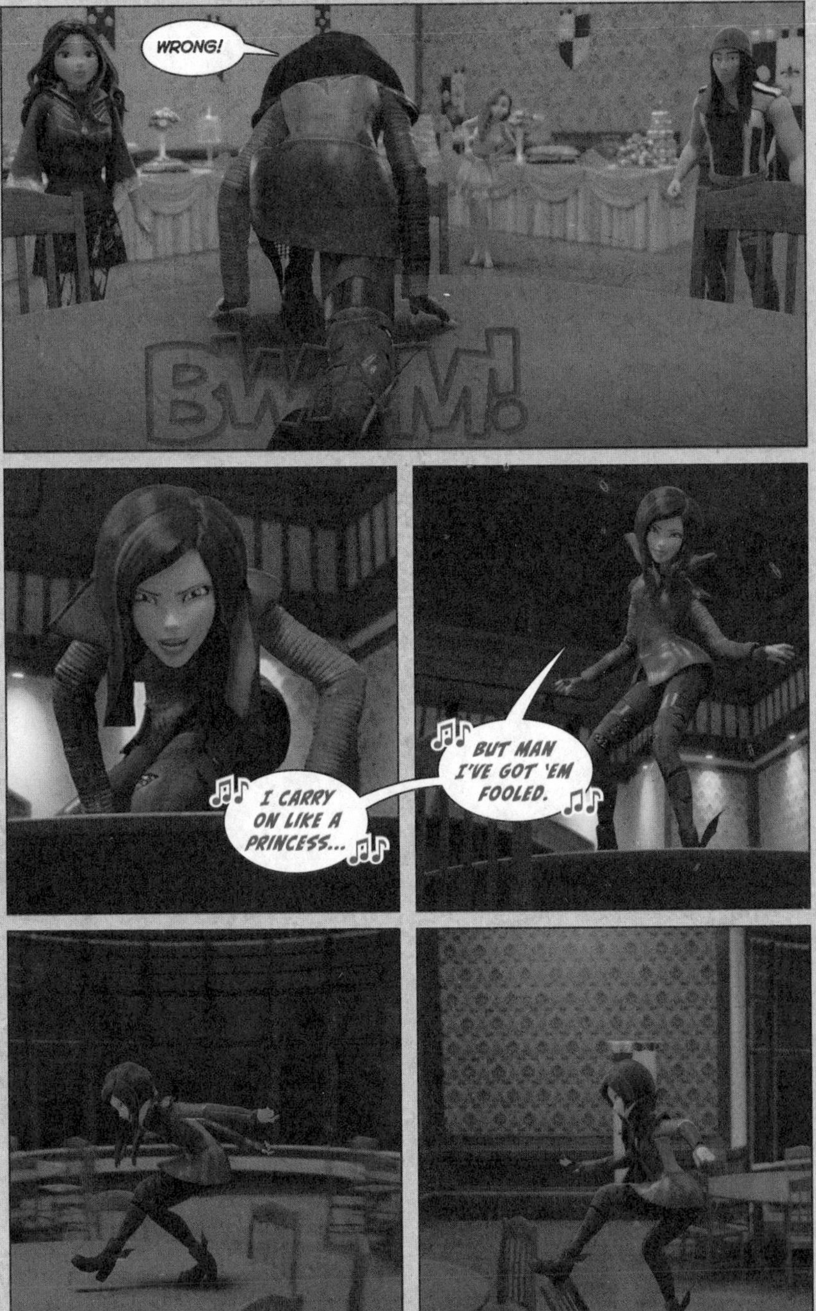
WRONG!
I CARRY ON LIKE A PRINCESS...
BUT MAN I'VE GOT 'EM FOOLED.

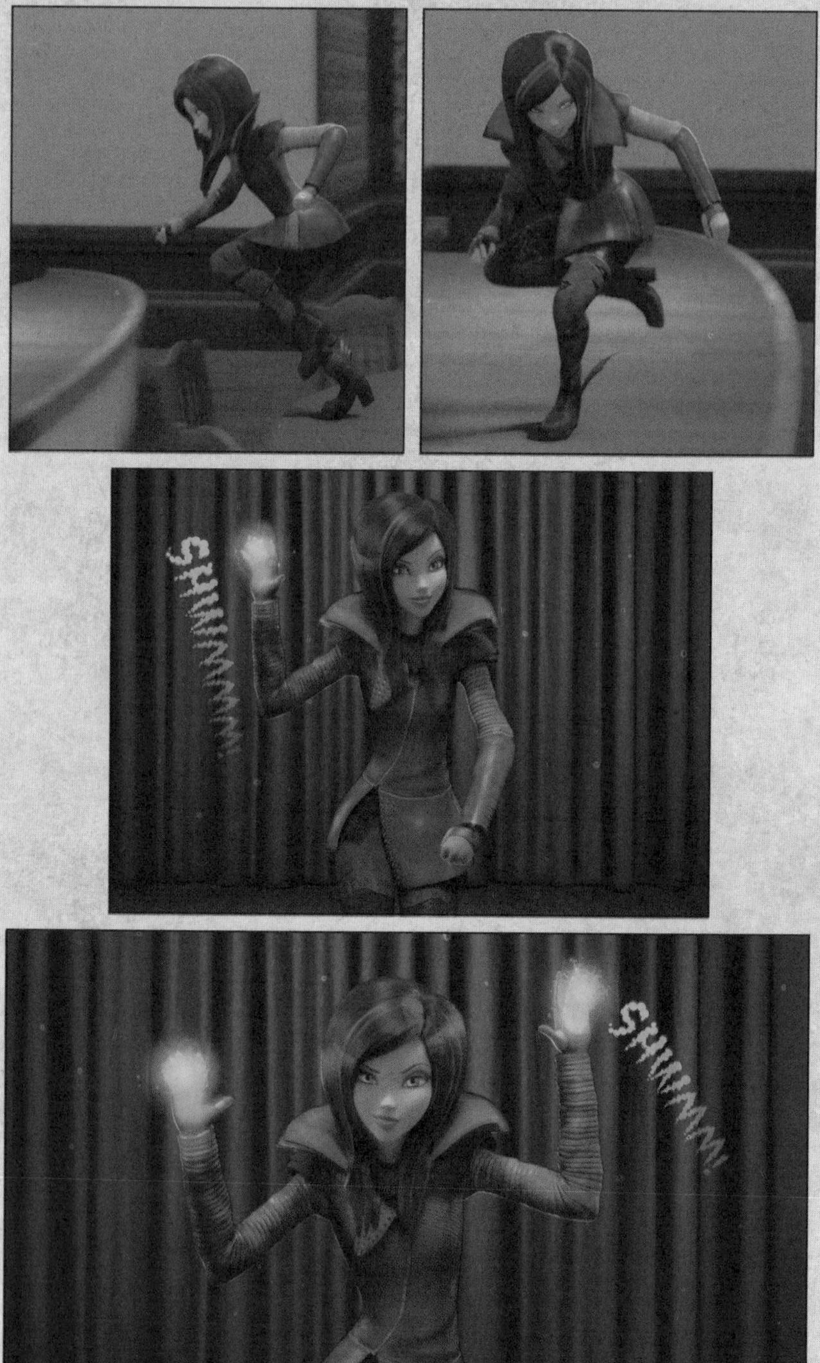
SHMMMMMM!
SHMMMM!

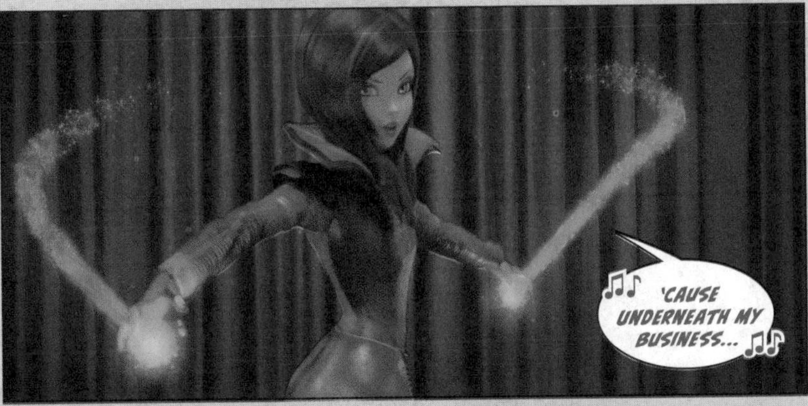
'CAUSE UNDERNEATH MY BUSINESS...

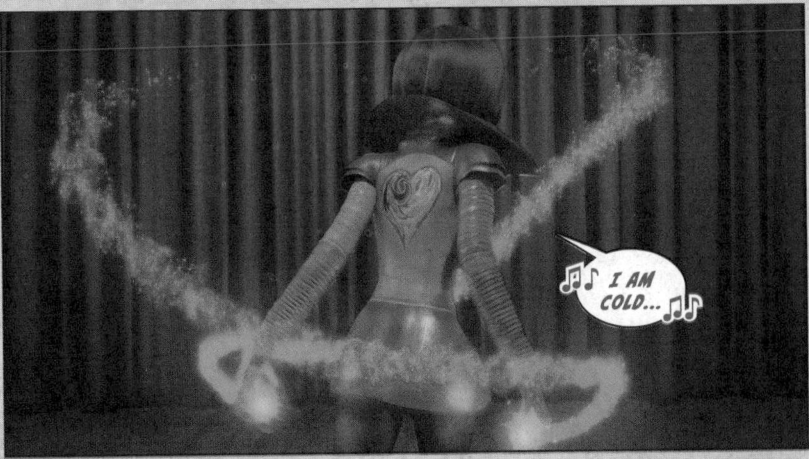
I AM COLD...

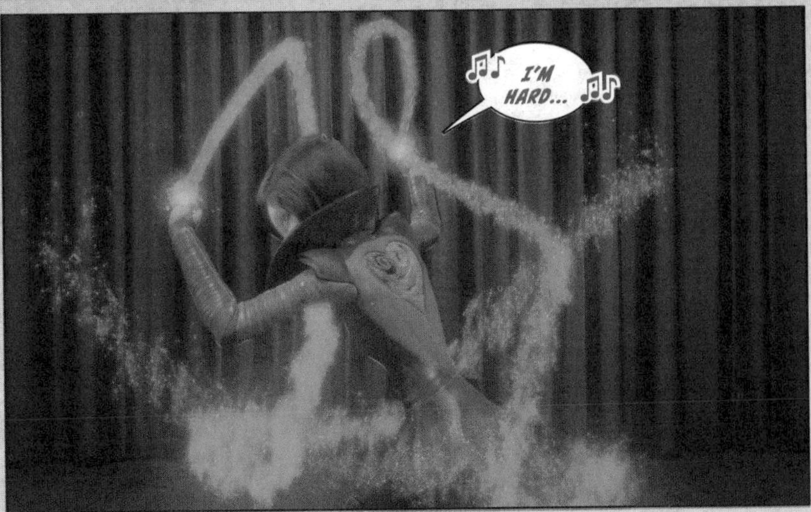
I'M HARD...

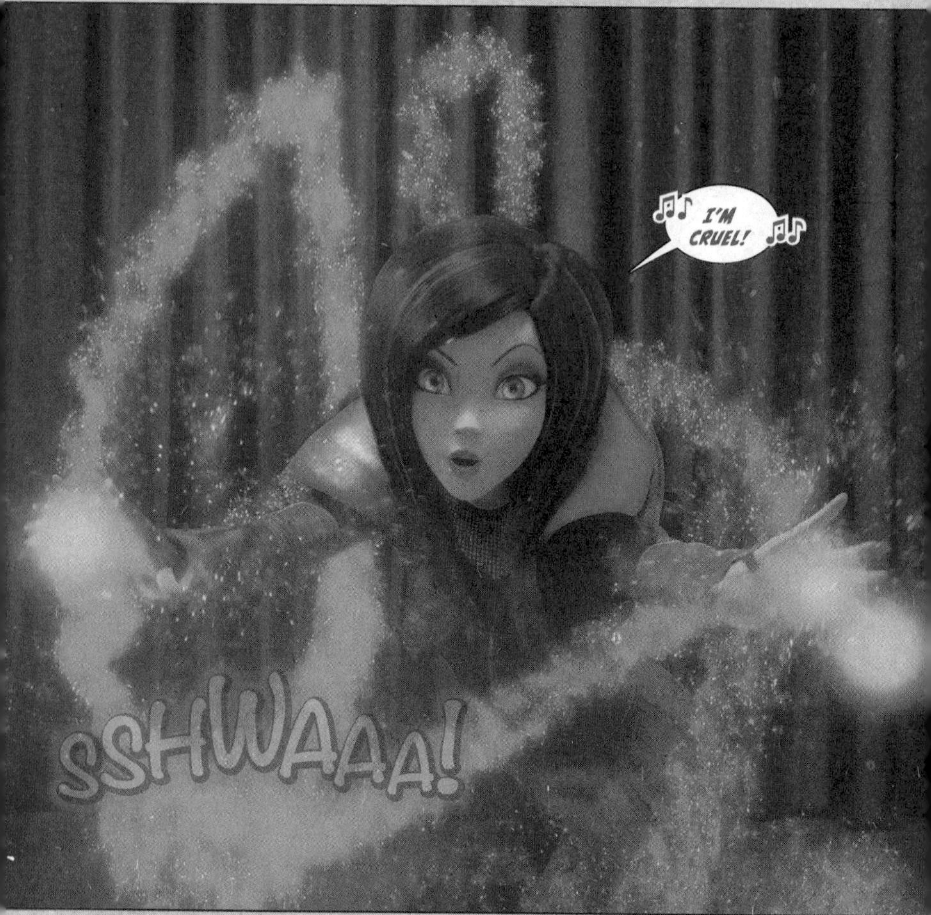
I'M CRUEL!
SSHWAAA!

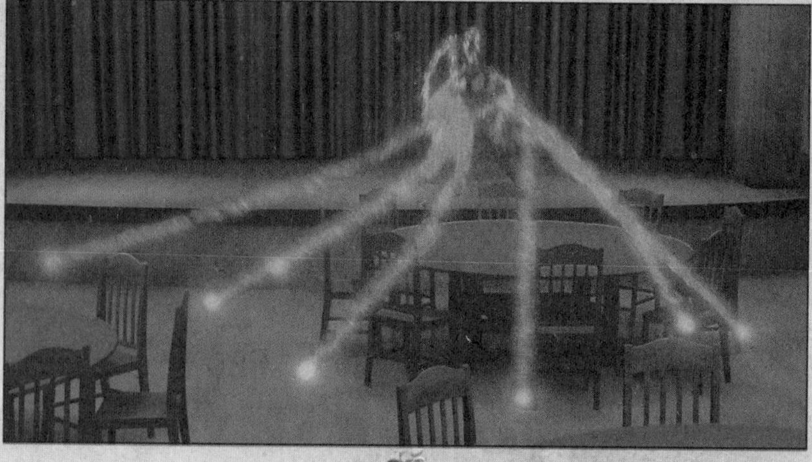

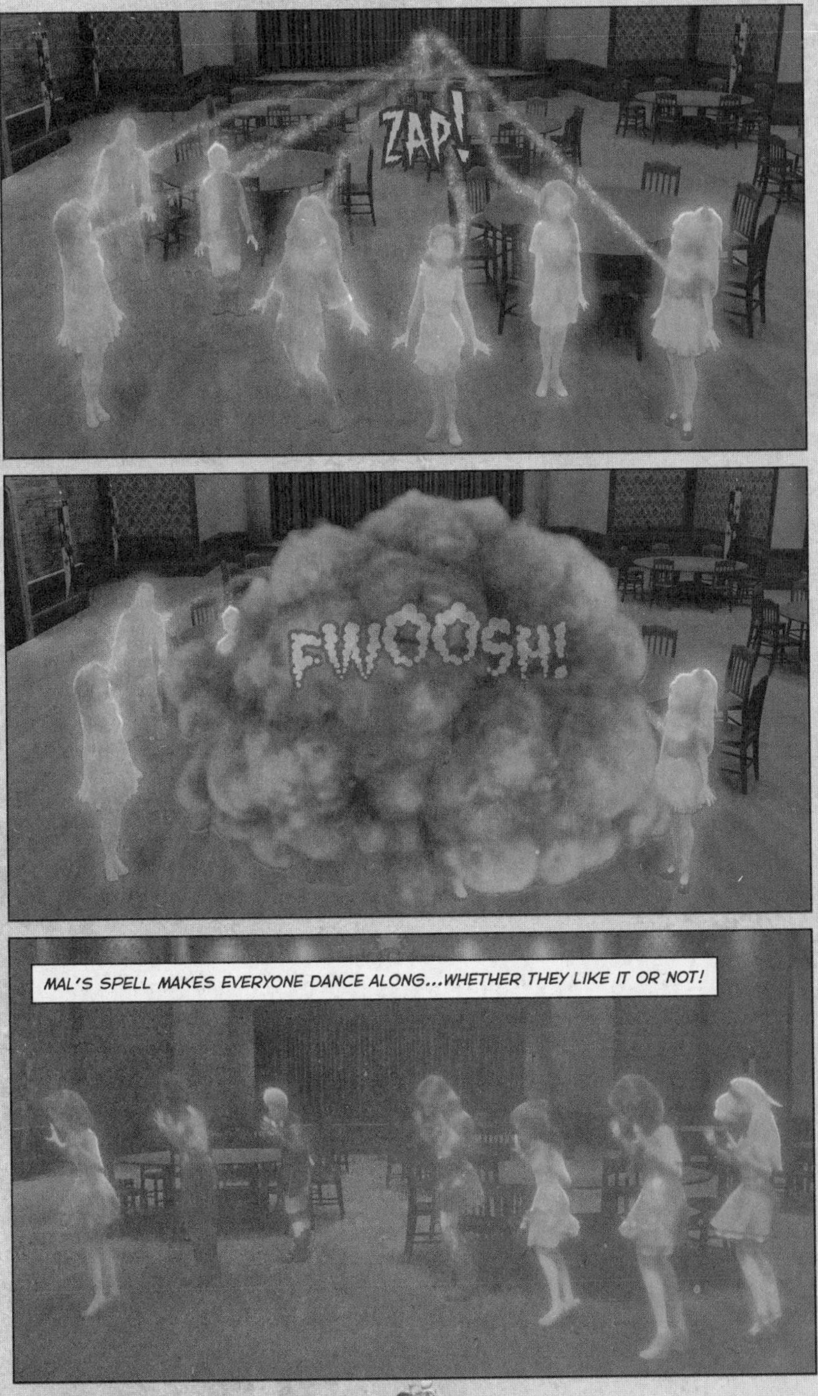
ZAP!
FWOOSH!
MAL'S SPELL MAKES EVERYONE DANCE ALONG...WHETHER THEY LIKE IT OR NOT!

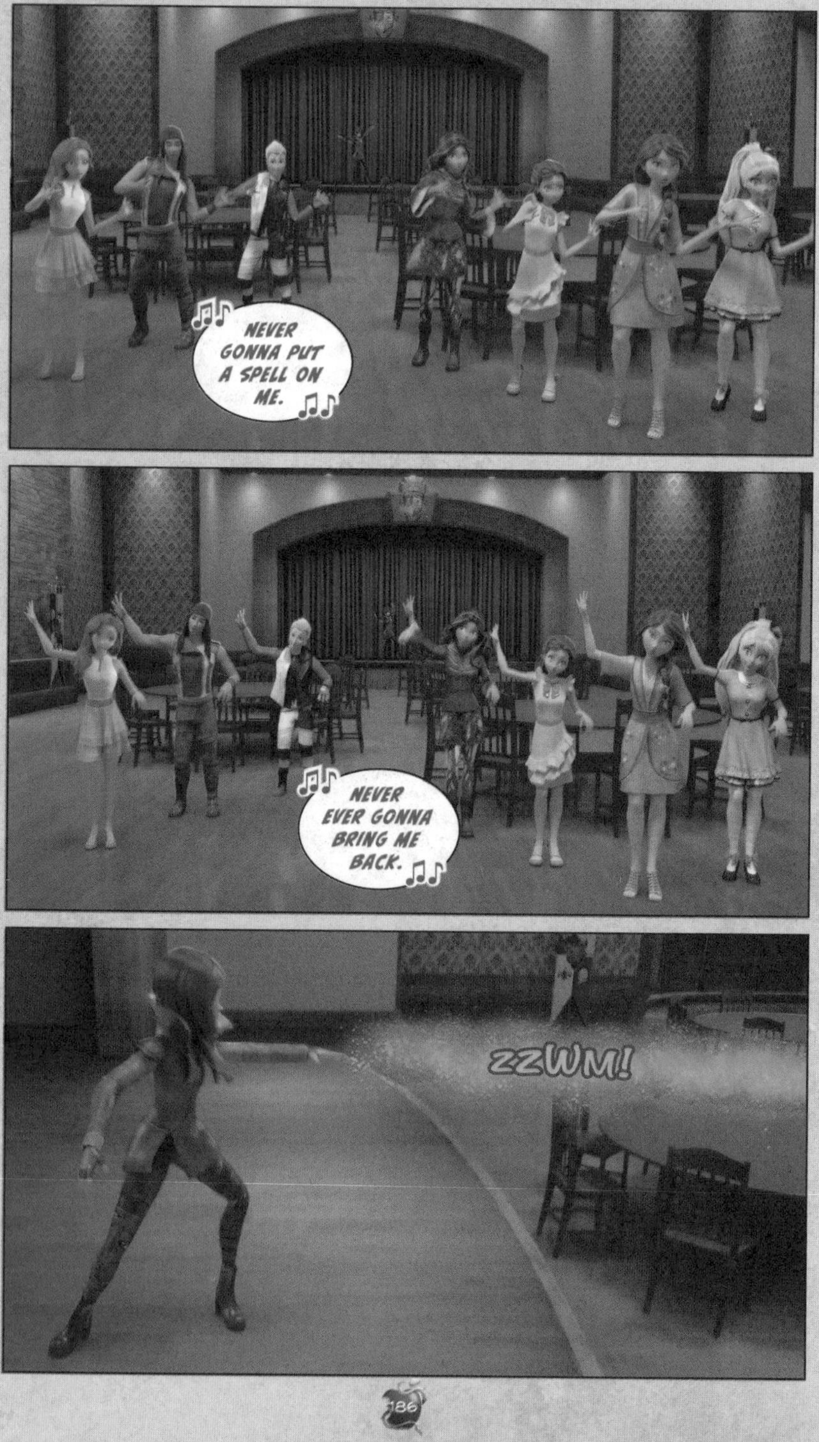
NEVER GONNA PUT A SPELL ON ME.
NEVER EVER GONNA BRING ME BACK.
ZZWM!

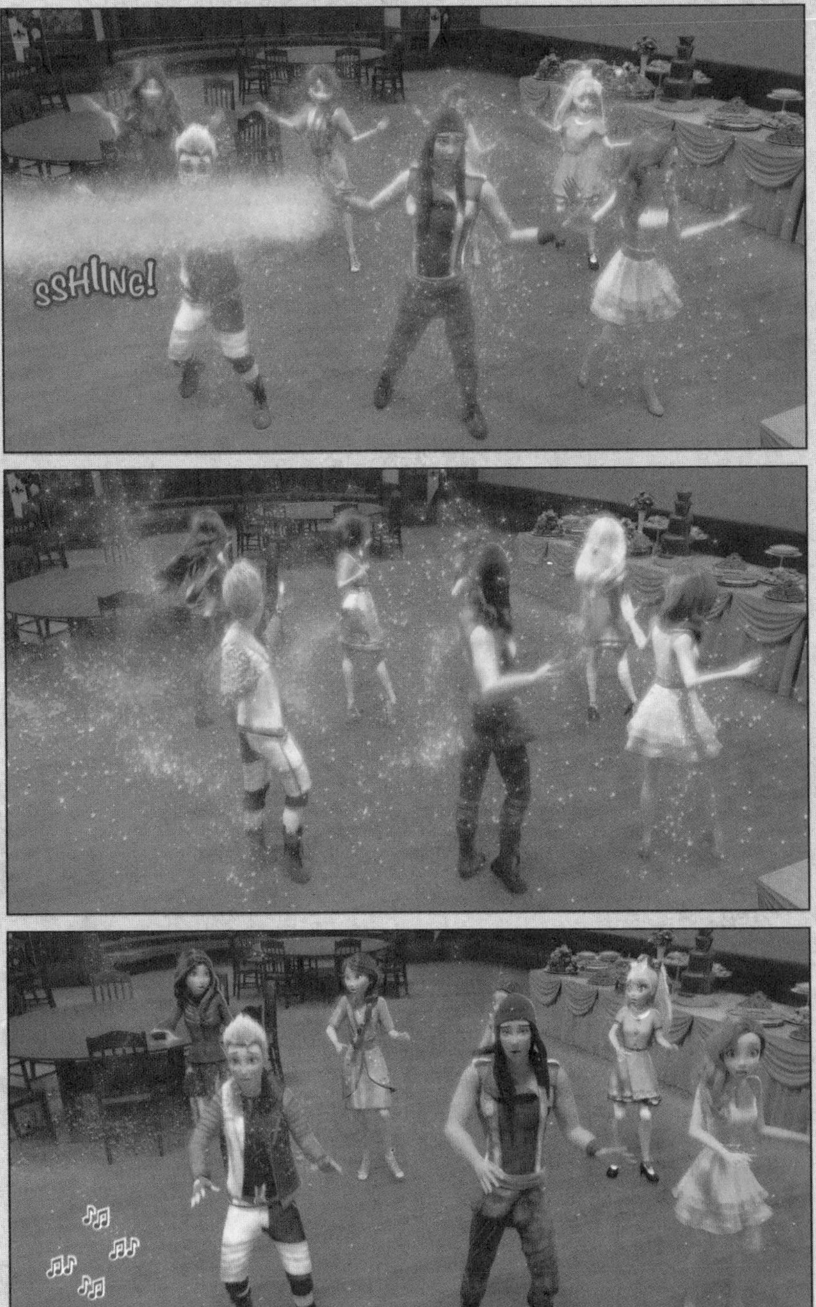
SSHIING!

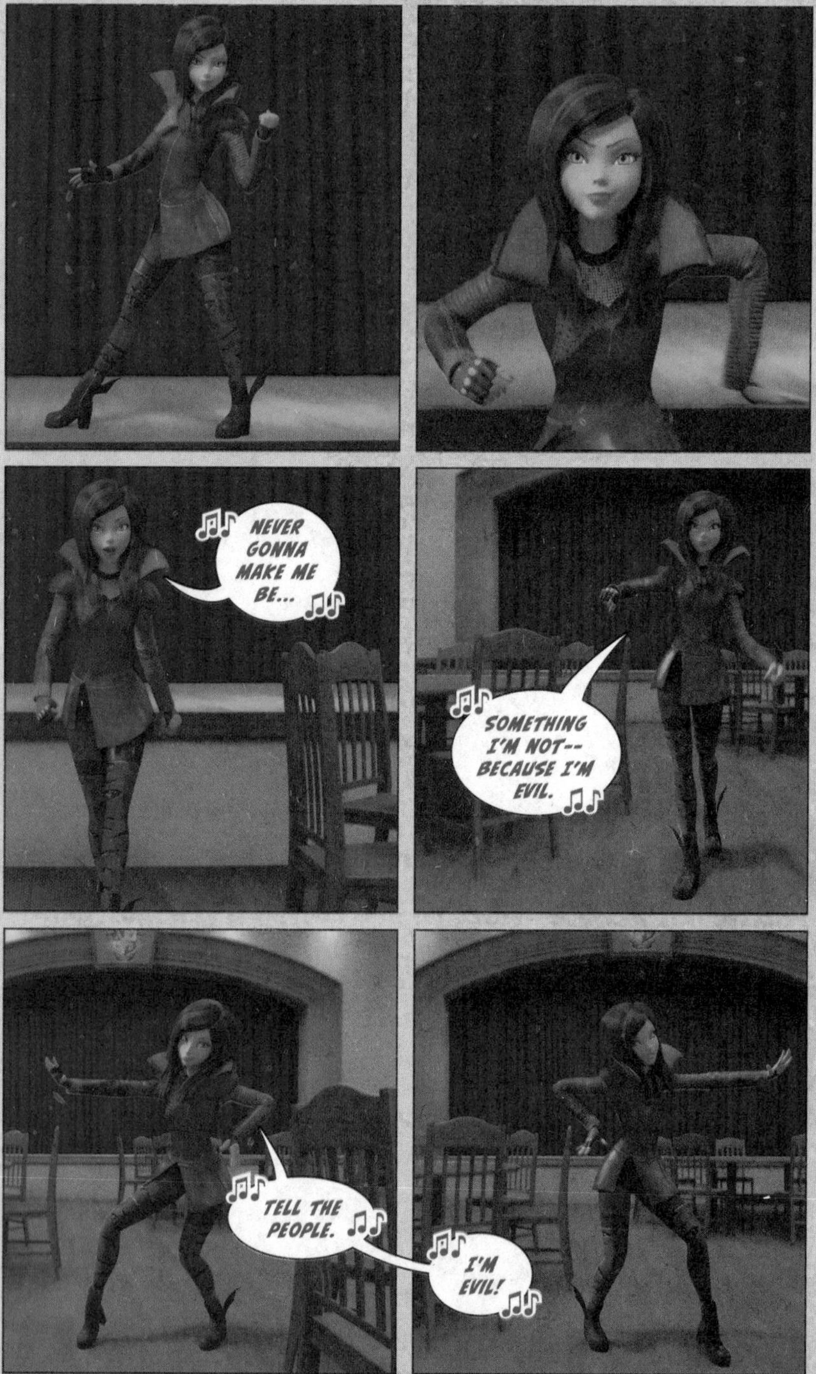
NEVER GONNA MAKE ME BE...
SOMETHING I'M NOT-- BECAUSE I'M EVIL.
TELL THE PEOPLE.
I'M EVIL!

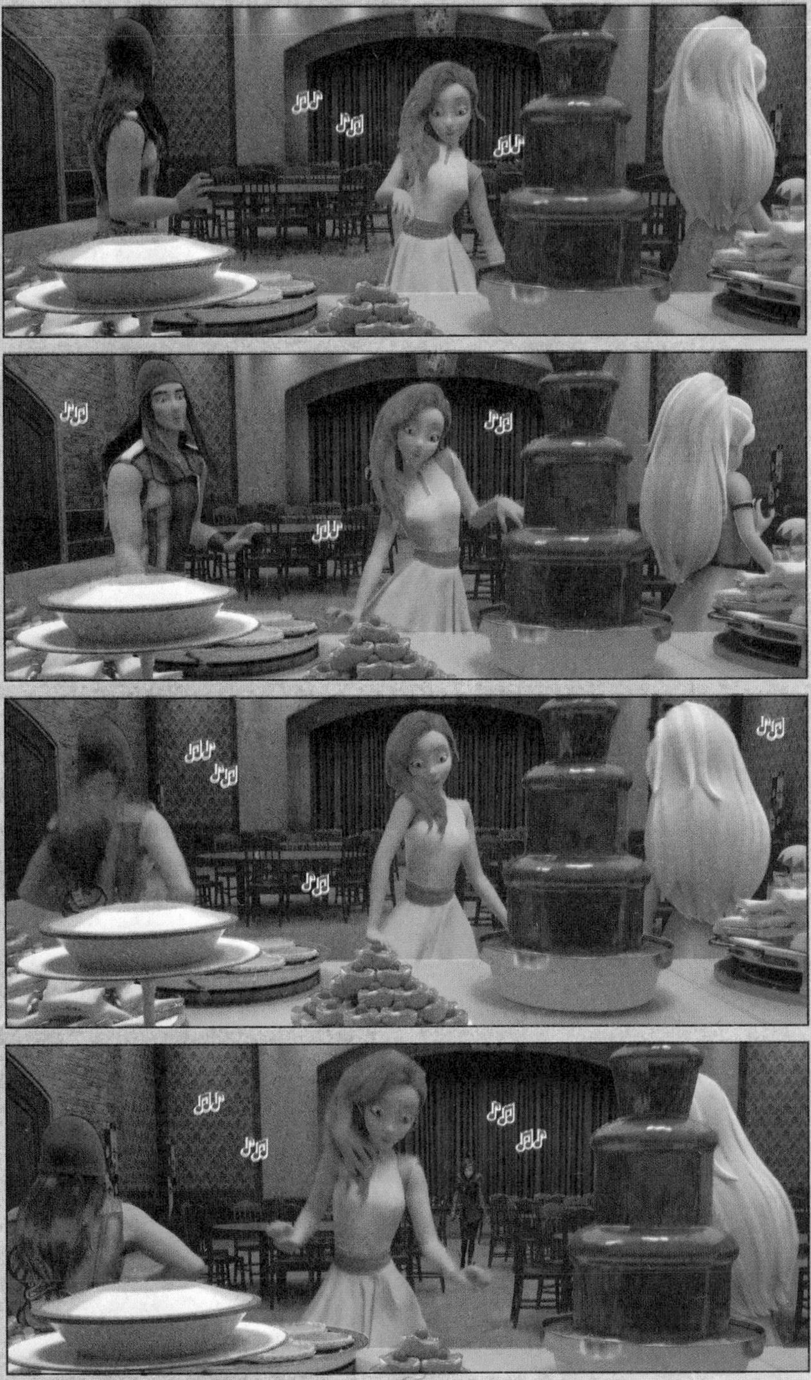

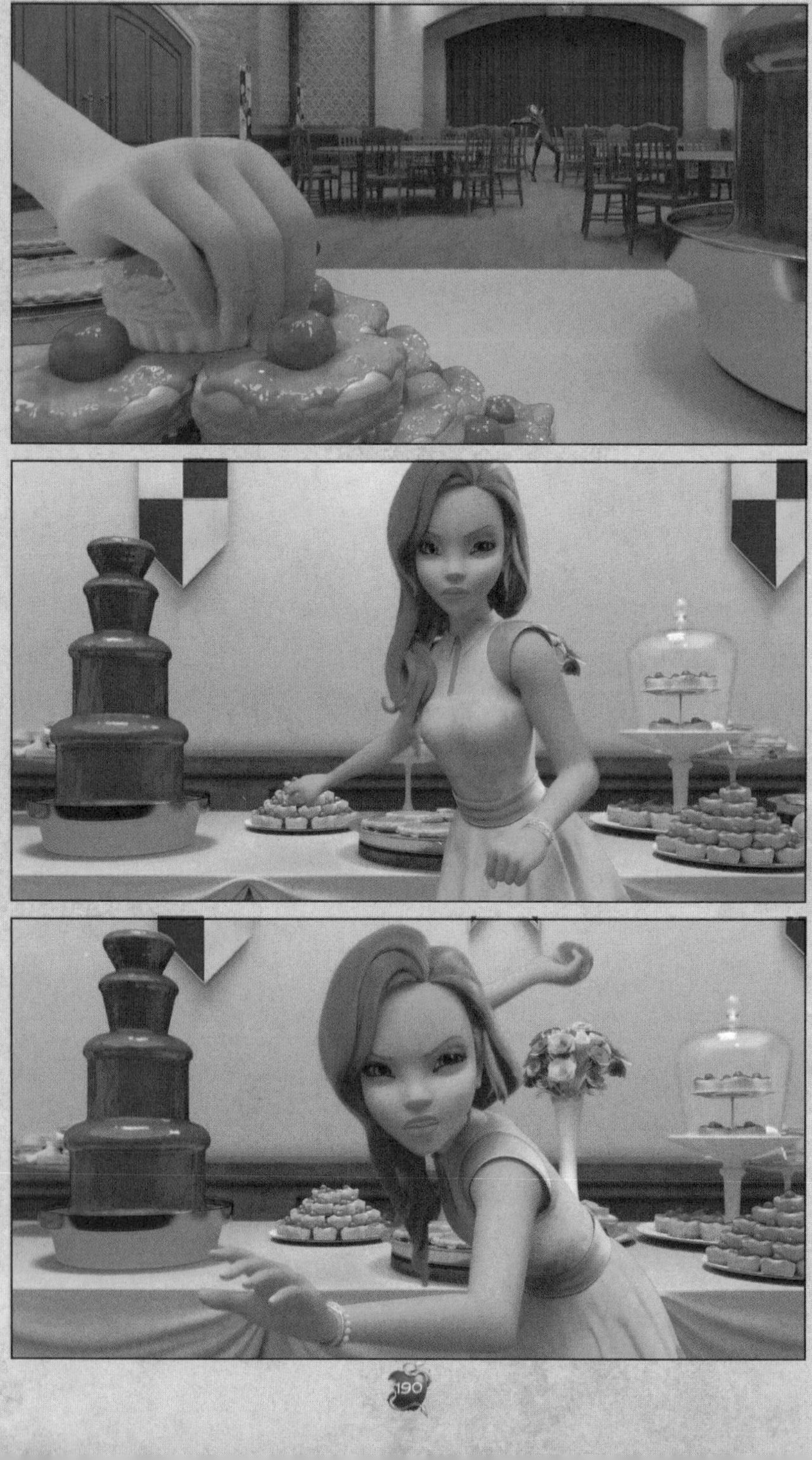

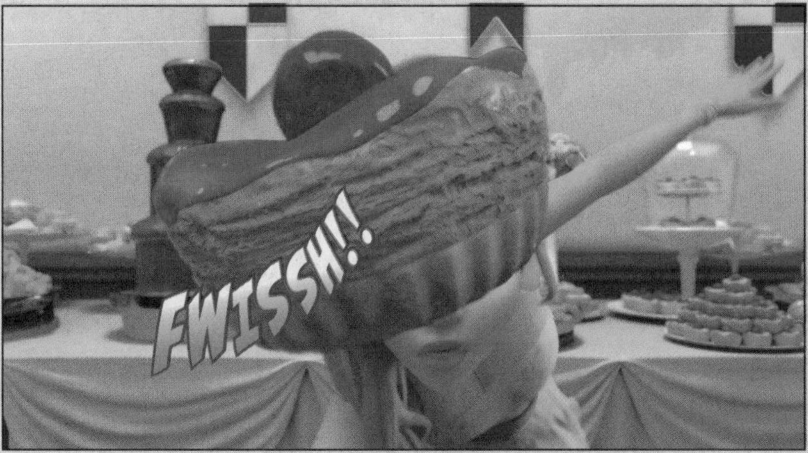
FWISSH!!

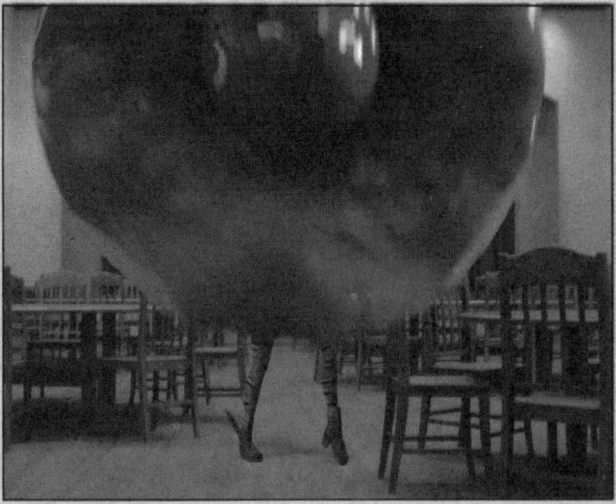

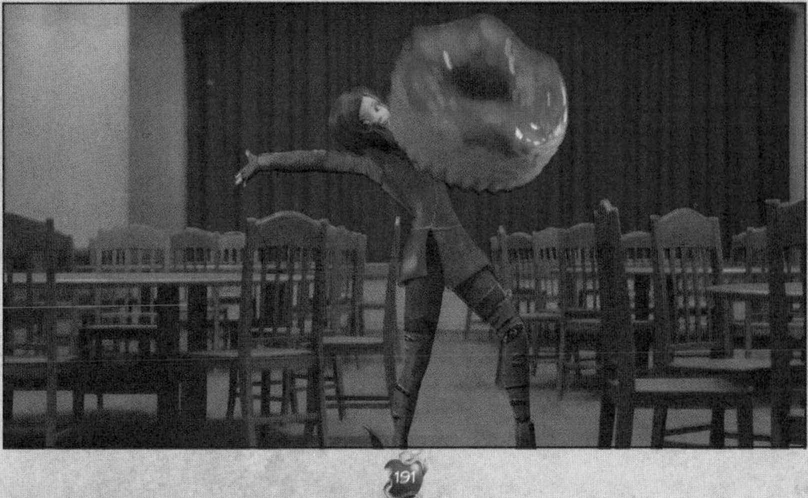

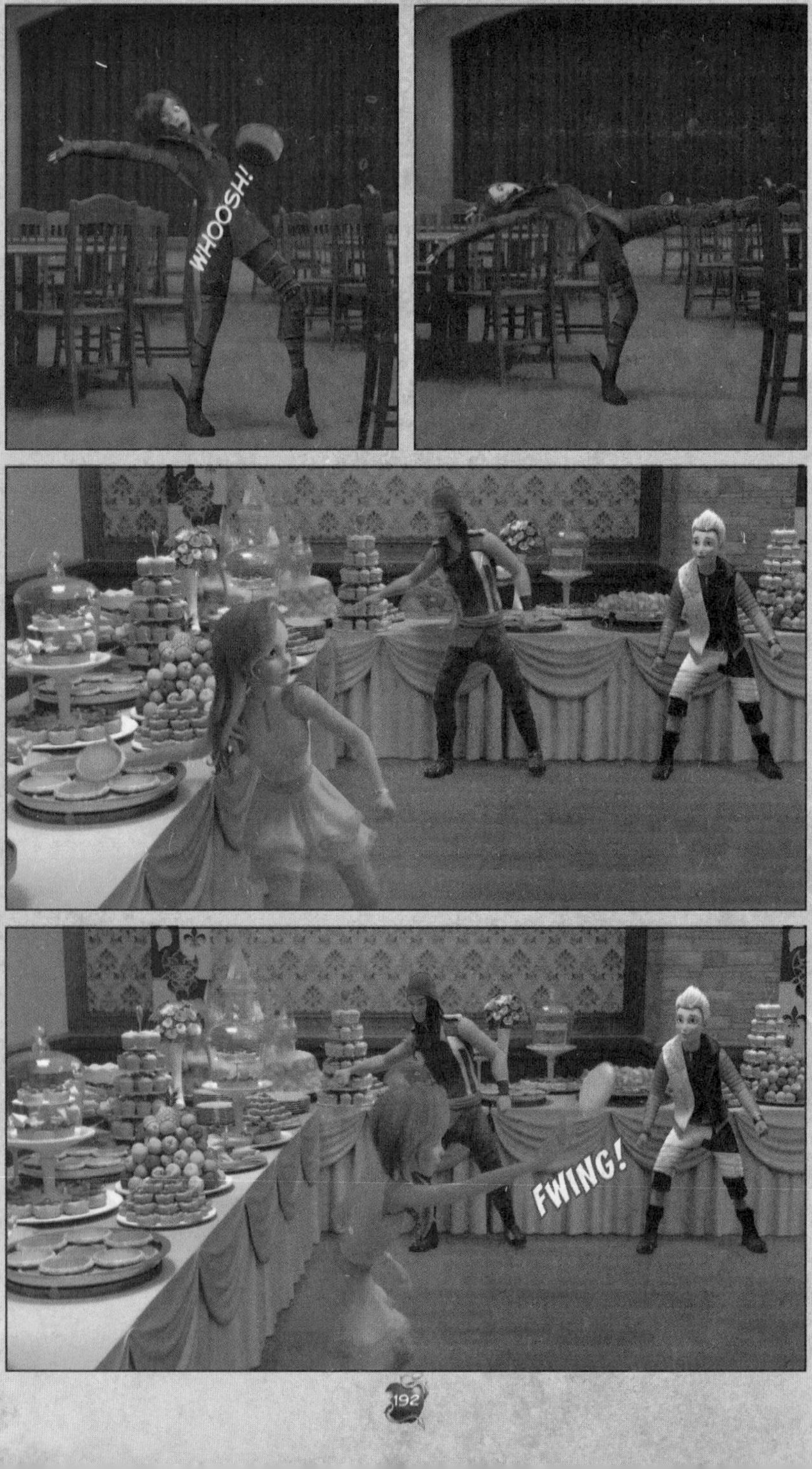
WHOOSH!
FWING!

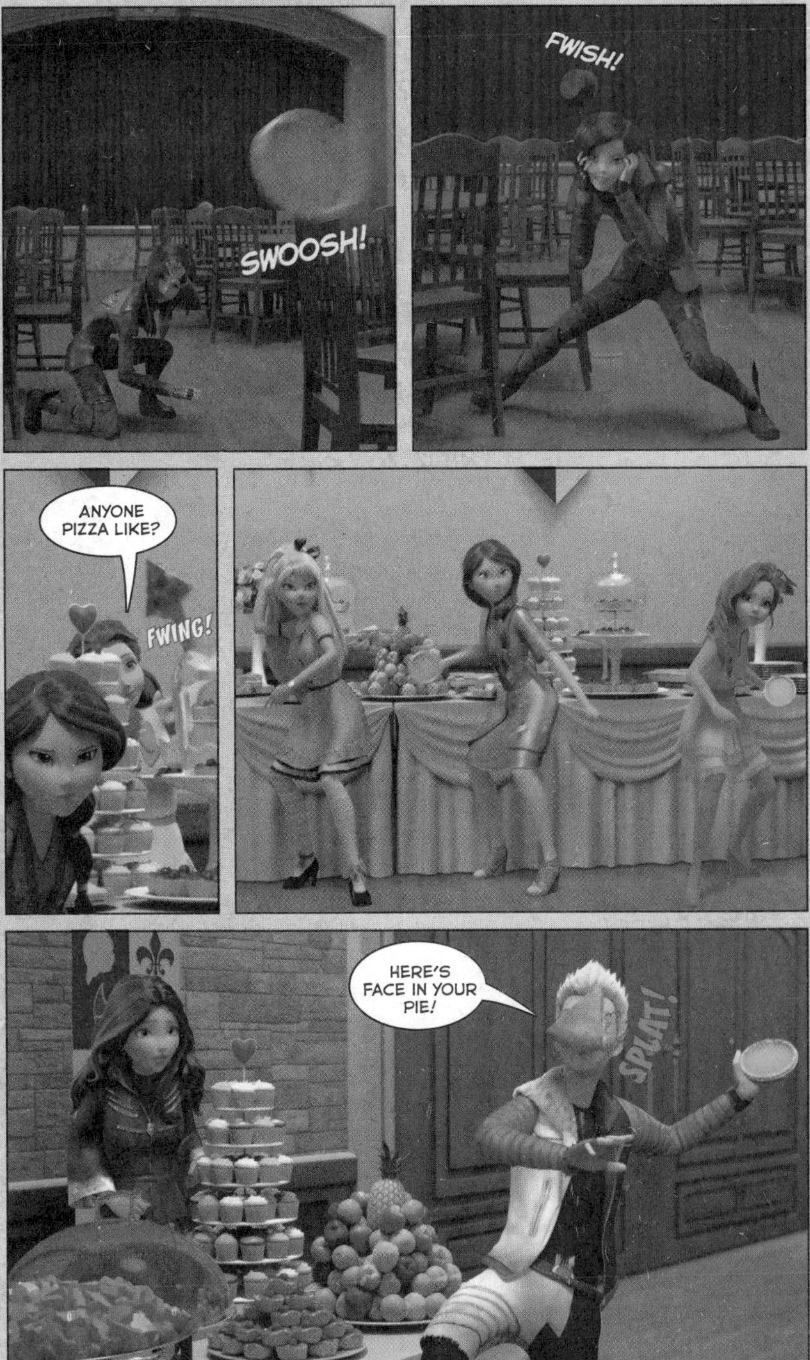
SWOOSH!
FWISH!
ANYONE PIZZA LIKE?
FWING!
HERE'S FACE IN YOUR PIE!
SPLAT!

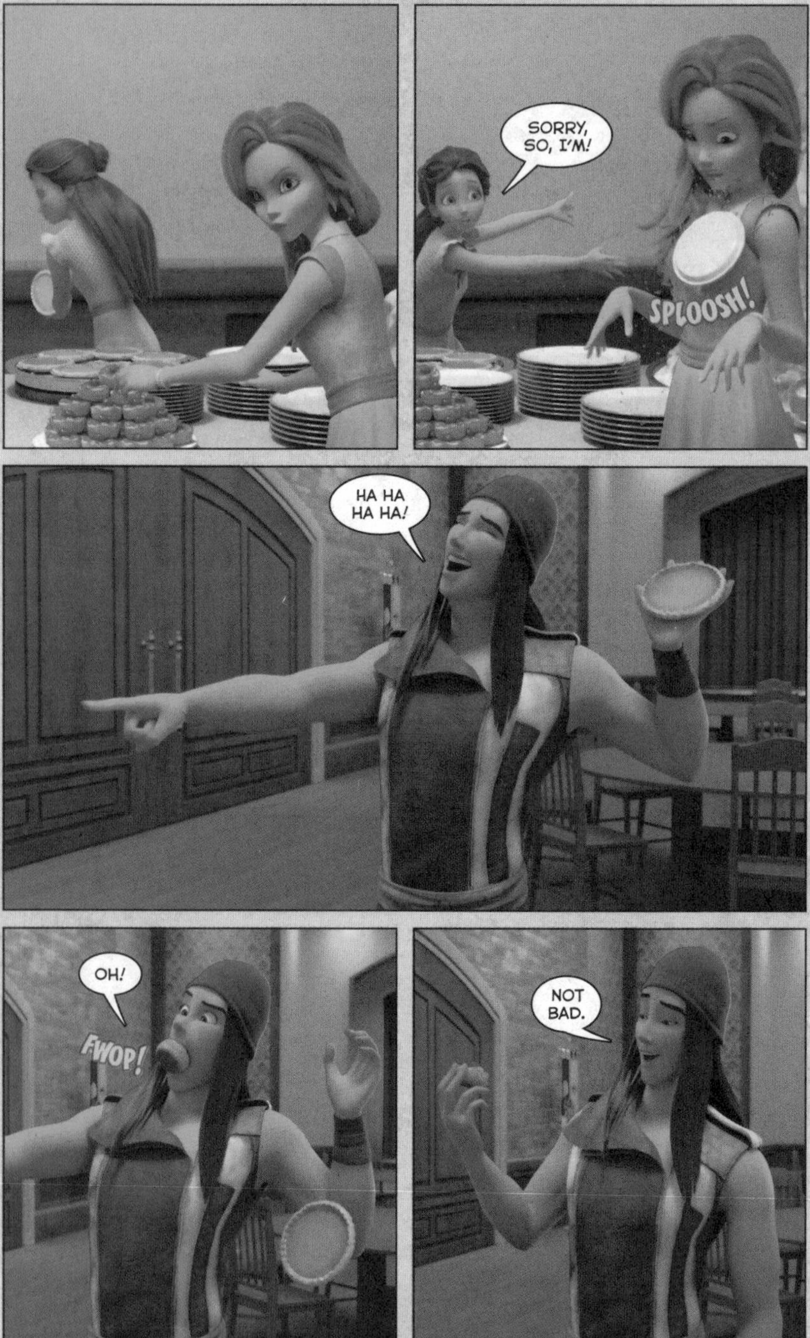
SORRY, SO, I'M!
SPLOOSH!
HA HA HA HA!
OH!
FWOP!
NOT BAD.

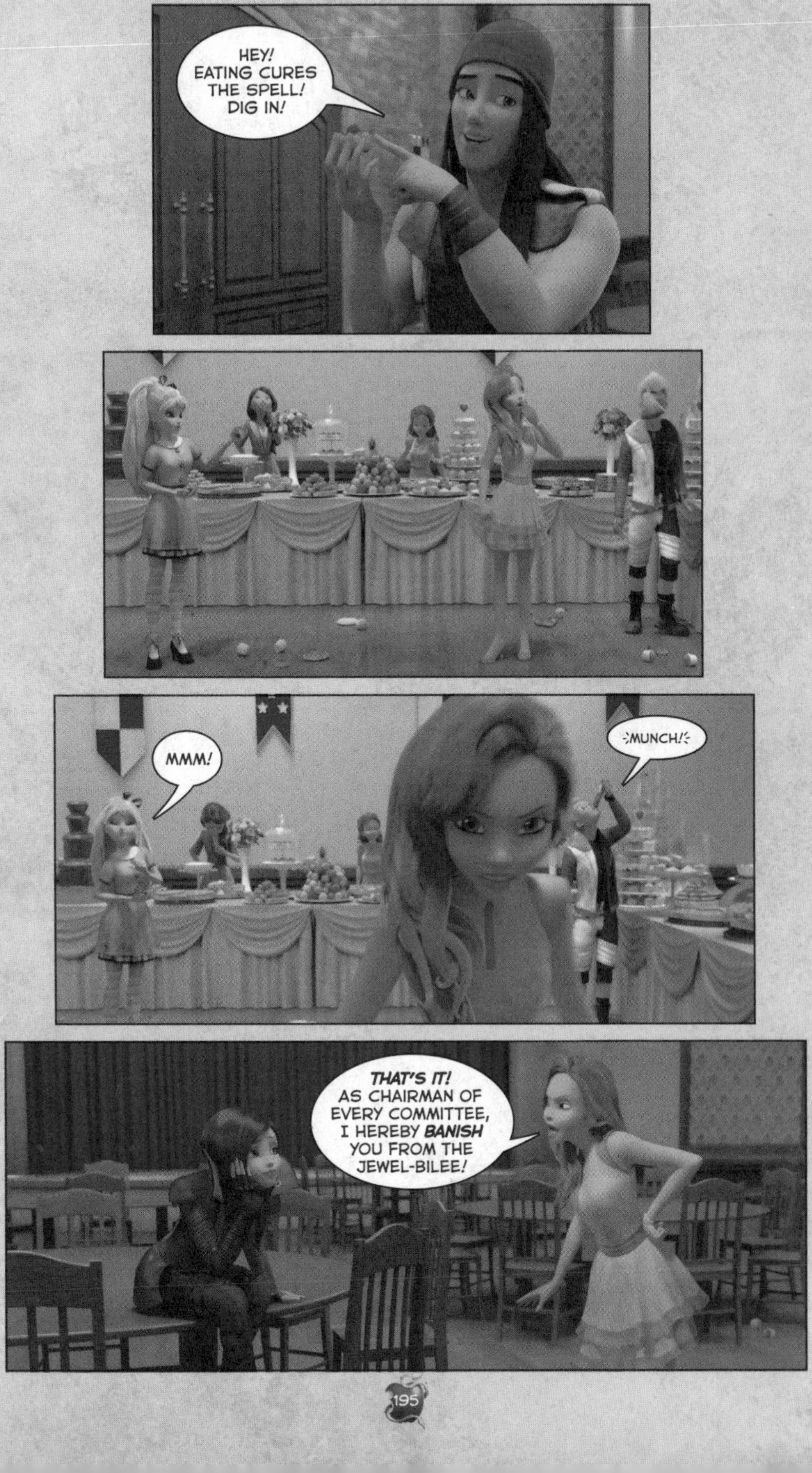
HEY! EATING CURES THE SPELL! DIG IN!
MMM!
MUNCH!
THAT'S IT! AS CHAIRMAN OF EVERY COMMITTEE, I HEREBY *BANISH* YOU FROM THE JEWEL-BILEE!

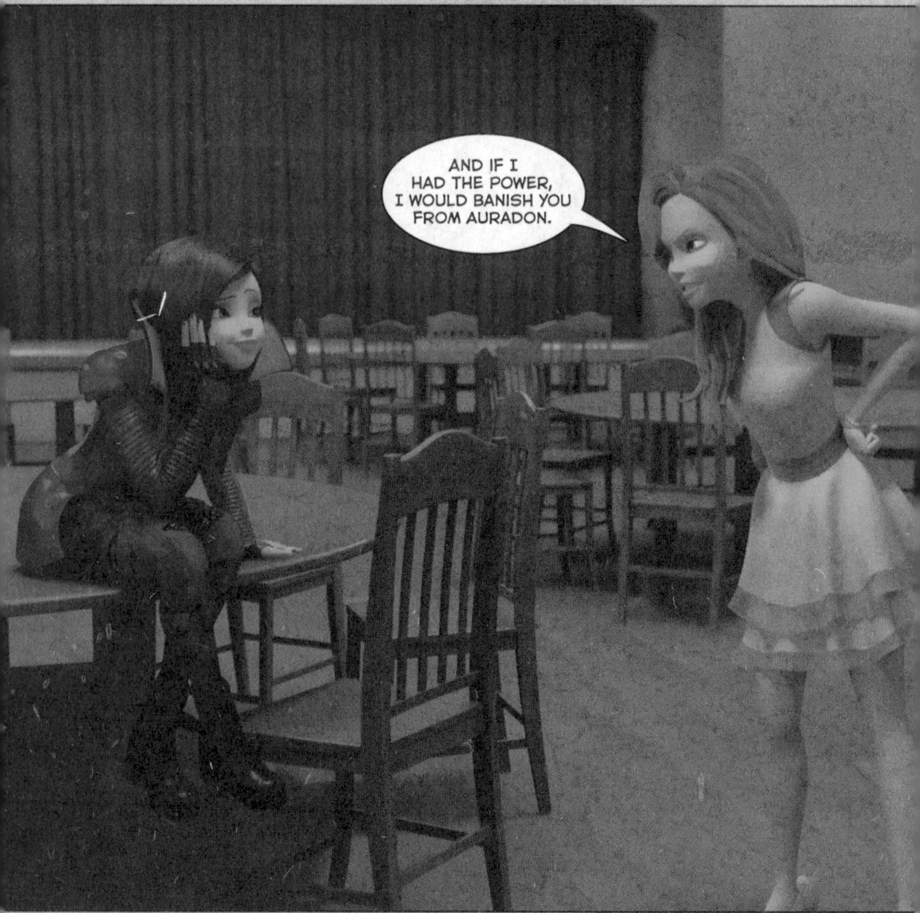
AND IF I HAD THE POWER, I WOULD BANISH YOU FROM AURADON.

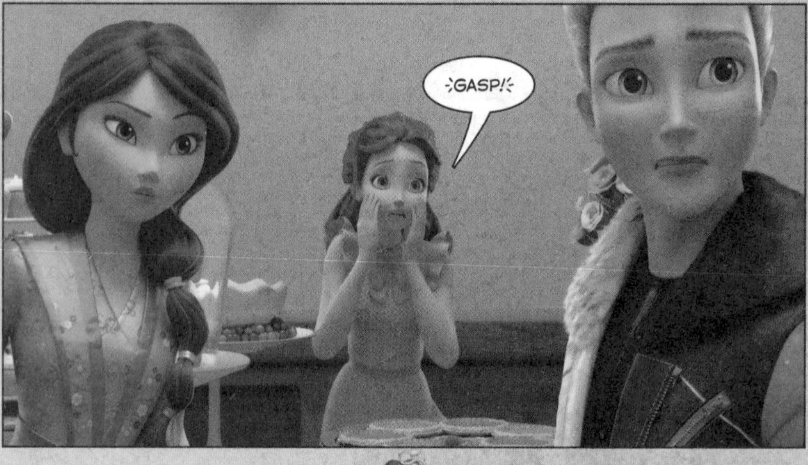
GASP!

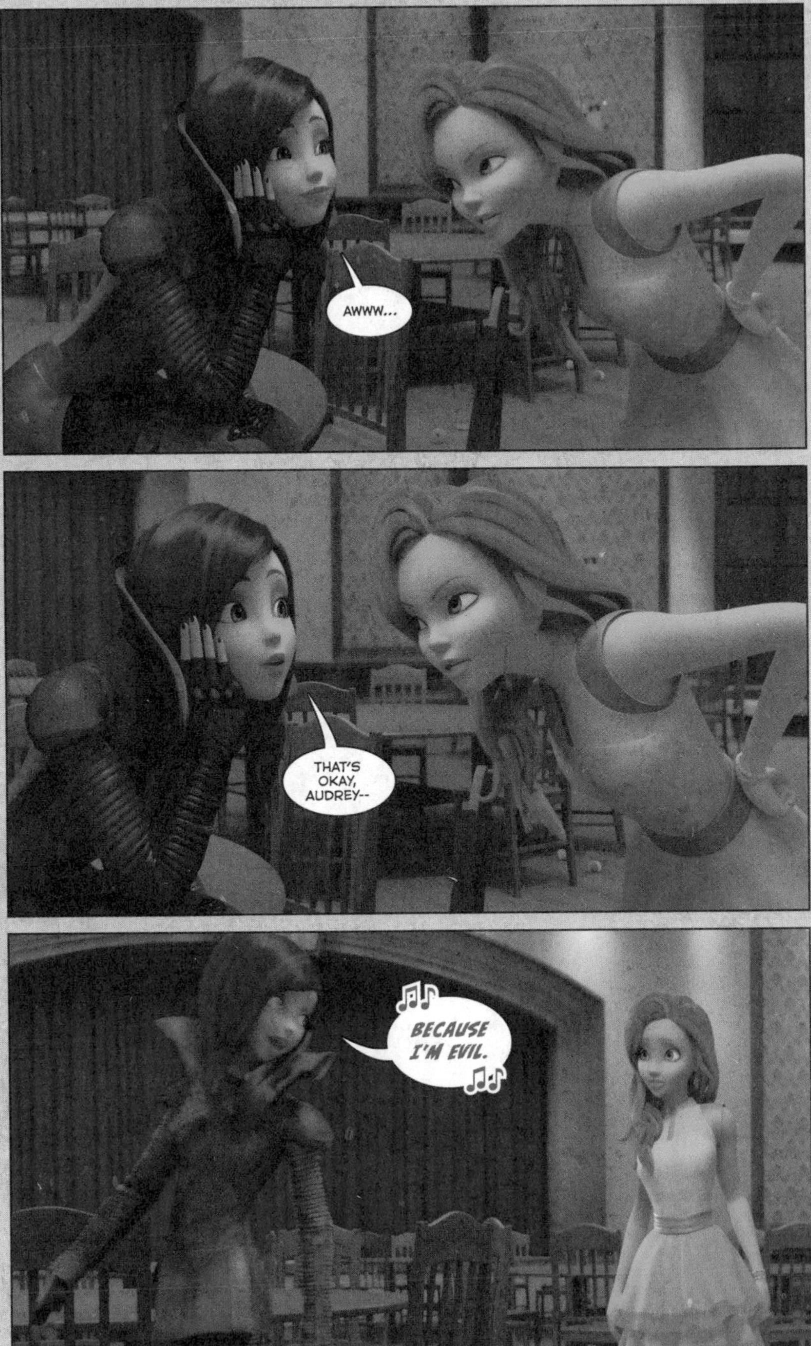
AWWW...
THAT'S OKAY, AUDREY--
BECAUSE I'M EVIL.

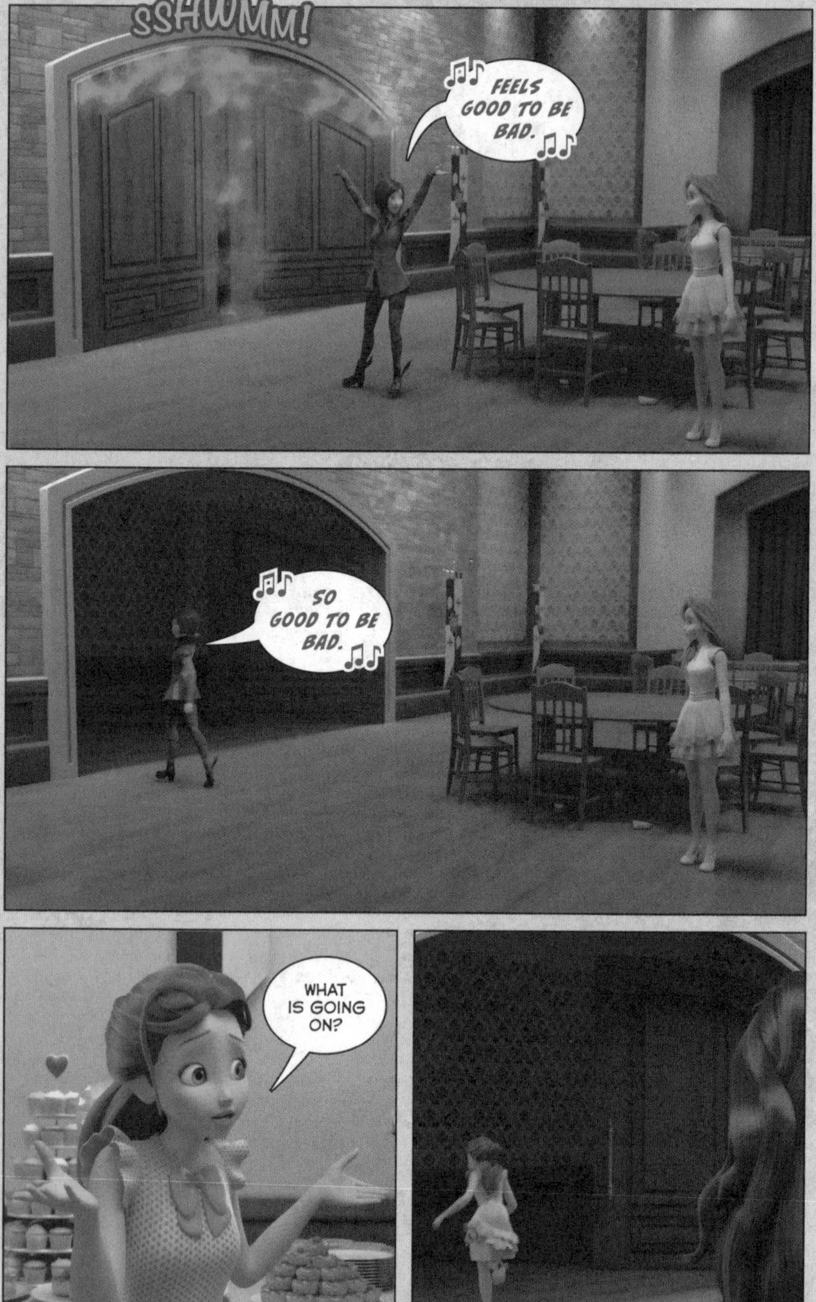
SSHWMM!
FEELS GOOD TO BE BAD.
SO GOOD TO BE BAD.
WHAT IS GOING ON?

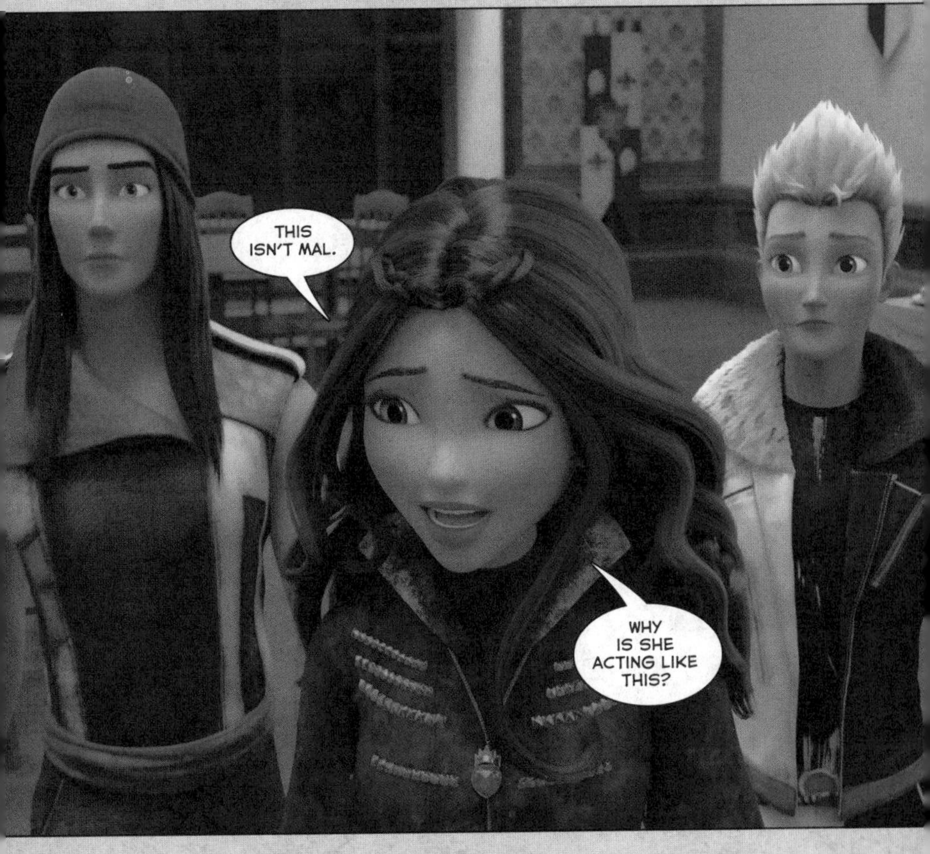
THIS ISN'T MAL.
WHY IS SHE ACTING LIKE THIS?

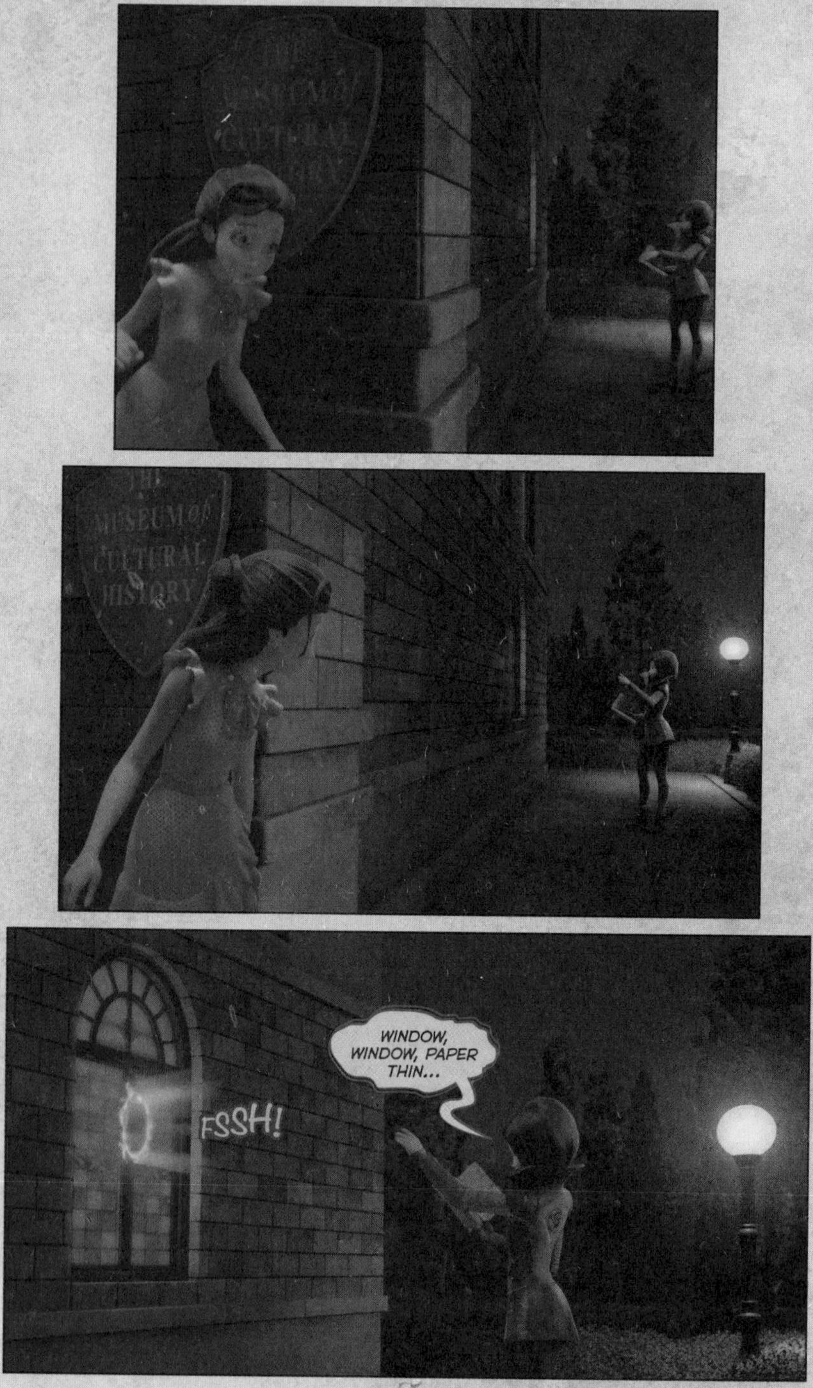
THE MUSEUM OF CULTURAL HISTORY
WINDOW, WINDOW, PAPER THIN...
FSSH!

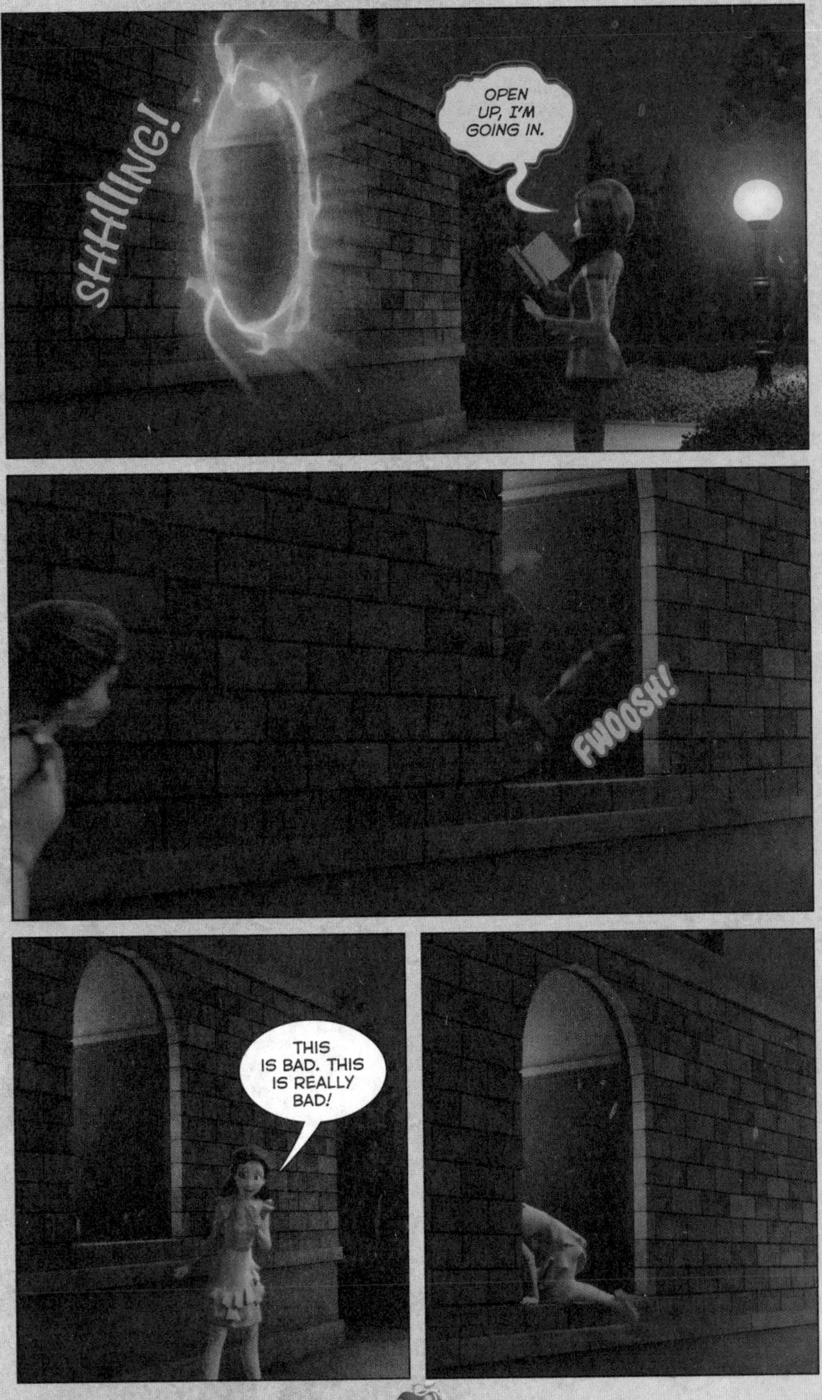
SHHIIING!
OPEN UP, I'M GOING IN.
FWOOSH!
THIS IS BAD. THIS IS REALLY BAD!

Chapter 25: Steal Away

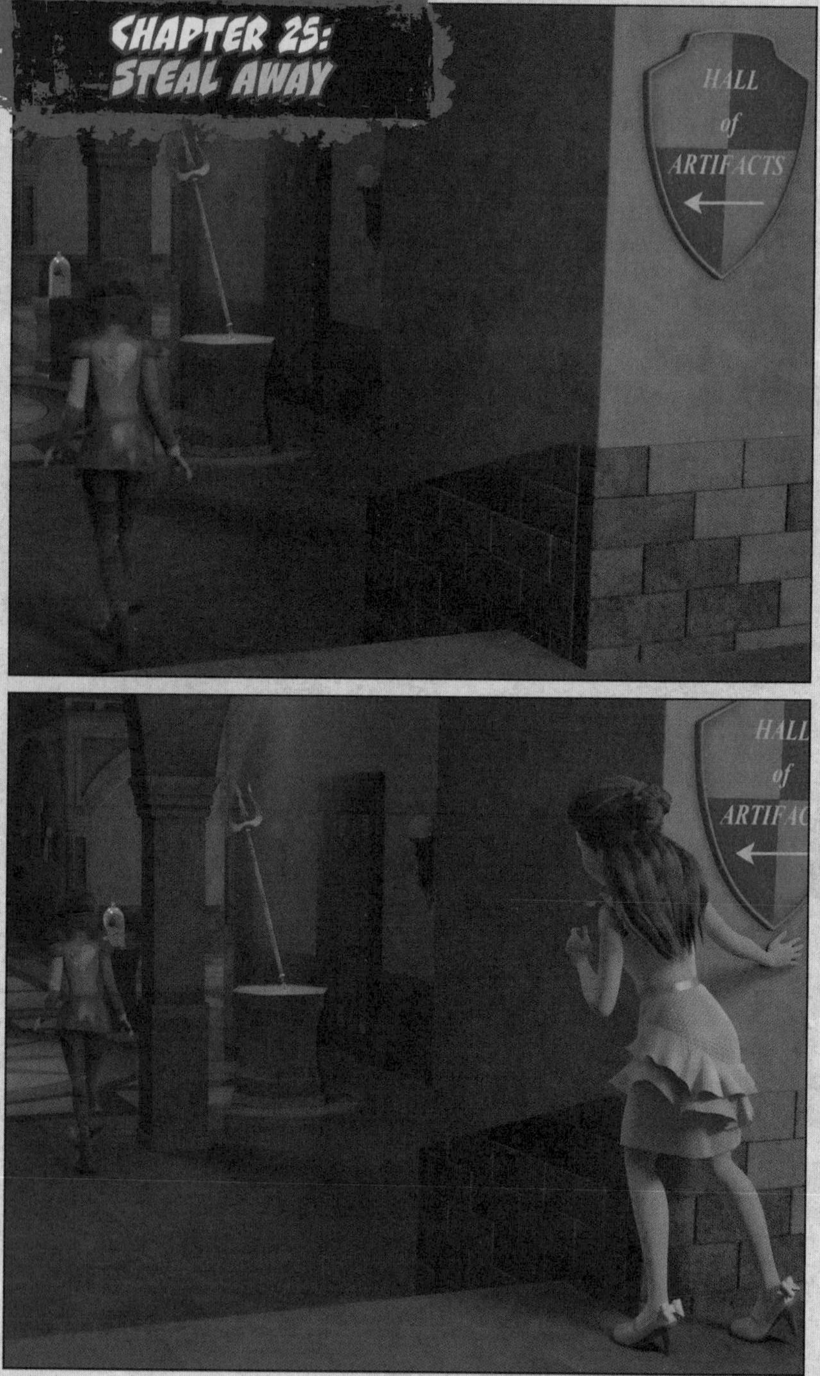
HALL of ARTIFACTS

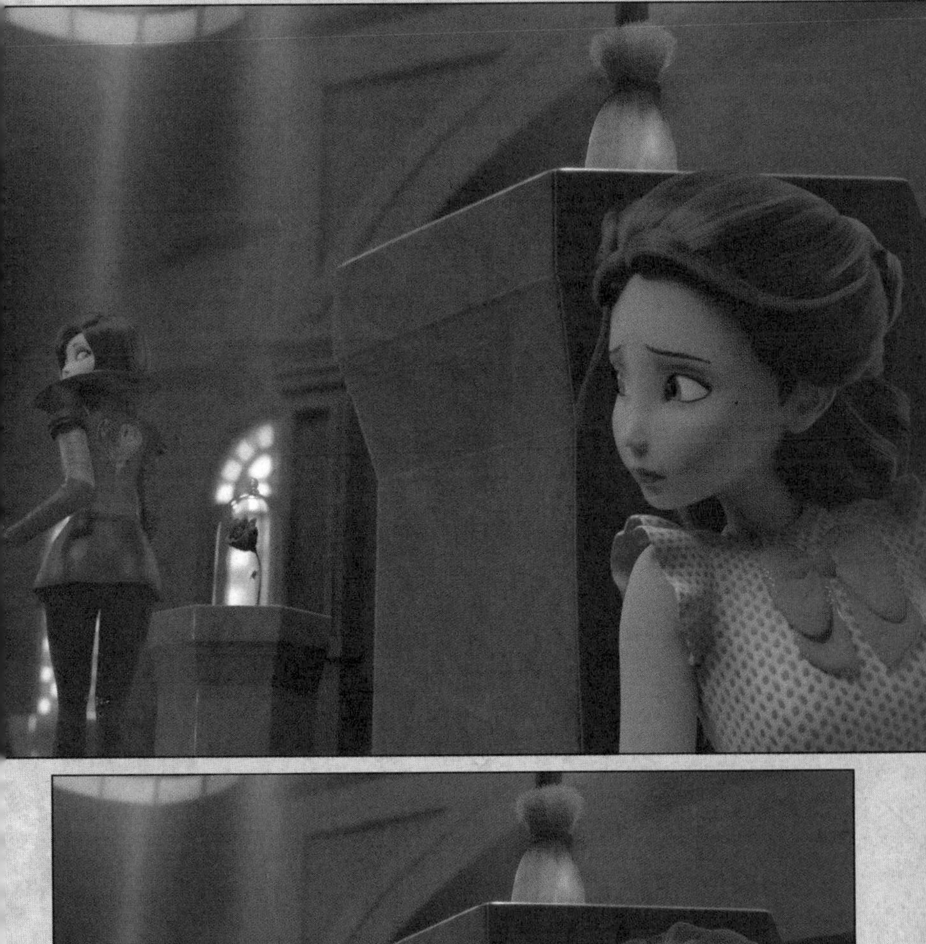

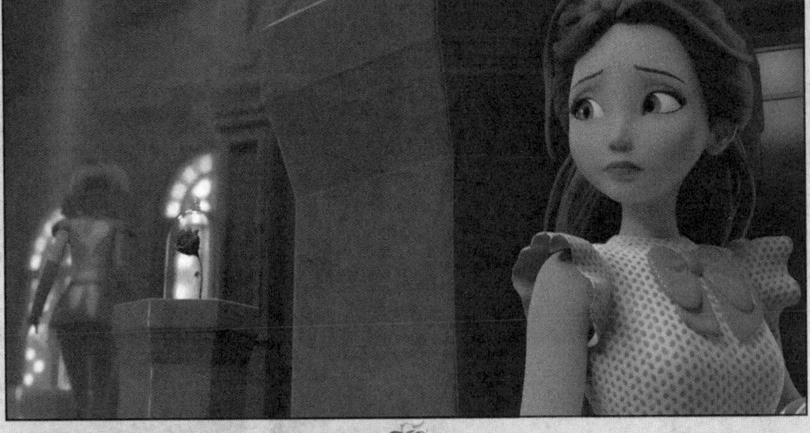

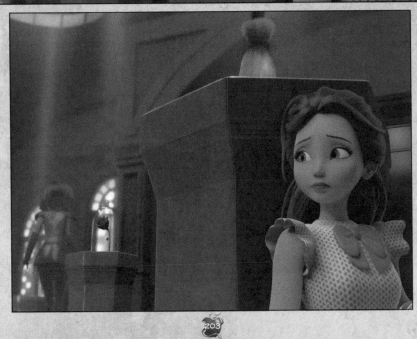

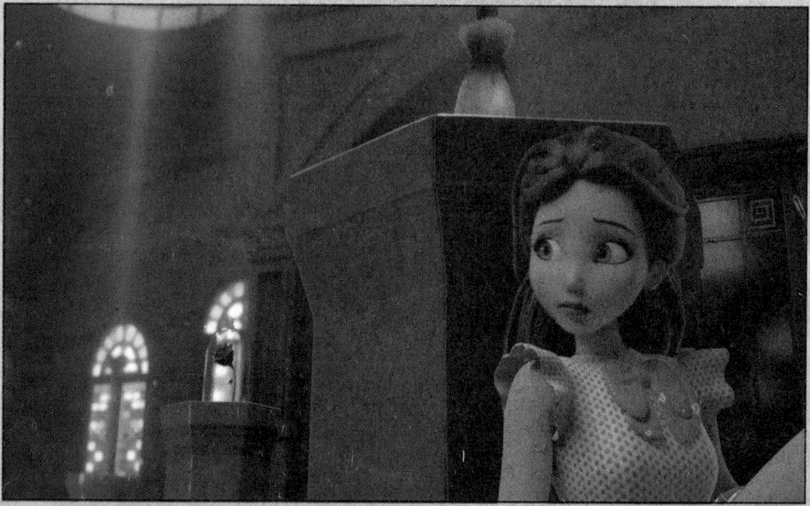

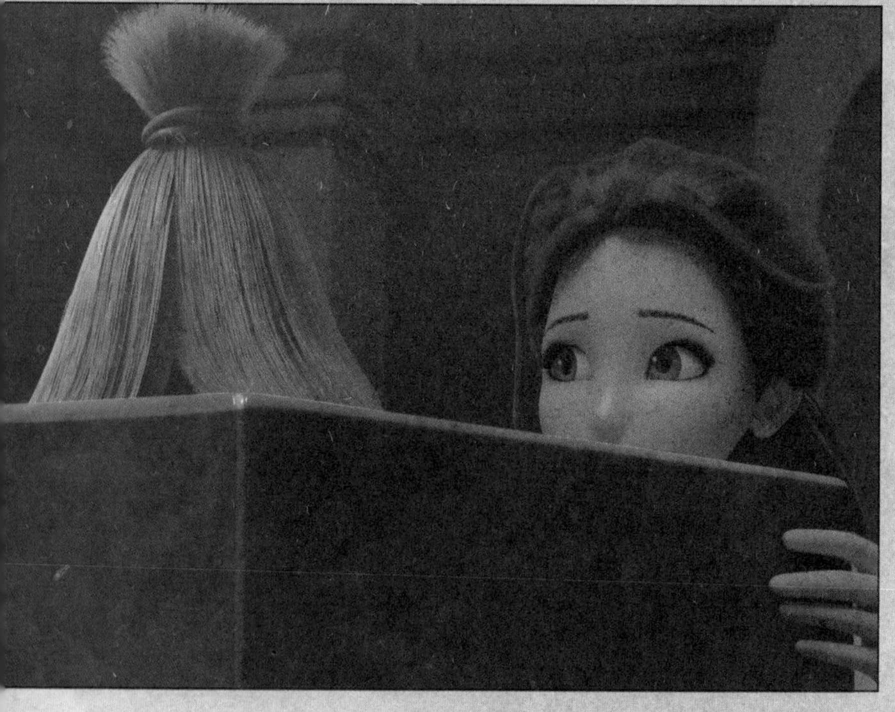

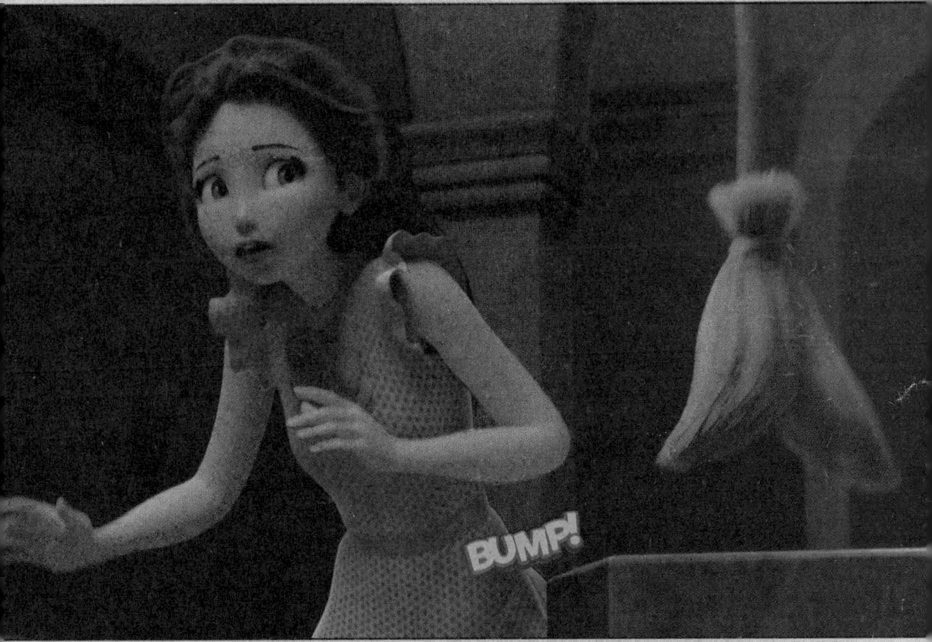
BUMP!

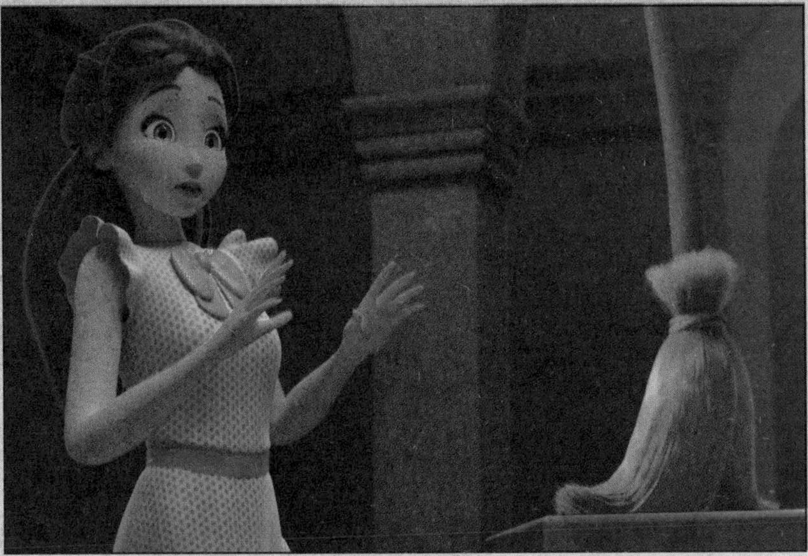

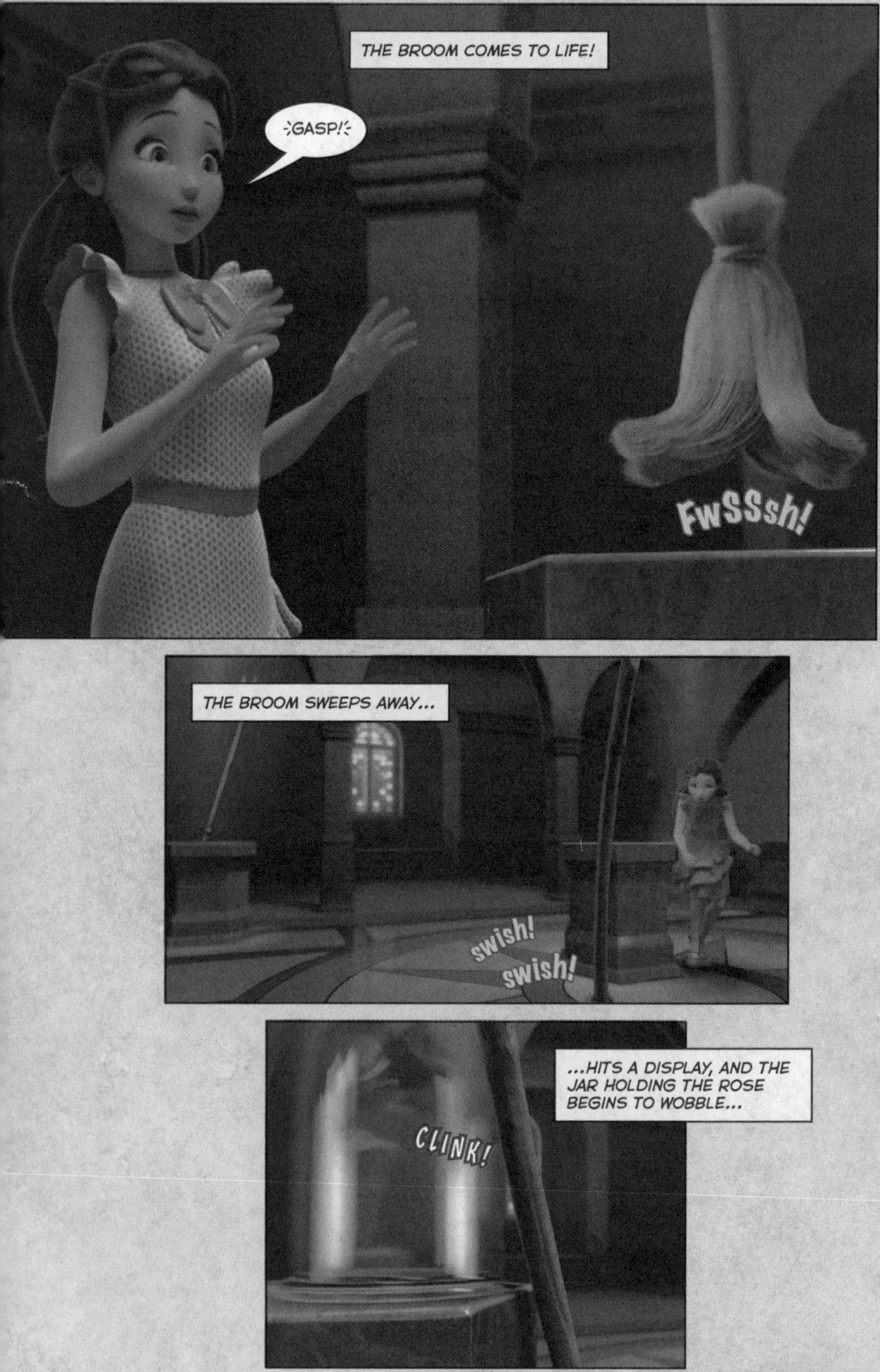
THE BROOM COMES TO LIFE!
GASP!
FWSSsh!
THE BROOM SWEEPS AWAY...
swish!
swish!
...HITS A DISPLAY, AND THE JAR HOLDING THE ROSE BEGINS TO WOBBLE...
CLINK!

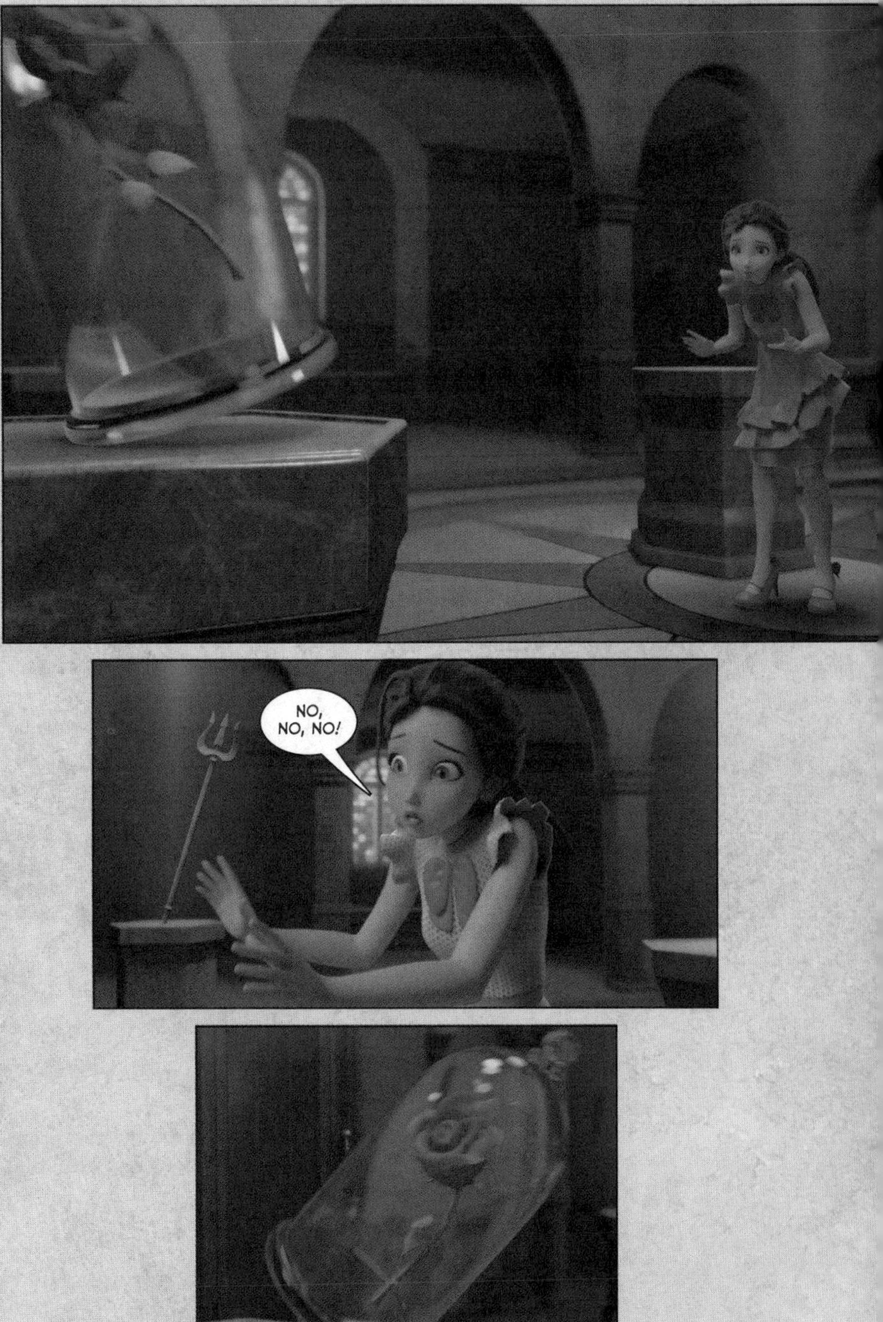
NO,
NO, NO!

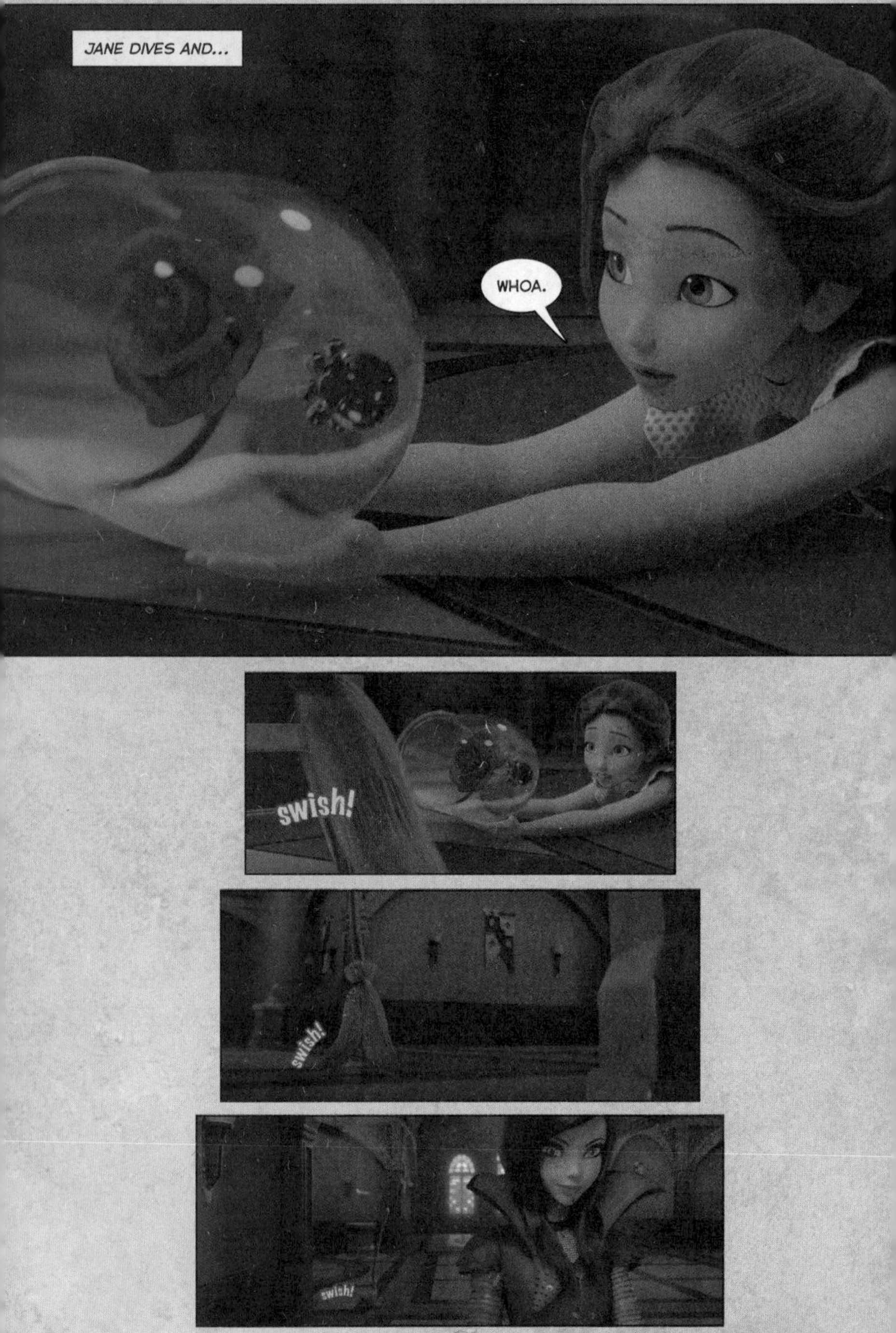
JANE DIVES AND...
WHOA.
swish!
swish!
swish!

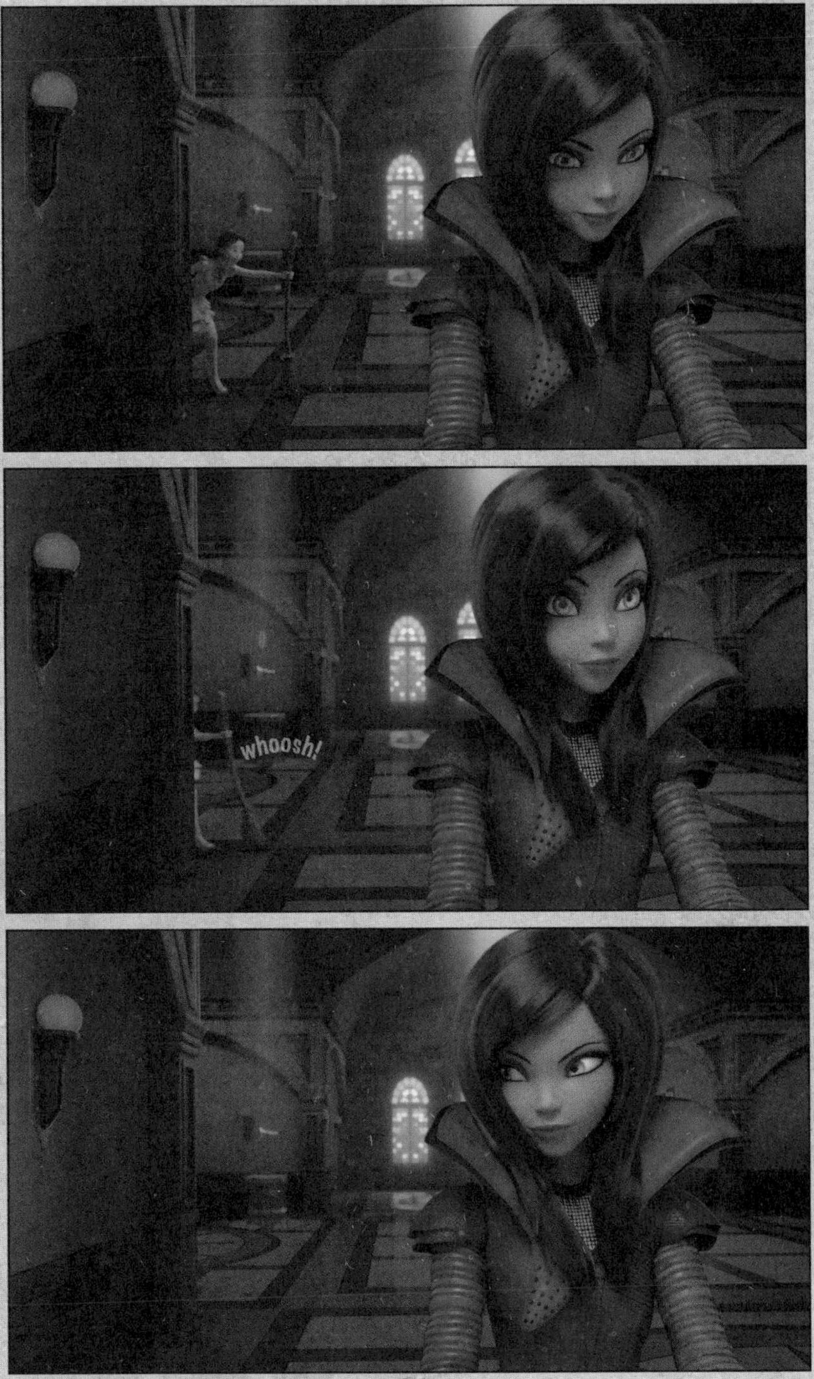
whoosh!

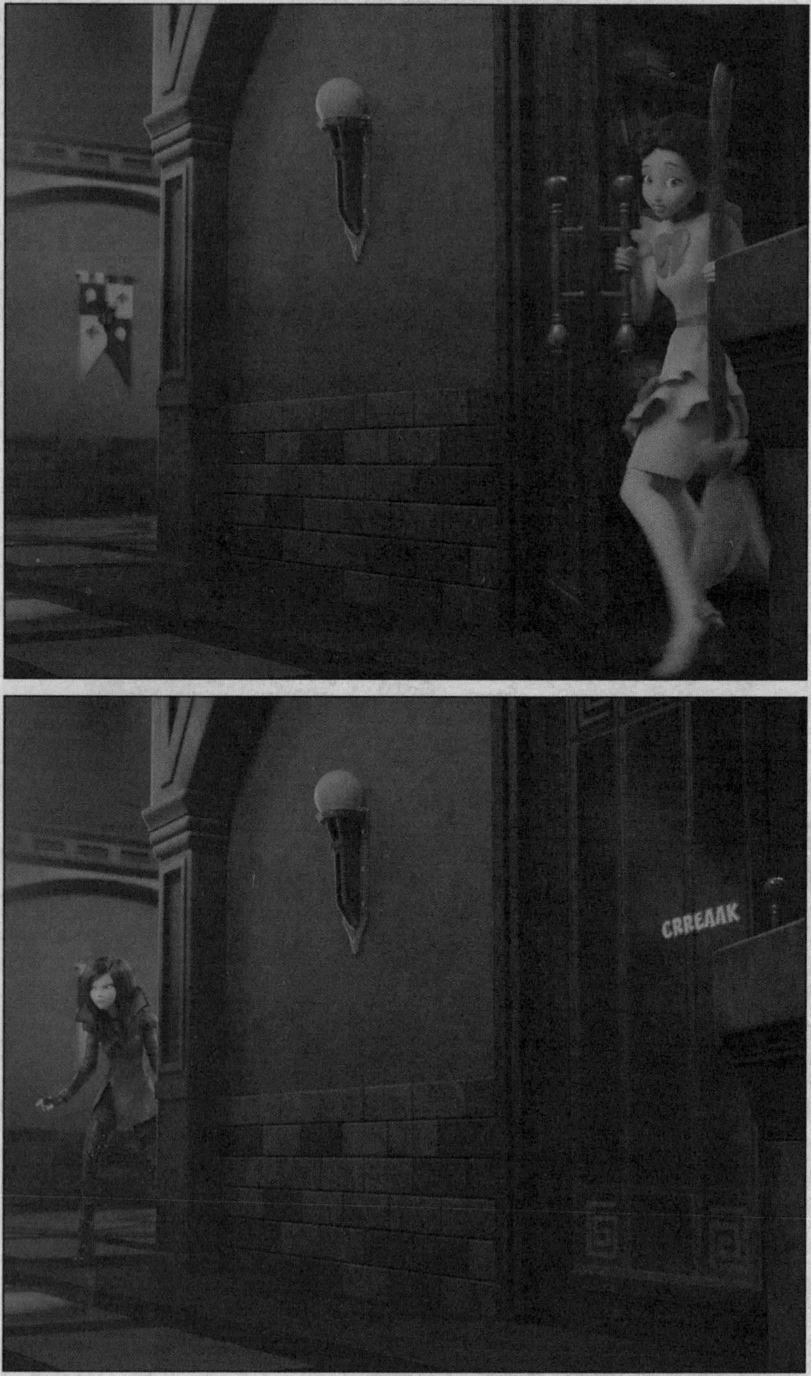
CRREAAK

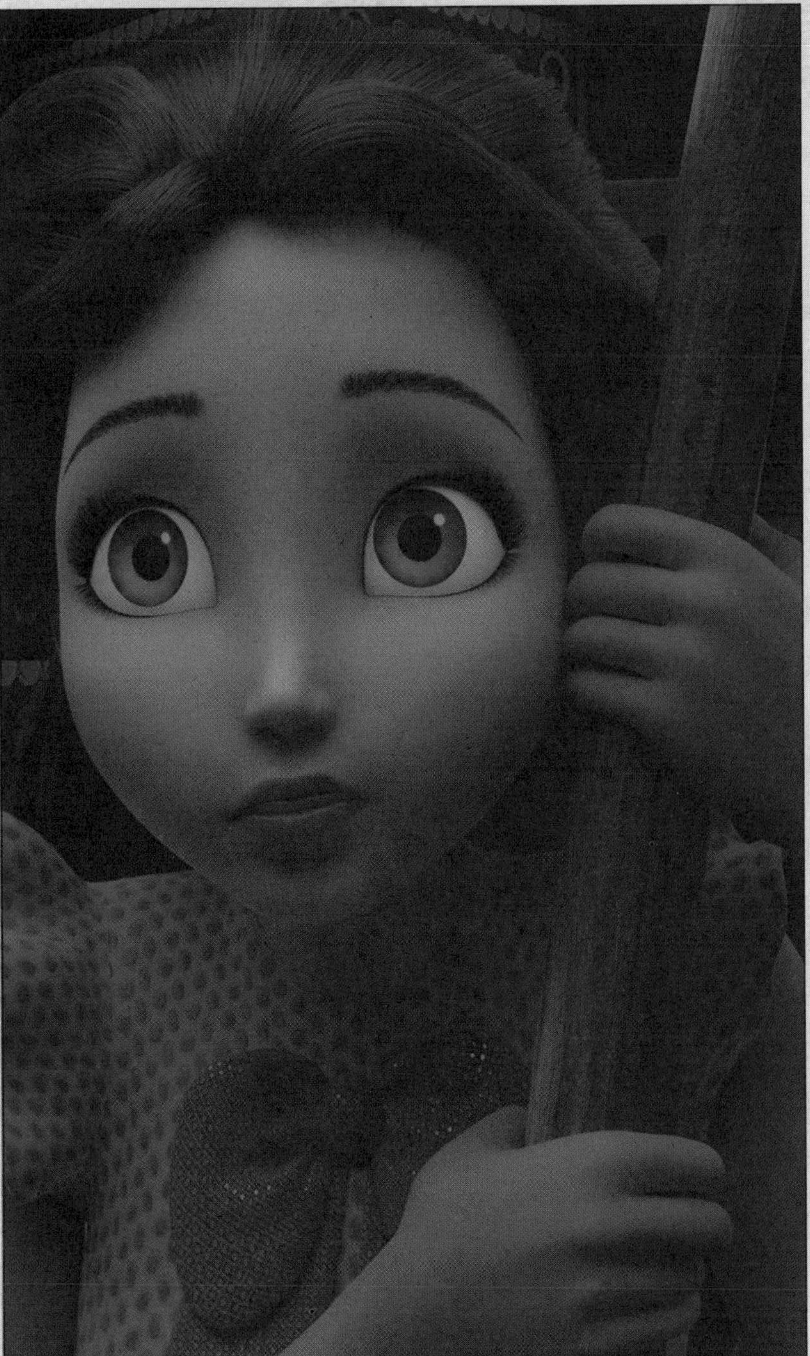

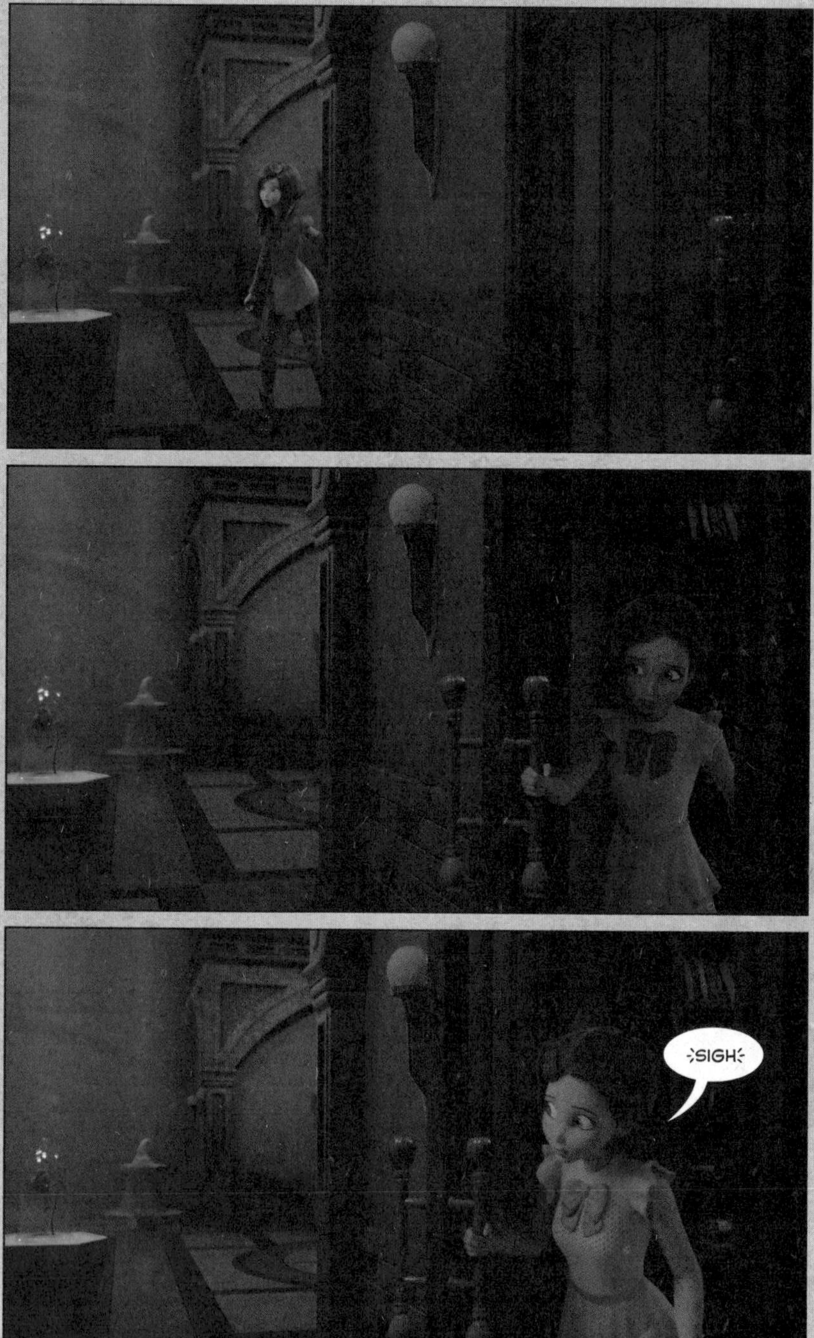
SIGH

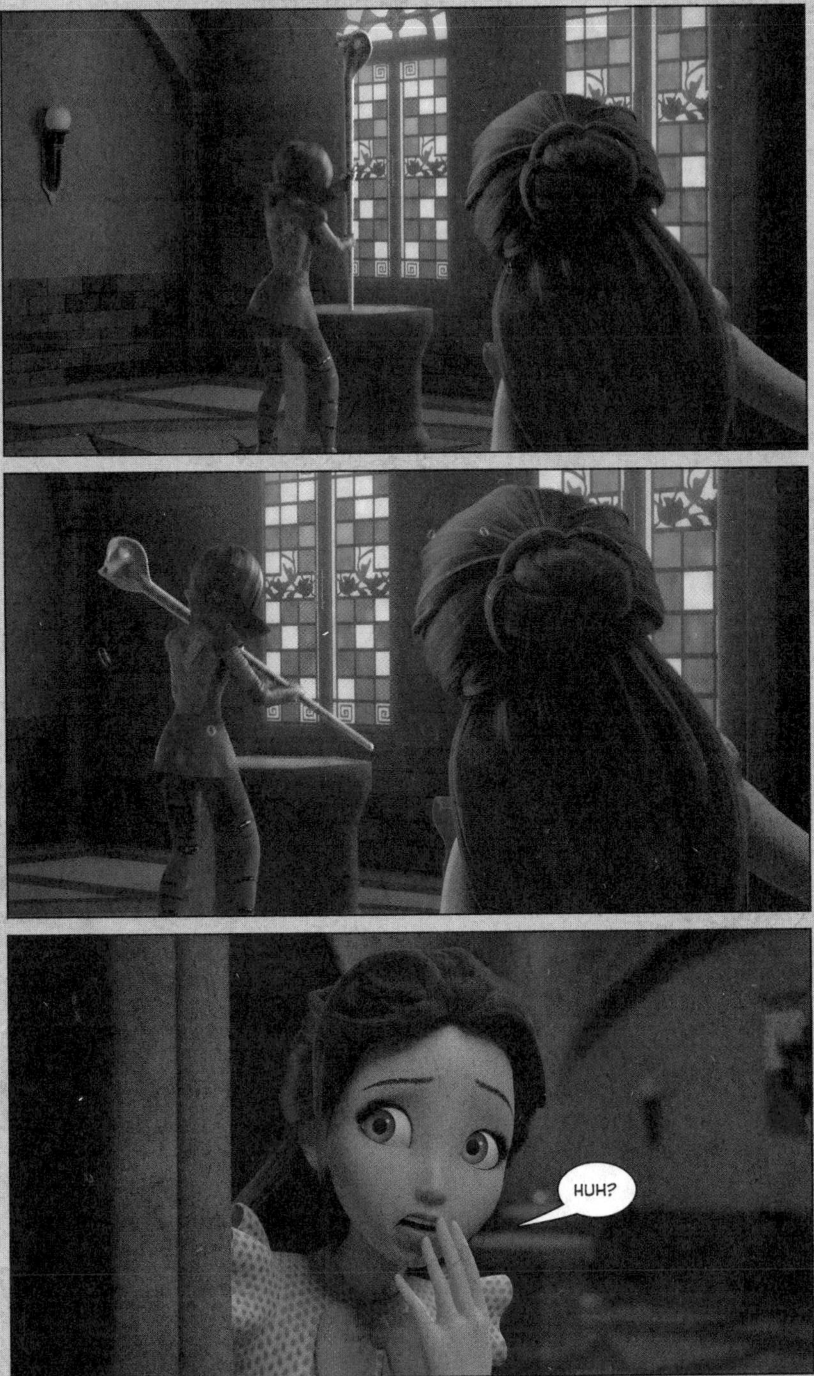
HUH?

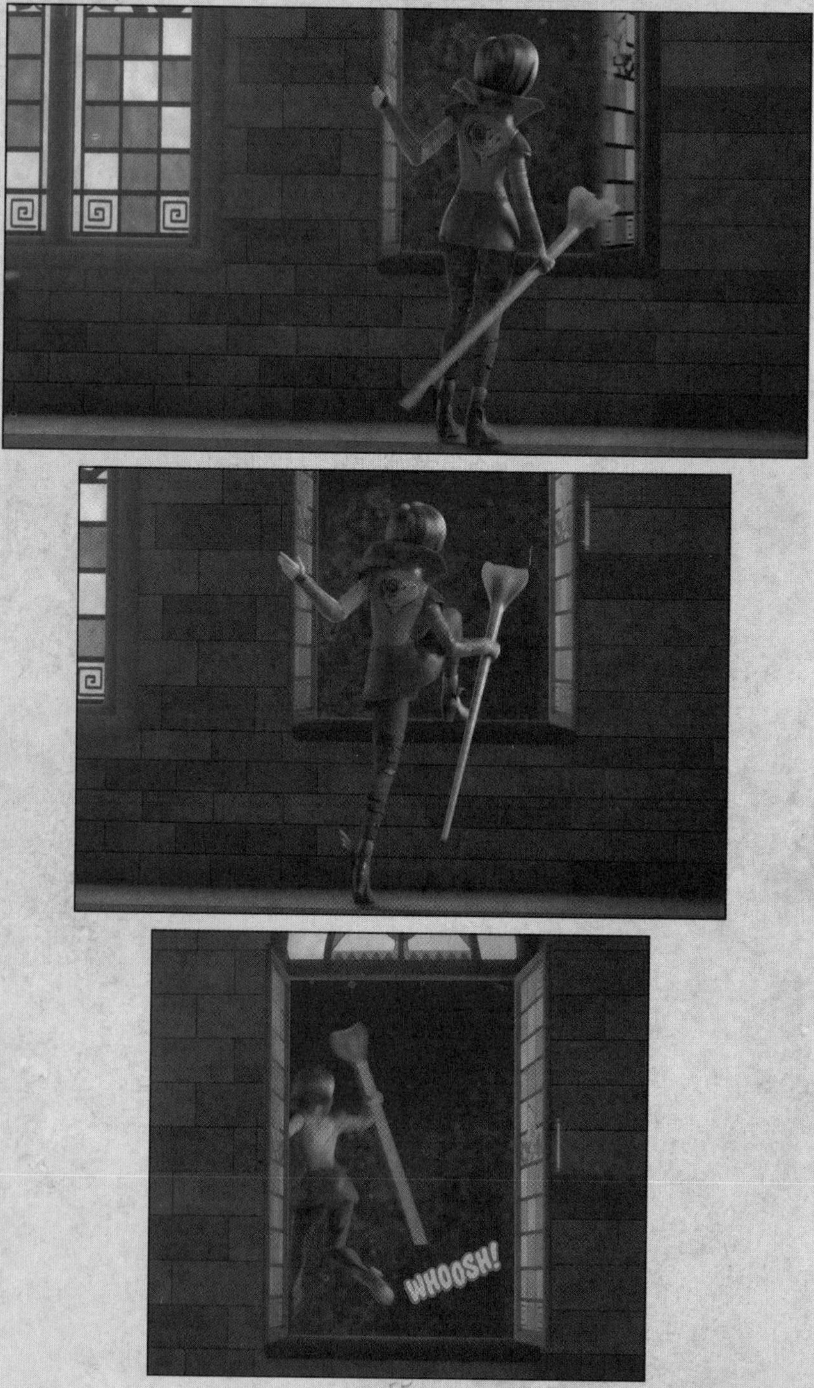
WHOOSH!

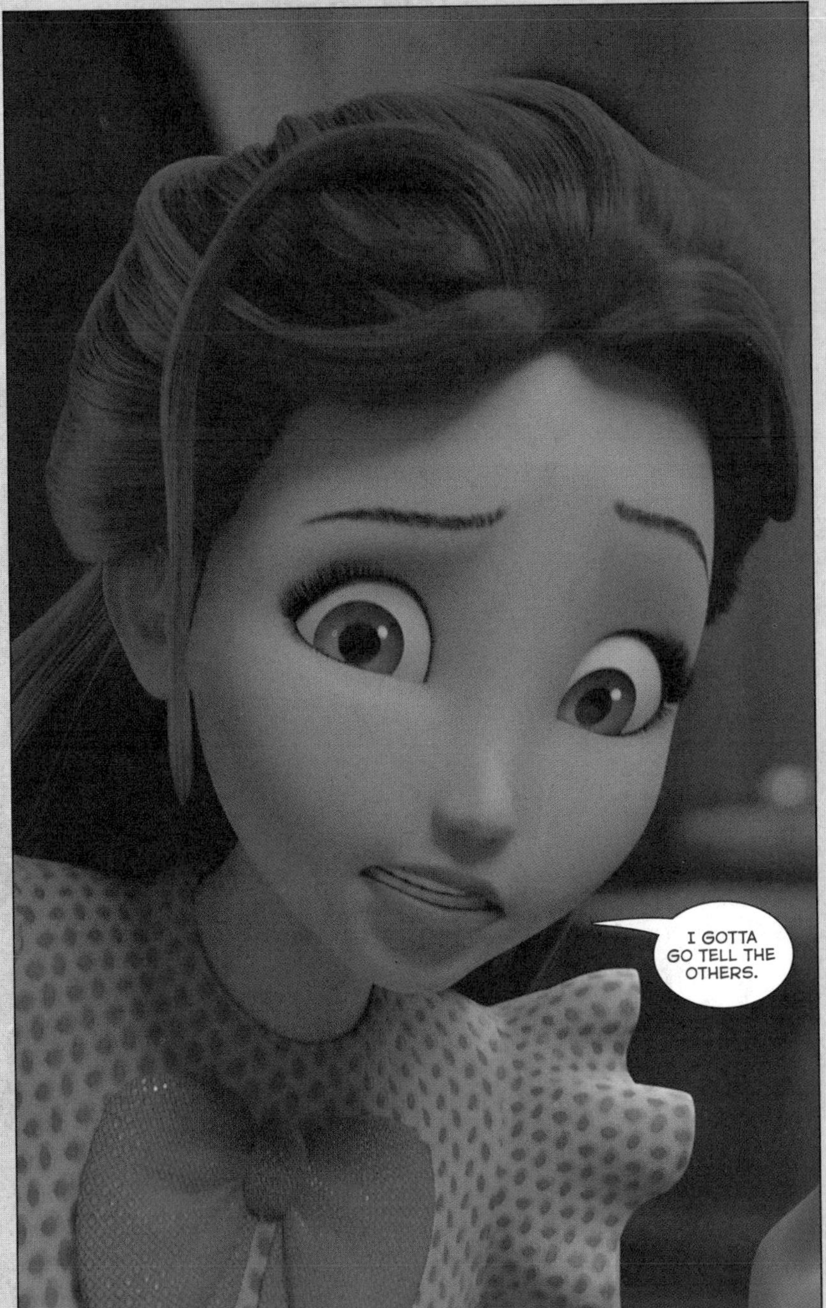
I GOTTA GO TELL THE OTHERS.

LONG LIVE EVIL.

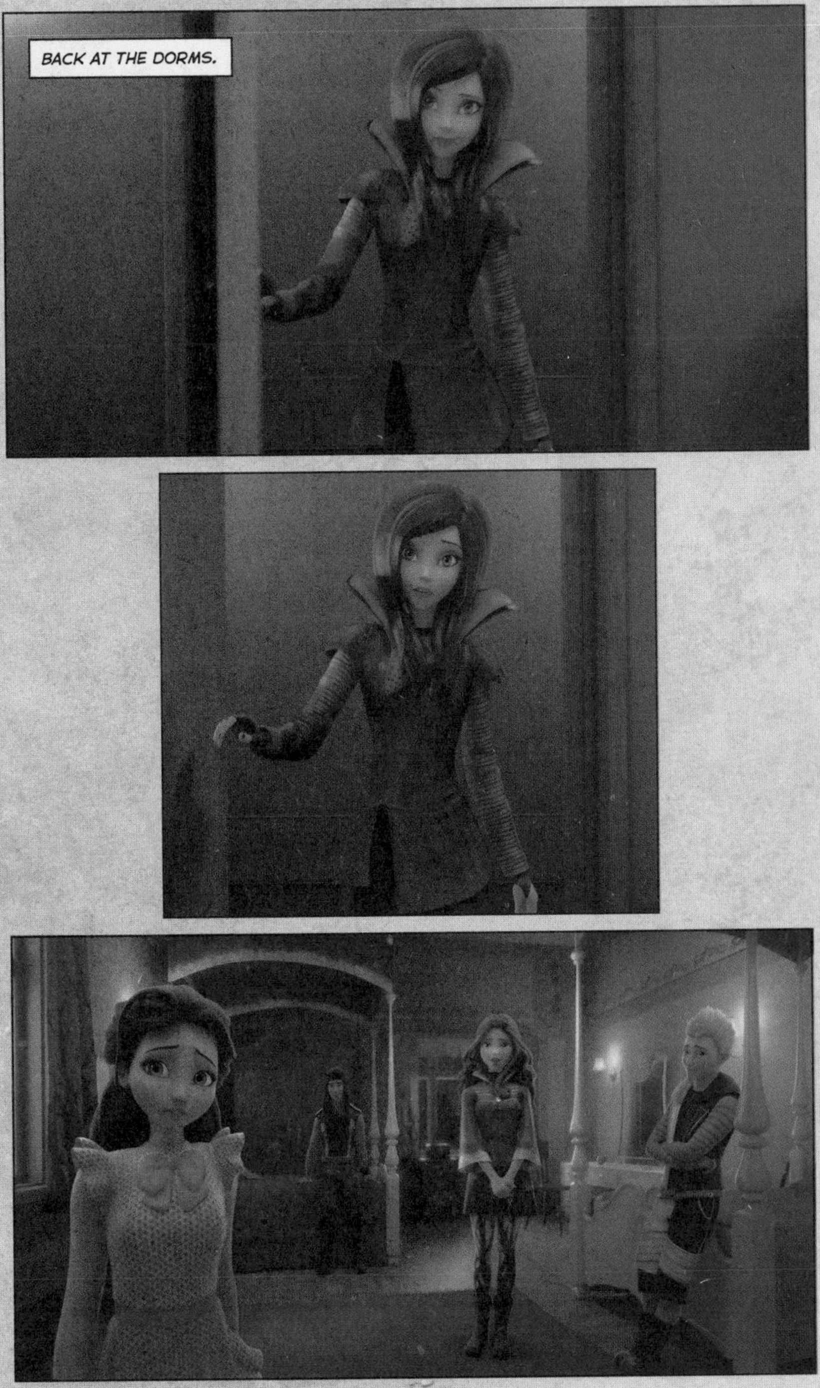
BACK AT THE DORMS.

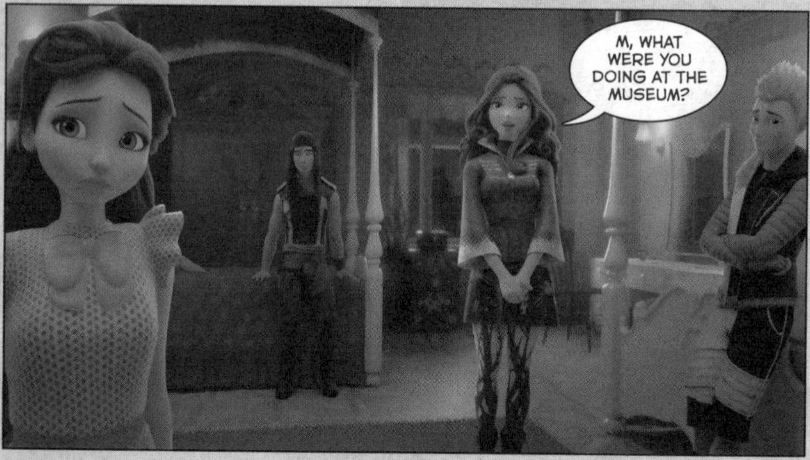
M, WHAT WERE YOU DOING AT THE MUSEUM?

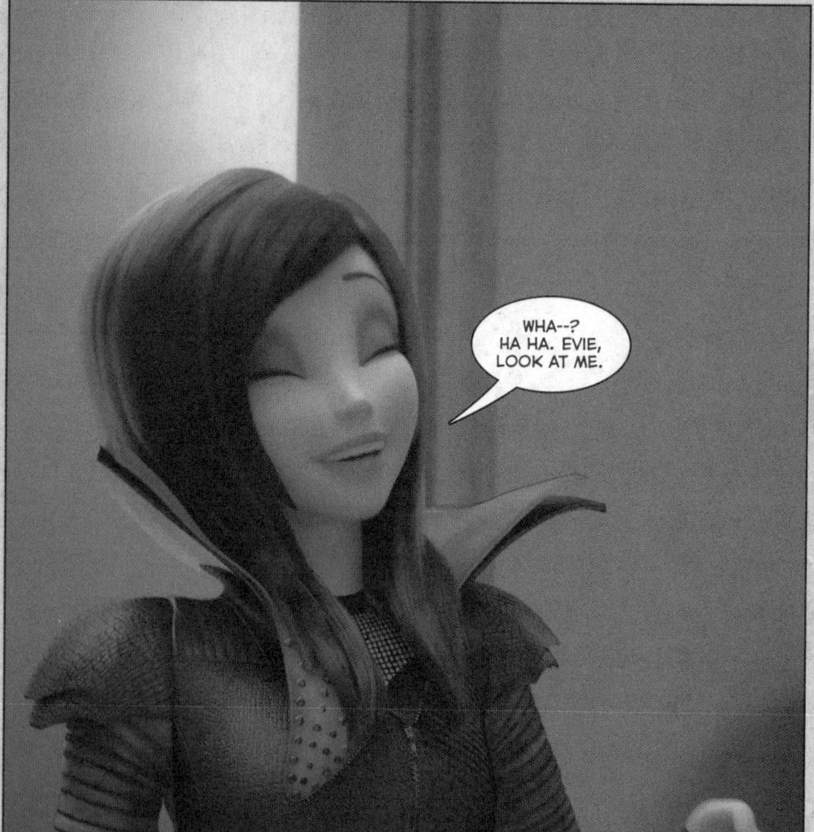
WHA--? HA HA. EVIE, LOOK AT ME.

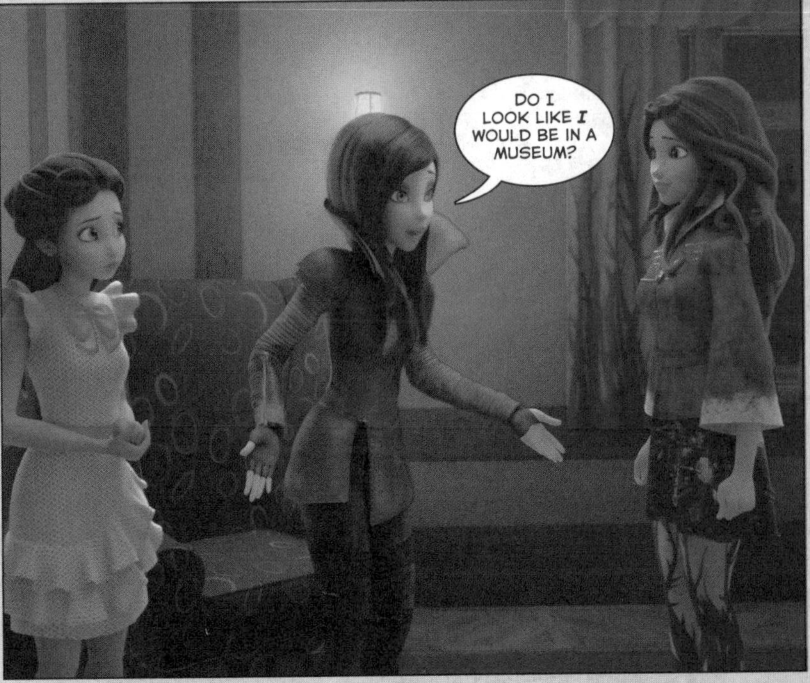
DO I LOOK LIKE *I* WOULD BE IN A MUSEUM?

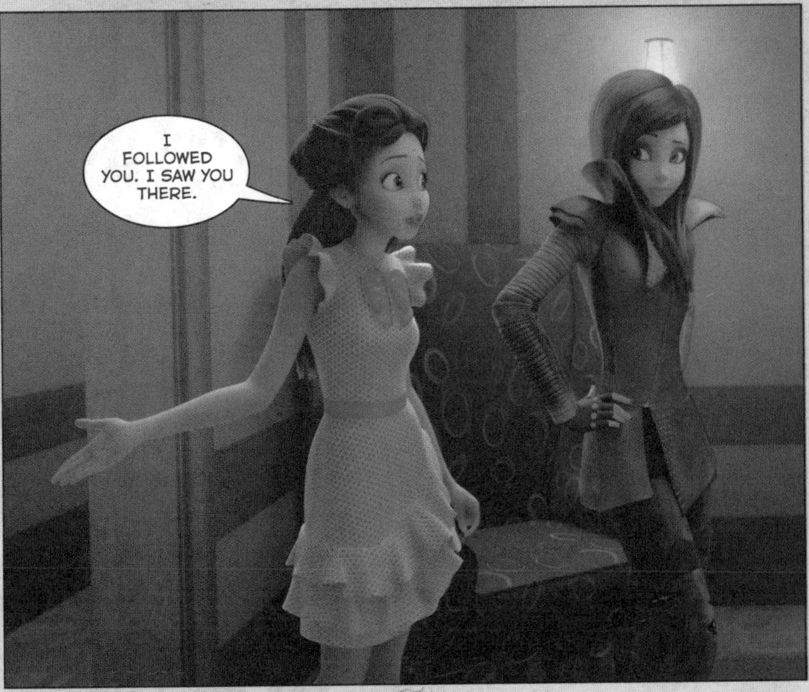
I FOLLOWED YOU. I SAW YOU THERE.

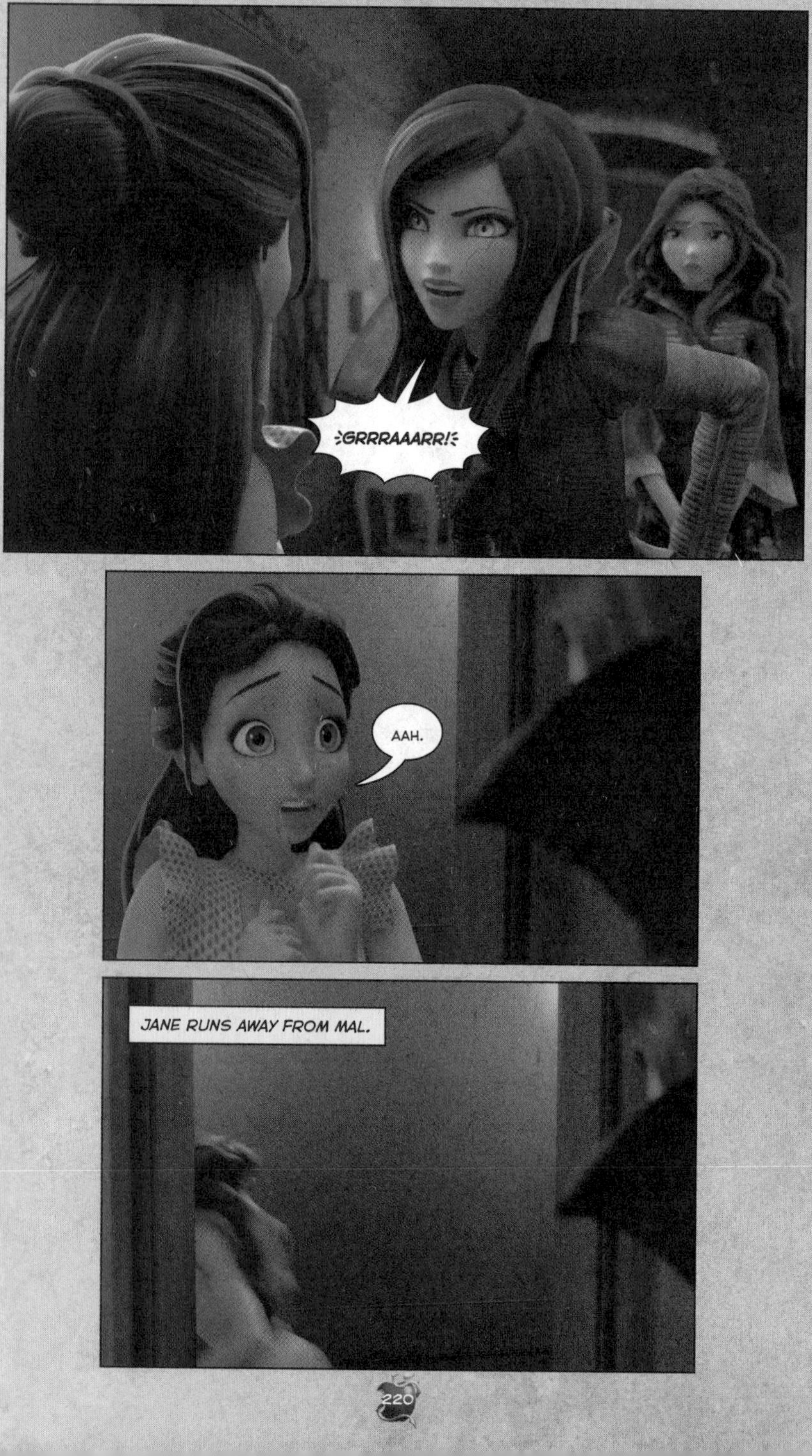
GRRRAAARR!
AAH.
JANE RUNS AWAY FROM MAL.

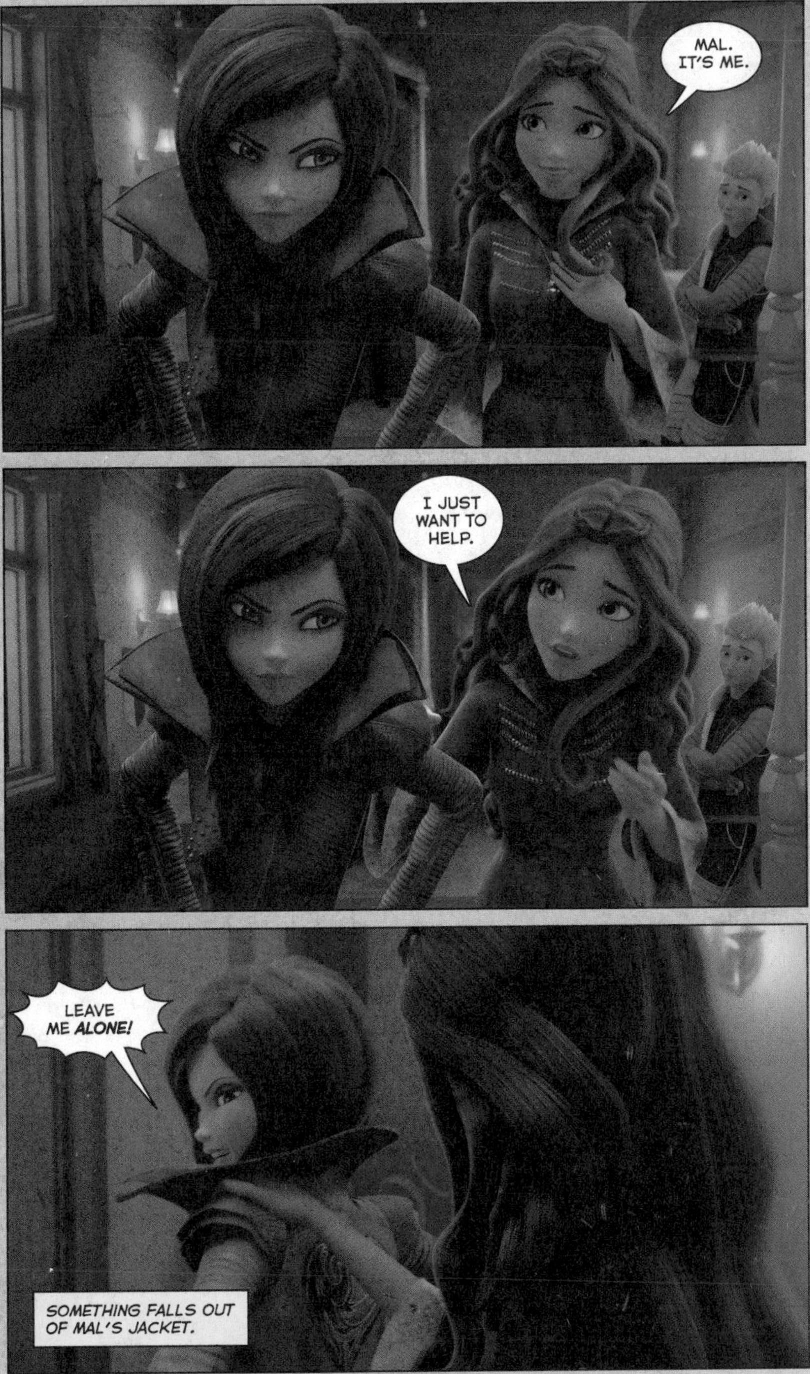
MAL. IT'S ME.
I JUST WANT TO HELP.
LEAVE ME ALONE!
SOMETHING FALLS OUT OF MAL'S JACKET.

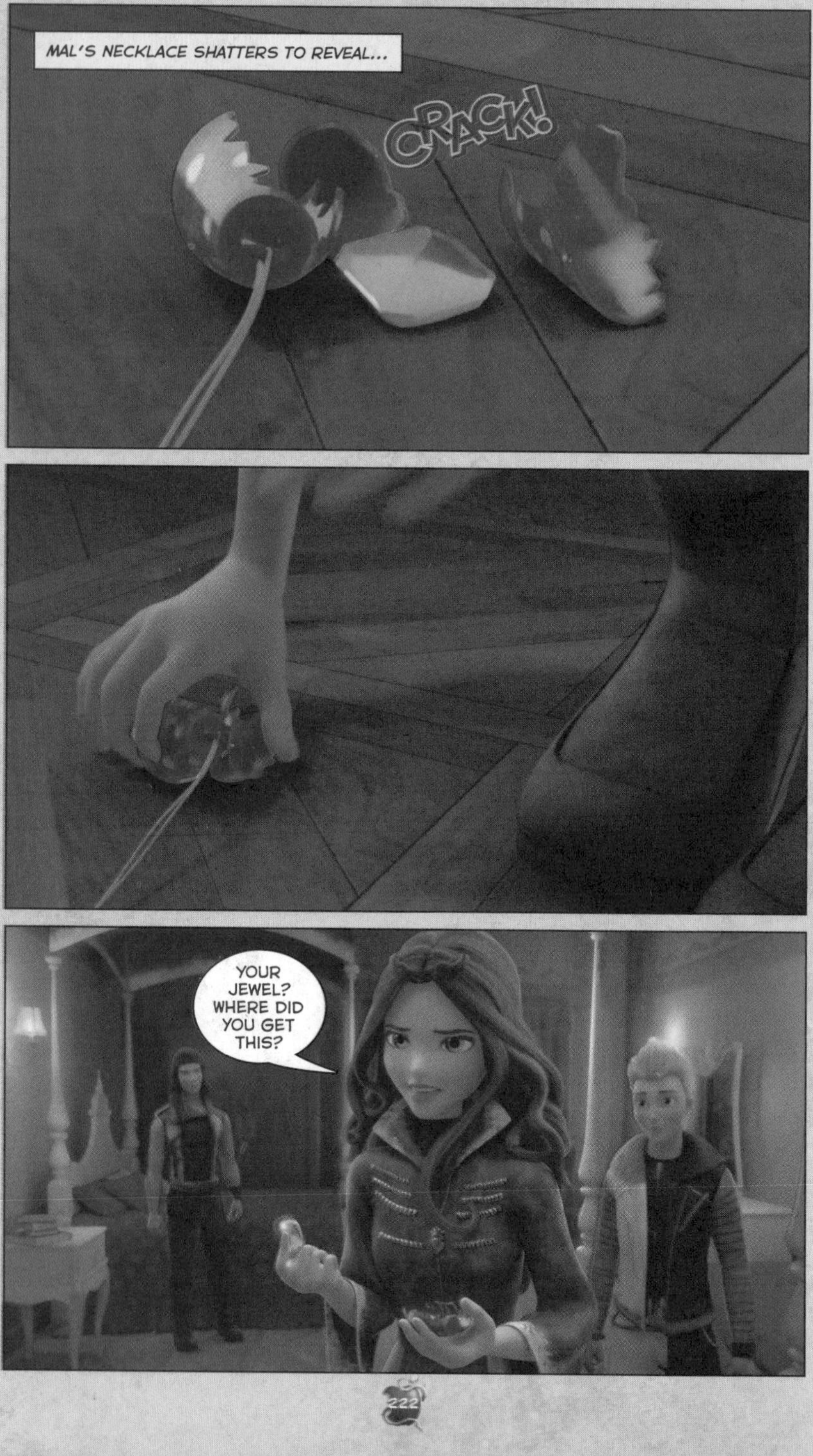

MAL'S NECKLACE SHATTERS TO REVEAL...
CRACK!
YOUR JEWEL? WHERE DID YOU GET THIS?

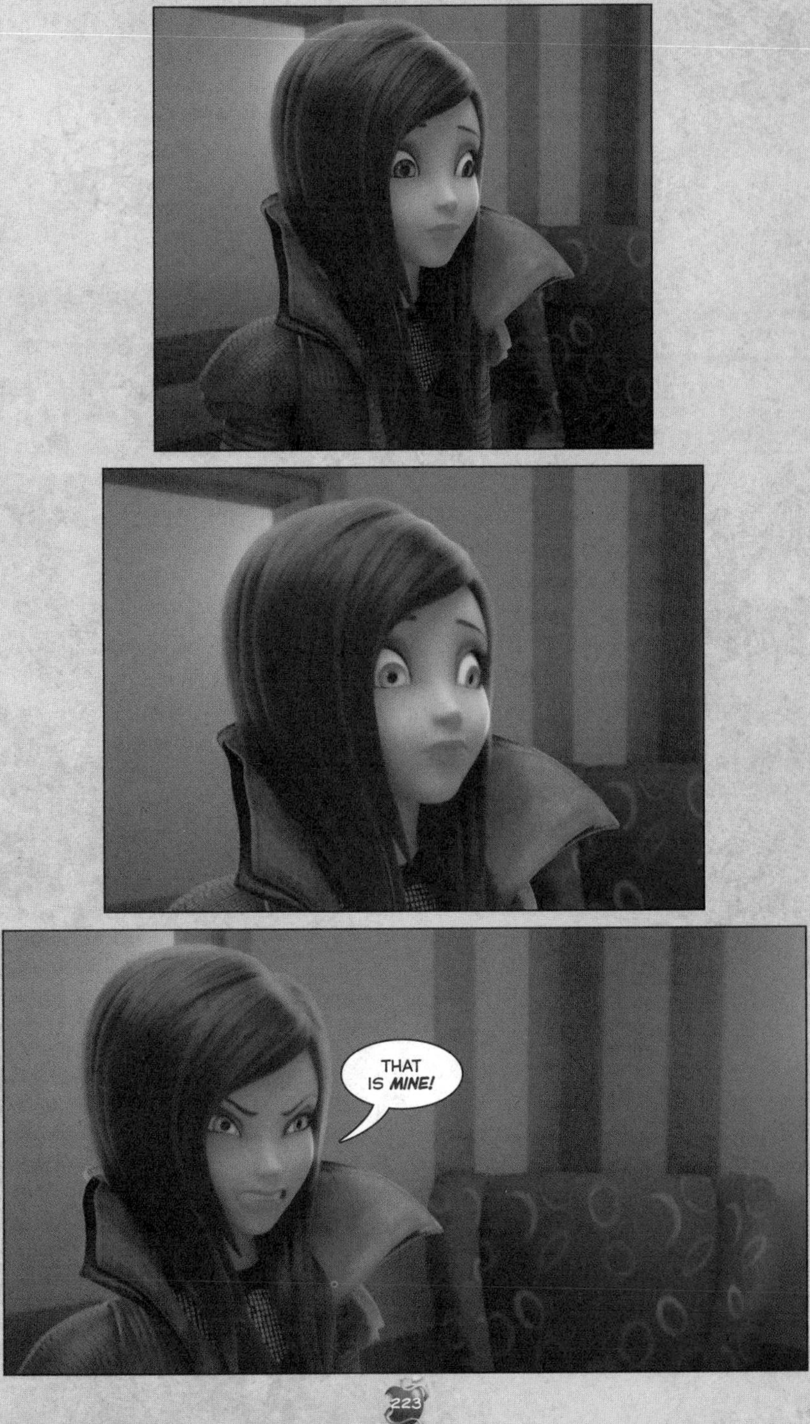
THAT IS MINE!

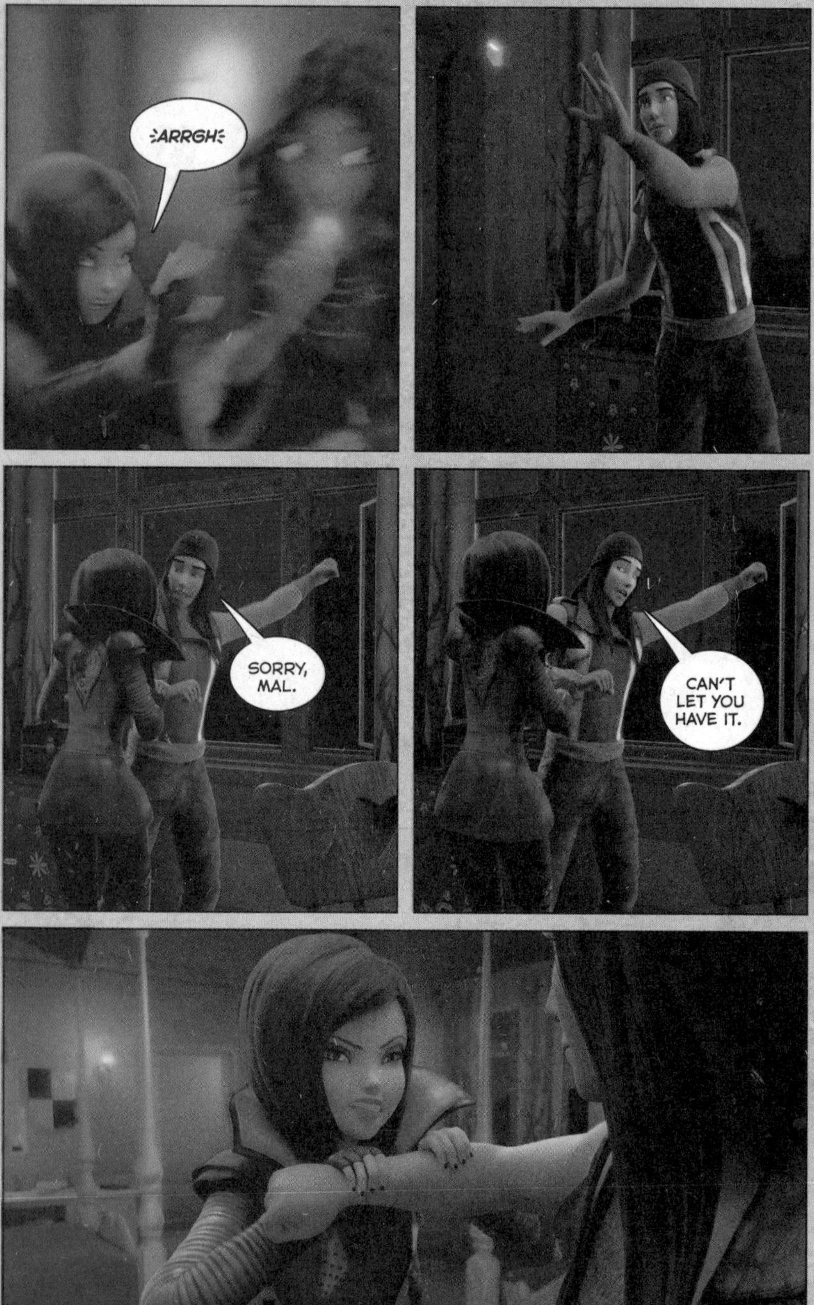
ARRGH
SORRY, MAL.
CAN'T LET YOU HAVE IT.

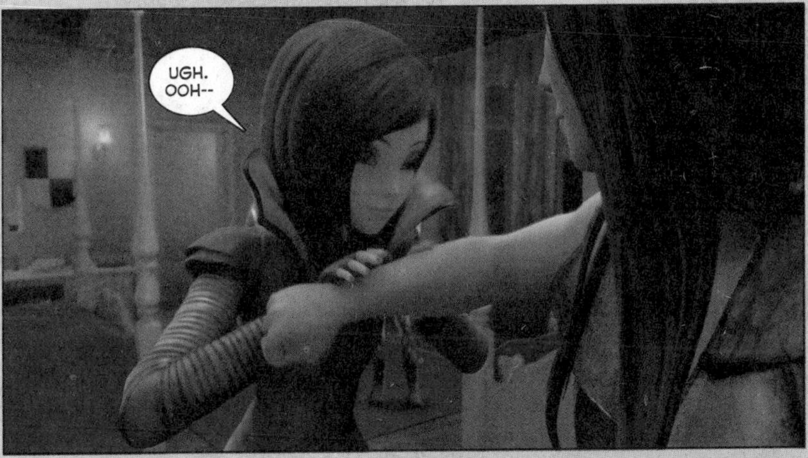
UGH. OOH--

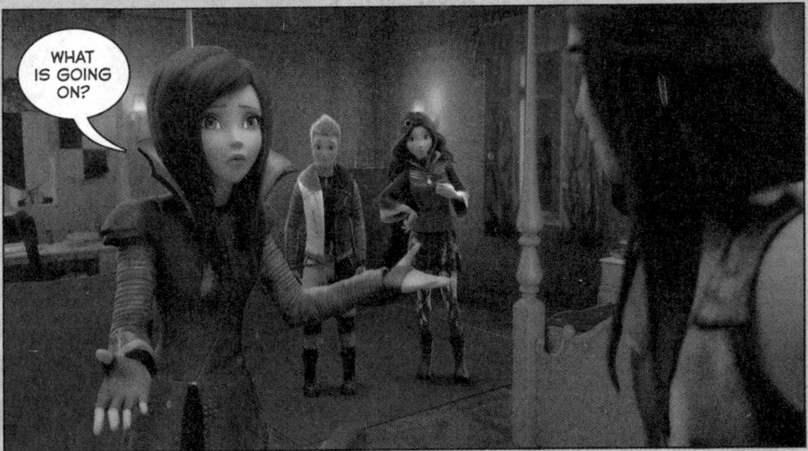
WHAT IS GOING ON?

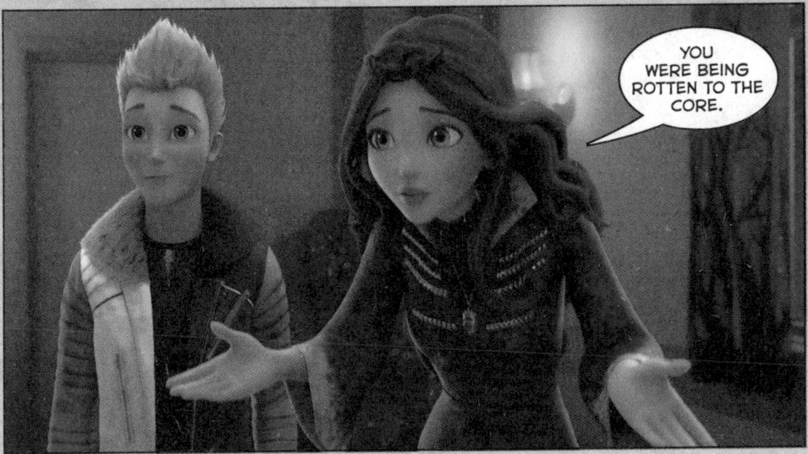
YOU WERE BEING ROTTEN TO THE CORE.

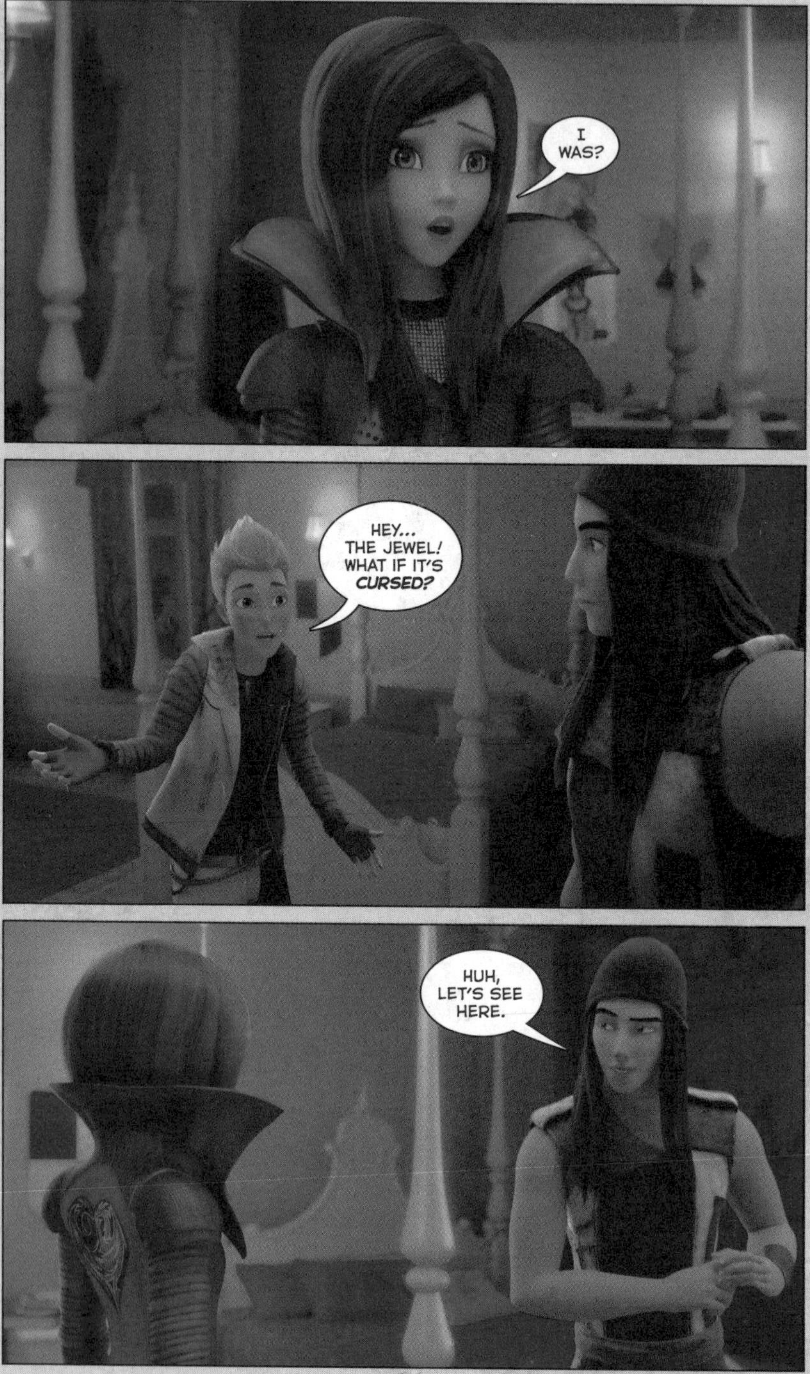
I WAS?
HEY... THE JEWEL! WHAT IF IT'S *CURSED?*
HUH, LET'S SEE HERE.

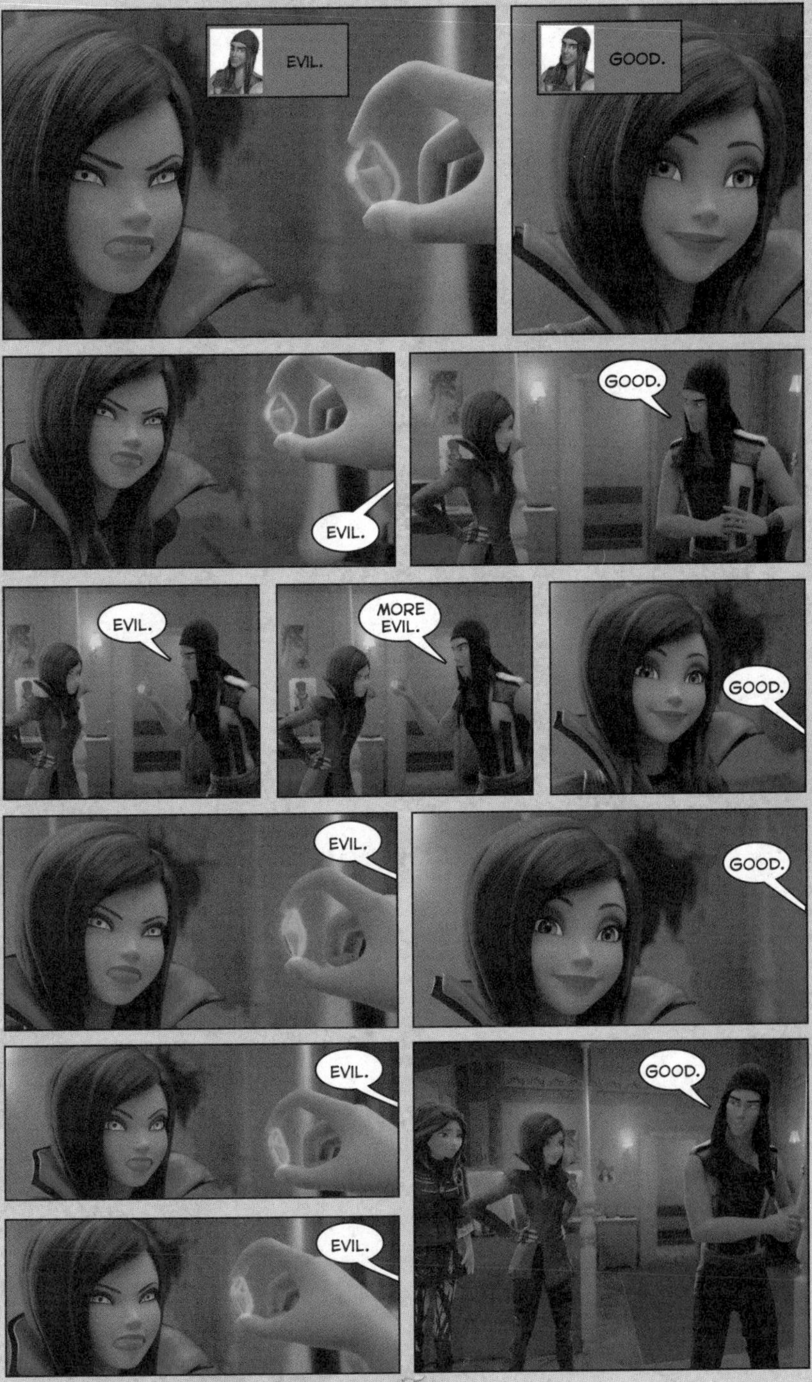
EVIL.
GOOD.
EVIL.
GOOD.
EVIL.
MORE EVIL.
GOOD.
EVIL.
GOOD.
EVIL.
EVIL.
GOOD.

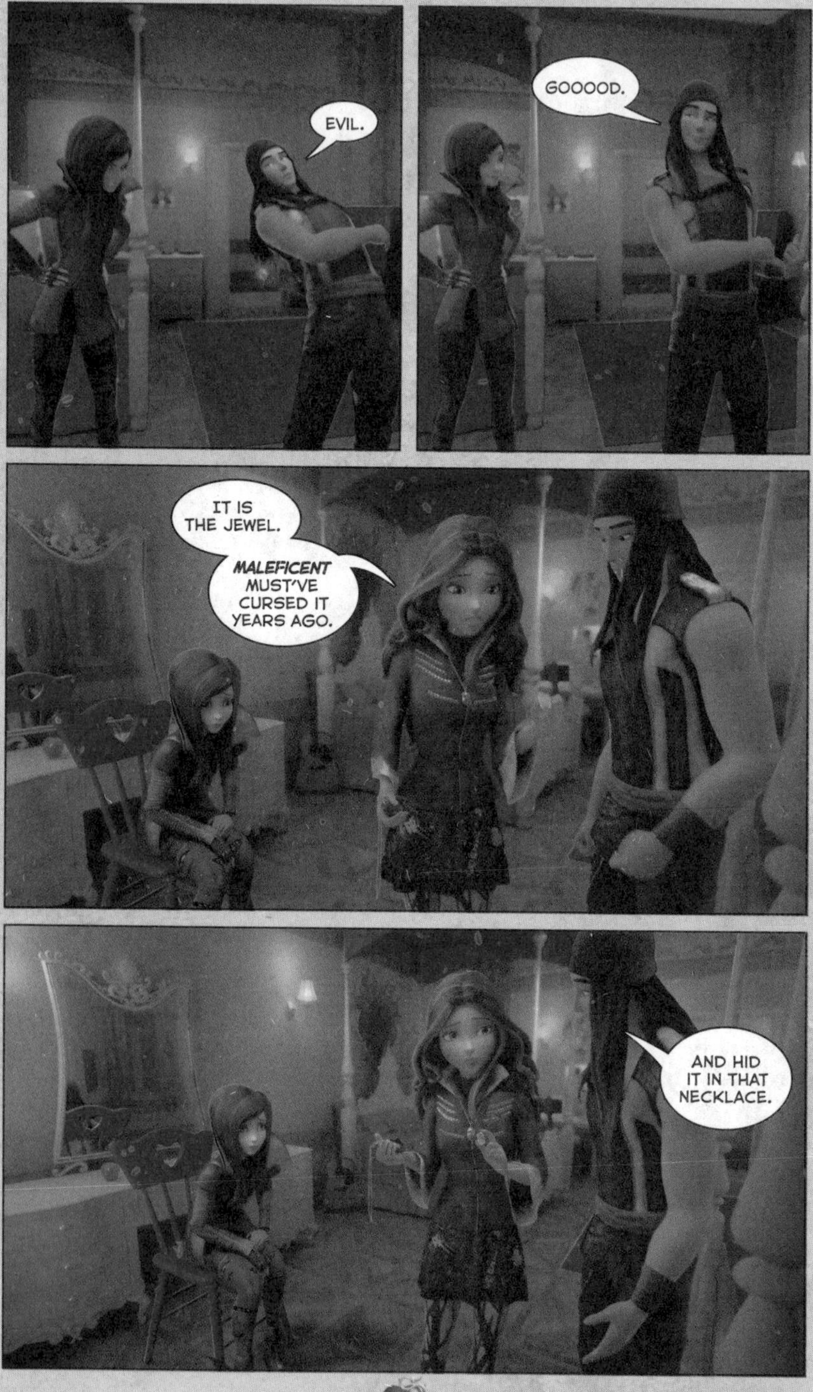
EVIL.
GOOOOD.
IT IS THE JEWEL.
MALEFICENT MUST'VE CURSED IT YEARS AGO.
AND HID IT IN THAT NECKLACE.

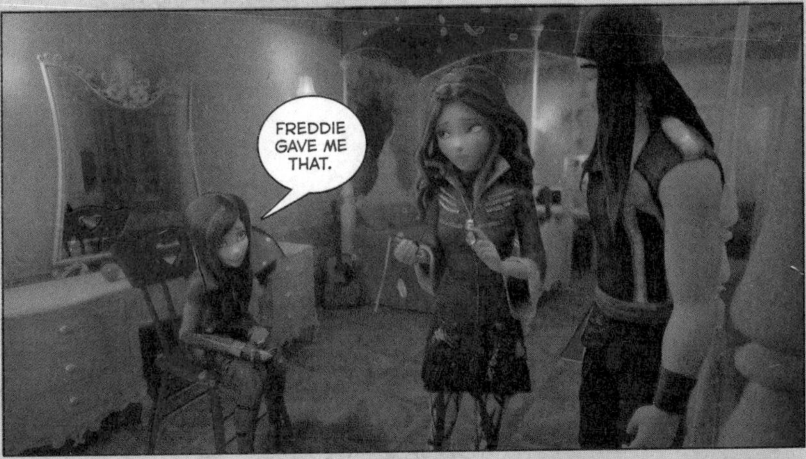
FREDDIE GAVE ME THAT.

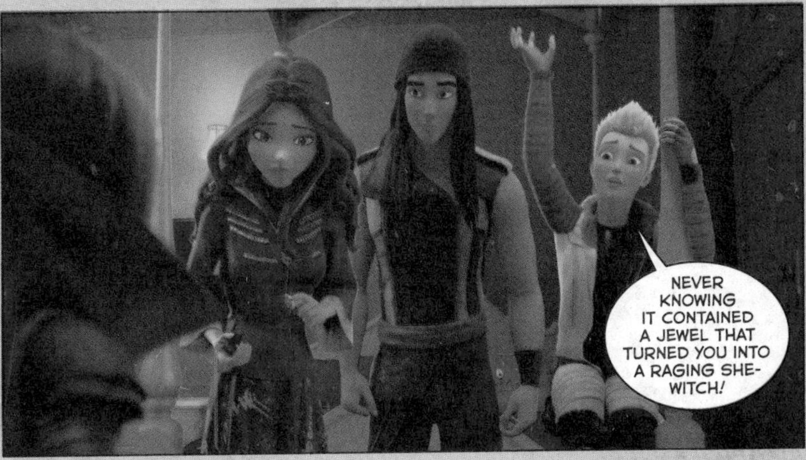
NEVER KNOWING IT CONTAINED A JEWEL THAT TURNED YOU INTO A RAGING SHE-WITCH!

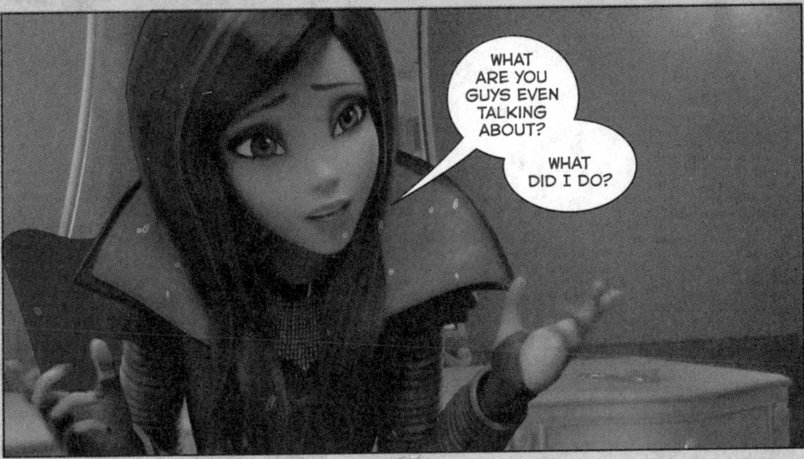
WHAT ARE YOU GUYS EVEN TALKING ABOUT?
WHAT DID I DO?

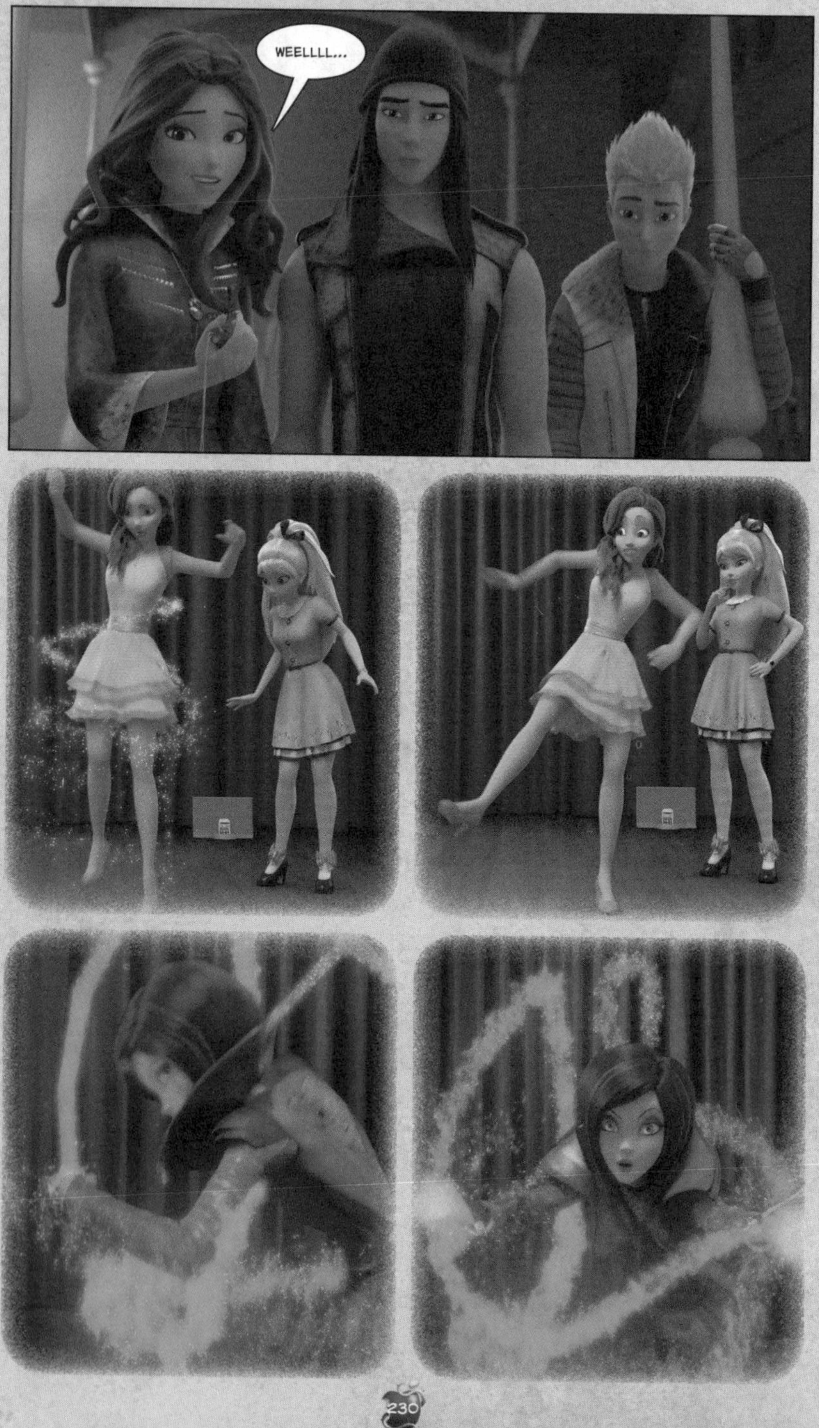
WEELLLL...

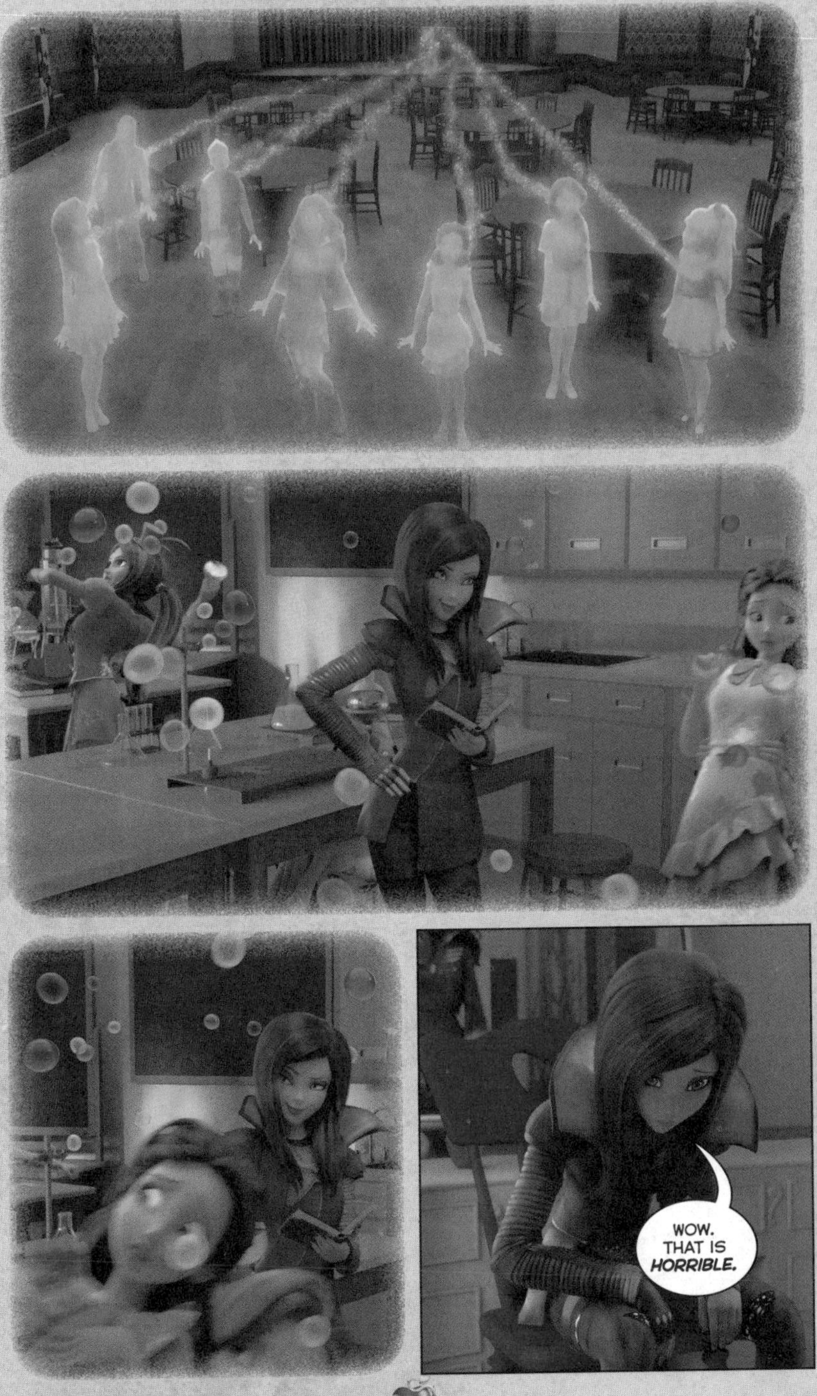
WOW. THAT IS *HORRIBLE.*

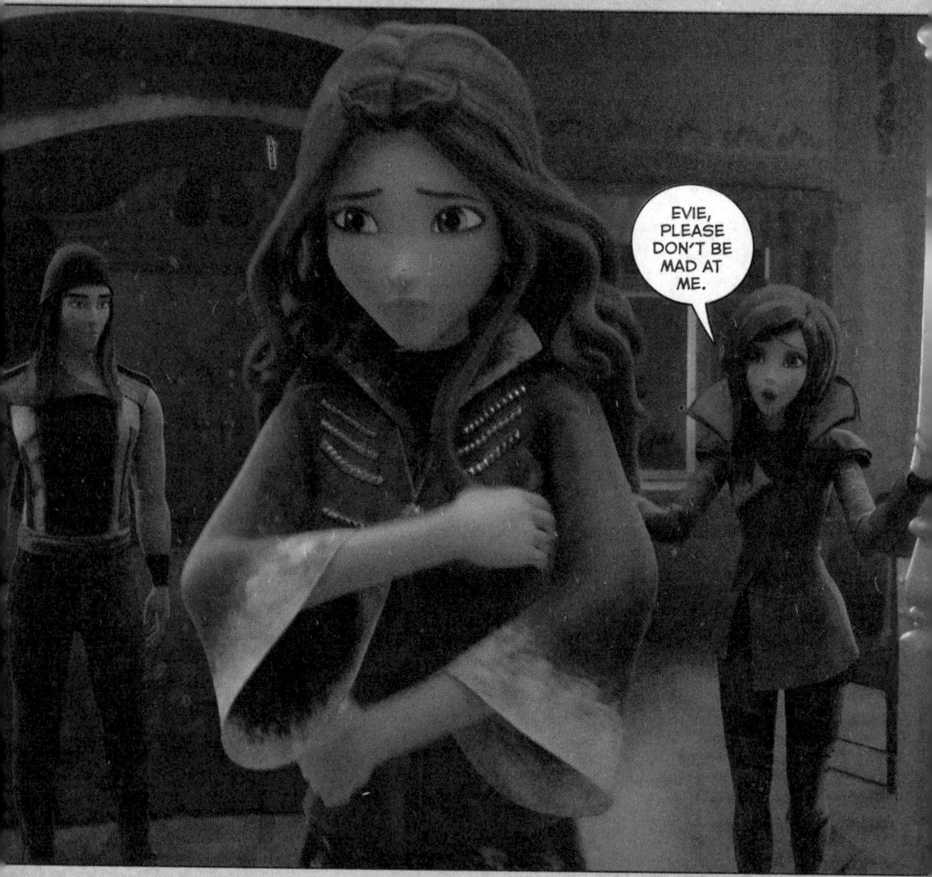
EVIE, PLEASE DON'T BE MAD AT ME.

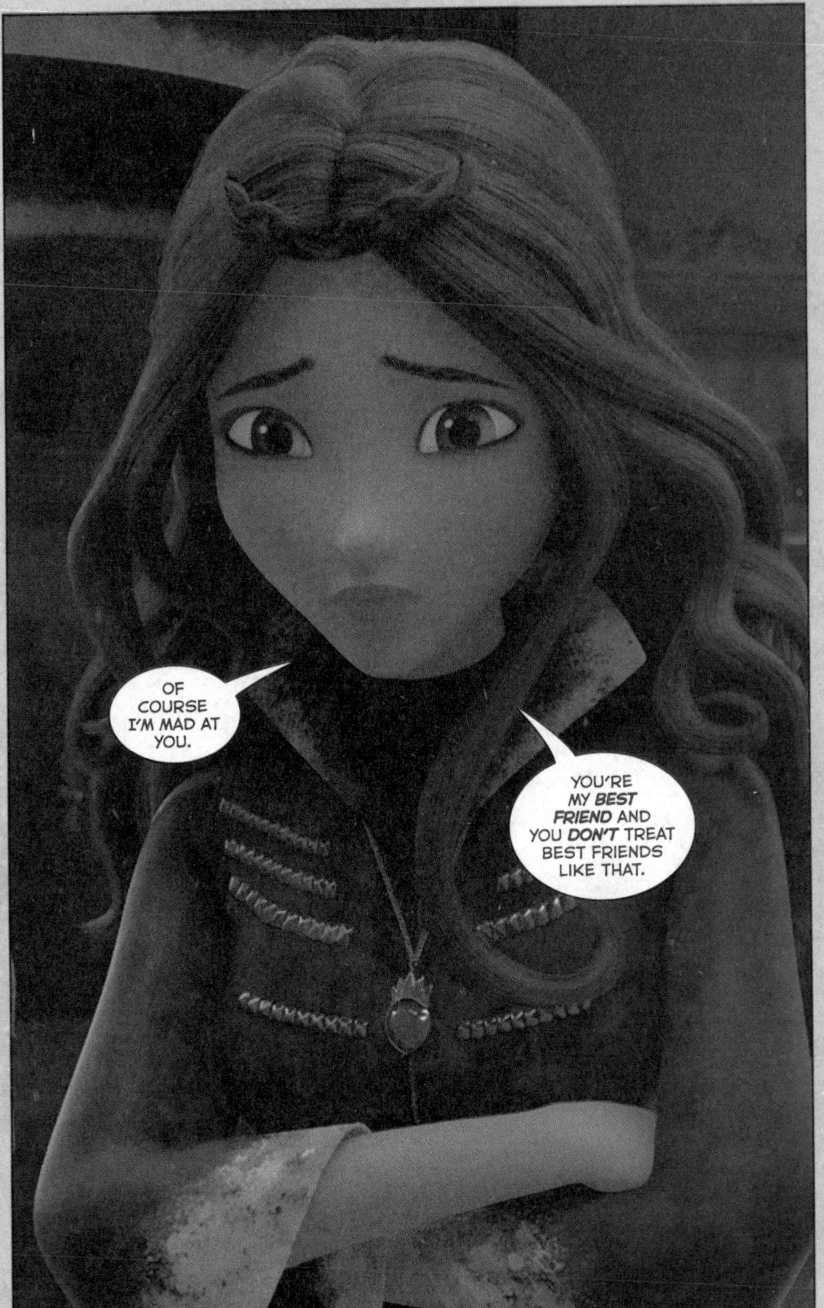
OF COURSE I'M MAD AT YOU.
YOU'RE MY ***BEST FRIEND*** AND YOU ***DON'T*** TREAT BEST FRIENDS LIKE THAT.

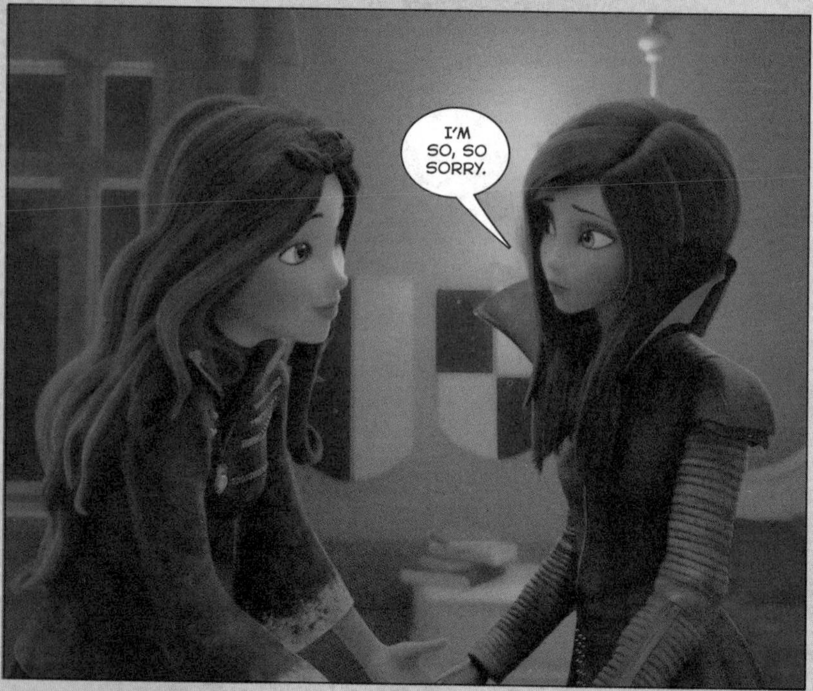
I'M SO, SO SORRY.

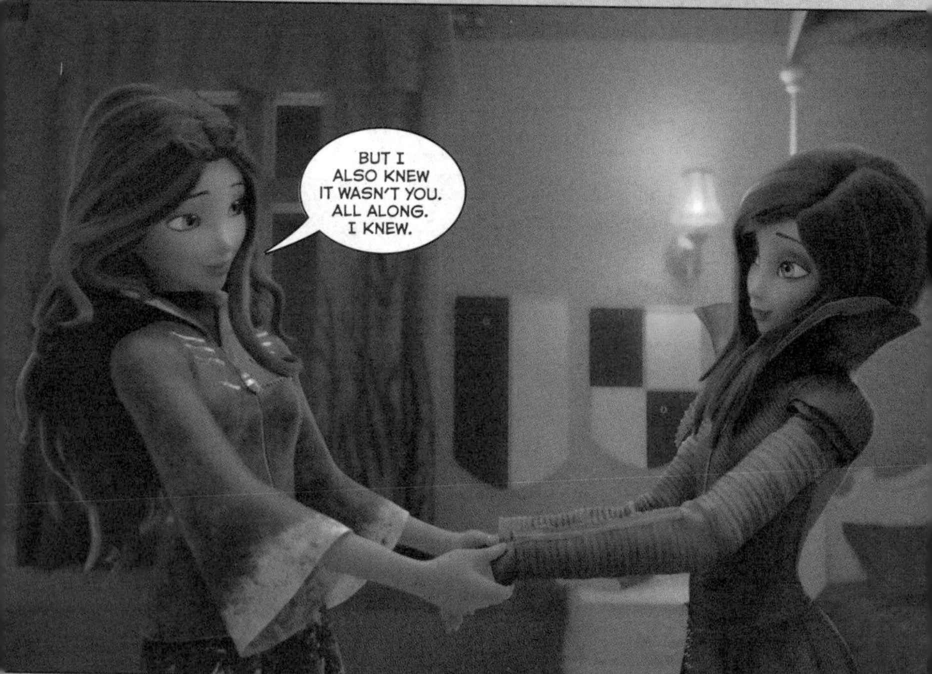
BUT I ALSO KNEW IT WASN'T YOU. ALL ALONG. I KNEW.

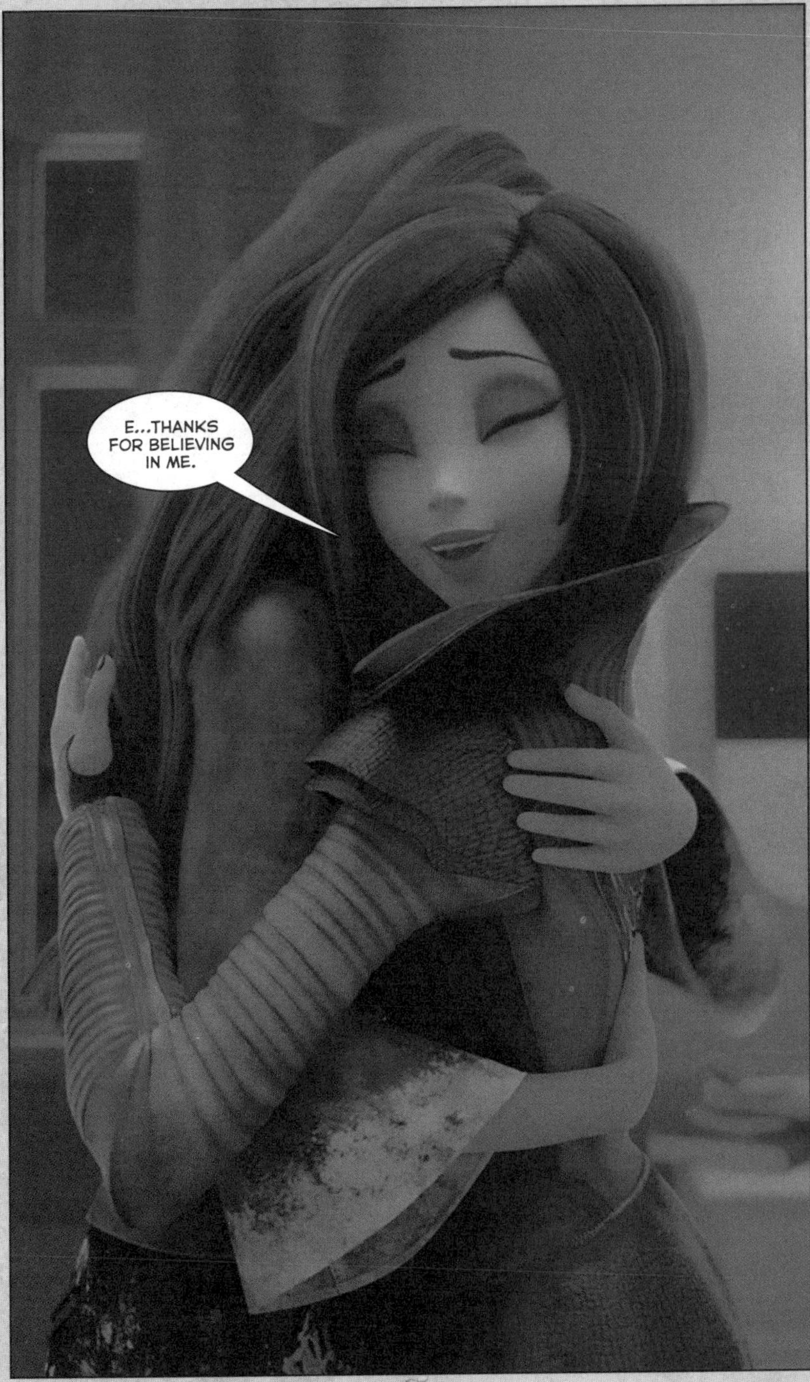
E...THANKS FOR BELIEVING IN ME.

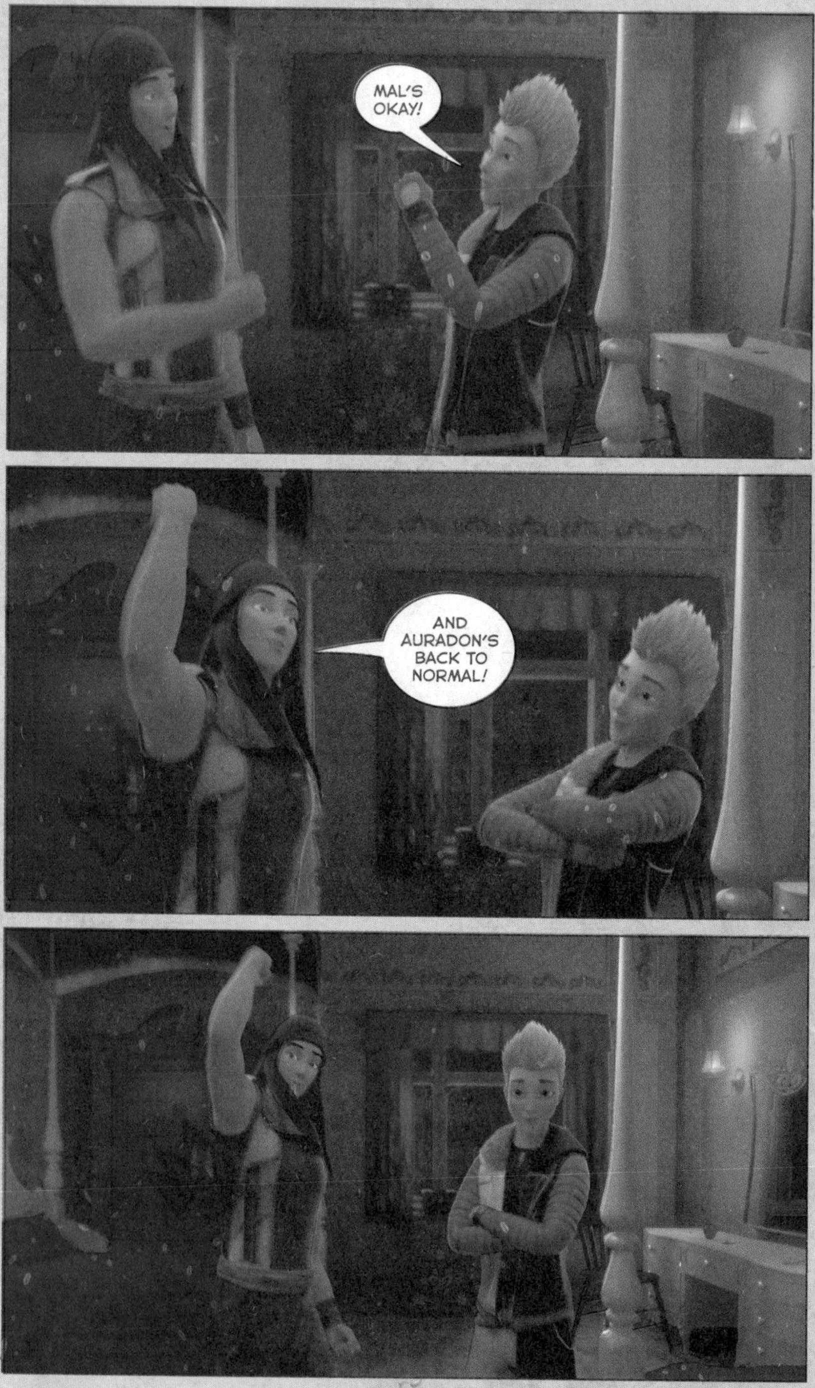
MAL'S OKAY!
AND AURADON'S BACK TO NORMAL!

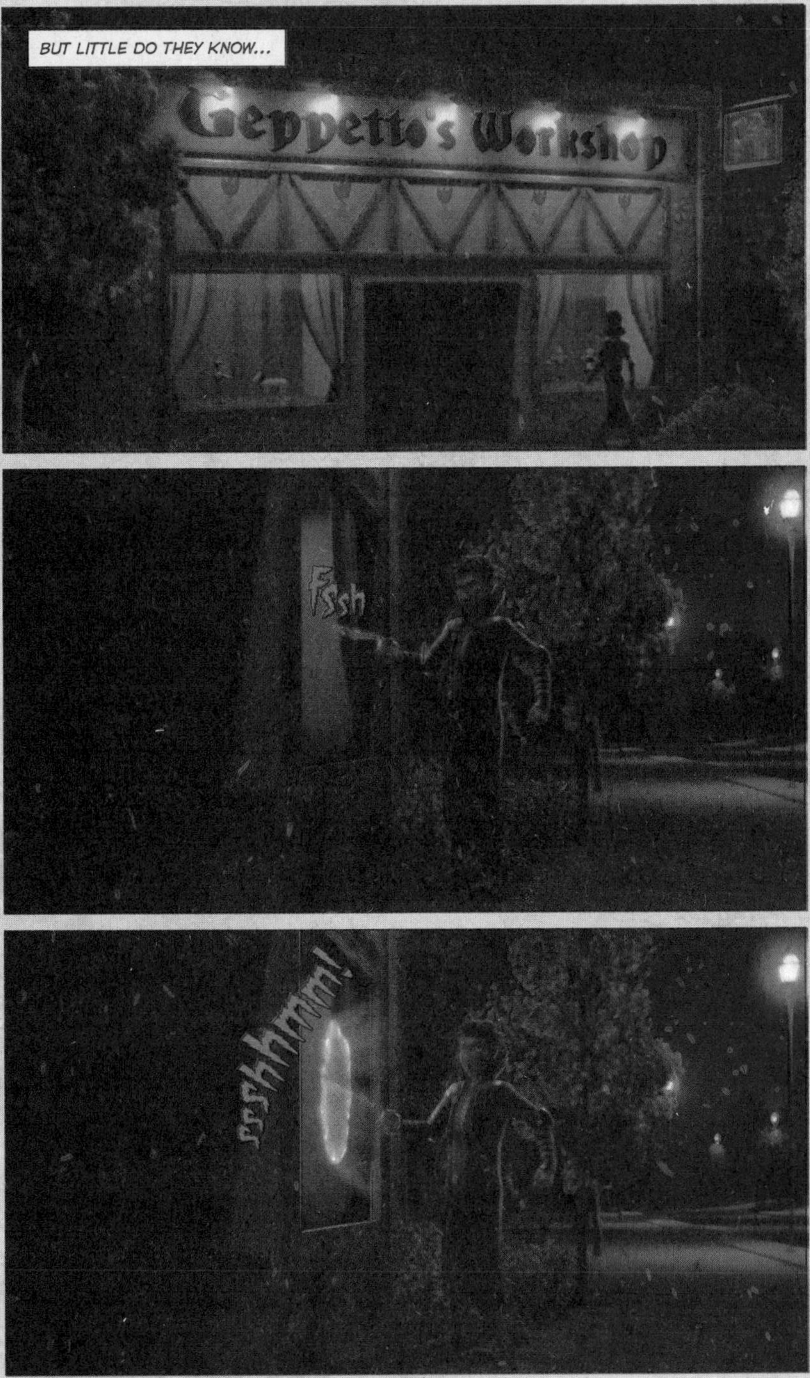
BUT LITTLE DO THEY KNOW...
Geppetto's Workshop
Fssh
ssshhmmm!

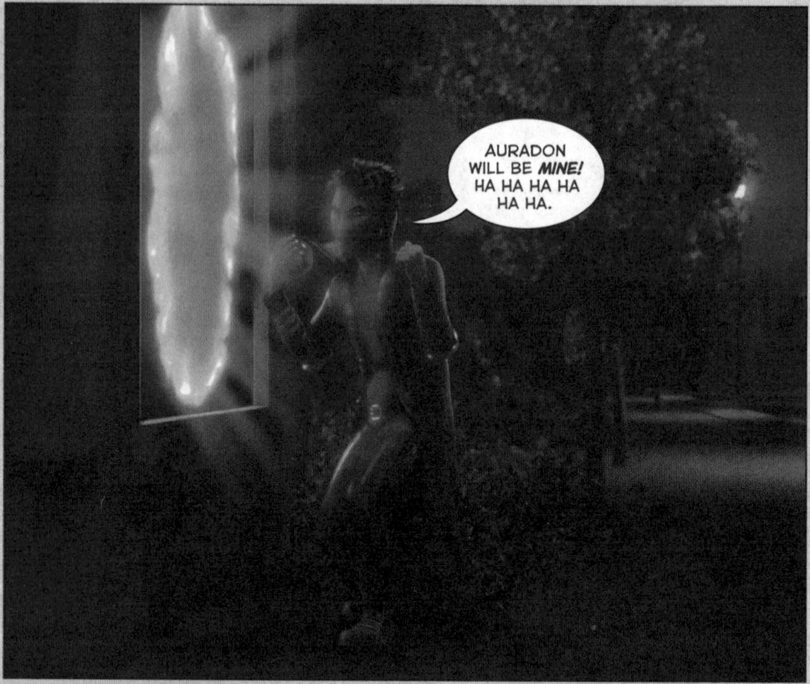
AURADON WILL BE *MINE!* HA HA HA HA HA HA.

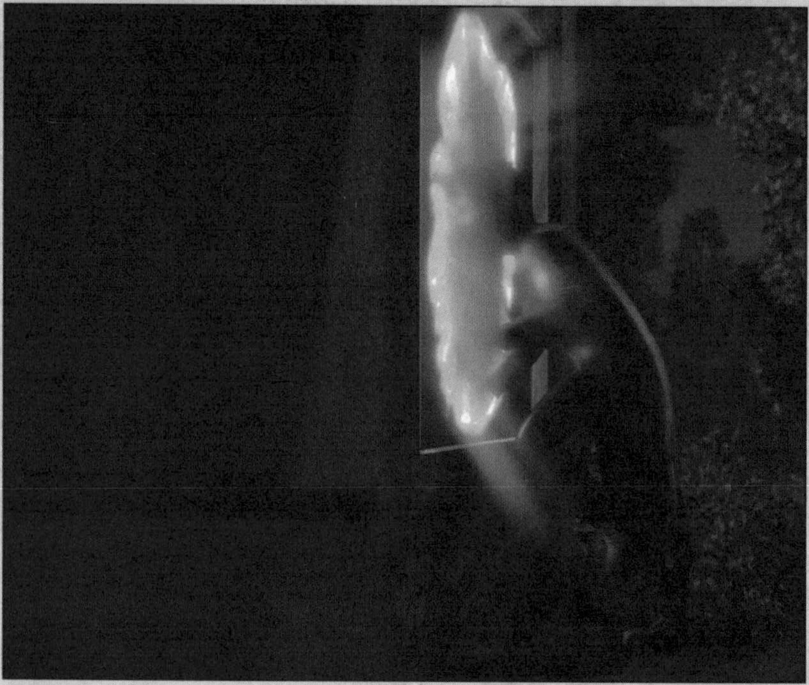

Disney

Descendants

Wicked World

Disney Descendants Wicked World Season 2 Shorts

Written by: Scott Peterson

Director & Executive Producer: Eric Fogel

Executive Producer: Carin Davis